BUCKET OF BLOOD

KIM BANNERMAN

FOX&BEE
STUDIO

ISBN 978-1-9994156-4-8

This book was created in Canada.

For more information, contact kim@kbannerman.com.

Created with Vellum

BOOKS BY KIM BANNERMAN

The Lizzie Saunders series

Bucket of Blood

Mark of the Magpie

Agony of Saint Alice

Other titles

The Tattooed Wolf

The Fire Song

Love and Lovecraft

The Blackwood Papers

Aeterna

To Dad, who cherished Cumberland
and all who called it home.

PROLOGUE

THE BOY'S father had been a military man, as precise as a chronometer, and this was naturally reflected in the boy's strict, unyielding upbringing. For a child, he was very observant, aloof and clever, with sharp, darting eyes that noticed any indiscretion. In his mind, he kept a tally of all insults thrown against him by his betters; whether the insult was real or perceived did not matter. Every slight was chewed upon and digested slowly, so that the taste grew bitter.

One day, when he was still only in knickerbockers and had not yet been fully breeched, his father took him aside and warned him that a woman's love can never be trusted. "They are not constant," came the explanation, "They are wanton, fickle creatures, driven by an insatiable lust. The serpent offered the apple to Eve because he knew, wickedly clever thing, that a woman cannot ignore her curiosity, and will fall to temptation with the smallest provocation."

His father seized his wrist and shook him. "The only constant is a man's devotion to duty, to Queen and to country. It is folly to trust a woman, for they are incapable of loyalty. Be vigilant, my son, for they will always find a way to destroy you, if you let them."

These words stayed with him, all through childhood and into his days as a young man. He knew it to be true; he had no reason to doubt. He saw fickleness in all women he passed, from the post mistress to the match girls on the corner.

So why, then, was he so surprised when he arrived home early, only to discover his beloved entangled in another's arms?

Such a rage he had never felt before – filled with insult and disgust, he surely thought he would burst into flames. And such rage, she had never before witnessed in him, though she'd oft before considered it a possibility. He was the quiet sort, very mindful of appearances, but he possessed a streak of cruelty that lurked just below the fragile veneer of his fine breeding. As the red flush coursed up his cheeks and his lips tightened into a slash of white, she realized with sharp dread that she'd unleashed the full onslaught of his restrained temper. He'd been willing to ignore the hints and clues of her indiscretions, but she had been too careless. The startling vision of her affair, laid out baldly before him in a swirl of cast-off petticoats and stockings, was too much for him to bear.

He seized her lover's hair in his hands, wrenching the terrified arms out of her grip.

"No, don't—" she begged, but he kicked her aside. His face remained stony. His eyes became discs of slate: dark, impenetrable, reflecting nothing.

There were screams of protest, cries for help, quickly silenced by his hands tightening around the long, pale throat. The body, only moments ago warm and moving in her embrace, collapsed dead to the floor.

He took a moment to catch his breath and smoothed back a lock of hair that had fallen out of place. "Now then," he said, looking down at the sobbing woman, "I will not abide by this behavior. Do you understand?"

She sobbed too hard to answer, so she nodded her head and clutched her arms around her naked knees. So quickly, it had happened so quickly --

"Never again!" he spat, "You are an affront to God! You disgust me, do you hear me? Disgust!"

She reached out one hand across the carpet to caress her lover's fingers, half-curled and turning blue.

But he seized up the corpse's feet and dragged it away, to deal with it as he saw best. She heard his boots thump down the stairs, her lover's head resounded upon each step in reply, down into the basement where the kindling was cut. She heard the click of the ax as he plucked it from the paving stones, and she cried until the sound of chopping stopped.

1

"LIFE AND DEATH appeared to me ideal bounds, which I should first break through, and pour a torrent of light into our dark world." – Mary Shelley, *Frankenstein*

FEBRUARY 20, 1898

MRS. MARGARET ANNE SAUNDERS, nee Worthington, of Cumberland, has regrettably passed into God's keeping after a lengthy illness. The deceased was born in Wiltshire in the year 1861 to father Captain Horatio Worthington and mother Gertrude Anne Worthingon (nee Dawkins), and sailed to Canada in the year 1890 with her husband and two daughters. Her husband's appointment as supporting physician with the Union Colliery Company brought the family to Cumberland, and since their arrival, Mrs. Saunders has been a vibrant and memorable citizen of this fine city. Her passing was not wholly unforeseen, for she had suffered many years with a number of long-standing ailments, and she will be missed by her beloved husband, physician Dr. John Saunders, originally of Wiltshire, and her two daughters, Violet Anne Saunders and Amaryllis Elizabeth Saunders. Funeral to be held, weather permitting, on the morning of February 20. All friends welcome. - *The Weekly News, February 15, 1898*

THE MORNING of Mother's funeral boasted a light trace of frost upon the windows and a fresh skiff of snow across the yard. The previous night had been bitterly cold but, as the sun rose, the air became refreshing and bracing, almost pleasant, and the light danced merrily across the glittering fringe of icicles that adorned the eaves. Over the housetops, the pale smoke from the chimneys drifted straight as chalk lines into a dove-grey sky. The eastern horizon embraced the newborn sun in a cloudy cradle of vermillion and pink, like a bed of rose petals curving across the wide expanse of heaven, and before the last stars had fully vanished, I could feel the promise of a crisp, clear sunny day in the motionless air. It smelled clean, and invigorating, and--

"By all the stars in heaven, Amaryllis! Close the window!"

I let out my breath in a sigh and put my shoulder to the wooden frame. Half-pulling, half-pushing, I dropped the pane of glass between myself and the world.

"Letting out all the good coal heat!" Violet nattered, "Do you have no sense, Amaryllis? It's as cold as a penguin's toes in here!"

"Father has as much coal as he wishes, Vi," I reminded her, "He's paid a portion of his wage in coal. But I need a breath of fresh air, and I didn't think he'd mind."

"A lady shuns fresh air, Lizzie, for that's how disease is borne! God's teeth!" Violet huffed in frustration. "You'll come down with consumption and die and be buried alongside Mother, and I should be shamed to have a little sister so stupid!" Her throat hitched. She sniffled a little behind one hand, and reached for a handkerchief with the other.

My sister scoffed at education for women, but she'd studied the art of theatrics like a master. The ague that she'd suffered in Panama had never fully left her, and Violet had fashioned her illness into a virtue, transforming it into a frailness that men found irresistible. Now, in deep mourning, Violet appeared more delicate than usual, as precious as the first snowdrop of spring. Her oval face, with a slight blush on her white cheeks and a rosy pink hue to her lips, appeared almost angelic. Grief had stripped her of her normally capricious, flirtatious nature, and transformed her into a regal beauty.

"Oh, for the love of... Please don't cry again, Vi," I said. "Look, I've closed the window, just like you asked!"

She hiccoughed into her hanky. "You haven't shed a single tear for Mother," she accused, "I think you must be a little stupid, Lizzie, and don't have a sense of what has happened."

I winced. "I know exactly what's happened," I replied.

"Not stupid, then," Violet sniffled, then added with thinly-veiled disapproval, "Only heartless!"

I leaned against the window frame as she dissolved into tears again. "I have cried, Vi," I admitted, "I spent the night in tears. I will cry again, no doubt. But this public display of sorrow –"

"You must not hide yourself away to cry! There is no shame in grief!"

"Did you just accuse me of feeling shame?" I countered.

Violet laughed, but her mirth was as cold as the icicles outside the window. "Oh, how much you are like Mother! As calculating as a snake; as womanly as a stone. You've never felt a lick of shame in all your life; why would you start now?"

She cried for a minute or two. While she sobbed out her anger, I waited. My sister could be caustic and mean, but Mother's death had struck her a fierce blow, and I saw plainly enough that her insult was born of sorrow and not malice.

"I'm sorry, Liz," she said with a hoarse throat. "One ought not speak cruelly of the deceased." She sniffled and wiped her nose. "But Mother's madness was a burden we all bore. You must admit, her death brings a sense of relief." She took a deep breath, straightened her spine, and tipped up her chin. "Now, come help me with the lacing, would you?" Violet offered the lacing of her corset, a fine piece of black bombazine with whalebone struts that were so crisp and new, they squeaked when she moved.

My own dress remained unbuttoned and my gloves lay rumpled on the end of the bed, but I breathed on my stiff fingers to warm them and took the corset's crossed laces in hand. With the heel of my right palm against the small curve of Violet's back, I jerked the cords tight.

"You... are....very....good..." Violet encouraged, grunting with each savage pull.

"Hold your breath, now, while I tie it fast."

I secured the corset. Violet took the black silk dress from the table and slipped it on, then pulled the long gloves over her hands and wrists. She swung a short wool jacket over her shoulders and finally finished the outfit with a fine angora shawl. Violet regarded herself in the mirror with a congratulatory smile.

A little pang of jealously prickled at my heart. I had to admit, she looked lovely. The outfit gave her curled tendrils of blonde hair an unnatural luminescence.

But then, she rounded upon me like a rabid dog, and her smile melted into a scowl. "Oh, Amaryllis! You're hardly dressed at all! Here, let me help you prepare."

"It's no bother." I pulled at my stockings, "I'll only be a moment."

But Violet would not be dissuaded; she saw an opportunity to fuss and cluck over me, two years her junior and a world less experienced. "This is a bit more complex than your regular trousers and shirt, Lizzie! You can't simply throw on today's outfit with mere seconds to spare!"

"This is a bit more involved than I'm accustomed," I agreed.

I silently wished that trousers would have been acceptable. I could get away with such indiscretions while raking the yard and pruning the apple tree, but wearing pants to my own mother's interment asked too much of society.

No, in truth, it asked too much of Mrs. Gunn. Our housekeeper had been positively gleeful when charged with the duties of laying out the girls' clothes for the funeral because it gave her an open opportunity to muscle me into a dress. I hadn't worn a frock since, well.... I cast her mind back. "Y'know, Vi," I mused, "I haven't worn a dress in over a year."

Violet aligned my body directly before her and, with feet braced, yanked the corset ties so fiercely that I almost felt a rib crack. Violet pulled and prodded, I grunted and cursed until, at last, the garment was tightly tied.

"Mercy!" I huffed, but Violet would hear no complaints.

"Come along, put this on," she insisted as she slipped the black blouse over my arms. She snipped the pearl buttons closed with practiced precision, and snuggled the gloves over my outstretched hands; the fine silk snagged on my calloused skin and dirty fingernails. At last, she snatched a brush from the dresser to tame my unruly tangles of ginger hair. There were times when I suspected that my hair, Gorgon-like, had a million serpentine minds of its own.

"Goodness! Unbelievable!" Violet muttered to herself. She twisted pins into the mess until my wild tresses were braided and smooth. "It is our duty," Violet said, examining the shape of my head with narrowed eyes, "Our DUTY, Lizzie, as young English ladies, to bring civilization to the wilderness, not succumb to it!"

I wobbled my head from side to side. So many pins nailed the braids to my scalp that my head actually felt heavier.

With a flick of both wrist and fabric, Violet flourished the silk jacket over my bony shoulders and wrestled and pushed and shoved until, her Herculean task complete, she stood back to regard her work, panting slightly.

And I, half afraid of what I'd see, glanced sideways into the mirror.

The black clothes accentuated the tawny sun-brazed color of my face. They made my hazel eyes appear dark and sharp and cunning, like those of a woodland mouse. Violet might look more celestial in her flowing black garment, but the same outfit made me look decidedly more terrestrial.

"There's not much I can do to help you, Liz," Violet said as she studied the flat, stark and unfeminine lines of my form. She was unable to mask the pity in her voice. "We've managed to stick you in a dress, but doesn't quite work."

"It was worth a try," came my despairing reply.

"I blame Mother, you know," she said, "You're like one of those strange Japanese fish that grows to accommodate the size of its container. Mother allowed you to wear trousers, and you've had no opportunity to grow except to look awful in a skirt."

I regarded myself in the mirror with utter dismay. My hair had adopted a fiery red tone in the warm glow of morning, which only accentuated the smattering of freckles across my small nose and the flecks of green in my eyes. I was plain and lean, ropy and muscular and angular. With my dirty nails and nut-brown complexion, acquired after long hours out-of-doors, I decided that I looked more like a faun from classical mythology than a prim and proper lady.

I couldn't suppress a sigh. "Lordy, I make an ugly girl," I decided.

Violet grabbed her clutch purse from the table and a folded black scarf from the shelf by the door. "Rest assured, Lizzie dear," she said, "You make an uglier boy."

We descended the straight, narrow stairs to the ground floor. Violet moved with grace and poise, one gloved hand outstretched to the balustrade to guide her descent. I tromped heavily, mindfully, with every ounce of concentration dedicated to avoiding a trip and fall over the unfamiliar, ankle-length hem.

"No one will fault you for your attempt, Liz," Violet consoled over her shoulder, "But years of heavy chores have taken their toll on you – why Father never hired help for the yard, I'll never know. It was unkind of him, Lizzie, to condemn you to a boy's chores. Simply unkind."

"I've never thought of it as unkind," I replied, "Only necessary." Hauling water was so much easier while wearing boots and pants. I couldn't imagine attempting my chores in this bloody awful corset.

"I remain committed to the fact that our parents' indulgence with your eccentricities is cruel." Violet waited at the bottom of the stairs for me to reach the last step. "They ought never to have perpetuated your ridiculous, ridiculous wardrobe."

When we reached the main floor, I heard Mrs. Gunn in the kitchen, humming a gusty tune to herself. The copper pots clattered as she prepared the luncheon to follow the service, but upon hearing our leather boot soles on the wooden floor, she poked her round, ruddy face through the kitchen door.

"Och, me wee lovelies!" she exclaimed, pressing her clasped hands to her bosom, the volume of which strained the durable fabric of her apron. Agnes Gunn was a busty rhinoceros of a Scotswoman, formidable in size and presence, with not a single dainty attribute to claim as her own. I mused that, without Agnes' perpetual white apron tying her all together, that broad and bountiful porridge-filled frame would lose all definition and any semblance of human shape.

Agnes Gunn had been the Saunders' maid since our arrival in Cumberland, and at times she seemed to be a fixture of the house, rather than an employee of the family. With an ease borne of familiarity and buoyed by her imposing size, she bustled through the rooms, perpetually dusting or tidying, preparing every meal in the immaculate kitchen. She kept a jealous account of the contents of the parlor and outbuildings; one could be forgiven for thinking that the money spent on supplies was her own. Dr. Saunders was often busy with his career and Molly had been in no fit state to care for children, but Agnes fawned and fussed over Violet and me with the same smothering affection she ladled on her own seven sons.

Her slab of a face, as delicate as the back of a shovel, was topped by a closely-cropped crown of silvery curls. When she smiled, the expression was quick; this morning, of all mornings, must not be wasted in frivolity. She was, in her own acidic way, a thoughtful and loving woman, although she possessed a propensity to speak her mind with a lusty, God-fearing and self-righteous vigor. She had never kept secret her disdain for Mrs. Saunders' madness, and she felt that Dr. Saunders tolerated far too much when it came to his wife's queer notions and his youngest daughter's free and easy will. Now, with the death (albeit tragic and sad, God rest Margaret Anne's tortured soul, sign of the cross hastily made over the hurdles of a body's bumps and valleys), the family was free to return to normalcy. I could dress as a girl befitting my station. Mrs. Gunn, with only a masculine brood to clothe, had collected a number of dress patterns from her neighbors and appraised the fine woolen weaves in Simon Leiser's Big Store. A bolt of cotton, olive green to match my hazel eyes, was already on order.

"Twa bonnie beauties!" she cooed, slapping the flour from her broad palms before she took my hands in her own. "A fair maiden hides in there yet, I do believe it!" she said. She turned to Violet. "And, you! Looking as noble as Her Majesty the Queen! All the boys heads will be a-turning!"

"Thank you, Agnes," Violet said, blushing slightly.

I fussed with the hip of my corset, which bit into my thigh. I hadn't thought of Queen Victoria as the kind of woman to turn a boy's head. "I don't need to wear this awful thing, do I?"

"For shame!" Agnes admonished, "Your mother not even in the grave, and already you're grousing!" She slung her arm over my shoulders and guided me down the hall, toward the parlor. "Let's try, just for today, tae exercise the feminine beauties that God hath bestowed upon ye!'

"But she's lacking in God's beauty," said Violet, "You can't blame her for being discouraged."

I wasn't completely sure if I ought to thank Violet for the support, or deck her in the jaw with a closed fist. Instead, I decided to bite my tongue and suffer through the morning, pesky corset and all, in tortuous silence.

Cedar boughs adorned the hearth in the parlor. They lent a Yuletide flavor and a pleasing, sweet perfume to an otherwise austere room. Strips of black crape tied the curtains back, letting in a few rays of watery sunlight, and ivory-colored candles on the tables provided a gentle illumination, much softer and more quiet that the hissing coal-oil lamps. Between the parlor and the kitchen sat the dining room, where all of the furniture had been rearranged: the long table had been moved against the wall and Molly's closed casket, surrounded by more candles, sat silently upon it. Three wooden chairs faced the casket, where mourners could sit comfortably and contemplate their own mortality.

I had spent most of last night in one of these chairs, reading a book and listening to the ominous ticking of the mantle clock. In the bone-chilling dark, the waves of heat radiating from the small inferno of candles had made the dining room a very pleasant place to wile away the hours. Pleasant, of course, except for the silent company of my mother's mortal remains, lying on the table.

Mrs. Gunn's first task, every day, was to light a fire in the hearths. Already, the parlor was quite comfortable.

Violet sat on the couch by the fireplace, smoothing out the folds of her skirts with her palms. "Is Father ready?"

Agnes shook her head. "He's oot in the yard, in his surgery."

This came as no surprise. My father was prone to contemplation, and the surgery was his refuge. The little building of dun bricks sat in the southwest corner of our yard and had originally been a tool shed, but John Saunders had converted it into a private office for after-hour appointments and emergencies. It was small, neat, well-organized and secure, with a tiny four-panel window to the right of its wooden door. Outside, it appeared small and modest, but inside, my father had created a cozy and welcoming office, pharmacy, and personal study.

The surgery held only three pieces of furniture: a solid wooden table, a wicker chair by the door, and a locked cabinet of medications and ointments. The monstrous table was hewn from a single massive slab of oak, and it was strong enough to support the full weight of a man; here is where Dr. Saunders urged patients to lie down while he sewed up lacerations or assessed bruised muscles. The surface was carved and hacked by years of use, and Father had told me that he'd bought it from a public house for a very reasonable price. Patrons had whittled their blades on the edges, and someone had carved a name, "Robbie", in runic lines at one corner.

In direct contrast to the table, the wicker chair looked too fragile to bear anyone's weight, even a scrawny bone-rack like me. When Father set his medical case – a heavy split-handled bag fashioned from walrus hide -- on the chair, the delicate legs creaked and groaned under the burden. I thought the chair to be rather useless as a bit of furniture, but its seat had been upholstered with blue chintz to match the blue Persian rug that covered the floor, and Mother had claimed that the complimentary pieces made the surgery seem more professional, and less like an old tool shed.

I could not blame my father for seeking solitude in the surgery. He often sought refuge there from a house full of shrieking, nattering women. Today, it offered him a private sanctuary to collect himself before burying his wife.

"I knocked upon the door," Agnes continued, "And told him tae come, but ye ken how your father can be. He'll join us in his own guld time."

"But he must be here when the hearse arrives," Violet said. Her voice wobbled like a marble on an uneven floor. "It's only proper!"

"Aye, but you must agree, your father's heart has fair been crushed to have lost the missus," Agnes reminded, "Your guld mother was his everything." She tipped her chin in the direction of the back yard. "Your father has the guld sense to take a few minutes of solitude to hide his weeping. Ye can nae fault him for wanting privacy at a time like this. He's too much of a gentleman to show his emotions."

The hollow clopping of hooves against the frozen mud of First Street rang in the icy air. I hurried to the parlor window.

A matched pair of shaggy black horses rounded the corner. Stars of sunlight flashed off their polished harness. Clusters of purple feathers adorned their brows. They pulled a carriage which gleamed like polished jet, and they breathed white plumes into the frosty air as they tossed their noble heads. The driver reined them to a halt before the house as a small crowd of neighbors congregated in the front yard.

"The hearse is here," I said from the window, "And a number of mourners, too. Thirty, at least, and more coming up the street."

"And Father, no where to be seen!" Violet fretted, "God's teeth! We shall not live this down!"

"The crowd can wait," I replied as I stepped away from the

window. "Another minute more won't matter; Mother isn't going anywhere."

Violet gave a little squeal. "There is an order to these things, Liz! Every social occasion is like the theatre, and all people have their part to play, and all moments have their cue! And if we fail in our duty to bury our Mother properly? What then?"

"What then, indeed?" I replied, "The world won't fall to pieces."

The pallbearers crowded onto the porch, waiting for admittance. Agnes looked quickly to the door, her mouth set in a hard line. "Girls, girls," she said, "There'll be nae fighting between ye today! Please!" She touched her fingers lightly to Violet's cheek. "Never mind, ye bairn, I'll fetch him now, and you invite the pallbearers in. With your mother gone, tis your duty now to host them."

Violet visibly trembled as she stepped into the entrance hall. The doorknob squeaked as it turned under her hand, and the door opened to reveal six men on the front porch, waiting silently, their hats removed and their hands folded before them. She stepped aside as they entered, each bowing his head with silent respect.

I recognized them all: patients of my father's and upstanding members of the community. Alistair and Henry Gunn, Agnes' oldest boys, came first, followed by Hugh Donaldson, the son of the blacksmith. Then came Daniel Creekmore and Steven Hughes, company men, who gave their condolences with a tip of their felt top hats. Both men looked over my dress and smirked at each other, as if my costume were a grand joke, but who was I to argue? It seemed ridiculous to me, too.

Last to enter was Rufus McGregor, the deputy constable, a stout ox of a man with a thick mop of black hair and a lop-sided face, and a neck as thick as my thigh.

It was said that McGregor had once been a fighter on the circuit before a ham-fisted chop fractured his skull, broke his jaw, and rattled his brains, but as far as I could tell, McGregor's brains had unscrambled themselves just fine. His skull had healed but his face remained forever lumpy and scarred, gargoyle-like, and no matter how pleasant his personality, McGregor knew he was nothing pretty to look upon. When he smiled to me, the expression was awkward, twisted and toothy, painful to watch and poignant for its brutality.

But great kindness lived behind it. I smiled in return.

"I am very sorry for your loss, miss," he said, his hat in hand. "We all knew there was a sweetness in your mum rarely seen outside these walls."

"Thank you, Mr. McGregor," I replied. "She had her moments of lucidity."

Agnes drew close and took my hand in her own. "I stepped oot tae the surgery, knocked upon the door, and heard nae a peep inside." She sighed. "I've done all I can tae fetch your father, me love."

"He'll come," I replied quietly. "We wouldn't leave without him."

Violet gave a slight cough behind one gloved hand.

"Gentlemen," she began in a quivering voice, "I wish to thank you for all your help. You'll find my mother resting here."

She led the six pallbearers into the dining room, and they drew alongside the table, moving candles out of the way to grip on the coffin's brass handles. On the count of three, they hefted the casket onto their shoulders for Molly's final exit from the home.

Violet stepped to my side and her sharp elbow nudged my ribs.

"Bow your head, Liz: the coffin's going by," she hissed, "It's only proper."

Mrs. Gunn shed noisy tears and covered her mouth with her hands, and Violet began to weep, pulling a black linen handkerchief from the sleeve of her glove to dab the corners of her eyes. I watched, silent and solemn, as the men bore the casket out the front door. I tried, but found herself unable, to imagine my mother lying inside. Molly Saunders, who in life had been so exacting and persnickety, who had measured and managed her household with a fiery obsession, who had insisted on all things in their place – Molly surely could never lie still as a cold corpse. My mother had flown across the surface of the world, mad with precision, sorting and cataloguing everything in her path, bringing order to the chaos of nature. How could Molly lie still and silent in a box? She had barely laid still during the thirty-seven years of her life! She'd slept sparingly, at odd hours of the day and night, keeping to no schedule. Even when she grew tired, Molly propped herself in the horsehide chair in the corner of the parlor, where one could look right and see the front door, or look left through the dining room to see the kitchen and back door. Her hysteria caused her to live in a state of perpetual readiness, and her obsessive nature demanded that nothing be out of place. I could scarcely comprehend a force that could keep a woman like Molly still, but death had succeeded where all other treatments had failed.

The pallbearers shuffled down the steps, treading carefully on the icy path as they bore her towards the waiting carriage. As I watched them go, I felt, more than saw, my father step next to me.

Neither tall nor short, neither large nor small, John Saunders was a specimen of average physical attributes, but he carried himself with the assured bearing of a man comfortable with his station: gentlemanly, knowledgeable, confident. His folded hands were muscular, deft and graceful, with well-shaped nails and scrubbed knuckles. With his patrician features, dark brown hair and a neatly-clipped beard halfway between brown and grey, I thought he made a modestly handsome man, but his calculated manners gave no outward indication of vanity. His meticulous keeping was more a result of good hygiene and breeding than any attempt to attract the attentions of the opposite sex. But gossip is merciless in its swiftness: Molly had been dead for less than a week and already the idle chatter of Cumberland's housewives portrayed him as a poor widower in need of a wife.

Of course, I thought, this was the fabrication of bored mothers with eligible daughters – John gave no indication of replacing his wife of twenty years and, if he heard the gossip at all, turned a deaf ear to it. He already lived in a house filled to the rafters with women, he claimed: between Violet's doting, my conversation, and Agnes' housekeeping, he had no need of another female creature under his roof.

John followed the men into the street and waited at the door to the carriage as they finished securing the casket. His solemn face was pale with grief. When the pallbearers filed before him with heads politely bowed, he clasped their hands warmly between both of his palms to give them a firm handshake, and assured each with his gentle, sad smile that he greatly appreciated their assistance. Only after he clapped McGregor on the shoulder did he turn his attention to the women. He kissed Violet on the cheek and embraced Agnes, but he startled slightly to see me.

"You look remarkable, Liz," he said to me, "You've become the very image of your mother."

"Thank you," I replied, tugging at the edge of my corset, "But I confess, sir, it isn't very comfortable."

"To be perfectly honest, Liz, I don't think your mother was comfortable in her own skin, either." He held out his hands to us. "Come, girls, let's get the day done with, shall we?"

2

We took our place in the front of the carriage and wrapped a thick black bear fur across our legs. The driver snapped the reins. With the eggshell crackle of ice on the axles and an answering snort from the horses, the carriage began its slow, stately procession down the street.

Our home sat at the corner of First Street and Windermere Avenue, on the crest of the valley's north slope. The two-storey Queen Anne-style house possessed lovely gables and dormers, and clever fish-scale shingles that covered the upper floor, all painted a crisp blue with smart white trim. The verandah boasted large, square posts with a spidery lattice of clematis vines, and to the right of the main door, the west wall held a library seat, where one could sit with book in hand and look down over the side yard and First Street. Unlike the miners' shacks on the lower slope of the valley, our home was clean and warm, with windows that sat flush in their casings. The polished wood floors of our house still gleamed, and had not been pitted by hobnail boots or the scuffing of dog claws. The parlor boasted the newest technology in coal oil lamps, and in the kitchen sat a shiny black McClary Brandon stove.

The house was one of four which faced the grounds of the

Cumberland and District Hospital; all of these homes possessed a sweeping vista of the entire valley from the southward windows, and to the north, a view of the hospital grounds. The company had set these residences aside for their doctors, and truly, they made a row of fine and beautiful buildings: the Saunders family on the corner, then Dr. McNeil and wife next door, then Dr. Frank and his son. The final home lay empty, waiting for the newest appointment. Dear, friendly Dr. Duncan had succumbed to influenza last autumn, and his position had yet to be filled, but gossip said that a military surgeon in Esquimalt had been offered the position, and would be brought north and installed at the beginning of summer.

The funeral carriage turned at the empty house and progressed down the hill to Dunsmuir Avenue, the main street that ran straight as a hatpin through the city. Little clumps of warmly-bundled people appeared from under awnings, and like leaves whirling from the verges behind a passing cart, our procession gathered a flock of mourners in our wake. Violet kept her head down and dabbed at her watery eyes with her hanky. I couldn't help but glance over my shoulder to see who was following, but my curiosity earned me a stiff punch in the thigh from my older sister, with a lot of knuckle added to give it a breath-gasping sharpness.

"It isn't proper to look," she hissed. "Just grieve, Liz."

But I didn't feel much like grieving. Everyone else seemed terribly, terribly sad, but I'd cried myself out last night. Now, I only felt an exhausted disappointment, a numbness that stretched from my cold fingers into my heart. I felt nothing like Violet's dignified weeping. What would it take, I thought, to make me feel the depths of emotion that Violet experienced? My heart beat steadily -- but then, my heart always beat in the same easy rhythm. It rarely reached any sort of pitch, unless I'd run a mile or so.

"I don't think I can," I admitted.

Father looked at me, but not with disgust, like Violet did, or frustration, like Agnes; instead, he looked calm and patient. His voice, when he spoke, was reassuring. "Sometimes, we must pretend to be something we aren't," he said, "Bow your head, Lizzie, and hold your sleeve to your mouth, and no one will know you don't cry."

The carriage and its sad parade moved slowly through the town, passed the stores and the boarding houses, the livery and the blacksmith shop. Violet piously averted her eyes as the carriage rolled by the last house in town, an imposing two-story mansion with more windows than made good sense. Women of loose morals lived there, she'd once told me, and the building was a den of unimaginable sins. The slow and silent progression gave me an opportunity to study it as we passed. A thin blanket of snow covered the prime garden plots, the fence was neat and painted a crisp white. Curtains in the upper windows were made of expensive velvets trimmed with lace, while lamps in the lower rooms gave the house a cheerful warmth. All in all, I thought the house looked rather inviting, and not sinful in the least.

The frozen road led us through the company farm, a collection of swampy strips of fields where brown mules had been put to pasture. The brawny creatures appeared impervious to the wind and snow. They watched the hearse pass, then lowered their noses to the earth again, pawing at the cold ground to forage through the snow-dusted pastures for any edible blades of grass.

The road followed up a small rise, then circled the base of the hill upon which the Chinese buried their dead. Hundreds of wooden planks stuck up from the bald earth, each one carved with characters. Once, when walking passed the graveyard on an early morning stroll with my mother, Molly had whispered into my ear that those marks were the name and ancestral home of the men buried underneath.

"Why do they put their ancestral home on the marker?" I asked.

Molly had paused to shade her eyes from the rising sun. Her fair hair, braided and tied at the nape of her neck, became a golden crown in the sunlight, and her shadow stretched out behind her, narrow and thin, like the needle of a compass.

"Well," she began in her slow and methodical way, measuring her words, always seeking economy, "After seven years, the Chinese remove the bones and polished them. Then, they send the remains back to China to be buried with family. With a name and a place, the bones find their way home."

"The Chinese don't like it here much, do they," I said, "Even when they die, they want to leave."

"Most people have only come here to make a bit of money; they haven't come to stay. The Chinese are simply well-prepared."

"Will we ever go back to England?"

"No, Lizzie," she replied, "I'm afraid we're here forever."

I could almost hear my mother's words in my ears, the memory was so strong. As the funeral carriage left the Chinese graveyard behind, I looked over my shoulder to the square box in the back of the carriage. Here forever.

The horses broke into an undignified trot as the road dipped down into the forest. A cathedral of firs rose around us, giving shelter from the wind, and a pair of bumpy ruts curved between the dark trees. The hearse tipped back and forth with each exposed root, swaying like a ship in a squall, and Violet clung to the side with both hands to keep her seat. I heard bumping in the back, within the casket, but kept my eyes trained forward. Eventually the vaulted ceiling of branches yawned open again, and the carriage pulled into a small patch of open ground, dotted with tombstones. The cemetery lay welcoming and honest before us.

The pallbearers dismounted from the sides of the carriage. I found myself lifted effortlessly to the ground by Rufus McGregor.

The scent of ash and burnt wood rose like incense from the open maw of the freshly-dug grave. Yesterday, the gravediggers had built a fire over the plot to melt the frozen earth, to make it easier to delve, and the consecrated ground still showed signs of scorching. People clustered together against the wind and stamped their boots against the cold. As they clustered close, the mourners looked alike under the swaddling of their heavy coats, but I could distinguish the women by their furs and ruffs, the men by their thick felt scarves and caps pulled down over their ears. I could only see slivers of their faces, eyes squinting in the bracing cold and noses turned red, but I recognized most of them.

There were none I would consider a friend of Molly's.

The Reverend Father Edmund McGill took his place at the head of the grave. He cleared his throat and shook his white robes straight over his woolen undergarments, ruffling like a roosting pigeon. He was stately, regal and arrogantly proud of his congregation, and his pale eyes admired today's crowd from beneath a pair of sweeping white brows. We are taught from birth to trust our clergy but, I'll admit, I did not admire Ned McGill; his gentle and generous manners cloaked an inflexible personality. He possessed a hawkish nose and fine white hair that wisped around his pink scalp, and his mawkish mouth was permanently frozen halfway between a smile and a sneer. He was kind-hearted only to those he deemed worthy of his kindness. His hands were long and skinny with nails bitten down to the quick, and his knuckles popped as he withdrew his Bible from the folds of his robes. When he flopped it open, the leather covers audibly creaked in the cold.

"Life is but a fleeting shadow," he began. His deep voice swam like a fat-bellied trout through the clear air. "Though Margaret Anne Saunders was with us but a short time, our dear Molly's memory shall live on in our hearts."

I plucked at my bodice. It was itchy and confining. Under my coat, the black dress was a prison. I looked around at the downcast faces, all clay masks of grief and sorrow, and wondered with a measure of cynicism how many of these people would keep the memory of Mad Molly in their hearts. Were they here as curious spectators, struggling to catch one last glimpse of the doctor's eccentric wife before the ground consumed her? Even Ned McGill had refused to attend to my mother's spiritual needs during the worst of her fits; though he spoke kindly of her now, safely dead in the grave, my mother while alive had terrified the hell out of him.

How many were here to give their condolences, and how many were here to gather one last bit of gossip? Common consensus deemed Molly to be a harmless lunatic, but a lunatic nonetheless, and her husband's modest wealth and respectable position had done nothing but give her the security to pursue her insane notions with impunity. Many whispered that John Saunders would have been better served to leave her in an institution in Victoria but, if he'd left her in the care of another doctor, his professional reputation would have been irreparably harmed. Perhaps this is true, perhaps not, but I know it wasn't his career aspirations that kept Molly safe from the asylum.

Let me say it plainly: my father was too much in love to abandon her.

He wasn't afraid of her fits, he never questioned her odd behaviors. He took all of these as facets of her personality, and I believe he loved them equally. She was paranoid, obsessive, afraid of shadows, but she was loving, observant, and clever, too. Molly harbored nasty suspicions that neighbors were spying on the house, or that the well water was poisoned with strychnine, or that the night was filled with advancing armies bent on tearing our peaceful home apart. She had an irrational horror of disparaging objects; canned pears, ceramic vases, pomegranates. Once, a painting of a pomegranate in a Christmas catalogue sent my mother into a fit of rage, and she ripped the offending image from the book to cast it into the fire. "I do not like how they look," she had hissed to Agnes' stunned expression, "Their shape reminds us of Sin!"

But her mind was steely and she remembered everything. Molly was astoundingly precise when it came to concrete matters; she knew the exact number of dried kidney beans in the pantry, she kept a running tally of bread slices in the bread box, and she could recite the entire dialogue of 'Hamlet' without a moment's pause.

Of course, as Molly persisted with her fears, the suspicions became true: the neighbors *were* watching. I resented it, but I didn't blame them, for how could they not? By the strangeness of her actions, Molly made herself a target. She rebuffed every attempt at friendliness, deftly shut the curtains on visitors, and locked herself away.

When her illness came, it was a blessing. At last, there was no need for fumbling excuses. Dying gave her a legitimate reason for her seclusion, and she seized it with relish, and took ease that she no longer had to endure the pestering of her neighbors.

At last, the hard lines of worry that had scarred her face melted and vanished. She smiled more, she reclined on the couch in the parlor and drew back the curtain to watch the world pass by. It was only in illness that Molly had started to appear well.

And only in death that she found peace.

Few recognized my father's commitment to his wife and his enduring love for Molly. I don't think people thought it possible to love someone as crazy as her – the mad are only good for making matches or entertaining paying customers on a Sunday afternoon. Otherwise, one must keep them locked away and safely hidden, until they don't feel so insane anymore. No, my mother had no friends and kept no acquaintances, and didn't even have the decency to act like everyone else, yet her husband refused to lock her away like he ought. The public simultaneously hated her and talked unceasingly about her, and this funeral was their last chance to get a good, long look at the pathetic idiot before she was shunted back into ashes and dust.

A hot tear crossed my cheek, but it was borne of rage, not grief.

Father McGill's sermon concluded. Using strips of canvas, the pallbearers lowered the coffin into the grave. The first handful of dry, cold dirt spattered across the lid. All faces turned to the hole in the ground and the coffin, freshly planted, so I took my opportunity to pluck a smooth, round pebble from the ground. I fondled its cold surface between my fingers, then quickly tucked it in my pocket. Father brushed the dirt from his palm against the hem of his coat, then turned from the hole in the ground and gathering Violet and me under his outstretched arms.

"Now, my girls," he said softly, "Your mother is in God's keeping. Let's put this horrible day behind us."

As we reached the coach, I noticed one tall figure hurrying to catch us. In his dove-grey jacket, with his bowler hat tucked under his arm, Alexander Kelly cut a figure as stiff and proper as befitting any man in uniform. His lean and angular face, garnished with a trimmed moustache and topped by a cap of short red-brown hair, wore an expression of solemnity. His eyes, slightly tilted outwards, gave him a constant look of pensive thoughtfulness, made even more pensive and thoughtful by today's sad occasion. It was said that Constable Kelly's father had been a general in the Boer war, and had imparted to his son a bone-deep respect for decorum and precision. This I could easily believe: I'd never met another man with such a keen respect for the law.

He stopped before John and bowed his head crisply. "May God keep your beloved wife in His hand, sir."

"Thank you for your prayers, constable," my father replied.

Violet laid one hand on Mr. Kelly's arm. "You are most kind."

Perhaps the sun shone a little brighter on Kelly. His face took a ruddy luster and his brass buttons gleamed. The look of gravity on his face softened, just a bit, into a smile. "Sir, I appreciate the opportunity to give your family my complete support in your time of grief."

"I don't want to go back by carriage," said Violet. She smiled a little to me. "Father, would you allow Mr. Kelly to escort me home?"

"I think that would be fine," John replied, "If Sandy is in agreement."

Of course he is, I thought. A single glance at Alexander's shining smile told me, nothing would please him more.

"I would be honored, miss," he said to Violet, extending his arm, "We could walk back along the road—"

"I'd rather walk the path around Maple Lake," Violet said, slipping her arm around the offered elbow. "It is a little longer, perhaps, but I should like very much to see the frozen pond, and listen to the laughter of children skating there." She turned to Father. "Do you mind?"

"Not at all."

We watched them go, arm in arm, to collect Kelly's cream-colored horse from the fence where it had been tied. "Do you wish to walk back with them, too?" he asked me.

"Not at all," I replied. "I wouldn't dare!"

"Very sensible of you, Liz," he agreed, "Violet would never forgive you for intruding." He outstretched a sheltering arm and guided me toward the waiting carriage. "Let us go home, then, as fast as the hearse will take us. Agnes will have the fires stoked and a hot lunch ready, and I want nothing more than a scalding cup of tea to wrap my cold hands around."

3

A STEADY LINE of visitors graced the doorway all afternoon, offering words of comfort and condolence. They also brought generous offerings of food and advice, neither of which I had an appetite. Most came to speak directly to my father, and he entertained them in the parlor. He let the women prattle and cluck over him, seeing their mothering to be a need that must be exercised, but he would not accept any pity from the men, and truth be told, they had little.

When the housewives and husbands had gone, Father McGill and John sat in the dim library. The languid flicker of the low fire allowed a body to relax. "I feel a weight has lifted," my father confided. He cast a brief glance towards me, sitting in the window seat with my book in hand. "I'm sorry to admit it in your company, Liz, but it's true."

"Molly had her trials to bear," said Father McGill, sipping the warm glass of buttered rum which Agnes had provided, "And the Lord God knows, you have borne those trials with fortitude and husbandly love, John." He reached forward and patted a supportive hand on John's knee. "But that is over. The future lies ahead. You have two girls to raise, and they must be your focus now."

"My girls are well-equipped to make their way in the world," he replied, "Isn't that right, Lizzie?"

I cast him a brief smile over the lip of the book before dropping my eyes to the page.

"What are you reading, my dear?" said Father McGill.

I lifted the cover to reveal the title: "Frankenstein, or The Modern Prometheus".

Father McGill's accommodating smile faded somewhat, and he looked to John for guidance. "A German book? Not a seemingly title for a young lady."

"English, actually, and I do believe it was written by a woman," John replied, "And not much older than Lizzie, either."

"A children's book, then?" Father McGill approved, eyebrows arched. He settled back into the chair and folded his long hands over his stomach. "Perhaps the time has come to encourage Amaryllis to pursue more feminine topics?" He said this gently, as if plucking his way through a murky stream, "I know Molly held the opinion that Amaryllis need not pursue the same arts as other girls—"

The sentence stopped abruptly as John gave a small, polite but pointed laugh.

"Molly and I were in agreement as how best to educate our children," he stated. "Amaryllis may pursue whatever arts inspire her, and only she knows which ones are best."

The answer was so clipped, so steely and unyielding, that the minister reviewed the direction the conversation was taking. He decided to let it drop. This murky stream may, in fact, be a deep-flowing and treacherous river.

"Of course, of course. You know best how to raise your daughters, John," he said by way of an apology. "But a man, alone, with two girls, and all the mysteries of the feminine condition laid bare before him?" He whistled low. "If ever you need help, or have questions, please know that my home is always open to you, John, and my dear Esther available to assist you."

"Your kindness is greatly appreciated," John replied, settling back into the horsehide chair as his expression relaxed. "And Esther, too. Tell her that I will seek her advice as soon as it is needed."

A footstep on the porch proceeded a light, brisk tap on the door. Agnes hurried to greet whomever had arrived. A flutter of voices rose from the entrance hall, and I met my father's gaze with a look of exasperation.

"You'll forgive me, Ned," said John, standing, "But Peggy and Kitty have arrived."

McGill stood, too, as a pair of women entered the room in a flutter of lace handkerchiefs and skirts and fringed shawls, swaddled against the cold in broad-brimmed felt hats and plush beaver fur coats. Peggy Faulks, a portly spinster and the elder by ten years, soared into the parlor with arms extended, her face a frightful mask of misery, her tiny eyes almost lost under lids grown puffy with weeping. "Oh, John! Oh, dearest John! Oh, our dear sweet widower!" She gripped Father's arms in her talons and wailed, clutching him, caressing him, and causing the quiet house to tremble with her shrill notes. "Oh, you poor, poor, lost man!"

Peggy's perpetual shadow, her gaunt sister-in-law Kitty, ghosted behind with hands clasped in fervent prayer. Kitty's dusky voice was filled with reverence. "We shall implore God for His Eternal Forgiveness to shelter Margaret Anne in her Most Holy Time of Crossing Over."

"Thank you," said John, but Father McGill gave a gruff cough.

"We all shall pray for Molly's eternal soul," Ned stated bluntly.

Kitty Faulks looked askance at the minister, her eyes narrow and mean, her mouth pinched.

It was common knowledge that Kitty Faulks had, in the blossom of her youth, enjoyed a career as a pre-eminent theosophist in Chicago, and had entertained a steady parade of admirers, followers, and devotees with her séances. The public exposure of her theatrics came shortly before meeting her husband, Peggy's brother and a mine manager for the company, who had been traveling east on business. Yes, she admitted, she had used a few cheap tricks to keep her audience's attention, but her mortal deficiencies should in no way detract from the truth and vitality of the spirits that guided her – but her protests fell on a public whose confidence had been irreparably shaken. Spiritualism was on the wane, her career was fading. She had never recovered from her fall from grace.

So she secured a marriage to a man with a good position, gained a sister-in-law sympathetic to the spiritualist cause, and came west, where fads and fashions lagged a decade behind the cosmopolitan centers. Kitty and Peggy became inseparable allies in a world hardened against their psychic crusade.

As creatures privy to the secrets of the spirit world, Peggy and Kitty had little time for men in moth-eaten robes, who spouted Latin benedictions from their dusty tomes. Spiritualists walked their own religious path. There was no love lost between the dramatic Kitty and the dogmatic McGill. Kitty had studied the works of Blavatsky and Doyle during her adolescence in Chicago, had attended séances in London and New York, and was a fierce proponent of photography as evidence of ghostly activity, and in Peggy she had secured a firm supporter. McGill's efforts to return the two women to the Presbyterian fold would forever be thwarted, for she and Peggy together made an impregnable fortress against what they referred to as the Church of the Old and Tired. The best that McGill could pray for was that none of the ladies who joined the Faulks sisters for their séances, held most Saturday nights for a nominal fee, would abandon the Presbyterian tradition, too.

Kitty drew herself up to her full height, which measured slightly less than me. "Peggy and I, tonight, shall hold a vigil for your dearly departed," she announced loudly. If she had any sympathy for the newly-bereaved widower, the righteousness of her beliefs carried her above simpering and fawning. "Already, we have a number of guests who wish to attend. If you so desire to join us, dear John, I do believe we will enjoy success in speaking with our Beloved Spirit Guides."

These last words were said with profound respect. Kitty ignored the rolling eyes of the minister.

John returned her smile, but his expression was kindly, patiently. "Thank you, ladies, but no. My interests do not run to the spiritual, but remain heavily fixed on terra firma. I am a doctor, a man of science, and I'm afraid I might scare away your spirit guides with my brusque and boorish behavior."

"Oh, John, my dear man!" Kitty assured, "You are hardly a bore!"

"No matter, precious widower! We shall endeavor!" Peggy insisted, still clutching his forearms in fervent hands, "We shall ask for guidance, and appeal the angels to comfort you and your children."

He thanked them again as they left in a flutter of shawls and feathers and fur, like all of God's creatures rendered down into two bustling juggernauts. I drew the curtain aside with my fingers and watched them scurry away down the hill towards town, arm in arm to steady themselves against patches of ice.

"Oh, the perils of wayward women," McGill muttered into his mug of buttered rum, "There lies the path to Hell, I'm sure!"

"They're silly, but harmless," John replied.

"Harmless!" McGill harrumphed, "Is that not what the Devil wants us to think? To lull us into complacency? Bah! If Geoffrey Faulks is not willing to discipline the women under his roof, why must we all suffer?" McGill stood and set his mug on the side table, and slapped his hands together. "I ought to be away, John," he said, "But should you need anything, do send word. Your family is in my prayers."

"Very kind of you, Ned," John said, "Thank you so much."

"And I do hope we'll see you in church for tomorrow's service?" McGill added. The question hung in the air for a moment, suspended by doubt. "Though she had her trials to bear, Molly was a pious Christian woman, and we must honor her memory as she would wish by continuing her good work with the Church."

"Perhaps," John replied. "I've much to do in the office."

"You must never be too busy for God," McGill continued as he strode to the door. "Good afternoon to you, Lizzie."

I stood and curtseyed awkwardly in the skirt. "Good day to you, Father McGill."

Once Ned was gone, John settled back into the horsehide chair and held his hand to his forehead. He uttered an audible groan.

"Can I guess, from that groan, that we will not be attending church in the morning?" I said as I settled back into the window seat.

He opened one eye to me. "Your mother wrestled me into a pew every Sunday, and I only went because of my love for her – so to answer your question, Liz: no, we shall not." He closed his eye again.

"Do you think Peggy and Kitty will attempt a séance?"

"Once they set their minds, nothing can stop them," he replied. "The pair of them constitute a remarkable force for backwards thinking."

I snuggled my bookmark between the pages and set 'Frankenstein' on the window sill. "You don't believe in Spiritualism?"

"Not a whit," he assured. "Not a single solitary whit. As fleeting a fad as leeches and humors."

"The Faulks sisters seem very taken by it."

"Don't tell me," he said in mock warning, waggling his finger in my direction, "That you've become enamored with Spiritualism, too?"

I laughed. "No, no!"

"Good. I don't know what I'd do if you started talking nonsense of ghosts and goblins, Amaryllis. You are my hope for a new era, you know – a child of science and reason, rather than curious notions of hocus-pocus and mumbo-jumbo."

"And so you support my reading of this," I questioned, tapping the book cover with my knuckles, "When the minister would prefer me to read A Girl's Own Paper?"

"Ned McGill is as much a purveyor of mythology and magic as the Faulks sisters," he said, "Although far more pleasant to talk with. I swear," he said, massaging his arms, "I think Peggy might have fractured the bone!" He cast me a lop-sided grin that was loving and warm. "You already know that I should be very pleased if you followed in my footsteps, Lizzie, and I shall do everything within my power to support your education and aspirations."

"As long as they run towards medicine, and not religion."

"I shall consider myself a failure if you become one of those dreadful church ladies, with their temperance and cloying good-will and endless bake sales," he replied. "Doubtlessly, if I should find myself in Hell, it will be populated by purveyors of their inedibles."

"You'd better not let Father McGill hear you say such things," I warned, reclining in the window seat again, "The congregation will run you out of town. All well and good for Peggy and Kitty to scintillate the ladies with harmless parlor tricks, but quite another matter for one of the town's doctors to profess he doesn't believe in God!"

"Oh, I believe in God," he assured, "And the Devil too, when it comes down to it. I simply don't think McGill, or the Faulks sisters, or any of them, would recognize a higher power if it whacked them across the face with a rolled-up newspaper. They nurture versions of theology, but know not the facts of which they speak."

"Facts? How can you have facts about God or the Devil, or all those things which rely on faith for our meager understanding?"

"Faith! I put no stock in it! If I seek an answer to the question of God's plan, then I wish only the facts." He crossed his ankles as he settled in for a satisfying conversation, where he could speak openly without fear of retribution. "Mankind was given minds to seek the facts. It is in our nature; it is our celestial duty. If we don't seek facts, if we aspire only to repeat what we've been told, we can never grow and learn. We do a disservice to all of humanity."

"So, what do the facts tell you about God's plan?"

He laughed. "Ah, Lizzie, I have theories, but without evidence to support them, I can not claim to truly know anything. And though he may think he has all the answers, I refuse to follow blindly what Ned McGill tells me. Instead, I seek to educate myself. There is no pursuit more noble than the pursuit of knowledge." He took a sip of his buttered rum and said, "While we are on the topic of education... I hear you've been fighting at school again."

"Who says?"

Judging by the way his mouth kinked up in suppressed amusement, he had noticed that my sharp question was, in no way, a refusal. "Is it true?"

I did not sulk, I did not feel shame. My reaction to being discovered was to lift my chin in defiance. “Twice,” I said, then added quickly, “Only twice! And both times, they deserved it!”

“You can’t solve your problems with your fists, Amaryllis,” he said, and shifted forward in his seat to rest his elbows on his knees and cross his wrists. “First of all, it is not tolerated by the school officials, and you will be asked to leave, and you are too bright to cast aside your schooling so lightly. Secondly, there will come a day when the boys are bigger than you, and you’ll find yourself laid flat on the ground with a split lip, and then where will you be?”

“Then I’ll just have to keep practicing, and make sure I’m faster than them.”

He shook his head in disapproval. “I can’t condone your violence, Lizzie. It simply isn’t—“

“Don’t tell me it isn’t becoming of a young lady,” I warned, “Because Violet already told me that, after I knocked Buster Gillingham to the ground.”

“Buster Gillingham!” He looked astonished. “He’s quite the lad already! How ever did you fell him?”

“He’s got a glass jaw, if you hit him right.” I tipped my head and tapped my finger to the point of my own chin. “He carries his mouth to the left, and he protects it when he scraps with the other boys. It wasn’t difficult to lay him low, with a fist to the right spot.”

John opened his mouth to praise me, then held himself in check, and remembered his fatherly obligation. “Lizzie, it simply isn’t wise to draw such attention to yourself. You already set yourself apart with your wardrobe. I will tolerate the pants, the shirts, the boots, but I can’t tolerate fighting. It makes no sense for you to beat up the boys of the Cumberland, only for me to stitch them back together.” He reclined in his chair. “People will think I’m trying to drum up business.”

“You haven’t asked me why I hit Buster.”

“Frankly, I don’t care,” he replied.

I left the window seat and took the chair which Father McGill had left empty. I still wore the corset and dress, and I sat stiff and supported by the wretched whale bones, but I extended my feet to the warm fire crackling in the hearth and tried to relax. "The girls say I'm destined to be as crazy as...." The words snagged in my throat. "As Mad Molly. Buster repeated it: he said I ought to be locked in an cell. So I plowed him one."

"You don't hit the girls, too, do you?"

I pursed my lips. "I wanted to. But they're Violet's friends; she'd never forgive me."

He looked at me with pity. "You need friends of your own, Lizzie."

"I don't want them," I replied, "Especially if they're like Violet's. A bunch of fussy, simpering fools, all of them! I bet they couldn't climb a tree if their life depended on it." I stared into the fire. "I've got my books and the woods to explore. I don't need anyone else to slow me down."

Together, we stared into the fire in comfortable silence.

"You are like your mother in many ways," he said at last, "She was never one for friendships, either. Damn pesky things which need always to be nurtured and tended like the most delicate bonsai... that reminds me. Molly may not have had friends, but she had acquaintances, and I've asked your sister to sent out the death notices; will you help her? She's most distraught, but you've managed to retain your composure, and I think she'll appreciate your level-headed assistance."

"Of course," I replied. I almost spoke further, but held my tongue.

John caught my hesitation. "What's wrong?"

What, precisely, was wrong? I had pondered this question all morning and had yet to divine a satisfactory answer. I felt as though nothing was wrong, when all logic told me otherwise. Shouldn't I be upset? Shouldn't I dissolve into tears at the mere thought of my lost mother? Shouldn't Molly's death have caused me some small measure of distress?

"Well, it's my composure, as you put it."

John drew his brow together, confused. "I'm sorry?"

I tried to explain as best I could. "I'm sad – really, I am. But I don't know if I feel grief like I ought. Violet is upset, and crying, and misses Mother, but I feel like all of the grief in me is buried under a big pile of sand. I can hear it, far away, but I can't feel it in my heart or my bones. Why can't I cry, like Violet?" I shook my head in bewilderment. "Why do I get so angry so quickly, but feel no sadness?"

"You are rational and not given easily to histrionics," he replied. "Do not see it as a deficiency, Liz, for it isn't."

"But Violet weeps and crumbles under her overwhelming grief. Father, there's something terribly wrong with me." I wrinkled my nose. "Maybe Buster's right: I am destined for the mad house."

"Of course not," he replied sharply, "You feel exactly as you should! Do not belittle yourself because you're different from all the rest! That which sets you apart makes you stronger." He clapped his hands around his knees. "Violet, Buster, and all the rest – they don't understand you, but that is their shortfall, not yours!"

I smiled at him. "Really?"

"That being said," he added, "You still must not fight them. When they question your lack of emotion, you must feign it, to put them at ease. Feel pity for them, Liz. They just don't understand the scientific mind."

"You say I should act the part, but as she lay dying, Mother instructed me to be true to myself."

He sighed as he curled again into the curve of the chair. His eyes were sad. "But Lizzie, your mother had me to protect her from a world that didn't understand her. I'm not asking you to be anything but what is natural to you; I'm simply saying you must be more careful in choosing those to whom you show your true nature. Does that make sense?"

I must be true to myself, but hide myself from those who wouldn't appreciate the truth? No, it didn't make much sense to me, but I nodded to reassure him.

He smiled. "Now, will you help Violet? I know she would appreciate it."

"I'd be happy to help."

"I have only a few people to notify: professional acquaintances of mine, mostly in Victoria, and a few in Nanaimo."

I selected my words with care and kept my question short. "None in England?"

The reply was equally careful and short. "No."

I returned my gaze to my feet, watching the flickering fire between the V of my silk slippers, but then mustered my courage and said, "But what of—"

"None, Lizzie," he insisted. "None. You will not contact Captain Worthington, am I clear?"

"Yes, sir."

"I absolutely forbid it."

"Yes, sir."

"You promise me, you will not," he demanded. "Promise."

My brows knit together, my mouth pursed in confusion. "How can I promise that?" I replied, "Shouldn't Molly's own father know she's dead?"

But John's face drew down blackly, and the shadows from the fire now played over an expression that was, all at once, determined and angry and remorseful. He shook his head. "Believe me, Lizzie, the damn stubborn bastard won't care."

I pouted a little. "Maybe they're dead by now. It's been almost ten years since you last spoke to them. Perhaps this ridiculous feud between you and Grandfather is at an end, and you don't even know!"

"The captain made it clear to me that he already considers us dead and gone." John stood, signifying that this topic was at its end. "A letter to Horatio Worthington is a waste of a penny stamp, and I want your promise that you'll only send notifications to those I've asked. Please, Lizzie, promise me."

I grumbled but finally muttered, "I promise."

A solid knock upon the door rang out. As Agnes hurried to the door to admit the next wave of mourners, the determined set of his jaw softened and he shared with me a look of warm affection. He stood and took my hand in his. "You are as stubborn as your mother, my girl. I have long suspected that you take after Molly, and she was very driven, very clever, and always very private with her heart."

"She was crazy, too," I said.

"Her reasons weren't always... apparent," John said carefully, "But all of her best qualities, I see in you." He brushed the palm of his hand over the curve of my cheek. "And I recognize in you a reflection of my own curiosity about the world. I hope to nurtured it, like a tiny spark which I might, given the right conditions, coax into a roaring inferno." He leaned forward to place a kiss on my forehead, a rare gesture for my father to share. "I'm proud of you, Lizzie. Proud beyond measure of all that you do."

4

THE AMBITIONS of one lone man, Robert Dunsmuir, created this place.

That's what Miss Marsh, the school teacher, told our class. She said that, before Robert Dunsmuir's arrival, this island was nothing but wilderness, nothing but a rock shrouded with untamed forests, latticed with rivers rushing through narrow chasms towards the Gulf of Georgia. The rugged, misty coast had sat in a state of stasis for millennia. Deer, bears, wolves, and noble savages lived on its surface, oblivious to the riches over which they lived.

Miss Marsh said that the coal hungered for a glorious man to notice it, to organize the workers required to free it from its terrestrial prison, to set the gears of industry whirling and bring civilization to this primordial Eden. Dunsmuir recognized the riches that the primitive landscape of Vancouver Island horded to its greedy bosom. In 1869, he endeavored to liberate the coal and lumber by claiming the prospecting rights over 1000 acres. He obtained financial backing, took on partners, and as the *Dunsmuir, Diggle and Company*, began to mine the rich coal seams along the east coast of the island.

By God's grace, the colony of British Columbia owed this debt to the Queen. She had welcomed this wretched backward land into her

Empire. She had brought prosperity and technology to the far edge of the world; the least this colony could do in return was support itself with its plentiful resources. Dunsmuir, wielding a emperor's power over all the bounty it offered, had perfectly positioned himself to make a fortune.

The Wellington Mines, just north of Nanaimo, proved to be a huge financial success for Dunsmuir, and he began to look farther afield. The lands of the Komoux and Pentlatch peoples caught his eye. Three major river valleys and countless streams, rivulets and creeks cut a venous path from a single inland lake to the curve of the ocean shore. The lake was glacial fed and steep-sided, bounded with granite cliffs and rumored to be bottomless: an endless source of fresh water, then, as Dunsmuir saw it. The canyons between rugged mountains, where the lake's waters gushed down to the sea, provided home for deer and elk: a supply of food waiting for hunters to cull. Where the rivers joined, flooded and swelled over their banks and dropped the silt they'd brought from the highlands, there was a wide alluvial plain: fertile agricultural land, good fishing in the bay, and plenty of resources to harvest. Most importantly, and to Dunsmuir, important above all things on this good green earth, here in this valley and on the shores of the lake lay the hallmarks of luscious coal seams lurking below the surface.

He bought out his partners from *Dunsmuir, Diggle and Co.*, sold shares in the renamed *Union Coal Company*, and took as new partners his sons, James and Alexander. In 1883, he contracted with the federal government to build the Esquimalt and Nanaimo Railway in return for $750,000 and a land grant of almost 2 million acres, encompassing the entire southeast quarter of Vancouver Island. All mineral and timber rights belonged, now, to the industrious Robert Dunsmuir, and the northern jewel in his crown was the valley by the Pentlatch and Komoux lake.

In the harsh winter of February 1888, a prospecting party determined the most lucrative area for mining, a mile or so east of the lake. Here, outcroppings of dark, oily coal slanted into the hillsides at a 12 degree angle and promised deep, rich seams underground. When they sent the good news back to Victoria, Dunsmuir immediately dispatched engineers and builders. They plunged shafts into the ground, erected cabins for miners, laid bare the earth and ravaged it.

When Miss March reached this part of the history lesson, I noticed that she became a little breathless.

Dunsmuir called the settlement "Union", and the nearest deep-water bay was selected as a shipping port, called "Union Bay". The company immediately dispatched teams of men to survey an 18-mile railway between the two destinations. Chinese work gangs arrived from other Dunsmuir operations, both as miners and to build the train tracks. They were housed in shacks build on the swampy lowlands while the company officials occupied a camp on higher ground.

By August 1888, the Union Colliery Company was incorporated, and by the end of 1888, the railway was completed. With the arrival of three locomotives, the production of coal from the mines could begin. The first 21 tons of coal were brought from No. 1 mine and No. 2 mine on the 25th of May, and in early July, the San Mateo steamed from Union Bay's harbor with its 4500-ton shipment of Comox coal.

But Dunsmuir never saw the culmination of his work: he died in April, 1889. The company fell to the management of his son, James.

When No. 4 mine opened in 1890, it provided a greater wealth of coal that the previous three mines. The humble camp and swampy Chinatown now grew into sizeable communities, capable of supporting the hundreds of miners who came to work. The Union Coal Company's growth, and the fortune of the Dunsmuir family, was assured.

As the company's prosperity was assured, so too was the future of the town now rising up from the slag heaps and ashes of industry. Men must eat, and clothe themselves, and have a bed to rest their weary limbs. They require succor, and liquor, and entertainment. They have needs that cry out for a community, and hearing that cry in the pay checks and prosperity, a community came -- first called "Camp", then named "Union", and then, in 1898, with the official status of a city placed upon it by the provincial government of British Columbia, entitled "Cumberland".

THE CITY of Cumberland that I knew was little more than a grid of dirt streets scratched out of the wilderness, surrounded by dingy pocks of coal mines and lumber yards. The whole community -- mines, sawmills, homes, shops, school, boarding houses, train tracks -- nestled in a narrow valley between mountains mantled in cedars and firs. At first glance, one could be forgiven for mistaking it for the end of the earth. The savage Pacific rainforests crowded in, resisting gentrification, and the lowest basin of the valley remained damp and swampy and choked with vegetation, even during the hottest months of the year. Where men had logged the slopes to provide timber for the mines, salal creepers and wild blackberry briars grew thickly, taking full advantage of the sunlight and stumpage to grow unhindered. The brambles rose up so deep that, in places, they could swallow a horse and rider whole. Everything grew vigorously, eager to live. A cleared field was replaced by shrubs within a season, and a man could barely keep pace against the relentless reclamation of the wilderness.

The woods were thick with life, all size and shape: herbivore, carnivore, omnivore. There were insects as big as a girl's hand, shaggy deer, packs of wolves, families of black bears, and solitary mountain lions. There were rats and voles, stoats and squirrels, snakes and frogs. In my estimation, the trees sheltered an infinite zoo of creatures, all of whom rebelled actively against humanity. Beasts peered out of the thickets with slavering lips, waiting to undermine any effort to tame them. So, yes, Cumberland was a city, but a city under the constant assault of nature. Its citizens knew that they must remain vigilant, work hard and secure their footing here, lest the forests grow up around us and brute Nature evict us.

That's what I love about Cumberland. Existence here is precarious. My mother knew it, the Chinese men who dig up the bones knew it. We're hanging on by our fingertips, no matter what we build, excavate, or destroy.

And nothing is ever clean here. A constant miasma of thick, dark coal smoke hangs in the air, perfuming everything with its heavy acrid scent. Mineral dust tints the coats of the mules and stains the wooden buildings. Some of the buildings are white-washed, and some are painted a rusty red, but all wear the same dusty grey film, no matter how old or new. On a still day, the air boasts a palpable thickness that sticks in the lungs and burns the back of the throat.

But no one dares complain because the stench is the dizzying perfume of industry. Plenty of people keep the Camp houses occupied, and more arrive daily seeking money and jobs and a chance at prosperity, and the coal dust that settled over everything, road and laundry and gardens, is the glorious byproduct of money to be made.

But even a girl like me knows, the money made is never equally shared. Within this sheltered bubble of gentility, surrounded on all sides by the unruly chaos of the natural world, stratification is the best method of instilling order and peace on civilized society. Dominion society lies in carefully constructed layers. The Englishman reigns over all, for he is the representative of all that is good and holy on the surface of the earth: this is generally accepted, enforced by the Company and unquestioned by local government. Below him exists a complex and Byzantine hierarchy, so dense and complex that the Englishman gives no thought to its structure. Let the unfortunates bicker and squabble amongst themselves. The Englishman is too busy with the exhausting chore of ruling the world.

THE NUCLEUS of Cumberland sat on the boundary between the old Camp settlement and the new city neighborhoods. Here was the Union Hotel, a massive boarding house where a perpetual rotation of new bachelors passed; the Union and Company Mine Clinic, to whom all company employees paid a monthly insurance fee of 50 cents, and where the four Colliery doctors would hold office for a week each month; a slanted two-story building with a barber on street level and a candy store in the back; and finally, the Company store, a three-story false-fronted establishment. A platform ran the length of its rear entrance. A short arm sprouted from the railway tracks and ran alongside this platform, which doubled as the Cumberland Station.

In Camp's earliest days, these four buildings had been the entire commercial district, but as the mine sites developed and the population grew, a rollicking economic boom struck the settlement. Where there's miners, there's money; where there's money, there soon comes those eager to take it. From all corners of the globe, hundreds of men arrived and took jobs with the Colliery. They brought their families and their brothers and their cousins. In the late 1880's, Union Camp had been a transient place, but the town began to spread eastward, where the valley slopes were less severe and the land easier to clear of trees. As people tried to put down roots, the camp solidified into a town of buildings, homes, parks and churches.

Boardwalks flanked the dirt streets. These were an absolute necessity for any town of good standing. The roads were easily passable for fine people only at the apex of summer, when the sun baked the dirt hard, and the depths of winter, when January snow froze the mud. All the rest of the year, the roads were ditches of filth that reached up to a child's knee, scattered with wads of manure and rutted deeply by wagon wheels. Boardwalks offered pedestrians a safe and clean path to stroll. Ladies with long dresses could walk from shop to shop, examining the wide array of goods which filled the windows, without fear of ruining their hems.

Dunsmuir Avenue, the main street, became a bustling hub of commerce. There was a small hip-roofed school that held 200 children, affectionately known as the Cottage, and a stout city hall, a livery stable, and an undertaker's. On the south east corner of First Street and Dunsmuir, a tall narrow building provided the constable with an office and jail. Upstairs, he was given a modest apartment.

On the south west corner of Dunsmuir and First sat the Masonic Hall, then the theatre, then a series of further shops, with Mr.

Samson's tinsmith shop on the corner of Dunsmuir and Second. Along the north side of the street ran a line of boarding houses -- a prosperous business in a town where men seemed to flow like water. A constant tide of new miners needed a place to sleep before they snagged themselves onto some permanent fixture in town, like an enviable management position, perhaps, or a wife. Some of the boarding houses rose as high as four stories with balconies on the upper levels. They had names like the Vendrome, the Cumberland Hotel, or the Waverley. The Eagle was a popular choice for migrating Americans, following the tales of gold and prosperity, but it had a reputation of being noisy and rowdy, and a place where virtuous ladies did not linger outside.

Public houses sold the migrant workers nourishment and entertainment, and the most notorious of all was the Bucket of Blood, which occupied the main floor of the Vendrome boarding house. Because its neighbor, the Waverley, was a temperance house of high regard and steel-clad morals, the Bucket of Blood managed to pull clientele from both establishments. On a Saturday night, the noise that issued from within was heard as far away as the west end of Camp. The Vendrome faced on Dunsmuir Avenue, but it backed onto Penrith Avenue, otherwise known with a wink and a grin as Church Row: the tall and stately Presbyterian spire on the west corner, the squat wooden Catholic tower on the south, and a full range of devotions in between. The humor of the town planners showed plainly. On Saturday nights, the Blood rocked with the drunken revelry of easy men and ladies of loose morals, but on Sunday morning, when the bells began to chime, it was impossible to remain passed out on the floor. Guilt had a miraculous way of dragging even the most ill and hungover to the chapel service of their choice.

Houses, churches, school, halls and livery: of these things, Cumberland was comprised, but it was not the whole of the equation. The Camp road, straight as a pin, led westward down a hill until it bumped against the railway line leading to No. Four mine. Most of

Cumberland's citizens considered this junction, where road met railway, to be the end of town.

But the road continued on the other side of the tracks, for the rail line was not the end of habitation. It was the boundary between West and East – the division between the Queen's dominion and the rest of the strange, dangerous world.

British coal miners of the lowest standing, even the dispossessed from the poorest slums of Northumberland, were given homes in town and knew themselves to be superior to those who lived outside Cumberland's boundary. On the other side of the railway were four distinct communities, carefully segregated from one another and, more importantly, from the upper crust of British management: first Chinatown, then a Japanese settlement (called, more out of economy than disdain, 'Japtown One'), then a small collection of black Americans fleeing the strife and racism of California. Finally, hugging the shore of Comox Lake, there sat a little group of cabins occupied by Hungarians, Italians and Polish families. 'Japtown Two' snuggled against the northern edge of Cumberland, providing accommodation for the Nipponese men who worked at the coal face of No. Five mine.

But these people did not often come to town, and if they did, it was surely for nefarious purposes. As Violet was fond of reminding me, fine ladies did not cavort with members of lesser races. To do so was a disgrace, not only to their family or their friends, but the entire regal heritage of their glorious British blood. "The Good Lord has placed us here to educate them and humor them," she would say, if ever she caught me looking too long at one of those foreign faces. "But we are not to befriend them, or accept them, or pollute ourselves with their absurd and ignorant ways. Beware, Lizzie," she would say in a hushed whisper, "They will drag you down and destroy you, if you let them."

5

March 9, 1898

Cpt. Horatio L. Worthington
12 Eden Vale
Westbury, Wiltshire
United Kingdom

Dear Grandfather,

No doubt but that you are questioning the identity of this strange woman who is so bold to write you and so brazen as to call you 'grandfather', but though many years separate our acquaintance, our ties by blood can not be so easily forgotten, and I hope you will forgive me for my forthright greeting. My name is Amaryllis Elizabeth Saunders, and I am the youngest child of Dr. John Saunders and Margaret Anne (nee Worthington) Saunders, which makes me your youngest granddaughter.

It has been ten years since last we spoke, and as I am almost sixteen, that would ensure that you are a stranger to me, but perhaps

I am not so much a stranger to you. Your memory of me might be fresh, though erroneous, for I am no longer the little sprite who played upon the hearth or dangled from your arms, seeking childish affection, or whom you took on rambles through the Wiltshire countryside. I am now a young woman living in the colonial colliery town of Cumberland, on the westernmost edge of the Dominion of Canada, and my ways are no longer that of a silly and frivolous toddler. My sister, Violet Anne, is a fine young woman. As the next year turns and leads us towards the new century, I hope to follow her example and become a graceful, accomplished and respectable woman, too.

The reason for my letter is, as you can see from the black edge of this paper, a sad and grievous one. While we have spent many years *in absentia* from your company, my heart persists in telling me that I must inform you of your daughter's untimely demise. In the last weeks of January, she fell grievously ill with a weakness of the heart and lungs, and succumbed quietly and without pain to her illness on February 12th of this year of our Lord, eighteen ninety-eight. It was a natural death, performed with grace. I hope this knowledge will, in some small measure, ease the pain you must surely feel upon reading this letter.

Father continues to practice medicine, and does his duty to Queen and Country with as much fervor as he can muster, but the loss of our Mother has struck him mortally, and he has grown withdrawn of late. I fear for Father's professional reputation and for his bodily safety, but I trust that time will heal these wounds, as our elders so often assure us.

Please remember me to grandmother, my aunts and uncles, and all of my cousins, to whom (it is my enduring disappointment) I am not acquainted.

God save the Queen,
Amaryllis Elizabeth Saunders

6

MARCH 13, 1898

"LIZZIE!"

Agnes Gunn's cannonball voice shattered the tranquility of the back garden. The plants still slept under frost-prickled earth but, I mused as she bellowed my name again, maybe Agnes could wake them.

"Lizzie! Where are yeh?" The barrel-bodied woman stood on the back porch, holding her brown shawl to her throat as if a tempest of Shakespearean proportions threatened to rip it from her shoulders. Her eyes widened when she caught sight of me, sitting in the wheelbarrow under the apple trees. Her scowl deepened. "Oh, ya neep-heid!" she proclaimed, "What are yeh doing oot in this weather? You'll catch yer death!"

I stood and closed the book in my hands. "I found a quiet spot to read," I explained, "It's not so chilly outside, once you're used to it." A few puffy clouds dotted the sky but the air was dry and clear. I wore a grey woolen sweater and trousers, a felt jacket, and a pair of heavy boots on my feet, and these insulated me well from the cold. Besides, the fresh breeze provided a welcome change from the stuffy, dry heat of the parlor, where the scent of the cedar boughs lingered and reminded me of death.

"God Almighty!" Agnes shook her head. "The last thing I wish tae do is nurse you back from the edge of pneumonia, you daft fool! Get ye in here, where it's warm!" As she shepherded me indoors, she muttered, "With Molly naught a month in the grave, and you, a-dallying tae join her!"

"I'm fine," I protested, but relented to her fussing as Agnes stripped the jacket from my shoulders and, holding it disdainfully at arm's length, hung it in the broom closet by the back door.

"I thought ye'd agreed to put *these* away," she said, ranging her eyes down my body to show what, exactly, she meant. To mention the clothes would only bring attention to them, legitimize them; if Agnes referred to the trousers obliquely, they held less power and were less real.

"I never agreed to anything, except to wear a dress to the funeral," I replied as I unlaced my boots. I set them neatly to the side of the kitchen stove, so that they would be warm and cozy when I next put them on. "Besides, Mrs. Gunn, I was chopping kindling before I stopped to read. I can't rightly do that in a corset, can I!"

"A lady can perform all sorts of miraculous feats in proper dress," Agnes snapped, "And you'd be wise tae grow accustomed tae it, for you won't be young forever, my duckling, and there'll be less folks who forgive you your strange notions, once you're grown." She set her hands on her hips. "Now, enough of this! Get you dressed proper, and help Violet. She's the one looking for you, not me."

I sprinted up the stairs to the second floor, and peered around the corner of the first doorway.

Violet sat at her desk by the window, her throat as pale and radiant as a moonbeam against the black lace of her neckline. A neat stack of envelopes lay before her, and in one hand, she held a little wooden brush. She gazed across the street to the hospital gardens but, hearing a soft footstep on the landing, Violet roused herself from her quiet contemplations and smiled to see me standing in the doorway.

"Come in, Liz, come in," she bid.

I sat on the edge of her bed. "You're still preparing the announcements? It's been almost two weeks!"

"This is not a task to be rushed, Liz. To draft a suitable letter is an art! It demands a woman's proper attention and care."

"I'm glad you're doing it, then, because I don't have the patience."

Violet smiled with pride. "I'm almost done. Will you run them to the post office with me?" She leaned forward. "Alexander Kelly leaves the constabulary at the stroke of four, and I should like very much to meet him in the street, purely by accident." Her smile was sweetly devious. "But I dare not go alone, lest he thinks I'm pursuing him. If it's the two of us, he'll think he's merely met us by chance, out on an afternoon stroll."

"What else would it be?" I feigned naivety with wide eyes, "Of course it's an afternoon stroll! It's a fine afternoon for a stroll."

Violet giggled at our scheme. She sealed the last envelope with a daub of glue and put the lid back on the glue pot. "I've been cooped up in my room all day, Liz, and I'm dying to stretch my legs. Is it cold outside?"

"Cool and brisk, but very pleasant."

"Good," she replied, "Maybe spring is on its way, after all. I can not fathom how we spent so many long days locked inside as wee children. A couple of caged birds, without any thought to how it must feel to fly!"

"It was natural to us, then," I replied, "We didn't know anything else."

"There was no reason for us to question Mother's ideas," Violet mused half to herself, then grinned, "But, thank goodness we escaped from that ugly life! When I return to London, I can't wait to visit every museum, gallery and gathering that it has to offer! Imagine it, Liz! It will be grand! Parties, music, dancing, a promenade around Hyde Park in the spring--" Violet stood and gathered a plum-colored coat from the wardrobe. "What larks!"

"You can keep it," I laughed, "I don't think I'm cut out for England anymore."

"Well, to that, I whole-heartedly agree," she said, leaning to the mirror to best pin a compact velvet hat to her hair. "Head uncovered, man's coat, trousers two sizes too big for you, an old leather satchel slung over your shoulder. England wouldn't know what to do with the likes of you." She clucked in the back of her throat. "I'd say you'd gone native, Liz, but even the natives know their place."

I said nothing, but cast my eyes aside and folded my arms.

"What?" Violet said, "Do I not speak plainly?"

"I have a hard time stomaching the thought that anyone has 'a place', as you put it."

"But of course we each have a place," she said absently as she adjusted her hat, "Every one of us, from the lowest urchin to the highest king, has part to play in this grand stage performance called Life. You are in constant struggle against your allotted role, Liz; that is why you are so terribly unhappy."

"But I'm not unhappy," I protested.

"Oh, I know you are terribly sad inside," Violet replied with a pitying smile.

"If you really wish to know how I feel, Vi, then let me tell you: I'm repulsed by your idea that some people are better than others, for no greater reason than the place of their birth."

"Lizzie, poor dear," she cooed, "If God wanted them to be privileged, He would have made them English."

At that, I barely contained a sharp, incredulous laugh.

But she ignored me; it was her preferred method of debate. "There is an established order to things, Liz, and it does no one any good to pretend otherwise." As I followed her down the stairs to the main floor, she added over her shoulder, "It's the truth, and there's nothing nasty about the truth."

I pulled on my boots, toasty and warm from their place next to the stove, and grabbed my leather satchel from the coat cupboard. We bid Mrs. Gunn farewell and left through the back door. The slight breeze had mellowed, and a few more clouds had appeared on the horizon. Perhaps it would snow tonight, but the weather would remain clear for a few hours yet. Our leather boot soles thumped on the frosty street as we walked, arm in arm. I considered arguing further, but honestly -- what good would it do?

As we rounded the corner onto Dunsmuir Street, I unfurled my arm from Violet's embrace and asked, "May I see Mother's announcements?"

"Why?" she countered, "Do you not trust that I've finished them? You saw me apply the last strokes."

"I want to admire your handiwork," I consoled, "To see the letters, to feel them in my hand: I think it makes it more real to me, that Mother's actually dead and gone."

From the protective depths of her beaded purse, Violet withdrew a little parcel of letters, bundled together around the middle with a short length of white string. Each envelope had been carefully edged with black. She placed them carefully in my outstretched hand and we continued to walk as I leafed through them. "Most are bound for Victoria, and I wanted to ensure they looked as lovely as possible," said Violet. "Wouldn't it be horrible for them to look provincial and rough? I couldn't bear it, to have Mother's last announcement appear unfashionable." She gave a little shudder.

"There aren't many," I noted.

"Father gave me only a few names to contact, mostly in Victoria, so I've sent one to the British Colonist for good measure. Do be careful, Liz! The last thing we need is your smudged fingerprints all over them!"

One name seemed to be written with more of a flourish that the others. "You've sent one to Mason Briggs, I see."

Did a blush give color to Violet's alabaster cheeks? "Father asked me to," she said, her face down.

"And I'm sure it was a pleasure to write," I needled, snuggling the envelope back amongst the others. "You would have notified him, even if he weren't on Father's list."

"It's only appropriate that Dr. Briggs know," she defended, "He lodged with us last summer; he and Mother got along very well."

"As did you and he, if I recall," I said. "And the fact that he is a wealthy, well-established bachelor with a thriving practice in Victoria had nothing to do with it." I grinned. "Oh, come on, Vi. Don't be embarrassed. He's a handsome fellow; I'd be concerned if he HADN'T caught your eye."

"He proved to be enjoyable company last summer," she said weakly, "That's all." Violet outstretched one gloved palm. "Now here, give them back, I'll keep them safe."

But I hesitated. "Can I hold them? Please? I really didn't do much to help, and holding them makes me feel as if I'm helping in some small way."

Like a patient mother doting on a foolish child, Violet consented by snapping her purse closed. "Just be careful," she added. "Put them in your satchel, to keep them safe. Unless you've carried something terribly dirty in there – have you? Rocks and twigs? Jelly sandwiches?"

"Only books, Vi, to and from school."

This satisfied her, and she seemed visibly relieved when the letters were safely tucked in my bag.

Our leather boots tapped musically on Dunsmuir's wooden boardwalk. We passed the hotels, parlors, greengrocers, two butchers, a furniture craftsman, a livery. Even under the dull light reflected by the overcast sky, the streets were crowded and colorful. Afternoons on Dunsmuir Avenue produced a strange mix of demographics: women in fine dresses shopping, gritty men changing shifts at the mines and mill, boisterous children playing with jacks and marbles in the dirt, dogs urinating on the boardwalk posts, along with a team of mules driven in from the Company pastures. As we crossed the intersection at Second Street, a pair of oxen dragging a lumber cart paused to let a hansom cab jingle merrily passed. A crier on the corner sold today's edition of the Islander News, and Mr. Samson called out to his stock boys, who struggled to carry crates of supplies inside his tinsmith shop.

In the early afternoon, the bars plied a brisk trade in lunches, pails of beer and entertainments. A crush of men wearing brown workman's overalls moved along the northern side of the street, filing into the beer halls. They had spent the last ten hours digging the shaft at Number Six mine, dredging up buckets of greasy soil and pulverized rock, and their faces were black with dust and sweat. When they emerged from the earth, rattling six hundred feet up to the surface, the men all looked the same. Chinese, Japanese, Scottish, Hungarian, Italian: black with dust, they became identical.

The surge of miners outside the Bucket of Blood attracted Violet's attention. I noticed my sister hold the beaded purse more tightly to her side as the we stepped aside to let a boisterous knot of young men, half-starved and thirsty, hurry passed.

"Goodness," Violet said in a hushed voice, "Such rough fellows."

"And without them, this place would crumble, and the doctors would have nothing to do," I replied. "And more are coming – Father says the company is bringing in more Scottish workers."

"I suppose it will be nice to have a few new faces in this town," Violet said, her hands folded at her waist. "And I'm pleased to hear that they're coming from Scotland – there are simply too many foreigners here already, don't you think? Mrs. Gunn told me that, after the problems in Nanaimo, the Company is less inclined to let their Chinese workers near the explosives."

"As I figure it, we're foreigners too, Violet."

"Oh, Liz!" She wrapped her hand over my elbow. "This is the Queen's Dominion, and we belong here. More than anyone!"

I opened my mouth to disagree but was interrupted by a hearty guffaw. "Good day to yeh both, me wee lassies!"

The man standing directly behind us was round and small, and covered in a thick crust of dirt from his ankles to his armpits. His bristly beard, normally a rusty red, had turned a dull grey with coal dust. When he tipped his cap, a puff of fine grit rose from his hair. The only thing that seemed clean about him were his teeth, which gleamed white.

"Good morning, Mr. Gunn!" I said brightly. "How are you today?"

"I am right well, now that the day is done for me, and I can head home tae a good hot bath and a good hot meal!" he chortled. "And you, lassies! How're you this fine day?"

"Very well, thank you," Violet replied, "I was just telling Lizzie, your wife has said there will be more of your countrymen arriving to work in Number Six."

"Aye, true!" he replied, "This summer, once the bellows are up and running."

"And Dunsmuir won't be hiring any more men from Asia?" I asked, "Is that true, too?"

Hamish Gunn gave a snort, then spat a wad of black phlegm over the side of the boardwalk and onto the street. "Is that what Agnes told ye? No, no, Dunsmuir'll hire more. He can save his money, with Celestials on the roll – they'll work for half the wages with nary a complaint, and sleep six tae a bed. Fewer houses, less money? Aye, he'll bring 'em on, that's for sure."

Violet scoffed. "They ruin the quality of the town."

"Well, there's no help tae be done for it," Mr. Gunn continued, "Not while there's seams tae be dug, and money tae be made, and bloody Celestials tae take the lowest wage and work twice as long." He slapped his filthy hands across his thighs. "But pay it no mind, girls. The heathens keep tae themselves, and go back tae where they've come once the Company's worked the good years oot of them. They don't warrant a thought from the likes of fine, upstanding ladies." He glanced at me and his grin broadened. "I keep hope and pray tae God that there's an upstanding lady somewhere in that get-up of your's, Miss Amaryllis."

"I doubt I'll ever become a lady, Mr. Gunn, when there are so many opportunities to be a rogue and a pirate," I replied.

He laughed. "Oh, ye'll meet a fine lad, and want tae turn his head, and I wager ye'll be in the skirts and finery faster than spit, me lassie!"

"God's teeth, wouldn't that be a marvel!" Violet laughed.

I tipped my chin towards the mine site below. "You said the new shaft will be open in summer?"

"Early September, most likely, if the weather co-operates." His eyes glittered. "We've dug almost five hundred feet of shaft, and already we've hit coal. She'll be a fine operation, this one, and they'll need many hands to help with the digging." He looked toward the entrance of the Eagle, where a cluster of men flowed in for a nip of food at the bar. "The word travels fast in the Old Country that the Union Coal Company needs laborers. There's no work in the coal fields of Fife and Culross, so they've naught tae leave behind, and already there's been a guld number filling up the boarding houses and signing on for work."

As Violet and Mr. Gunn discussed the mine, I slipped my hand into the leather satchel at my hip. My fingers seized upon the touch of paper within; a single black-edged envelope which had waited for three days, all by itself in my bag. Without making any overt movement, I slid the free envelope smoothly into the midst of Violet's letters, still tied by their single length of string. I kept my eyes on Mr. Gunn, nodding at his comments and smiling at his jokes, and only when I was confident that my letter was hidden amongst the others did I withdraw my hand from the satchel.

"—my brother and his family may be joining us." Mr. Gunn continued, "And Agnes has asked her own brother tae come, too, but he's a salt man and business is brisk, and what would he do oot here?"

"Do you mind working with the Chinese, Mr. Gunn?" I asked.

He followed my gaze, southwest. There was nothing beyond Number Six but wetlands and Chinatown and the train to the lake, and clouds of mosquitoes as dark and thick as smoke. "Tae be honest, lassie, I've no real problem with them. A quiet lot, and they keep tae themselves, which is fine by me. They've got curious ideas in their heads, you know – idolatry and odd food, worse than the Japanese." He ran the back of his hand over his beard, knocking loose a curtain of coal dust. "At least the Japanese bring their wives and children, and don't scurry about with secret societies and silly nonsense like that."

The mention of food, no matter how exotic, caused his stomach to gurgle. Violet held her hand over her mouth to hide her smile.

"We've kept you too long," I said, "You have a hot bath and a hot meal waiting."

"Me wee lassies, tis been a pleasure speaking with you, but my bones are weary," he said, and added with a grin, "Awa wit ye, then!"

We left him and continued east down the short hill, towards the new brick building known as the Willard Block, where one could find a dentist's office and a photography parlor upstairs, and on the main floor, the local postal counter. I held the door open for Violet, but as she entered, she gave me a sharp look of disapproval.

"What have I done now?"

"Pirates? Really, Liz, be reasonable. You're almost full-grown, and such talk is highly inappropriate for a lady."

As we entered the postal office, the musty scent of paper, wool and wax filled our nostrils. Two women stood at the counter. Behind it, a skinny mail clerk in white shirt and cap gathered their packages from a neat pile of boxes, recently arrived from Nanaimo. He looked fretful and harried; as the bell above the door heralded our arrival, he cast us a rueful glance.

"Mr. Gunn took amusement at the thought," I said.

"He was only being polite." Then, half to herself, Violet said, "But he's right; we ought to find a fellow for you – that would make you see the error of your ways!"

I rolled my eyes.

"You dismiss the thought now, but the time will come when you'll seek a man's protection, and only God knows who might attract your eye." We stood alongside the mail counter and Violet clasped her hands primly before her, waiting politely for the clerk to finish his tally of today's letters. "You must change your ways, Liz, if you want a partner of any quality. Let me be frank: who would accept your odd dress and rough hands? You've set yourself up for nothing better than a rough and uncaring sort of fellow."

"Perhaps I'll meet a wonderful man -- a great adventurer, a traveler -- who doesn't care a whit if I'm in trousers."

Violet only laughed.

"You don't seem concerned for your own future." I replied.

"Me? Oh, Liz, any man would be pleased to have me! Seventeen, the eldest daughter of a surgeon, educated and delightful and pretty?

I have no reason to stoop to desperation." She waggled one gloved hand to the clerk, to hurry him up. "Between Mr. Kelly and Dr. Briggs, I'm sure I will secure a prosperous match, and be a bride before the year is out. Now, give me the letters, and I'll post them."

I slapped the bundle into Violet's hand and, as she spoke with the clerk about the destination of her letters, I peered at my own refection in the window, superimposed over the hustle and scurrying on the street outside. I found myself strangely comforted by the return of Violet's boundless pride. Compared to my sister, I was plain and roughly hewn, but when I grinned at my reflection, my smile held a certain mischievous quality that could not be erased or tamed. "You're right," I decreed as the mail clerk took the letters to weigh and measure them, "I shall be my own worse enemy in the search for a husband."

"Oh, you're fine enough. Hardy as a thistle. And surprisingly sturdy," said Violet absently. She waggled her fingers to dismiss the comment, a gesture used to shoo away pesky flies. "Wash your face, and I'm sure someone would be happy to have you."

I threw an impish grin to her. "Maybe, but I haven't yet decided if I shall marry."

"Liz!"

"Well, why should I?" I continued, "To become some man's property, to give up my rights of ownership? To be little better than Agnes is to us? Endlessly cooking, cleaning, washing--"

"A family, a home, a place in the community! How else can you fulfill your responsibilities to society?" Violet huffed. "An unmarried woman is a burden upon society, at best!"

"And at worst?" Lizzie prompted.

"An adventuress, a nymph of the streets," she hissed. "A common whore."

I laughed.

"What's so funny?" Violet asked.

"Let's agree to this, Vi: you shall marry well, and I shall live with you. There -- all parties will be satisfied."

Now Violet laughed. "Perhaps my husband shall not."

"He has absolutely no say in the matter."

The clerk tossed the letters into a canvas mailbag and handed a slip to Violet with the price, then called one of the assistants from the back room. The boy pulled tight the sack and hauled it away. Glancing at the slip and finding the price agreeable, Violet requested that the postage be added to Father's tab.

With that, my letter to Captain Worthington was sent. I felt jubilant, and a little sly, but there was a sense of relief in my heart, too. It seemed only right to me that our grandparents know of Molly's death, so that they could include her in their prayers and no longer wonder what came of their daughter.

Never, in a million years, would I've foreseen the damage that one small letter can do.

7

March 15, 1898

Where I Was Born, by Amaryllis Saunders

I was born in London in the year 1883, in the upstairs bedroom of a brown brick townhouse on a street called Magdalene Court, situated only a block or two from the north bank of the Thames River. My mother was Mrs. Margaret Saunders and my father is Dr. John Saunders, and at the time that I was born, he worked in St. Bartholomew's Hospital, which everyone calls Barts. People in London never call anything by its right name. My mother was called Molly and I am called Lizzie, and the street we lived on sounded like "Maudlin", instead of the name of Mary Magdalene. Even though they invented the language, the English have a funny way of speaking it.

I did not like London very much. It is a stifling, stuffy, oppressive place. It reeks of butchered pigs, and blood sausages, and rotten horsemeat, and unwashed bodies, and when the water runs low, the Thames belches forth the most horrific stench a nose can ever smell.

All the buildings are smeared with black soot and there are many, many rats, everywhere and in all directions, huddled in the doorways and scratching in the basements. They eat up the trash in the gutters, which means that the rats never go hungry, even if some of the people are starving. London is so full of hidey-holes and crumbling buildings and overcrowded courtyards that I can not help but think the city was designed for the comfort of vermin. Sometimes, when there had been a lot of rain and the sewers were full, thousands of rats ran through the streets, and their undulating backs flow like rivers of brackish water. If you look up, the buildings in London are very pretty, underneath all the soot and grime, but no one bothers to wash them off because they will just get dirty again. However, if you look down, you are bound to see unpleasant things, such as a multitude of rats scurrying over your boots.

Because we left when I was five, I do not recall very much of London, but I clearly remember that it didn't feel like a very safe place. My mother was often afraid. A lot of sick people live in London, and she feared that we would contract cholera or typhoid, so she kept my sister and I inside all day and night. London was awash with poverty, the likes of which I have never seen since, not even across the isthmus of Panama. My father wished to shelter us from the evils in the world, and yet we were growing up in the heart of it, in the most vile and loathsome pit in the civilized world. We never went out to visit friends or acquaintances, and we never visited the park, and I don't have a single memory of breathing fresh country air until we moved to my grandfather's estate in Wiltshire. While we lived in London, Violet and I spent our days playing with our dolls in the attic. We hosted tea parties and garden parties and fancy dress balls without ever setting foot outside or speaking with another child our age. I wonder, now, if the neighbors even knew that two little girls lived in No. 4 Magdalene Court, for we certainly never spoke to them nor stepped into the courtyard.

Of course, we knew a great deal about them. We watched them come and go from the attic window, which overlooked Magdalene Court and the adjoined Warwick Street. We pieced together snippets of information overheard from adult conversations. Mr. Hardwick was a man of law, and lived in No. 3 with his pretty wife, whose name remained a mystery to all, and his three massive wolfhounds, named Tip, Tupper and Edgewater. He would call and yell and reprimand the dogs, so that their names were often heard on the early morning air. His wife, in direct opposition to their enthusiastic canine companions, was a silent and taciturn beauty, who treated her wealthy husband with a coolness that bordered on dismissal. He didn't seem to hold much fondness for her, either. I don't think Mr. and Mrs. Hardwick spoke to each other.

Mr. Jacob lived in No. 5, with his two teenaged sons and his old, decrepit mother. He'd been a dentist, I believe, though no longer possessed a single tooth in his head and refused to wear dentures; he sat on the step to smoke his pipe and gaped a empty smile at passers-by. His mother was a wretched hag with a hump on her left shoulder -- a wizened witch with a foul temper and a nasty tongue, ripped from the pages of a fairy tale. She took in laundry to supplement their income, but the boys were in the habit of spending freely, and it was not uncommon to hear them pleading with their grandmother to unlock the door, to let them in during the early hours of the morning, after they'd spent her hard-earned coins on drink, cards and amusements.

It was in this way, devising fictions based on our neighbors' schedules, that Violet and I entertained ourselves at the attic window. I was fascinated by the tiniest human interactions playing out on the street below. The prospect from that window was a living, breathing, ever-changing theatre, with myself occupying the best box seat: the lovely, glossy cabs pulled by high-stepping horses, the flower sellers and the match girls plying their wares on the corner, the news boys bringing the daily broadsheets to the doorstep. In the morning, just after breakfast, the dustmen arrived to empty the ashes from the back garden, and by noon, an Irish tin smith named Mr. O'Connell popped by to fix objects that might need mending. There were rag-and-bone men, too, who bought the kitchen scraps. Our attic room was still and quiet, but outside, the world was in constant motion.

London is like the eternal revolving of a great clock, with all of its gears and wheels working in perfect choreography.

My father kept a man named Mr. Ogden as a butler and a small black boy named Hamel to run the low errands. I lump the two of them together, although I never figured out the nature of their relationship -- Hamel was obviously of no blood relation to Mr. Ogden, but they held a close companionship as would any father and son. If I remember correctly, Mr. Ogden was an efficient manservant who never required reprimand. He was a tall, hunched man with a somber, equine face. Hamel was ten or twelve years old, and possessed a narrow, gaunt, half-starved frame. He had knobby knees and elbows, and his spidery limbs too long for his torso. His brown eyes, as big as saucers, were flecked with gold like a jungle cat's. He always seemed dirty, covered in dust from the basement or wood shaving from the kindling or hay from the yard, and Mr. Ogden regularly scolded him for keeping his clothes in such poor condition. Invariably, Hamel listened to Mr. Ogden's words with a good-natured grin. I wonder, now, if he even spoke a syllable of English.

In addition to Mr. Ogden and Hamel, we kept a staff of three housemaids. Hannah, Pauline, and Mary Anne. The trio kept the house tidy and Mary Anne cooked meals. From dawn to dusk, they swept the floors, pounded the dust from the curtains, cleaned the fire grates and polished the wood adornments. They slept in rooms downstairs, close to the heat of the kitchen stove. Only Pauline, the eldest, was allowed to dust the fine porcelain decorations in the parlor. She was older than my mother by more than twenty years, and there was great animosity between her and Mr. Ogden, whom she often muttered was a drunkard, though I never saw any evidence of weakness on his part. Pauline hated him with a passion, but she was a professional, too, and kept her opinions hidden from my father.

Mother allowed Hannah to act as our nanny, which I loved very much. Hannah taught us our letters and read books to us, and she seemed more jolly (and more intelligent) that either Pauline or Mary Anne. Hannah knew a multitude of tricks to keep two housebound girls entertained. She told us funny stories about her brothers and sisters, of whom she seemed to have an unending supply, and she told us wondrous tales of the Fae, who live in hills and steal away lovely children. Hannah possessed a very merry laugh that reminded me of a nightingale's cry, and she wore her black hair in a braid coiled on top of her head, tied up with blue ribbons. Her expression possessed an air of gay levity. She had a tiny nose and a mole on her chin. The world seemed sunnier with Hannah in it. She made my mother laugh, too, and act like a normal person, which is more than anyone else has every done.

The servants wore black uniforms, but my mother allowed Hannah to wear a dress of purple satin. I think this was because Hannah was more of a tutor than a maid, and the dress set her apart from the other girls. It would have been difficult to run after two high-spirited youngsters in a prim black dress and white apron. Besides, the rich purple color accentuated the glossy jet of Hannah's hair, and made her look very pretty indeed.

When I was five, Hannah left our employment, and not long afterwards, so too did Pauline and Mary Anne. Without Hannah, my mother slipped back into her previous unhappiness and she distrusted every human face. Her paranoia grew in leaps and bounds; even my father was forced to bear the brunt of her screaming fits, her nervous hysteria, and her foul temper. My father tried to avoid her by working more, spending days at a time in the offices of Barts, sleeping at the gentleman's club and eating in restaurants, and eventually he relieved Mr. Ogden and Hamel of their services. The house was now utterly without staff, and therefore, without any of the bodies needed to keep it in running order. A three-story town house requires a staff of at least four, yet my mother insisted that no one enter our home. She covered the furniture with sheets, sealed off the basement and lower floors, and refused all social visits. Friends dropped away. Alone, Mother could no longer bear the burden of looking after the house by herself, and so we lived in the attic, and ate cold meals, and wore unwashed clothes that stank of sweat and filth. For the hot month of August, we lived like paupers in a fine home, without a single member of staff to attend us.

When Mother suggested we move to Wiltshire and live with her parents, if only for a while, my Father reluctantly agreed. He could not contain my mother's frantic nature, and perhaps he believed that a return to the home of her childhood would restore her good health. Our family left London on the first of September, and joined our grandparents on their estate in Wiltshire, and though we no longer had servants of our own, I liked the countryside of Wiltshire very much. I believe my father detested the idea of leaving his city practice and his patients at St. Bartholomew's Hospital, and he made no secret to anyone that becoming a country doctor was a shameful demotion, but my mother had grown more and more ill, not only mentally, but physically. She couldn't bear the burden of caring for us alone. He reluctantly submitted to the new path for his career, but on the single condition that he return to London weekly to see his wealthier clientele.

Both Violet and I loved Wiltshire. After years of living under London's dismal shadow, locked in an upstairs room like two tragic princesses in a grey stone tower, we were finally able to run through sun-drenched fields, play in daisy-speckled meadows, and bask in the fresh air of the countryside.

Not only were we liberated, but we were surrounded by people again; friends, family, servants. Our grandfather had been a senior officer in the Queen's navy, now retired to a small estate in a town named Westbury, where he raised sheep and lived a quiet, pastoral life. Captain Worthington had great flowing white walrus chops and sweeping snowy hair topping a solid, sturdy seaman's body. He'd been a decorated man in the Navy, and his stories came from all corners of the globe. The dust of Australia, India and Canada had settled on his feet, and I found the breadth of his experience awe-inspiring.

His estate, White Cob Hall, provided room enough for all of our family. The house was large and well-staffed, with a stable of ponies and a kennel full of friendly, slobbering border collies. It sat on acreage west of the town, and from the windows of the library, one could gaze out over fields to a gentle rise in the land, where someone had long ago carved the turf, revealing the chalk below to shape a massive white horse. I remember the horse as breathtaking, mystical, and a little frightening.

Our family lived at White Cob Hall for almost a year, but my mother insisted that Violet and I be schooled at home, because she couldn't abide by the idea of her cherished children learning shoulder-to-shoulder with rustic farm pups. A tutor was hired, Mr. Grindley, and our lessons (which were not even half as fun as Hannah's lessons) were conducted in the library. Through the window, I often found myself studying the distant horse, and imagining myself astride the giant beast, riding away.

But if Mr. Grindley was strict and unyielding in our schooling, our grandmother spoiled us. Jolly, flighty, and forgetful, Gertie Worthington bustled about the grounds like a flustered hen, showering guests and staff alike with gifts and affection. She could barely remember her own name, and she ran the estate in a haphazard way, yet her staff was so honest and experienced, and all of them loved her so dearly, that there was little fear of thievery or pilfering. Besides, if the servants helped themselves to extra flour or soap, I doubt that my grandmother would have begrudged them the need. She was filled with Christian charity, a good soul, and loved the sound of children's laughter filling the stately, stuffy corridors of White Cob Hall. She ordered the staff to never speak of London in our presence, for it was a nasty brutish place, and our futures were so full of sunshine and happiness that we must be encouraged to look forward and never look back.

Sometimes, if I was good in my studies, the Captain took me on rambles through the forests and downs, pointing out the den of a fox or the scat of hedgehogs, and if I was especially good, he would carry me up the hill to the White Horse itself. My father says this was his first hint that I contained a scientific mind – I learned more from my forays into nature, where I could observe the vast array of flora and fauna with my own two eyes, than from any musty volume of Mr. Grindley's. The Captain and I would stand on the hilltop as all of Wiltshire unfurled at our feet, and he would tell me about the patterns of clouds and weather, or the ancient Britons who once held blood sacrifices on these earthworks. It was they, he said, who first carved the horse into the turf.

From our vantage on the hilltop, the carving adopted a strangely distorted perspective. When I stood at the nose of the horse, the close vantage turned the majestic creature into a stretched, flattened patch of green grass and white dirt. I dearly loved the rambles with the Captain, but it bothered me, to see the horse like this. It was meant to be seen from far away, where it was beautiful and proud. Looking at it close made it ungainly, ugly, squashed. It was like seeing a pretty woman with her make-up removed: it wasn't proper, and perhaps a little embarrassing for both parties.

I do not know exactly why we left Wiltshire. Perhaps Mother decided she was not happy. Perhaps she decided we would be better off at the edge of the empire, as far from England as we could possibly be. Perhaps she wished for us to be free of the polluting ideas of the modern age. Perhaps, like the White Horse, our lives looked graceful and contented from far away, but from a closer vantage, they were uncomfortably wrong. I don't really remember, for I was only six at the time, and my recollections of Wiltshire are painted in the carefree, innocent palette of childhood.

My grandfather introduced my father to Mr. Wadham Diggle, who lived on the opposite side of the vale, and who had been a business partner to Mr. Dunsmuir many years before. Through him, my father secured employment in Canada. We sold all of our furniture, except for my father's great iron-bound traveling trunk and medical tools, and bought passage on a ship to Panama, and crossed the isthmus by train. My sister and I were ill in Panama, and had to stay there for almost a month to gain our strength, but then, we caught another ship and sailed to San Francisco, then Victoria, then to Cumberland. But this essay is about the place I was born, and that was London, so I shall not talk anymore about Wiltshire or our travels here.

In conclusion, I do not miss London, because I was not allowed to be free there. It was dirty and stinky and full of people whom my father calls 'unfortunates', and who are loud and brash and sick and very poor. My father says that he likes me to be free here, and tells me that my excursions are the natural outlet for my curiosity. "I appreciated my own freedom, in my youth," he says to me, "And I would never dare to clip your wings." I like this metaphor, because Violet tells me that we were like caged birds in London, but here, I am able to spread my wings and fly.

Sometimes I feel badly for our housemaid Hannah, because I wish she could have come to Cumberland with us. She was very poor, but she was not sick, and I liked her very much. I would rather be poor here, where there is at least fresh air and good water to drink, and many trees all around, than be rich in London, where one must hide away and only watch the world pass by from an upstairs window. London is a great prison made of brick and iron, where people walk around with the illusion of liberty, and never recognize that they are slaves to the city. The End.

VERY WELL-WRITTEN ESSAY, Lizzie, but off topic and some spelling errors. C-

8

MARCH 17, 1898

THE DREAM HAD BEEN PARTICULARLY ARRESTING, full of London's vibrant scents and sounds. It wrenched me from a deep slumber, and as I woke, Hannah's merry face retreated into the mist of my vanishing sleep. One minute, I dreamt of busy streets and tall buildings, and the next, I found myself staring out the window at a dark, star-speckled sky. Through the half-opened window I heard the gentle, rhythmic sound of the distant mine bellows marking out the minutes, but nothing more: no traffic, no horses, no bustling crowds nor hawkers. The real world was peaceful and serene. I was alone.

I folded my hands under my head. London had been so different. There, Molly kept the windows closed to block the stench, but the glass could not muffle the perpetual din of pedestrian traffic on the street below. There were always the cries of peddlers with their wares, or rag-and-bone men asking to purchase the detritus of the household, or the maids chattering away in the back court as they washed the laundry and hung it to dry. Hannah and Pauline and Mary Anne had seemed like otherworldly creatures to me – free to come and go in the world. To a five-year-old locked in the attic, the women were to be envied.

And Hannah was the most envied. She came and went as she pleased, though she must have been a good worker, too. I couldn't remember a single time that our mother raised her voice to Hannah.

As if flaunting her freedom, Hannah had been there one day and gone the next without a word of warning to anyone. The bonny, blithe, black-haired maid in the purple dress had slipped into that river of humanity and been swept away by the millions of unfortunates. I never heard from her again, not even a letter. I envied her, but I loved her, too, and yet she was lost to me forever.

'Where is she now?' I thought, staring at the stars, 'How has her life turned out?'

I slipped from my covers and pulled the tin biscuit box from its hiding space under my bed. The battered, dented lid was difficult to open, but when it did, there before me lay all the treasures of my short life, crammed into the box on a bed of green velvet. Each item represented a moment of consequence, a turning point, a pivot; I ran my eyes and the tip of my finger over the objects, too numerous to count. I felt the range of textures, took comfort in the memories that they held. There was my mother's cameo necklace, the pebble from the funeral, the small glass vial which had held quinine and saved Violet's life in Panama. Here was a wizened pansy blossom wrapped with red ribbon, which I'd plucked on my first day of school in Cumberland, and a tuft of fur from our first cat, and finally, a small red canvas marble bag, which held nine dollars and fifty-two cents of horded coins, found in the gutters or given at Christmas. Childish trinkets to some people, maybe, but to me this tin box was a reliquary of comfort, within easy reach in the darkness of night, when anxious dreams startled me from slumber.

I rifled my fingertips through the objects until they brushed against a filmy scrap of linen. I carefully withdrew the handkerchief, edged with delicate lace. Hannah had adorned this bit of fabric and given it to me as a gift, two days before she'd abandoned our family.

When I held it to my nose, I caught the faintest trace of Hannah's peppery scent, still trapped amongst the fragile fibers.

The longer it was exposed to the air, the more Hannah's smell would fade, so I folded it with the utmost care and returned the handkerchief to the bottom of the box, underneath the other bits and pieces of my life. I carefully stashed the tin box out of sight.

Then, on bare feet I padded out of my room and across the hall, and slipped into Violet's bed to curl up against her. The spring moon, only a few phases from full, cast a gentle glow through the gauzy curtains.

Violet woke as the bedsprings jostled. "Mmm...Liz? R'you okay?"

I spoke gently, softly. "Do you remember Hannah?"

"What are you talking about, Lizzie?' Violet rose to one elbow. "You mean our maid-of-all-work? Back in London?"

"She was so pretty, with her black hair all tied up with white ribbons," I mused, "And her tiny little nose, and the mole on her chin."

"You're half-asleep, Lizzie. You're dreaming."

I rolled on my back and closed my eyes, not to sleep but to better remember Hannah's face. "Miss Marsh asked us to write an essay about where we were born. It made me think of London."

Violet didn't sound angry to be disturbed, only very tired. "Yes, I do remember Hannah. I think she made the best rose pound cake in all of England."

"But she left so quickly, and mother said that Hannah had found other employment elsewhere." I opened my eyes and propped myself up on my elbow. "Why did she leave us? What had we done?"

"We hadn't done anything, Liz," Violet soothed, "You were, what.... five when she left? We were too little to be responsible. Go back to sleep." She curled her arm around my shoulders to drag me under the covers, and pulled the quilt up to our chins.

"What did mother do, then, to chase Hannah away?"

"Maybe nothing. Mother was becoming more difficult... maybe Hannah decided to find another employer. One who wasn't so unpredictable and paranoid."

Yes, I thought, perhaps it was true. Pauline and Mary Anne left soon after Hannah, refusing to work any longer for their mother, who had become almost impossible to live with. She asked too much of the housemaids; she demanded to know what rooms they'd cleaned and when, to know the exact moment they'd arrive or depart, to be given a list each day of who had entered the house and what objects had come or gone. Every book, every newspaper, every pamphlet must be recorded and brought to her first, to be catalogued and censored and burned in the grate, if she felt the information within was not proper for the family. I gave a small, helpless sigh and closed my eyes, gleaning comfort from the warmth of Violet's embrace.

"Our mother was a curious specimen of womanhood," said Violet politely.

"Hmph," I replied, "Curious, like a two-headed cow."

THE NEXT MORNING, at breakfast, I waited until Father had finished his cup of tea and had begun leafing through his day's agenda before I posed the question that gnawed at me.

"Why did we leave London?"

Violet almost choked on her toast.

At first, he made no immediate reaction. He continued to look at his schedule, then set down his papers and affixed me with a calm, collected mien. But his finger tapped against the table, agitated. "Why do you ask?"

"Because I wasn't old enough to understand, then, why our lives were so sharply uprooted. I think I am old enough now."

He breathed deeply. The finger ceased to tap. "Leaving London was the best decision we'd ever made. Do you not like it here, Liz?"

"I like it here, very much," I answered, "But you haven't answered my question."

John's eyes fell to his plate, and he gathered his napkin up to dab at his moustache. A score of long seconds passed before he said, "Between your mother and I, it was decided that London was no place to raise healthy children. It is a den of poverty and sin, populated by all manner of nefarious characters haunting the shadows." He set down the napkin, and folded his hands over them. "We sold all of our belongings to start afresh, and your grandfather offered for us to live with him on the estate in Westbury – he felt his farm and holdings were was big enough to accommodate all." He chuckled ruefully and added under his breath, "How mistaken he was!"

"Why? What happened between you and Grandfather?"

"Goodness, Lizzie, you are full of questions this morning!' he laughed. "Violet, what are your plans for the day?"

Violet opened her mouth to speak, but I interrupted. "Why do you refuse to answer me?"

His fingers drummed against the table again. "Liz, your curiosity is noted. But some things are best left in the past." And dropping his shoulders in the manner of a man defeated, he added, "Sometimes, it isn't easy to live with another family, even when they are kin. And, let me assure you," The corner of his mouth kinked upwards. "Wiltshire is too small to accommodate your grandfather's prodigious ego."

"So you came to wear on each other's nerves."

"I think that would be fair to say," John replied, "He could be a tiring fellow."

"I remember him as being very supportive," I replied, "I remember long walks with him, up the hill. He always acted kindly to me."

John's lips tightened and his fingers became a fist. "He took you on long walks when the house became too cramped for all of us, especially when I was home from London for the week." His voice strained. "You were small, Lizzie, and I doubt very much if you remember the tension. We will speak no more of this, understand?"

I parted my lips, but Violet said, "Of course, Father. Hush, Liz!"

"I only wished to say, I have a hard time imagining anyone disagreeing with you," I said to Father.

"That's very kind of you," he said, "But the fault did not lay with me." His expression softened, his hands relaxed. Perhaps he felt he'd trespassed too far against a figure of whom I held happy memories, for he continued in a tone that was softer and more forgiving than before. "Some of the fault may have been mine. You must understand, Liz, that I continued to practice medicine, but the distance forced me to take fewer and fewer contracts in London and more in the neighboring town. A country doctor holds a different place on God's earth than a city doctor, and I grew restless. Both your mother and I longed for the prestige and social circles of my previous appointment, but with my daughters and wife in Wiltshire, I could rarely attend club functions. I could feel myself slipping away from friends, clientele, and acquaintances. I may be a rational and calm man, but even I can be discontented." He reached across the table to pat the back of my forearm. "I'm afraid I was too harsh with the Captain, and he viewed my restlessness as a dire character fault. He claimed I was weak, I claimed he was obstinate, and between the two of us, it became clear that we could not stay under his roof."

"And that's when Mother introduced you to Mr. Diggle?" said Violet.

John leaned forward in surprise. "Good Lord, and now Mr. Diggle enters the conversation! I'd not thought you'd remember so much!"

"He was a very jolly little man, and difficult to forget." She poured herself more tea and warmed my cup, too. "Besides, he pointed us here. You have your current appointment because of him. Yes, I remember him quite well, indeed."

"Well, Mr. Diggle was a good fellow indeed," John said as he stood. "Let's end the discussion on such a gentleman, shall we?" His eyes flashed to me; I read a silent warning there.

"Yes, Father," I said, trying very hard to sound meek. "If it angers you to talk of Wiltshire, then no more shall be said."

9

March 25, 1898

Miss Adele Kelly
136 Fort St.
Victoria, BC

Dearest Adele,

I hope my letter finds you and your mother in good health. I think back fondly to my last trip to Victoria, and our day together in Beacon Hill Park under the shade of the oak trees, and I wish now that I had your merry company today as I did back then. Your cousin Alexander continues his post here with great efficiency and is such a comfort to us all. However, I find myself wishing for a good friend such as you in my immediate circle – never have I longed to visit Victoria more, if only for your good council!

You remember my sister Amaryllis, no doubt. She is proving to be troublesome yet again, and casts a pall of disrespectability over our family. Glory, how she vexes us!

Let me regale you with her latest indiscretions.

A few days ago, she took it into her fool head that our maid-of-all-work from London has abandoned us; yes, our maid, from nigh a decade ago! I have told her, it is not good form for house staff to keep in touch with their employers after they've left the home. Why should we expect a poor, uneducated scamp like Hannah to invest in a penny stamp to communicate with us? Doubtlessly, that money has gone into a glass of gin.

Yet still Lizzie persists. She pesters Father for information, and he has grown quite vexed with her. She remembers very little of our leaving because she was so small at the time, and I am unsure if I should tell her what I remember of those far-ago days, or if I should follow Father's example and demand her to cease her queries.

What do you think, my friend? Your opinions mean much to me.

Let me share with you how we came to be here, to this horrid parochial outpost in the midst of the coal fields. If I tell you, I shan't be so eager to share it with Liz, and it will be easier for me to tell her that I don't recall the details when she pesters me again. My dear Adele, I am greatly concerned for her, for she exhibits some of the signs of my mother's afflictions, and the last thing I wish to do is nurture a growing dis-ease in my sister's brain.

The place was my grandfather's Wiltshire estate, and I was six or seven years of age. As I recall it, Mother took us from our after-dinner studies with Mr. Grindley and dressed us in our finery, and introduced us to a merry round elf of a gentleman. He said his name was Lieutenant Wadham Diggle. I curtseyed and told Mr. Diggle that it was my great pleasure to make his acquaintance. Lizzie gave a clumsy bow and said it was a fine thing indeed, to meet a man named Waddy. Her silliness drew a laugh from all in attendance but, God's teeth, I nearly died of shame!

Mr. Diggle owned the country house on the opposite slope of the river from White Cob Hall. He was grandfather's age, long since retired to pursue rural pleasures, but with a retinue of stories filed away in his spry memory of past naval campaigns and worldly adventures. An evening between Diggle and grandfather proved to be a series of come-uppances, each one trying to out-pace the other with narratives of dashing derring-do. Every glass of port brought forth another harrowing tale from some far-flung savage corner of the world. I was certain that the two of them, and only they alone, had saved Queen Victoria's Empire from impending doom.

Once their tales were exhausted, Diggle set his cut crystal glass down on the side table. His jolly cheeks lifted in a smile to my Father, sitting across from him on the couch in the drawing room. He said, "You have been most quiet, sir."

Father had long since been abandoned in the conversation due to his lack of Herculean heroics, which was hardly good form for gentlemen of grandfather's and Mr. Diggle's station. But he was prim and polite in his reply. "I have not the experiences to share," he said, "My meager life pales in comparison."

"Sir, I have a prospect for you, if you'll hear me." Mr. Diggle replied, trading an amused glance with Grandfather. "How would you care to embark upon an adventure?"

My Father was polite to feign interest, and if he was surprised at such a bold invitation - and I have no doubt he was - he concealed it admirably. "I shall like to hear it, first, before I agree," he said, which was very prudent indeed.

"I have approached the son of a former business partner of mine in Canada, and he has expressed an interest in procuring you for his employment, for he has much need for learned men on Vancouver Island. The Old Rooster, here," and Mr. Diggle guffawed at Grandfather, who took the nickname with a tip of his glass, obviously well-acquainted with the title, "Tells me that our gentle countryside is not to your liking."

Grandfather's voice boomed, "And nor should it, at your tender age! You have a great opportunity to go forth into the world! Why, in my thirties, I'd already crossed the Atlantic more times than I could remember!"

Mother sat in the enclave at the edge of the parlor, playing a tune on the piano. Her music ceased, her hands dropped to her lap.

Canada! The thought fair made me cry! Mr. Grindley had told us of Canada, for his sister had been married off to a man in Montreal, and he was of the opinion that there was no worse place in the world! He said it was perishingly cold and populated with grizzly bears and French men. Now, while a Parisian gentleman is certainly fine company, Mr. Grindley had assured me that the rustic French are little better than the Irish, and resist all attempts at decent education, and are to be avoided at all cost! And here, Grandfather and Diggle had conspired to send us hither, to a place full of boors and brutes? The wild creatures of Wiltshire gave me concern, and what's a hedgehog or a fox compared to a grizzly or the French? My fingers trembled so!

But, Lizzie was all ablaze with the prospect! She leapt to her feet and scurried to Father's knee, crying "Oh, please let us go to Canada!" with such passion that it was obvious to all, she knew not of what she wanted.

All three men turned their faces to Lizzie: Mr. Diggle, ruddy and jocund, with a warm encompassing smile; Grandfather, hiding his lips behind his glass, but with a guarded wariness in his eyes, at odds to the easy merriment he'd only moments ago expressed; and Father, handsome and youthful, with eyes turned dark, half hidden in the shadows cast by the flickering fire.

"Lizzie, you and Violet ought to head to bed," Father said to us.

And, as I remember, Lizzie protested his orders, but he shushed her and turned to Mother to say, "Molly, take the girls. This discussion is not for their ears."

"But if we are going to Canada, I want to know now!" Lizzie persisted. Even then, barely a toddler, she was much too willful and stubborn for a child of good breeding! I ought to have known she'd turn out so poorly!

"If I decide that we will go, you'll be the first I'll tell," Father said with a half-smile, but I could tell, he was not eager to leave the comforts of England. I believe he wrestled with his shock at this crude, unsolicited offer. As Mother shepherded us along the hall to our rooms in the west wing, I said as much.

"It was horribly unkind of Mr. Diggle to spring such a ridiculous prospect on Father! No letter of invitation? If I were Father, I'd be furious!" I turned to Lizzie. "You do not want to go the Canada, Liz. It is not a decent place."

"But there's bears there, Vi!" Lizzie whispered in awe. "We could see bears!"

"Yes, there are bears," said Mother. "And many fine people, and all sorts of beauty in the landscape. It would be a splendid place for us."

"How can you say such a thing!" I cried, but Mother smiled patiently at me.

"Because England has grown too small for us, and we need space to roam and grow."

"But Father did not know Mr. Diggle was asking on his behalf!" I said.

Mother opened the door to our bedroom. "No, he did not."

Lizzie measured Mother's expression, and said, "But you did."

Molly held a finger to her lips. "You hush, Lizzie, and keep your observations to yourself." She sat at the edge of our broad bed as we changed into our nightgowns, and when we crawled into bed, Lizzie snuggle close to me. "Your father is not happy here," said Mother as she tucked us in, "And he'll find a greater purpose for his gifts in a place where he is needed. Wiltshire boasts an abundance of country doctors. He must go further afield to find his place."

"And Grandfather and Grandmother?" I asked, "How do they feel about us, leaving?"

"This is their home, not ours. We must make our own place. I think..." and she gave a small sigh, "I think a position as a doctor in Canada will be far more suitable to your father's talents. And you'll have space to exercise with plenty of fresh air to breath, and forests to explore, and more children to play with than you have here. No, the journey will do us all good, and a new beginning in a land freshly-borne will be the remedy to all our troubles."

I thought I might cry, and my chin quivered. "Will we see wolves? And Indians? And snow?"

"Most likely. It will be a long and arduous adventure, but wonderful, too, and I promise you, Violet, that you'll see all sorts of marvels. Tomorrow, I'll show you on a map."

After she left, I wept a little. Lizzie put her arms around me and tried to comfort me, but it was difficult for she was so very excited by the prospect.

"Father will refuse," I said at last, "He must!"

"He can't," Lizzie replied. "Did you not notice, Vi? Mama spoke of this if it is happening, and I think it really is."

"What are getting on about, Liz?" I snuffled. She was so small, but she spoke with such confidence.

"Mama doesn't doubt our adventure at all. I think she has made it happen, and Father will go along with the plan because it is already set in motion."

And not long after, I discovered that she was right. The men might argue about the little details, but Mother had already bought passage on a boat, sold our possessions, agreed with Mr. Diggle that Father will accept the position, and written a letter of introduction to the esteemed Mr. James Dunsmuir, who would be Father's future employer. Mother could, when her madness seized her, work with utmost proficiency. If her actions had not been tainted with paranoia, obsession and sly manipulations, she might have been considered a wonder of Victorian efficiency.

I hope you understand, Adele, that I dare not tell Lizzie this story for it only highlights her keen sense of perception, and I do not think such a trait should be cultivated in a woman. Mr. Diggle was very kind indeed to set Father up with a good appointment here. We owe a great deal to his generosity. And yet I can not help but think, life would have been far sweeter in England. We would never have passed through Panama, and I would never have caught ague, and I would be married by now to a fine young man with an estate and a good position.

I ought not dwell on what can never be, but my heart aches at the thought.

Dear Adele, I can not wait to see you again this summer! Do write to me with your good opinions. Pass along my best wishes to your dear Mother, too, of whom Mr. Kelly speaks with longing. He is a true gentleman, and bestows great honor upon your family name with his noble spirit and strong sense of goodness.

YOURS TRULY,
Violet

10

April 6, 1898

March flew by in a tempest of storms, then relented to April's sudden warmth so decisively that people held their hands to their eyes and blinked cautiously at the brilliant, instant return of the sun. Every lick of golden light held a palpable summery warmth. The world shook off the drudgery of February and March like a dog dislodging fleas.

The small schoolhouse sat with its back to a grove of maple trees. Cumberland's growing population required a larger school, and construction of a three-story school house with bell tower was planned to begin in May. This meant, of course, that these trees were slated to fall within the week. I often brought a book and my lunch pail and ate in the shelter of the grove, and the thought that it was about to be razed made me feel queasy, but there was nothing one small girl could do to hold back the juggernaut of progress. I wandered between the narrow trunks, running my fingers lovingly over the bark and fondling the soft tips of the branches between my fingers. The maples seemed to sense that something dire was coming, and had bloomed with more jubilance than in years past. Every twig burst into a froth of green buds. Holding an ear to the lowest branch, I swore I heard the leaves crackling and popping as they raced to unfurl.

A stick snapped behind me, and I heard the soft footfall of a boot on the loam.

"Hey, Dizzy Lizzie -- what's the tree sayin' to ya?" said a voice.

I turned to see Buster Gillingham standing a few paces behind me, his arms crossed over his skinny chest. He had an oval head made wider by a pair of big ears, which (with the sunlight hitting them from behind) caused the thin membranes to glow pink. He stood almost a head taller that the two boys who flanked him, Donny and Bill, who followed around in his wake like a pair of exuberant, slavering hounds.

"What's it saying?" repeated Bill. Donny nodded his head.

I released the branch in my fingers. "It says, when Buster pees behind it, he's got a gnarled-up willy the size of a peanut." I crooked my pinky finger towards him, and waggled it suggestively.

Donny and Bill snickered, then quickly stifled their laughs. Buster was not amused.

"My pa says yer just as crazy as yer muther," he replied, "And this cinches it."

"My mother was perfectly fine," I replied, but my voice wobbled, betraying any confidence in the statement.

"Your mother was a god damned crack pot," Buster said, "I saw her, a week or so b'fore she was taken up to God, and she was wringing her hands and staring at the new miners comin' out of the Vendrome, and making the sign of the cross over her heart."

"That doesn't mean anything," I snapped.

"My pa said she didn't wear no underwear," he continued. "And at night, she'd sleep in the alleyway behind the Bucket of Blood, so's every man could see her Gates of Heaven."

"She did not!" I said, "Your father's a god damn liar! She never left our house after dark!"

"My pa says, Mad Molly used to hide in the garden of the whorehouse," said Donny, "And spy on the prostitutes and scare away the business 'til Mr. McGregor took her home one night and gave yer pa a good talkin' to. Ain't no good lady's business what happens in the whorehouse, and every man in town was gettin' mad with Molly standing in the way between him and a decent fuck."

"She never!" I said, clenching my jaw.

But talking of sex and men had left Donny emboldened. "Sure is true, sure as rain!" he insisted. "Mad Molly didn't even have the good sense to stay home when she was told."

"Everyone knows, she wandered in the woods like a heathen, talking to the trees," quipped Bill, "Just like you."

"You ain't got no hope, Liz," Buster said with mock pity, "Yer ma was Old Mad Molly, and you're Little Mad Lizzie," he sang, "Old Mad Molly and Little—'

Rage flared in me. I threw aside my lunch pail and my book, and clenched my hands. I moved fast, faster than any of them anticipated, and Buster's sentence was chopped short with a hard right to the jaw. I heard more than the clack of teeth; there was a crunch, too, followed by a moist smacking. A chunky red substance sprayed out of Buster's floppy lips, which splattered across the ground and revealed itself as fragments of teeth, accompanied by a sliver of freshly severed tongue.

He staggered back, clutching his mouth with both hands. His eyes pinwheeled in their sockets and bugged wide. With one solid left to his temple, I figured I might knock them both loose, and they would roll across the grass to be snapped up by a hungry crow.

But before I could unleash my left hook, Donny and Bill seized my arms. Roiling waves of pain rolled up from my stomach as Bill's fist buried itself in my gut. The breath whooshed out of my lungs in a gust of air and moisture. Donny's fist caught me in the face. Stars burst across my field of vision.

But rage dampened these physical feelings, and I stared through the pain at Donny. He faltered for a moment, transfixed; maybe he'd never hit a girl before, or maybe he'd never acted without Buster first approving the movement. His hesitation gave me just enough time to yank my knee skyward until it stopped abruptly, cramming the soft bulge of adolescent testicles against the solid arch of his pelvis. His fingers, gripped around my right wrist, slackened. He yodeled out a strangled howl of agony.

I wrenched my arm free and buried my fist into Bill's nose. He stumbled back with a high-pitched cry. I reeled on my boot heels and ran.

11

JOHN ARRIVED home from the his morning rounds to find the house in a state of disarray. A young woman in a prim brown dress with white blouse sat in the parlor, clenching her hands in her lap. Her mouse-brown hair was pinned to the top of her head, but a number of wisps had fallen free, and her plump lips were pulled down in a disappointed scowl. Agnes plied her with tea and cookies, but when John entered the foyer, Agnes flew to him and clucked at him, her Scottish accent made so thick and impenetrable by her flustering that he could barely understand a word she said. He managed to pluck 'Lizzie' from the verbal tangle.

And when I appeared in the kitchen door, a black bruise neatly ringing my left eye, he understood.

He set his walrus-hide bag by the chair and sat across from the woman in the parlor, bracing himself for the inevitable. "Good morning, Miss Marsh," he said. "Can I infer that Lizzie has been in some sort of trouble?"

"I'm told Buster Gillingham will now speak with a pronounced lisp," she reported, her pinched face a map of disapproval.

John pursed his lips, tented his fingers. "And Lizzie?"

"We simply can not continue to welcome Amaryllis into our classroom if the danger exists of her harming the other children," Miss March proclaimed, "She is a bright girl, gifted and observant, but... her temper! And now, with three children injured, and a day's worth of lessons disrupted—"

"I'm sorry," he interrupted, "Did you say three?"

Miss Marsh nodded briskly. "Buster, Donny and Bill."

"Four, then, were hurt in the scuffle," John corrected, "For it looks like Lizzie has not come out of this unscathed."

She harrumphed. "This is the third time this year that Lizzie has been unable to control her temper, and I can not allow her to distract classes further. Some of the younger children are quite frightened of her, Dr. Saunders! I can not allow her beastly outbursts to continue!"

"Yes, but she does well in her studies—"

"Every time I send a child home with a bruise on his face, I must explain myself to the Board of Trustees, and if this persists—'

"Your reputation is suffering, is it?" he said dryly.

Miss Marsh pressed her fingertips to the centre of her brow. She was not a weak woman; she spent every day in the company of uncouth ruffians, and when her mind was made up, very little could be done to change it.

"I'm sorry, Dr. Saunders," she said, "But Lizzie has shown that she can not conduct herself in a seemingly manner. I must insist that she be evicted from our school roster."

He grumbled but nodded.

Father waited until Miss Marsh had left before calling me into the parlor. He gestured with a sweep of one hand for me to sit opposite him, then he looked me over, noting every bruise and laceration.

"I warned you, one day the boys will be bigger than you, and they'll not have any mercy."

"It took three of 'em."

"I don't care if it took a whole army," he said, "You must not fight."

"They said—"

"I don't care," he replied patiently. "Amaryllis, you can not fight like this. You've put your education in jeopardy with this outburst, and now what am I to do with you?"

"I hadn't meant to," I murmured.

He leaned forward, narrowed one eye and trained an ear in my direction. "Let's be clear," he said, "You hadn't meant to fight? Or you hadn't meant to get hurt?"

"I hadn't meant to get caught."

"Ah," he replied, leaning back, barely suppressing a smile. "I suppose most people don't."

He pulled the medical bag close and unlatched it, taking out a small, flat leather box. From this, my father withdrew his ophthalmoscope. Using used a manic series of concave mirrors and polished lenses, it focused ambient light through its brass funnel, and channeled it straight into my eyes. He examined one, then the other.

"I didn't really think of the consequences," I stammered as he looked at my pupils, "I was filled with the desire for satisfaction – I only wanted to hurt Buster, nothing more." I sniffed. The bruise prickled with pain whenever my mouth moved, but it hurt less in comparison to the ache in my stomach. "Honestly, Father, his face made such a lovely target."

John began to laugh, then reined it at the sight of Mrs. Gunn's disapproving frown from the door between kitchen and dining room. He tucked the ophthalmoscope in its case, and then returned it to the bag. "Oh, come now, Agnes," he said to the woman, "You've got to admit, Buster Gillingham's face does cry out for the addition of a smack or two."

"Dr. Saunders!" she gasped, "How can you say such things?!?!"

"Quite easily," he replied, "In truth, it comes naturally, as I look upon the bruised and battered face of my own youngest child."

Agnes clamped her mouth shut, but she was clearly displeased by every aspect of the conversation. She reeled around on her small feet and took respite in the empire of her kitchen.

"Well, Lizzie," he continued, "If you are no longer welcome at school, we must be resourceful and make the best with the situation." He rubbed his hand over his neatly clipped beard, carefully considering the direction of the conversation before committing his thoughts to concrete words. "I had expected to wait until after you finished the year, but Fortune has dictated that we begin now, so we shall."

"Begin?"

"I need an assistant. You'll do well enough."

My eye screamed in pain as I arched my eyebrows and stared at him in surprise. "You'll teach me to be your assistant?"

He nodded.

"God damn! I should've punched Buster ages ago!" I replied, which pulled another laugh from him.

"First of all, I ask that you clean up your language. You have an occupation, now, and it is unbefitting for a member of my staff to speak in vulgarities. It's all well and good for men to speak thusly while working on the picking table, but not in a hospital."

I nodded, still dazed with the rapid turn of my day.

"And secondly, this is no holiday from the rigors of school. Quite the opposite. You will spend your days working with me, and your evenings reading what I require you to read. There will be no time for play. Your lessons have not ended, Lizzie. In fact, they have only started. Understand?"

"Yes, sir."

This pleased him. "This afternoon, I will show you the facilities, my office, my surgery, and you will accompany me as I meet with my patients. You will need to be neat, and clean, and professional."

"Do I have to wear a dress?"

"Are any of your pants freshly laundered?"

I shook my head. "If I put them in the laundry, I'm afraid Agnes will burn them."

John frowned at this. "I shall ask her to keep your clothes, all of your clothes, safe and well-mended, then. I have no objections to whatever you choose to wear, but for this afternoon, a frock will do. Nothing so mad as a corset to bind you, Lizzie – I'll need you to be capable of lifting and steadying patients, and you can't perform labor in one of those horrific contraptions." He rummaged in the medical bag, pulling out a skein of small, onion-skin papers. "But immediately, Lizzie, I have an errand for you. After today's fight, are you in any form to run?"

Honestly, I felt that I could run to the moon and back, I was so happy.

The pages were scratched with Latin words: diagnosis, perhaps, and notes on methods of care. As Agnes entered the room to collect the tea cups and biscuits, John selected one paper and handed it to me. I read the graceful handwriting. It was a list of flowers and herbs.

"Take this list to Mr. Tao," he instructed, "And bring the items back as soon as you can. Do you know which apothecary is Mr. Tao's?"

"You took me there, last time you visited Chinatown. His shop is the one at the end of the alley, on the lower street, right?" For good measure, to prove that I knew my directions, I added, "Not the one in the house with the pigs in the garden. That's Mr. Han's apothecary."

"You're sending the girl down Chinatown?" said Agnes, "What folly is this, Dr. Saunders?"

"No folly, Agnes," he replied with easy leisure, "Some of these items are for Peggy Faulk's tonic. She's happy to consult the spirits, but they don't help much with her migraines."

But Agnes huffed like a disgruntled cow. "Really, Dr. Saunders, ye can nae think it would be wise to send a wee gurl—"

He looked up at the formidable woman, now standing with chubby fists on her wide hips. "I'm sorry, Agnes? You object?"

"I most certainly do!" she flustered. Indignation flashed in her wide, shocked eyes.

John's face barely changed, but I caught the slightest flush over his skin and the smallest hint of one brow raised, and sensed his anger like one might perceive a faint odor on the breeze. Agnes was too offended to notice John's reaction, and she was too forthright to pay attention to social decorum. A housemaid was supposed to function as a pliant and pleasant addition to the room, and refrain from questioning the judgment of her employer; it was not proper.

"Tis an affront tae all that's good and dignified!" Agnes insisted, "Sending a wee bairn down Chinatown – do ye nae ken the depravity that occurs there? The debauchery? I'll nae spell it out for ye, Dr. Saunders, for you are a learned man and there are innocent ears present!"

He appeared more curious than angry at her horror. "I do not fear for Amaryllis' safety. She's a bright girl, and the day is fine and sunny, and my reputation will shelter her."

Agnes sputtered. "Oh, dear sir, you do think highly of yerself! The Celestials don't care a nought for the niceties of a polite civilization – they are bloody heathens, and more than capable of whisking your wee child away from ye without a thought to the Queen's law! I implore ye, Dr. Saunders, hire a boy from town to go, or better yet, take your business to one of the fine pharmacies in town. Can ye nae see the peril in which you put our dear little Lizzie, if ye send her like a lamb into those foul dens of iniquity?"

John set his chin. "Agnes, your opinions have been noted, but this is my house, not your's, and it is I who make the rules."

"But, sir—"

"I do not know how a house is run in Argyll," he began, "But in England, a woman in your position would never dare to broach the running of the house. You have, in my opinion, overstepped your bounds, Mrs. Gunn."

She blanched, but was not chastened.

"With all due respect, sir," she began, "This is nae a question of a housemaid overstepping her bounds. This is a question of you, sending yon innocent lambie into the mouth of the dragon. Aye, I might make a poor maid in your estimation, but it is my Christian duty to speak for the safety and moral sanctity of a wee child, e'en if it means losing my job!"

I burrowed into the pillows of the chair, watching as the tension between them ratcheted up like the cogs of a clock's wheel.

"And might I add, sir," Agnes continued, "That my Christian duty also begs to remind ye that you've been negligent in your duties to bring up yon girls in God's pure light. Only last Sunday, Father McGill asked when he might have the pleasure of seeing you again, sitting in the first pew."

"Religion does not interest me," he began, but Agnes was like a boulder rolling down a hill – it would take more than mere words to stop her.

"Are ye so blind to the shame that follows ye? As a doctor and a learned man, a gentleman, you are beholden to provide a guld Christian example to the rest of the town, for they look to you, sir, for guidance. Aye, I wuld cross my boundaries and speak out of turn, but at least I ken my failings, sir, and recognize the risk I take by speaking my mind. You are well-liked here, sir, and your work is quality. No one takes fault with your position. But they whisper that ye fail your daughters in raising them, and that only Violet shows promise of being a good and wholesome woman." Agnes affixed me with her blazing, black eyes. "If you send Amaryllis into Chinatown, there will be talk."

An ugly silence filled the parlor, thick as treacle.

Then, John laughed.

And laughed.

And, when Agnes' face contracted into surprised offence, he laughed some more.

"Oh, good Lord," he finally said, leaning forward and resting his elbows on his knees. "Oh, Mrs. Gunn, you give me great entertainment!"

"It is nae my intention—"

"Of course it isn't," he chuckled, "That makes it all the more amusing. Mrs. Gunn, I have never cared a whit for what others think of me, or my daughters, or my household. Let them talk! It doesn't matter to me."

Agnes fumed. "Then doubtlessly, you'll be much amused to ken, they already talk about our dear Lizzie behind her back. They say she'll be as neep-heided as her mother."

John's smile extinguished. His face fell dark with the first hint of anger. "Molly's condition has no part in this conversation, Mrs. Gunn." He folded the napkin and set it aside, and straightened his shoulders. "I don't care what anyone says about Amaryllis. They can burn in the fires of Hell, for all I care."

"Dr. Saunders!" Agnes gasped, bringing her fingers to her mouth, but he would not be abated by her show of sensitivity.

"If Molly had borne me a son, I'd have sent the boy for my errands, but two daughters is all I have, and so I must make due. Violet has neither the fortitude nor good sense to visit Chinatown unscathed, but Lizzie has both in spades."

I suppressed a smile.

But Agnes jutted her chin, and would not be dissuaded. Perhaps she figured her job was already lost, and there was no harm in speaking the fullness of her opinions.

"You wuld do her nae good service to treat her like a wee urchin," she spat, "You'll only make a disgrace of her. Everything about her is unbecoming, from her filthy boots to the callous on her fingers, and I'll tell ye truly, she'll amount to nothing if ye let her persist so." Agnes mustered strength for the rest of her assault. She drew up her mountainous bulk and looked down upon me. "Dr. Saunders, sir, with all due respect, you ought to care what others say about Lizzie, because she's a reflection of your good judgment, and nary a person would dare visit a physician they ken to be incompetent and incapable of upholding e'en the most basic morals."

At this comment, John glared at the woman. "How dare you call into question my integrity?"

"*I'm* nae calling it into question," she replied.

"But you think others are?" he asked. John now stood, and as he rose to his feet, his movement was smooth, fierce, graceful and calculated. He advanced a single, slow step towards the woman, and while his face remained placid and rational, the movement of his body betrayed the tempest of rage seething in his core. It now became startlingly apparent to the self-righteous Agnes that Dr. Saunders was not merely affronted by her opinions, but furious.

Agnes retreated a step as John fixed his calm, impassionate expression on her. He was quietly imposing, as solid as a stone wall.

"Is this so, Mrs. Gunn? Have you heard such rumors?"

She stammered slightly. Her cheeks flushed. "Not in so many words, sir," she replied, humbled, "Nae, I can honestly say I've heard no such blatant havering, but..." She let the thought trail away, fade into nothing.

John glanced out the window as he thought. His eyes blazed with anger but his face remained cool.

"If they never called your integrity into question for mother's indiscretions, I don't see why they'd do so for mine," I said. "She was far more outrageous than me."

"But ye agree that you're outrageous," Agnes snapped, peevish.

"I take a great deal of pride in it," I replied.

"Lizzie, hush," said John, returning his attention to the woman standing in the hall. "Mrs. Gunn, your concern for the well-being of the family has been noted."

"I shall collect my things, sir," Agnes said quietly as drew back into the hall.

John narrowed his expression, confused. "Why?"

"You'll not be asking me to leave your employ?"

From the look on his face, the thought had not even occurred to him. "Of course not. Don't be daft, woman -- who would make me such delightful scones?"

Agnes brightened, and her breath left her lungs in a sigh. "So... so you'll reconsider? You'll no send Lizzie into such peril?" The hope in Agnes' face was reflected by the dismay in mine.

But he smiled distantly to me. "I need those medicaments, and I have no time for hiring a boy to help. In future, Mrs. Gunn, I'll reconsider my lax judgment and poor parenting, but not today."

12

"AND LOOKING over the list of farmers and residentiary owners here, working their own lands, it is a remarkable fact that these are the very men who been as laborers of one sort or another, but have nobly carved out for themselves an independence by their won indomitable industry and hard-handed toil. These then (the very most desirable of colonists), will either pass out or not approach, discouraged by reasons of wages being reduced to a minimum. For, the question at the very root of all this contention is not that wages must stand at a maximum, but lest they tumble to a minimum and stay there. But further, if interest binds the colony to the European immigrant, and to the negro too, honest, civil and industrious as he is, also possibly, ere long, to the Japanese immigrant, honor and humility alike bind our colony to consider well in the case of the Aborigines. Now, it would be a most inconsistent action on the part of the Dominion or Provincial Government, after proving so humane and thoughtful of the interests of the Indian population in many ways, if in the way of cheapening labor to the lowest point, these should become sufferers, just at the time when their old resources by flood and field have ceased to be as productive as before. Then, indeed, would they settle down in disgust and despair of progress or pecuniary resource.

"But should considerations of this kind be overlooked, what will the final result be? What else by a population of Mongolians, numerically predominant, who will remit their earnings out of the province, who will practice exclusive dealing, and never permanently attach themselves to British Columbia, or become identified with her laws. And then what stronger justification can be given of the current censure of the inconsistency, contained in the taunt, that what was once "British" was made "Chinese Columbia"." - Nicholas Flood Davin, Esq., Secretary, Chinese Commission, Victoria BC, October 1884

The Chinese vendors hauled their goods on their backs into Cumberland because Chinatown was not a place for men and women of high standing to be seen. In huge wicker baskets, strapped between their hunched shoulders, they carried vegetables, fruits, candies, and trinkets to market – a bazaar of exotic items which might, on a good day, earn them a few extra dollars. Miss Marsh once told her youngest students that the Chinese vendors put naughty children in the baskets, to carry them back to Chinatown; if any child dared to misbehave, she would summon up a Chinaman, like a genie or devil, to whisk them away to an unspoken fate.

I often wondered if Chinese parents scared their children into submission with tales of prim Miss Marsh, who would lock them in stuffy classrooms and force them to recite the kings of England until they cried with boredom.

When Mrs. Gunn had retreated into the back garden, John pushed the list into my hand, and said, "Do hurry; I have an appointment with Mrs. Faulks this afternoon, and she requires these tinctures."

"I'll be as quick as I can," I promised, and tucked the paper safely in the satchel slung over my shoulder. I hesitated at the door, then turned back to the parlor. I stretched upwards to kiss his cheek.

He startled. "What was that for?"

"Thank you," I replied, knowing that any admission of love or gratitude would only fluster him. I gave his hand an affectionate squeeze before releasing it and scampering out the door.

I ran passed the new mine site, the Colliery offices, and the rows of small white Camp houses. Laundry flapped on the lines, streaked with blue from the coal dust in the air. I dashed through stunted orchards of apple, pear and plum trees, and the road dipped down a long hill to the train tracks. Listening for an engine and hearing none, I skipped over them, and followed the road as it narrowed, then over a wooden bridge across a ditch. The road rose through a hedge of blackberry brambles, and when the brambles parted, a crooked collection of shacks appeared.

When the Company decided to bring foreign workers to dig the Cumberland coalfields, they allotted the damp, dismal hollow south of town as the site of Chinatown. Maybe they assumed the Chinese were content to live in moldy canvas tents, surrounded by skunk cabbage and ferns. More likely, they gave it no thought at all, and figured this to be a good use for land otherwise unusable by civilized men. But, sure as the day is long, the Company did not figure the work gangs to be resourceful and skilled, or to turn what had been given them into something habitable. These Chinese workers had surveyed Dunsmuir's railways and toiled in Dunsmuir's mines: through their years of service, they'd gained the engineering knowledge to turn a mosquito-infested swamp into a vibrant community. They plotted out the marshy swamp, pitched tents on the highest points, and began to drain the wet ground. They cleared spaces for vegetable gardens or pig pens, and where the water refused to subside, they drove pylons into the soil and constructed broad platforms. Up from the marshes sprang a village.

The bustling business centre clustered around two dirt streets: Ha Gai, or 'Low Street', and Shan Gai, or 'High Street'. Chinatown had a theatre, five or six butchers, stores of cloth and dry goods, a Christian church and a Buddhist temple, and almost a thousand men lived amongst this labyrinth of shacks and shanties; so said Mrs. Gunn with a certain amount of scorn. Men in shapeless grey suits pushed barrows of vegetables through the foot-traffic -- they called out the name of their wares in the lyrical language of their homeland. Signs painted on old sheets hung above the doorways, chickens scratched in the dirt for bugs, everywhere came the sound and smells of commerce. From the laundries wafted lye-scented steam, and in the valley, smoke from cooking fires and sweet floral incense hung in the air. The sweet, pungent vapors of opium floated from upstairs windows. Some of the buildings had no signs to mark their particular trade, and these were the busiest – places of ill repute, opium dens, whorehouses. Day or night, Ha Gai and Shan Gai remained in constant motion, with miners seeking establishments where they might spend their cash away from the eyes of the law. Anything one fancied could be found here, if one was willing to pay handsomely.

My father visited Chinatown once a fortnight to fetch herbs and medicines not easily gained elsewhere. Molly had contested his patronage of the Chinese apothecaries, for there were other businesses here, too, of which a man in his position should not be acquainted. However, when her nagging resulted in no change to his routine, she grudgingly consented to his visits as long as they were quick, purposeful, and restricted to daylight's hours. Violet found it horrific that Father made such frequent errands, and was scandalized when he brought me in tow. The mere fact that her little sister would agree so readily to a jaunt into the depraved alleys and filthy squalor of the Chinese workers proved, to Violet, that I possessed absolutely no scruples.

But I adored these visits, especially when he let me carry the exotic herbs and flowers that he'd purchased. And now, running through the streets of Chinatown alone, I felt as free as a sparrow. I knew exactly where I must go.

I ran along Shan Gai towards two buildings, each three-stories high. One was milk-washed and adorned with red silk lanterns, while the other was grey and surrounded by barrels of salted fish. Between them appeared an alley, barely a slit between their facades and only wide enough to admit the passage of a single person. I dipped sideways to keep my satchel from thumping against a building. A deep twilight replaced the sunlight, as if a curtain had been drawn in haste, and the two buildings crowded close together and arched overhead. The sky became a distant narrow thread of bright blue, sliced and obscured between clotheslines.

I followed the alley to its end. To my right was a slanted doorway, and above, on the lintel, a small wooden dragon had been carved. The workmanship was exquisite, if measured out in a tiny portion and displayed in an unassuming, almost invisible place. The entrance was covered by a heavy woolen curtain, so patched and mended that it was difficult to tell the fabric's original color.

I pushed the curtain aside and stepped into the dark room.

The air was close and cloying, thick with the heavy fragrances of spices, herbs and soot. Boxes, green glass bottles and wooden crates crowded the edges of the rectangular room, and on three walls, sheets of yellowing paper with curled edges had been pinned up crookedly. On each poster was a drawing of a human form, outlined with points and pathways. Directly across from the entrance, a worn tapestry covered a door leading farther into the building, and even this tapestry portrayed the life-sized image of a stylized man, naked except for a red cloth around his waist. Small arrows pointed out regions of particular interest on his body. In the farthest corner, an iron brazier contained hot white coals, over which a sliver of fish slowly roasted and a tiny, doll-like kettle softly bubbled. To my right, a long counter carried large glass jars, and behind the counter, shelves carried a hundred small glass vessels, each one filled with twisted roots or dried flakes or mysterious crystals of resin.

Light came from a few tallow candles in dishes on the long counter. Shards of flickering candlelight glinted off the flasks and jars, giving the illusion of stars scattered around the room.

I paused at the first jar on the counter. Inside, casting a pale metallic sheen, I saw the tangled limbs and smooth thoraxes of dried insects, each the size of my index finger. The illegible script on the parchment label looked, to my eyes, like a further tangle of insect limbs, pointing in all directions.

I took the ceramic lid off the jar and reached in. The legs of the bugs were sharp, prickly, like a nest of needles. I took one smooth abdomen in my fingers and lifted it gently, noticed the warm mahogany pattern on its toffee-colored head. Dried and preserved, it was as delicate as a pressed flower.

"Those are golden cockroaches," said a man in a low, measured voice.

Though he startled me, I did not drop the insect. In fact, I did not move at all, except to raise my eyes to the source of the words.

A young man stood in the interior doorframe, holding the tapestry aside with one hand. He was no younger than twenty and certainly no older than twenty-five. As he stepped into the room and entered the circle of candlelight, his movements held a lean, graceful strength. His face remained cautious and closed, but I marveled immediately at the beauty of his wide-set, dark eyes under strong, defining brows. He strode to the counter, his bare feet silent on the wooden floor, and he did not wear the shapeless grey flannels buttoned up the front like most Chinese men hired by the company. Instead, he wore a white collarless shirt and black pants with a ragged hem. His black hair was tied back in a queue, the braid reaching passed his waist, but his tonsure was not shaved and a few stray locks of hair framed his brow. A narrow scar, white in the low illumination, crossed his right cheek. Though I had only heard him speak four words, I recognized his English as flawless.

I pried my gaze from his face and turned the insect in my hand, studying it. "What are they for?"

He drew next to me, almost a head taller, so close that I could feel the warmth of his skin. He smelt of apple blossoms and earth. Though quiet and reserved, I sensed a lithe restraint to his actions, too, like the crackle of energy in the air before a thunderstorm. "When ground up and added to tea, they assist with digestion," he replied, "They come from the gardens of Suzhou, where they're bred for medicinal purposes. It is said that they are the offspring of dragons." When he turned to look at my face, his gave a short gasp. "Zao gao! What happened to you?"

I raised my fingers to my bruised cheek, and the injury sang under my touch. "I was in a bit of a tussle." I grinned. "Considering the outcome, I think I won."

He whistled low. "Anyone who can smile with a bruise like that deserves respect." His smile was open and welcoming. "How can I help you?"

"I need some things," I began, then remembered my manners, said, "My father, Dr. Saunders, gave me a list…" I withdrew the folded onionskin paper, and handed it to him. "Here, a tally of everything I wish to buy."

The young man took it, unfurled the paper with athletic fingers, and read the list with furrowed brow. He seemed to be the same age as Violet, yet his eyes were thoughtful and clever, and he lacked the frivolous spark that my sister possessed. They might be the same age, but his experiences far outweighed hers. "I think we have most of these items," he mused, "Most, but not all."

He set the paper on the counter and began to pull jars from the shelves, one from here, one from there, placing each on a table in the corner next to the door leading within. A roll of brown paper and string lay there, and next to it, a knife with a wickedly curved blade as long as my hand.

"I was expecting to see Mr. Tao," I said.

"Mr. Tao is my uncle," he said. Without looking up from the list, he added, "Normally I work with the mules in Number Five, but jiu fu is collecting mushrooms in the hills today, and asked me to mind the store."

"Jiu fu…?"

"Sorry, yes, English," he reminded himself, "Jiu fu: my mother's brother."

"Jiu fu," I repeated, tasting the sounds as they rolled off my tongue. "Did I say that right? Jiu fu?"

He laughed. "The first time, yes, but the second time? No."

"I said it the same."

"No," he replied, "You said the first attempt correctly: jiu fu. But the second time, you rose your voice at the end. Jiu fu? That changed the meaning."

I crossed my arms. "How else am I supposed to ask a question?"

"You don't strike me as someone who ever has difficulty asking questions," he chuckled, "Now, this item, tolu balsam, we have none." He took a pencil from the drawer under the counter and made an X next to the item. "Tell the esteemed Dr. Saunders that he'll have to wait two weeks for the next shipment, or he can try Mr. Han's apothecary, but I doubt he'll have any luck in securing it. There was none in our order from Victoria, and they said the ships have had a hard time bringing it north from Peru."

From a drawer under the table, he pulled a little wooden case shaped like a long-necked violin, and set it next to a blue-beaded abacus on the counter. He untied the body of the case, opened it on fragile hinges, and withdrew the components of a delicate brass scale. As he constructed it upon the top of the table, his hands worked of their own accord, intimately familiar with the chains and weights and balance. A series of brass spoons appeared from the depths of the case. He began measuring items: powders, flakes of resin, sticky grains, and then folding each into triangles of wax paper. He took great care to clean the brass dishes and spoons after every measurement – clearly, it was a sin to pollute the contents of each jar with its neighbors.

"What's your name?"

"Chen Shaozhu," he replied, "And you?"

"Everyone calls me Lizzie." I strolled around the edge of the room, studying the strange maps of the human body, wondering what the lines meant and why everyone looked so stern. "I wish I spoke Chinese as well as you speak English."

"Please -- my Mandarin is horrible, and my Cantonese, even worse," he replied, still focusing on his work. The abacus alongside the scales clacked and clicked as he calculated weights and prices, jotting notes in pencil on my father's list. "I've been speaking English since I was four. My uncle claims I'm a disgrace to the family, I've forgotten half of the proper way to speak my birth language. Instead, I sound like one of you."

"Is that so awful?"

"Terrible," he replied bluntly, "When I return to Luoyang, no one will understand a single word I say."

I sat on the upturned crate by the brazier and watched him as he measured the items out with brass spoons, bundling each in brown paper envelopes. "Luoyang – it sounds so exotic!" I let my gaze drift across the hundreds of containers, but eventually, it returned to his face, like a magnetic needle towards north. "I imagine it must be beautiful!"

He laughed, and lifted his gaze from measuring herbs just long enough to take in my wistful smile and judge the state of his lunch. "Can you turn the trout for me? It'll burn, otherwise." He put the lid back on the glass jar with a musical clink. "It's been so long since I saw Luoyang, I don't remember what it looks like, but I remember the garden of my mother's house, and yes, it was beautiful. Jiu fu took me to San Francisco when I was four, and we ran an apothecary there, until it looked more profitable to head to Victoria."

When I turned the fish on the grill, a delectable smell rose from its flaky, seared flesh. My mouth watered. "Four?" I asked, incredulous, "You left your family when you were only four?"

"One less mouth for my mother to feed, and one more pair of hands to help jiu fu? It seemed the most profitable for everyone."

"I can't imagine leaving my sister behind in England, to come here, all alone. It must've been horribly frightening, Chen."

He brought the small envelopes, rounded with the fullness of their contents, to the counter. He piled them there before walking to the door and tying it aside with a length of jute rope. A gust of cool, fresh air wafted inside, although the narrow walls of the alley allowed for very little light. "My given name isn't Chen, it's Shaozhu. Chen is my father's family name, like Saunders." He dragged a second wooden crate closer and set it on its end, and sat across from me.

I liked his candor, and the way in which he spoke to me: not as a child or a woman, but as an equal.

"My apologies, Shaozhu," I said, "I don't mean to presume."

"I'll call you Lizzie, and you call me Shao. Agreed?"

I shook his hand. It was warm and smooth and strong in my grip.

From a cupboard to his left, he withdrew a small clay cup and, from the pot boiling on the brazier, poured out a generous portion of tea. "It was frightening, to leave home so young," Shao continued, handing me the cup, "But I didn't have much say in the matter, and I wasn't alone. I was with jiu fu, and he's an ambitious man, and has taught me much about business and medicine. I don't mind. I've seen the far side of the Pacific, while my brothers and sisters have probably been no farther than the borders of Henan."

I took the cup in both hands, for it was without a handle, and studied the fragments of leaves swirling in the dark liquid.

"Are there any ground-up bugs in it?"

He suppressed a chuckle to retain a dignified reply. "No. Only dried mint and green tea leaves." He poured a second cup for himself. "I'll save the bugs for your second visit."

I grinned broadly.

The fresh air that drifted in carried the scent of pig manure and roasted chestnuts, as well as the constant, pervasive musk of the swampy earth underneath the buildings. The tea tasted as sharp and sweet as candy canes.

"Do you keep in touch with your family?"

"Absolutely. It's why I'm here." he said, "The money I make, I send home to my eldest sister and her children. She has a small farm, but it doesn't produce enough to feed them, and they'd starve without me."

"I have a sister, but I don't think her hands have ever been dirty, and I doubt she'd ever accept my charity. She's rather proud. But she has lots of friends, and she's far more beautiful and accomplished than I can hope for, so maybe her pride is deserved." I laughed at his look of pity. "Believe me, I'm happy with the arrangement, Shao. I've never aspired to Violet's beauty or poise."

"You're content to be yourself? Then you've attained a state which most men never achieve."

"I'm not content to be myself," I corrected, "I'm just content to not be Violet."

He laughed, a low pleasant chuckle that put me at ease. His eyes ranged over my face and hands, and his distant expression softened as he studied my dusty pants and faded shirt. "I must admit, when you first entered, I thought you were a boy. My uncle has told me about you." He took a sip of tea, and over the rim of his cup, his dark eyes measured my reaction, "About Dr. Saunder's youngest daughter, who dresses in trousers, who pummels the boys and wanders in the woods. You're a bit of an eccentric."

"I'm just not fond of skirts."

"I can't blame you; I imagine they're rather impractical. Not to mention cold on the ankles."

I sipped the tea slowly, luxuriously, and our conversation effortlessly drifted from topic to topic, as though I'd known Chen Shaozhu forever. The minutes slipped passed as my cup emptied, then was refilled, then emptied again. I don't even recall what we talked about – the specifics don't really matter. I may have forgotten our first conversation, but I clearly recall one silent promise I made to myself: many apothecaries existed in Chinatown, but in future, I knew I would only visit this one.

13

FROM A DISTANCE, the Cumberland District Hospital looked nothing like a medical facility. It was made of timber instead of red brick, and possessed a large, inviting verandah that overlooked prim rose gardens, bounded by a white picket fence. The building had originally been planned as Mr. Dunsmuir's Cumberland residence, but as it was being constructed, Colliery officials successfully argued that a hospital was needed more urgently than a grand mansion on the crest of the hill. Their reasons? Coal production was increasing steadily, men arrived daily in droves, and the miners needed a medical facility to keep them in good working condition. Either turn the building into a hospital, or expect production to falter and the cemetery to grow.

Mr. Dunsmuir agreed with the mine managers and gave the building to the city, then opted to build a slightly-bigger, flashier residence farther east. The hospital opened to patients in 1894 without a single soul ever having lived inside.

As I mentioned, from a distance, the Cumberland District Hospital looked nothing like a hospital, but as one drew closer, one noticed little differences. The curtains in the windows were of the most utilitarian cotton, with no lace to soften their edges. On the verandah, two gaunt men in wool blankets slumped in wheeled chairs -- great iron behemoths with mahogany seats that were so heavy, they would sink in the dirt if they ever left the porch. In the side yard, a cook in white uniform rested his spine against the wall and smoked a clay pipe while ordering a boy with a coal bucket to replenish the supply in the kitchen. The building possessed no sense of welcoming – it was as formal as a factory, as indifferent to its occupants' comfort as a workhouse. This was a place of business, no matter how lovely its roses.

I raced up the garden path and took the front steps, two at a time, then shouldered open the front door and entered the main hall.

From upstairs came the sounds of pain: the moans of exhausted desperation or the shrieks of agony. Someone on the main floor yelled for help, for God's mercy, then suddenly fell silent. An older nurse, dressed in a white frock and cap, burst out of a door at the end of the hall and demanded morphine, and another nurse rushed down the stairs with glass vials in hand, narrowly avoiding a Japanese woman carrying a basket of sheets, freshly washed and ready to be hung outdoors. I stayed close to the wall, wanting to stay out of everyone's way, as I walked down the hall to my father's office.

Because he was the youngest of the doctors, or perhaps because his reputation was not as far-reaching as the others, the Board of Directors had installed Dr. Saunders in the smallest room on the north east corner of the building, next to the laundry and boiler. In the winter it was cold and drafty, in summer it was stuffy and humid. He did not complain but I know he much preferred the quiet privacy of his surgery to the busy circus of the hospital. I found his office door closed to keep out the noise, but I knew he was within: his shadow moved under the gap. I knocked politely and entered without waiting for his reply.

Afternoon sun slanted in through the window. The white walls gleamed in the light, and Father, garbed in black with a white apron to cover his clothes, leaned over the gurney in the center of the room.

"You've returned," he said without looking up. "Was your visit to Mr. Tao's apothecary successful?"

When he received no immediate answer, he looked up to see what was wrong.

I stood by the chair and the desk, where his papers lay in neat, precise piles. I noted the color – or, rather, the absence of color – in the office. Against the stark white of the room and its furnishings, the black of Father's clothes created almost an absence of light. The white flesh upon the metal gurney and the white towel covering the groin contrasted sharply with the black crisped edges of seared skin over the dead face. And loudest of all was the slash of crimson blood across Father's apron, double-tined like the tongue of a serpent.

"Lizzie?"

I blinked. "Yes?"

"You're staring."

"Am I?"

"Are you in danger of swooning?" He lowered his right hand. Sunlight flashed on the polished steel blade of his scalpel. "If you're going to faint, please do so in the hall, where the nurses can attend to you."

"I won't faint." I dropped the satchel on the top of the battered traveling trunk in the corner, next to the desk. I ran my fingers over the familiar surface, the worn leather-covered wood bound with stout iron. "I'll be fine – I was only a little surprised by the colors: black, white, and red. It's very pretty."

"Did you manage to get everything I need from Mr. Tao?"

"Mr. Tao wasn't there; his nephew helped me." I counted out his list on my fingers, "I got belladonna, digitalis and dried bachelor buttons. Everything you needed except tolu balsam," My tongue tripped over the word, "Which they do not have. They expect a shipment in two weeks. You could try Mr. Han, but Mr. Tao's nephew thinks even the other apothecaries will be out."

John gave a short huff, not of disappointment but of thoughtful consideration; he would need to be resourceful to devise some other method of mixing Peggy's medicines. From his walrus-hide bag, he took a triangle of white, heavy-grade cotton and carefully wiped the fluids from his scalpel blade. "Mr. Tao has a remarkable garden," he said, "But his business connections up and down the coast aren't always reliable. Considering tolu balsam comes from South America, I ought not be surprised that his stock is running low."

I reached for the latch of the trunk. "Shall I put them away? You keep your medicaments in here, yes?"

He put the scalpel aside. "No, no, I'll do it myself, Liz. I need to record the weights and measures in my log book... but here, Lizzie my girl, help me stitch this poor corpse up for his old widow," John said. He gathered a curved needle and black thread from the cupboard, and held his hands to the window to best take advantage of the daylight.

I stepped alongside the gurney, across from Father, with the naked figure stretched out between us. He had been a portly, pale man of about forty years, his pores peppered black with coal dust, his face grey and his lips blue. What little hair he'd possessed was almost all gone, burned down to the scalp, leaving a dome of raw, roasted flesh. A long incision ran from the base of his throat to the top of his slack belly, and a clamp held the edges open, revealing the twin pink footballs of his lungs, splotched with black like cowhide.

"I'm afraid he would've been dead in a year," said my father, "If not for the flash fire in Number Four this morning, he'd have drowned in his own dust-clogged lungs." John regarded the incision thoughtfully. "Poor fellow probably couldn't run fast enough to escape the flames. Huffing and wheezing, you see."

The raw, black-edged wounds that covered his head looked severe, but they would only have proven fatal after the inevitable, drawn-out bout of infection. I puzzled over them, then said, "It's a horrible injury, but would this kind of burn kill him so quickly?"

"It wasn't the flame that killed him." John used the tip of the scalpel to ease back the edge of the lung, displaying a murky sponge of sooty tissue. "Inhaling the smoke did him in."

I unscrewed the first clamp and set it in a metal bowl at the gurney's side with a noisy clatter, then washed the threads of its screw, rubbing away the blood and fluids in a bowl of water already pink.

"Does it bother you," I asked, "To cut open a man's body?"

"Not at all," he replied candidly. "I rather enjoy it."

I lowered the clamp and paused. "Really?"

"Perhaps 'enjoy' is the wrong word," he replied as he returned to the corpse's left side. The second clamp still held the flap of the stomach aside, revealing the multi-colored guts and ropes of intestines. "I *anticipate* what I might find. I look forward to the pleasure of exploring the inner secrets of the body. Here, look at this..."

He snaked one bloody finger behind the black-red liver, and eased it aside. A bubble of flesh appeared: pink-grey, shiny, and the size of a small nectarine.

"What is it?"

"Every body has unique features... curious things hidden deep within," John said, "Every time I perform an autopsy, I'm opening a precious gift. It is an honor and a privilege to discover the jewels hidden within its structure, which even the owner himself never had a chance to admire." He ran his finger over the sac. "This, Lizzie, is a teratoma."

"What's inside?"

"Let's see, shall we?" he said, picking up the blade again.

The teratoma's plump, glossy surface sprang apart under the sharp knife. A fetid scent wafted up. Inside, damp with blood, was a wad of tangled white hair.

I gasped.

"Teratomas are not so rare, but they are often overlooked, and yet, they're such curious things!" John said, "They're tumors which contain all manner of inconsistent tissues; I once heard of a fellow at Barts who opened one up and found an eyeball inside!" He teased out a few wisps of hair, curly and fair.

"That's amazing!"

"Isn't it?" he replied, his eyes bright. "I'm so glad you think so!"

"Can I.... can I keep it?"

The request startled him. "I don't think this fellow's old widow would be pleased, if you took a chunk of him home. But," John considered my request, "Even he didn't know about the teratoma, so she certainly won't miss it." He dipped his chin to the lower cupboard on the north wall. "Go on, then. Fetch me a glass jar. We can put it in spirits, and keep it here in my office. But you must tell no one, understand? It isn't good form."

I grabbed one from the lowest shelf, and returned to the right side of the body, holding out the jar as Father sliced the teratoma from the rear wall of the liver and plopped it in.

"So, you think you have the constitution for this sort of work, then?" he asked over the crook of his elbow.

"Running more errands?" I thought of Shao's warmth and easy conversation, and a little flutter like pleasurable nausea wiggled through my gut. "Oh, yes, I think so. I look forward to running more errands."

"No," he laughed, "Helping with autopsy, learning the secrets of the body. I know that you possess a strong, stable bearing, Lizzie, but you have a peculiar look upon your face, and you're staring at the corpse."

"It's been a strange day, that's all," I assured him, holding the glass jar with its macabre contents up to the sunlight. With hair and clear fluid dribbling from the tumor, the teratoma looked like a small, deflated mouse, turned inside out. "This morning, I expected to spend the day doing math equations and spelling lessons for Miss Marsh. Instead..." I let the sentence trail away, trying to find the most economical way to express the amplitude of my thoughts. "Instead, it's improved dramatically."

John chuckled as he unclamped the stomach and pulled the torso closed. "Well, if you promise never to faint or squeal in horror, you'd be a direct improvement over the rest of the assistants. I suspect that some of the younger nurses are here solely to ensnare a doctor with their charms. I want to pass along to you my knowledge, Lizzie. I've long nurtured hopes to train you and, in time, perhaps you could continue my work. Would you be interested?"

"Me? A doctor!"

"Does that seem so odd?"

I regarded the empty corpse between us, a man whose life had been sad and short, full of hard manual labor, and who had died to make money for a distant gentleman, most likely never met or seen. I puzzled over Father's optimism. "You don't think the small fact of being a woman might hinder me?"

He laughed. "There is a new era upon us, Lizzie. If a woman can govern the world -- God save the Queen -- I don't see why you can't perform an operation or two."

14

MAY 12, 1898

ATTN. Miss Amaryllis Saunders,
Cumberland Post Office
British Columbia

DEAR GRAND-DAUGHTER,

WHAT A PRECIOUS SURPRISE TO receive your letter, and to be re-acquainted with your bonny personality! It was with pleasure that I read your letter to your grandmother, who is in her decline, and who has often wondered what became of you and sweet Violet.

We were disheartened to hear of your mother's demise. In all these intermediary years, our fond memories of our daughter have eased the sorrow that comes with such distance, and I cling to the belief that our memories will continue to soothe us, now that her distance from us is greater than mere oceans and mountains, and spans both Heaven and Earth. We shall wear the crepe for her and extend to you and your sister our greatest condolences on the loss of your mother.

My dear granddaughter, I must implore upon you to refrain from contacting us further. It was for your family's best interests that you left for the west coast of Canada, and it would do no one any good for communication to resume between our households. Your grandmother can now pass happily into God's hands with the knowledge that you, Amaryllis, are safe and well, and I shall continue into my own twilight years envisioning you, living full and joyful, on your far and distant shore. However, I require nothing more from you. With your mother's death, all ties between us must now be severed. It would be folly to persist in our acquaintance, and any further letters you send to me shall go unanswered.

YOU MOST DEVOTED and absent grandfather,
Capt. Horatio Worthington, esq.

I DIDN'T READ the letter to Violet; I hadn't admitted to sending the first and, frankly, I hadn't expected any reply. I knew that Violet would be upset beyond measure to learn that I'd gone behind her back, written a notice to our grandparents, and sent it without ever entering into her confidence. I hadn't given her the opportunity to dissuade me; for that rudeness alone, Violet would never forgive me.

So I folded the letter carefully and pulled the biscuit tin from under my bed. I stashed the envelope and its polite, but firm, rejection in the tin, then fastened the lid with a squeak of metal on metal and pushed it out of sight.

The next afternoon, with Father's list of herbs and ingredients, I took Captain Worthington's letter to Mr. Tao's apothecary.

Mr. Tao was a gruff man, given to few words, and built like the back of a stage coach: wider at the bottom, giving him a stable stance, and boxy on top, with a square face permanently frozen in a calculating scowl. His black hair, slicked back in a queue that reached half-way down his back, contained long streaks of silver. His presence in the room sucked any possibility of mirth from the air, and at the first sight of him, the anticipation I'd felt at seeing Shao drained out of my limbs. I handed the list to Mr. Tao, lowered my chin and made every awkward attempt to appear demure; even though I was the only client in his shop, I was seized with the urge to hide. He gave a bearish grunt, jutting his jaw out as he looked over the handwriting, and took his time as he mentally tallied behind a pair of sharp brown eyes what items he could, and could not, spare.

"Yes. We have all," he muttered, and began the slow, methodical collection of jars and sundry from the shelves. He barely looked at me and there was not a single smile in my direction -- I suspect the expression is foreign to Mr. Tao's face. He handed me the wrapped parcel, I paid him and left, simultaneously thankful and disheartened, and the whole process took no more than twenty minutes, but when I stepped out of the shop, I took a deep breath of fresh air as though I had been enclosed for hours.

When I reached the end of the alley, a finger snagged my elbow.

Shaozhu stood behind me, dressed in his familiar white linen shirt and tattered pants, a pair of scuffed leather sandals protecting his feet. He had wanted to attract my attention but, now secured, he seemed unsure of what to do with it.

"*Ni hao*," I said after a silence that lasted a moment too long for comfort, and then added, "That's all I can say. It isn't much."

"It's a good start," he replied, "How are you?"

"I am quite well, thank you." I wrinkled my nose. "No, actually, not well. Can I talk to you? I can't go to Violet, and I certainly can't talk to my father, and I'm not sure who would care to listen to me. You don't know me very well, so please, say no if I'm asking too much of our acquaintance, but I thought—"

"Of course you can talk to me," he said without hesitation. With a sweep of his open palm, he offered me a spot on the top step leading from the raised porch to the dirt street. "I saw you from the upstairs window," he pointed to the window on the second floor, overlooking the alley, "And I came down here to talk to you. Nothing would make me happier than to talk."

The porch of the boarding house overlooked the dusty street, crowded with wheelbarrows and vendors. In the faint spring breeze, a line of paper lanterns swung gently along the eaves, and dun-colored mongrel dogs lounged in the shade cast by the boardwalks. A few rats scurried under the steps. The afternoon sun cast a mellow golden warmth over the wooden buildings. Even in this season of growth and new foliage, the swampy air released a fragrant perfume of decay and damp soil, mingled with the delicate scent of hawthorn blossoms and smoked pork from a butcher shop, farther down the street. Because my father had asked me to dress in a seeming manner to work at the hospital, I wore a plain black skirt of the lightest weight of cotton, and a blouse with high collar and long sleeves, but it was too warm for comfort in the spring sunshine, and I felt as if melting into the dust would be a mercy. Shao was bound by no such rules. He unbuttoned his shirt as he sat next to me, revealing a tawny, muscular body, strengthened by many mornings of chopping wood and hauling water.

I tried not to admire his lissome athletic form, his smooth skin, his leonine grace. That would be crude. I could practically hear Violet's disapproval at such vile and loathsome feelings.

So I tried to keep my eyes focused on Shao's face. His pleasant, open, accommodating, angelic face. His dark sympathetic eyes and strong brow and handsome chin and --

"You wanted to talk?" he urged.

"Uh, yes!" I stammered, and realized that I'd been staring. "I... uh... I sent a letter to my grandfather," I began, then gave my head a little shake to focus. I started again with more confidence. "Last March, I sent a letter to tell him my mother was dead, and I never expected a reply, but he did! He sent me a letter!" My eyes widened with the wonder of it, of receiving communication from the past, resurrecting a link with a far-distant home that I had never dreamed could be restored.

"That's wonderful!"

My expression soured. “Well, no, actually, it isn’t,” I admitted, “Because while he sounded pleased to hear from me, he’s asked that I never contact him again.” I fished the letter out of my pocket and handed it to him. I’d read it so many times that I could see every curve of letter and slash of ink in my imagination. “He wrote that they require nothing more from me. What does that mean?”

“It seems clear to me, Lizzie, ” Shao replied carefully, studying the words. “He wants nothing to do with you.”

“But why?” I insisted, “Why would they cut us out of their lives so completely?” I set my jaw, frowned in thought. “You still contact your family, yes?”

“I have every intention of returning home,” he replied. “Your father and mother left England and never looked back. Maybe your grandparents wished to do the same, no matter how painful.” He handed the letter back to me.

“Well, to be honest, my father and grandfather didn’t see eye-to-eye.”

“Then, there’s the answer to your question.”

“But it wasn’t me who had a disagreement with my grandparents,” I began as I folded the letter and returned it to my pocket. “It isn’t fair that they’d hold their grudge against my father over me, too.”

“They don’t really know you,” he offered, “You were too small when you left.”

“But what if I wanted to re-aquaint myself with them? What if I wanted to go back to England? If I were standing in their doorway, would they still reject me?” I slumped back against the stair and shrugged. “Ah, what does it matter. After being in Canada for so long, I wouldn’t fit in England anymore.”

He dipped his chin down and stared at the dirt, and chewed on his bottom lip. After a moment’s consideration, he said, “Travel changes a person. You can’t go back to how you were. Luoyang is only my birthplace; it’s no longer my home.”

“Exactly. London isn’t my home. This is my home.”

Shao shook his head. “This isn’t my home.”

“Where do you think you belong, then?” I asked, and his shoulders tensed. He clenched his hands into fists. I immediately regretted asking, but the question now hung in the air between us.

He said, slowly and with confidence, "I do not know where I belong." One fist tapped against his knee, each strike sharp with anger. "But not here, not this place. This is an ugly life to be trapped in."

I looked around at the buildings and the street. The setting was rugged and sparse, but set against the backdrop of forests, this place far better than any city. "I rather like Chinatown," I said innocently.

"This place is Hell."

The ferocity of his voice caused a shiver of surprise to skitter through my gut.

"You probably think we like it this way," he said.

I folded my hands over my knees. "I haven't given any thought to what you might like," I admitted, "But I can't imagine anyone would be content to live in a place they call Hell."

Shao gazed down the street at the vendors with their wheelbarrows. "See that man, there? With the barrow full of carrots? That's Luang Yi-Chen."

"He looks not unhappy," I said, studying the elderly man. Stooped to hold the handles of his barrow, he chatted with a friend in the shade of an awning. They punctuated their conversations with hearty laughter.

"Yi-Chen came here in 1891 to work in the mines. He left his wife and child behind to make his fortune, because he was told that he would find incomparable riches here. Have you been down a mine, Liz?"

"No, but Mr. Gunn has told me what it's like: hot, dark, crowded."

"Crowded… hmph." He looked at me briefly before returning his gaze to the man with the barrow. "Yi-Chen worked ten or twelve hour days in a seam that was no more than a foot high – he crawled two hundred feet on his belly to chip coal from the face, and only came to the surface after the sun went down. Yi-Chen didn't see daylight for seven whole months."

"That's barbaric!"

"One morning, he heard a hissing in the rock and felt a shift in the walls: imagine, lying on your stomach in a tunnel of rock, six hundred feet below the surface of the earth, and suddenly the walls and ceiling and floor begin to tremble. Yi-Chen knew that he was lying in his own grave. The tunnel was too narrow to turn around, so he began to back out when he heard a roar and a crack. A crushing weight bore down around him, and he remembers nothing more until he woke on a stretcher in the picking yard."

I watched Yi-Chen and noticed the lack of grey in his hair. "He isn't half as old as he looks, is he."

"Yi-Chen's only a few years older than me," Shao replied, "But his legs were broken in six places, and his shoulders crushed. He lives in constant agony. My uncle attends to his injuries, gives him opium to ease his suffering, but his bones have healed as much as they ever will. He'll never be whole again."

"Why hasn't he gone home to his wife and children?" I asked. "Surely his family would support him?"

Shao shook his head. "Yi-Chen would give anything to see the face of his wife again, but he'll die here, and he knows it. No matter how much agony he endures, he must make money, because he is burdened with a debt that must be paid. We are here, all of us, because we owe the Company."

"What do you mean?"

"The head-tax," he said, and was answered by my look of bewilderment. "Haven't you ever wondered why there are so few women in Chinatown?"

"Well, yes," I said. When I looked along the street, I saw only men's faces, "But my mother said it was because the Chinese planned to return to Asia, and don't want to settle here."

"Of course I don't want to settle here!" he exclaimed, "For twice the work, I make half the wage as a white miner! I'm expected to remain silent and say nothing, and do as I'm told, and be industrious and thrive in squalor! I don't even have a name, here – I'm just Jim boy, or Johnny Chinee, or a goddamn chink, if I get in their way." He spoke with teeth set, his brown eyes black with rage. "Why the hell would I want to stay in North America, where I'm not even seen as a human being? To the mine owners, I'm just a two-legged mule that doesn't understand a word that's said to me."

"But you keep working because of the tax?"

"I have to," he admitted. "When jiu fu and I arrived in Victoria in 1892, he discovered we had to pay a head-tax, and he didn't have the money to cover us – fifty dollars each! So he let an agent loan us the money, who then sold our contracts to the Company. And that's why there's so few women... a woman simply can't make enough to pay for her head-tax, unless she's a prostitute. What man in his right mind would bring his wife or sister to this god-forsaken place, to pass her around like a cheap slab of meat to the highest bidder?"

"So, if your contract was bought and sold, does that mean you're..." I didn't want to say the word, for fear of offending him, but he sensed what I was thinking.

"A slave?" He looked down at his feet and knocked the dust from his sandals. "Until I pay back my head-tax, that would be a good way to describe it. Of course," he cast me a sideways glance, "The Company would never use such vulgar language – zao gao, no! Slavery was something that heathens and Americans did. No, in the words of the Company, I am indentured. I am indebted. I am an honest worker, making an honest wage, to pay back a loan which I didn't choose to take." He laughed bitterly.

"How long, then, until you can buy your freedom?"

"Too long." From the way he answered, it was clear: this was a calculation he'd figured out and discarded as too depressing to keep in mind. "On a good day of hauling coal, I make a dollar. But I send half my wages home to my family in Luoyang, pay a weekly fee to my Benevolent Association, and give the rest to jiu fu. He insists that, as the head of the family, we pay his head-tax first, but I suspect more of my wage ends up on the gambling tables that in the pockets of the colliery officials." Shao snarled. "I don't think I'll ever be free, no matter how much I make."

"What's a Benevolent Association?"

"A social club, that helps if I'm injured, and affords me protection, should I need it."

"Oh! Like the Freemasons, or the Order of the Druids."

He nodded towards the end of the street, where a two-story building lurked innocently behind a higgledy-piggledy rampart of sheds, sow-sties and shops. "Jiu fu and I belong to the Guan Yu Tong."

"Are there many of these associations here?"

"Quite a few. And they don't all get along." He swept his hand out. "This is a whole community of angry, downtrodden, desperate, starved men, trying their damnedest to scrape out a living in a place that doesn't want them. There's a lot of rage here, and the associations pit themselves against each other because there's no one else they can hate so openly. It makes for...." He chose his words with care. "Interesting times."

I felt the weight of his last comment, marveled at the force of it, and wondered if I could ever feel as much raw emotion as Shao had locked away inside.

"You're so angry!"

"Wouldn't you be?"

"Violet says the Chinese don't feel anger."

His eyebrows arched. "Really."

Compared to Violet, Shao's personality was so strong, so real, so galvanized by experience. Violet only parroted what society told her. Shao knew from experience how brutal and unfair the world is, but it hadn't made him resentful or malicious. It hadn't twisted him into something ugly. It had made him wiser. It gave him substance and anchored him.

I blinked twice, chastened. At last, in a hushed whisper, I said, "I think you're absolutely beautiful!"

"What?"

"If I get any closer to you, I think I'll catch fire." I leaned back against the wobbling banister post and regarded him with open awe. "Your defiance, discontent, and indignation is absolutely fantastic!"

Only after I proclaimed my admiration did I realize Shao might take offence at my excitement, not share in my enjoyment, and indeed feel a bit offended by my naïve exuberance. To be honest, he looked a bit stunned. He cast about for something to say, and his brow knit together in an expression somewhere between disbelief and shock. I hadn't intended any insult – I hurriedly scrolled through a number of addendums to my previous sentence which, now that I matched my revelation with the humorously stunned expression on his face, he must have interpreted as inappropriate, glib, and downright rude.

"I only mean that you have such power," I stammered.

This word, judging by his steepled eyebrows and slowly closing mouth, was a good choice.

"And that you *feel* so much..."

The eyebrows drew together quickly, the corners of his mouth wrenched into the first twist of a frown. Not a good choice. Boys, I remembered, do not like to *feel*. Pointing out their feelings was like noticing a pimple: a fault best ignored, no matter how impossible.

"And that you are indescribably handsome when you are angry, like a general in command of a vast army, focused solely on your goal of victory in the face of indescribable odds."

I took a deep breath and paused, waiting for the result.

Shao collapsed back against the opposite balustrade, obviously winded by the maniacal carousel of my fumbling sentence.

"I don't quite understand," he said cautiously, "You like that I'm oppressed? Or you're suggesting that I ought to raise an army?"

"No, I don't like that you're oppressed!" I replied, "I like that you're mad about it! I like that you have an indomitable core of strength in you! I like that you want to change things! I wish I had that kind of power in me!"

"Oh," he said, laid low by my adoration. "Thanks, I guess." He pushed back a strand of blue-black hair that had broken loose from his queue and said, "Did you just call me handsome?"

I could not stop the blush from racing up my cheeks.

"I think I did."

"Oh." He tried, without success, to hide a bashful smile, so he looked away, down the road toward the stump-covered hillside and the virginal woods beyond. Two men carried a freshly butchered goat suspended on a pole between them, strolling around the corner from the lower street, Ha Gai. They shuffled passed, one whistling slightly, and had almost vanished at the end of Shan Gai by the time either Shao or I had gathered our wits enough to speak.

He cocked one eyebrow towards me. "I've never seen anyone get so excited by another person's anger."

"But your anger is real and concrete!" I insisted, "I feel nothing, compared to you!"

"Maybe you haven't had any good reason to be angry," he said pointedly, then grinned. He didn't seem to resent my wide-eyed admiration; far from it. He drifted closer to me, and said, "There must be something that makes you angry."

I pursed my lips as I considered my words. I liked Shao, I appreciated his sensibility and compassion. He was restrained and reserved, but his bearing was trustworthy. "Yes, there is. When the boys say my Mother was crazy, it makes me angry. But she was crazy, so I can't really argue with that." I rubbed one hand over the back of the other, putting into words what I could never say to Father or Violet. "And when they say I'm crazy, too, I wonder if maybe they're right."

He looked confused. "Why would they think you're crazy? You seem bright and healthy to me."

I shrugged. "I wear pants – because they make the most sense! And I don't cry as much as Violet – but why would I? She's a simpering twit!" I sighed. "It seems, whenever I do what seems to make the most sense, others tell me I'm acting as mad as a March Hare."

"Well, by all of my accounts, you seem fine to me, Lizzie Saunders," he assured with a wide, honest grin. "And while I may not be a doctor, I am an apothecary's apprentice, and I've certainly seen my share of sick men. You? I would never say there's anything wrong with you." He peered closer to the skin surrounding my eye. "In fact, I'd never suspect you'd had a black eye – the whole thing has clear up without a trace. You're quite lovely, without it."

My heart soared.

"I should be getting back." I said, and let him hold my hand and pull me to my feet. "I've agreed to meet Violet at the corner of Dunsmuir and First. As long as Constable Kelly is the only man in town worth her attention, he's all she can see, which means she must be seen walking by his office every afternoon, to remind him of her availability." I rolled my eyes. "Honestly, have you ever heard of anything so absurd?"

Shao's eyes widened and he sat upright. "Mr. Kelly – damn! I forgot....Will you do me a favor, if you're going that way?" He beckoned for me to follow him back down the alley, into the apothecary.

Mr. Tao had retreated further into the building; the room was empty. Shao dodged behind the counter and grabbed a small, paper-wrapped box from a shelf. "This is for Alexander Kelly. Could you carry it to him?"

"Of course, it's no trouble," I replied.

It was as large as an apple and tied with white string. I took it and tucked it under my arm, marveling at its heavy weight.

"What is it?"

"Mr. Kelly has a standing order with us," Shao said, "His position with the company demands that he refrain from coming to Chinatown for his..." There was a long, pregnant pause. "Medications."

"Opium?"

Shao held a finger to his lips. "Here, for your trouble." He pressed two pennies into my palm.

"You have more need of money than me," I said, resisting.

"You've saved me a good deal of trouble," he said, "I hate going into town. Besides, it's bad manners for you to refuse my money – it would be highly improper for you to do me a favor. It might mean we're more than business associates, and have actually become friends."

"Goodness," I grinned, "We simply couldn't have that."

. . .

On the corner of Dunsmuir and First Street sat the Constabulary, a two-storey building situated on the highest point of the main street. The main floor held the offices and jail cells. A narrow flight of wooden stairs ascended along the side of the building to the small entrance of Mr. Kelly's second-floor apartment, and a trail around the back led to the stable yard, where the city provided three good horses for the use of the Law. One of those horses, a cream-colored mare, was tied to a post at the corner.

I stopped to tousle the horse's mane. It gave an affectionate snort and bumped its nose against my shoulder; it was a lovely creature, well-groomed and straight-limbed, but its legs were covered in mud and bits of fern. Mr. Kelly had ridden through the woods, perhaps, and had not been back long enough to attend to his horse. "Good day to you," I whispered, scratching my fingers along its neck, then strode to the door of the building. I knocked twice to announce my entrance and found the door unlocked.

Inside, the space was divided into halves. The front section held two desks and a black iron potbellied stove, and the back half was portioned into two austere cells, each with a cot and blanket and a tin bucket for a chamber pot. Today, both cells were empty.

Alexander Kelly was the only man in the room. He looked up from his desk when the door opened, and laid his pen along his inkwell. Wiping his fingers on a handkerchief, he stood and straightened his grey jacket, and pulled down his sleeve cuffs.

"Miss Saunders, do come in," he bid, and circled his desk to offer me a chair. "How good to see you!"

His feeling about my visit were plain to read on his face: a visit from Lizzie might make a poor substitute for Violet's charming conversation, but it was better than nothing, and he was bound to learn a little of Violet's habits and health from her sister.

"Thank you, Mr. Kelly," I replied. "It is my good fortune that you only use the pale horse! I was pleased to see it tied out front – I thought you might be away on business, keeping the town in order."

He chortled. "Calliope? Well, she's a fine beast, that one. We've already been to the lake and back – strong, quick, as smart as a terrier, loyal to a fault. I couldn't ask for a better mount. She even keeps her head when guns fire."

"I suppose that would be very useful, given your line of work."

"Indeed!" he said, "Did you know, she'd been raised for the cavalry? That's what I've been told: originally trained for the 1st Hussars, but not tall enough for regulation." He chuckled at himself. "Look at me, chattering on; now you'll go and think my horse is smarter than I... please, do sit. How might I be of service to you on this fine afternoon?"

It was easy to understand Violet's infatuation with Mr. Kelly. In a town of drunkards and gamblers, he cut a dashing figure. He was charming, literate, and a champion for justice, and he managed to remain liked by both Company managers and miners – no small feat in a town where almost everyone nursed grievances against either their betters or their underlings. Father McGill voiced the opinion that Kelly was not tough enough with his criminals, and even John Saunders agreed that the jails were too often empty and the streets too full of despicable characters, but despite his leniency, Kelly kept the crime rate low. He was a moderator, a politician, and in general, a most congenial fellow.

Instead of taking the offered chair, I withdrew the brown-paper package from my leather satchel. "Actually, I hope I can be of help to you, sir," I said. I dipped forward as if imparting a great secret. "Chen Shaozhu asked me to deliver this to you."

His ruddy face brightened, his smile widened, his cheeks drew up into a pair of red cherries. "A most pleasant surprise!" He hurried to dampen his enthusiasm. "Did he tell you its contents?"

"No, he did not say," I replied, which was not technically a lie, for the words had never left Shao's lips, "But I suppose, a man of your standing would have need for medicaments. I imagine you acquire a number of aches and pains, chasing down ruthless criminals."

"And I would not want to bother your father with such little trifles," he replied. "There is a stiffness of the joints that comes upon me in this damp spring air. Nasty business."

I accepted his reasons with a nod. "I shall say nothing to my father, nor to any other. I wholeheartedly believe that the methods you use to improve your own health are your business and no other's."

A heavy pause filled the air. He weighed my comment, then nodded to show his own understanding.

"Very kind of you to think so, Miss Saunders," he said as he took the box from me. "Besides, I can assure you, I only take a spoonful to sweeten my tea. None of this smoking business – too much, and it renders a man useless!"

"I have never once questioned your ability to perform your duties, sir," I assured.

He stashed the box in the lowest drawer of his desk. His eyes sparkled, and his smile warmed. "My mind is eased to know that you will be discreet with this information."

"Why wouldn't I be?" I replied frankly. "Working with my father has impressed upon me the importance of confidentiality when it comes to a man's health. It would reflect poorly on me – and on my father! – if I were to tell every man and his horse about the patients we see!" I dipped closer. "Plus, Violet would never forgive me for trespassing against you. She is greatly fond of you, sir."

Did a flush of red skirt up from his collar? He gave a gruff cough and lowered his head to rustle through his desk.

Eventually, he pulled out a money box, from which he withdrew a small envelope that clinked with coins. "Will you see Chen Shaozhu again soon?"

"If you give me a reason to seek him out, then I look forward to it."

"Here, my girl." He handed me the envelope, and pushed a coin into my hand to seal my silence. "For your most cherished discretion."

A man's addictions were rarely a secret in this town, but neither were they the topics of polite conversation, and it mattered little to me what Mr. Kelly did with his money or spare time. Half the working men here sought comfort in one vice or another – if opium was Kelly's habit, it was no worse than prostitution, drink or gambling. If he dabbled in riding the dragon during his leisure hours, an act not technically illegal and only merely frowned upon, then I had no argument with Mr. Kelly. He was too likeable to hold responsible for long.

"I promise, sir," I said, "I'll return this to him immediately."

"He's a good fellow, you know." Mr. Kelly replied. "Quite clever, for a heathen."

My heart stuttered a bit; Shao was quite clever, indeed, and handsome and beautiful as the dawn and – I struggled to strangle my thoughts, the memory of his athletic shoulders, his black hair streaked with blue like a raven's wing, the flash of his cynical smile. I felt the blood rising up my cheeks. Instantly, my adoration was swept away by the embarrassment flooding through me, and the confusion of my own infatuation. I stuffed the envelope in my leather satchel "I really must go," I stammered, turning my back to him, striding to the door, "I promise, I'll take this to Mr. Chen right away."

"You'll give my regards to Violet?" Kelly asked. When I glanced back, his broad, prying smile only flustered me more.

15

PANAMA STANK of sweat and mud and rot; every breath tasted as if it had been inhaled through a wet sock. Even at the age of six, I recognized the stench of sickness. I fought to hold my breath as the train, a tottering bundle of old parts and rusted carriages, crept across the buzzing, burning, mosquito infested mountain core of the isthmus. The train's steady pace was no faster than a brisk walk -- this ensured that the engine wouldn't rattle itself back into its basic components over the wobbled tracks, or hurl itself over the precipice and into a newly-carved river chasm, but the pace turned the 48 miles from Atlantic to Pacific into a journey of titanic proportions. Father had called it 'the shortcut between oceans', but the effort required to cross this little snippet of land was completely out-of-scale with the smooth sea voyage on the *Papillion*, a White Star steamer from Liverpool to Aspinwall, which I had found easy and breezy and utterly enjoyable.

Mud sloped away at the edges of the track grade, disappearing into the morass of jungle creepers and palms. The dirt here was so infused with moisture, it looked fluid. Sometimes the train would crawl alongside a crowd of men, laborers on the French project, but they were like no laborers I'd ever seen. These were stick figures, undernourished and overworked. Red mud stained their pants to the knees and, in the crotch, flies billowed around crusted diarrhea. They struggled to march on the viscous surface, slipping back and crumpling to their knees, propping themselves up with crutches; the stinking, festering, moist heat made their progress no easier. They did not walk so much as wade through the thick air.

At least, in Aspinwall, the Atlantic air swept in during the early morning hours and brought a revitalizing freshness, salty but full of oxygen. I liked Aspinwall, so different from London and all I'd known. Americans had named the city after a businessman in the Pacific Mail Steamship Company, William Aspinwall, but everyone else called it 'Colon', and Father said we must take care to use the right name with the right person, lest we start an argument. The city sat on a marshy island called Manzanillo, and the whole area had suffered greatly during a recent civil war, with many of the old buildings burned to the ground and quickly replaced by new apartments and cabarets. Lively, shiny, and bright: Colon had become the gateway to the New World, and it had shaken off the drudgery of the Old with unrestrained joy. As we disembarked from *The Papillon*, I saw people of all races, religions, castes and creeds, gathered together in one place to make their fortunes, and my head whirled with the wonder of it.

But Father complained that the *Papillion's* arrival on Sunday proved to be poor timing, because fresh recruits for the French project, the Grand Canal, had arrived the day before, and they'd snapped up all the tickets for carriages heading west on the Transcontinental Railroad. To make matters worse, the ticket agent would not accept dollars or pounds but wanted to be paid in gold, and Mother was forced to give up her watch pendant to satisfy him. Father showed his impatience plainly, but I rejoiced that we must stay in Colon for ten whole days.

Then, to his horror, we discovered that almost every available room in the city had been rented. Father left us in the waiting room of the station while he hunted for lodging. We cuddled under Mother's arms, keeping guard over the whole of our worldly possessions: a carpetbag of spare clothes, the travel trunk of Father's professional supplies, and the grey-brown portmanteau of walrus-hide containing his medical instruments. We slept in our damp clothes when night came, hoping he'd met with no ill fate.

He returned at dawn. He'd managed to secure lodging in a hotel run by a surly Spaniard, who spoke no English and begrudgingly conversed with Dr. Saunders in a broken jargon of French, Latin, and angry hand gestures. I'd been so excited to see the streets of Colon but, for hot days on end, our mother kept us in the tiny upstairs room, so I contented myself with listening to fights erupting in the streets below. Molly mended our stockings and busied herself by organizing the clothes in our carpet bag, again and again. Father left us to scrounge for food and drink, and after long walks, he brought bread that was soggy with humidity and tepid water that tasted like iron, and a salty jerk made of meat that none of us could identify.

Almost two weeks after our ship had docked, we returned to the station and boarded a rusted train called 'The Westminster'. John staked a place for us in the second carriage -- four seats, far enough back to avoid the cinders belching from the steam stack but close enough to the front to miss the stench of the cattle cars. Standing passengers surrounded us, many of whom stank like rancid sweat and cheap cigarette smoke. Violet complained that her skin felt hot, and her stomach unwell.

"We are all terribly hot," Molly dismissed.

The old carriage bumped and rattled and shimmied its way out of the station, crossing the causeway to the mainland and sliding between slums of dark-skinned, desperate children and three-legged dogs. We had not yet passed the hump of Monkey Hill when I first noticed Violet's discomfort. She clenched her arms around her torso and shivered. Her teeth chattered.

Molly, too, noticed. "Violet, are you—"

Violet's eyes lolled back. A gurgled moan escaped from her blue lips.

Molly pressed a hand to her brow. "She's feverish," she said to Father, then plucked at the sleeve of a man by the window, who had leaned his head out to escape the sour stench of unwashed workmen. She glanced at the leather bladder slung from his satchel. "My daughter needs water to drink," she said to him.

He shrugged off her grip, not even bothering to glance at the wasting, trembling, damp girl. "Let go," he replied. His face, pocked and scarred, was a triangle composed of two gaunt cheeks and a pointed chin. Sweat plastered his black hair to his high forehead, and when he sneered, his gums had craters instead of teeth.

Molly opened her mouth to demand water, but Violet cried out as a fresh sheen of perspiration turned her grey skin glossy. The train hitched, then began to climb slowly into the jungle. I watched Violet transform before my eyes, melting from a lively girl into a pile of sodden rags in the corner of the train carriage, moaning with every shiver and bump.

John knelt at Violet's side and touched her brow. "Ague," he said to my mother, "Marsh fever. We stayed too long at the coast."

A strangled sob caught in Molly's throat. "Are you sure?"

John nodded. "Stay with Violet, I'll be right back."

He grabbed my hand and pulled me after him, to the front of the carriage, where our luggage was stowed. A pile of crates, boxes and canvas bags had been lashed down with jute ropes, and men who could not afford a seat on the train rested their backs against the pile. John shoved aside a couple of African laborers and a small knot of white men – from their curses, Germans and French -- who were traveling as far as the worksite of the Grand Canal. They glowered but stepped aside; my father's coat and hat marked him as a man of quality.

As I watched him search for our luggage, I noticed that my limbs felt stiff and quavering. "I'm hot," I whined.

"You will catch a fever, too," he said as a matter of fact.

I began to cry. "But I don't want to be sick! Violet is sick! I don't want to be sick!"

John bent down before me and took my hands in his. "Can I tell you a secret, Lizzie?"

I sniffled and nodded. In the crowded train, he pulled me close, and his breath on my cheek seemed cool next to the humid stink of the air. "Sometimes," he whispered, and his voice tickled my ear, "Sometimes, one sickness can cancel out another." He pressed a kiss to my nose. "It is better to have a little fever, now, than be very, very sick later. Do you understand?"

"No," I replied.

"I fear that you and Violet have a secret illness, one that you don't even know you have."

Cold, piercing dread flooded through my stomach, which had already begun to feel weak and rubbery. "I'm already sick?"

John held his finger to his lips. "You must not tell your mother; she does not know. But I promise you, Lizzie: a fever, today and tomorrow and maybe for a few days yet, will be good for you, and make you stronger."

"You want Violet and me to get sick?"

"I want Violet and you to get better," he replied, "I know you don't quite understand, but I will try to explain it to you, when you feel well again, and when we aren't in such uncomfortable surroundings. But, for now," he said, standing, "I need your help. Will you help me?"

Without a word to anyone, John dug through the belongings, ignoring the protests of other passengers at the poor treatment of their luggage. He uttered a small grunt of relief as he unearthed his leather-bound, iron-girded trunk.

He unlocked it and threw it open, and I heard him mutter to himself as he sorted through the contents. I did not watch him, for my attention was elsewhere: I studied the faces of the African laborers, who in turn watched me with equal fascination. The sclera of their eyes was an impossible white against the jet sheen of their skin, and when one smiled to me, his teeth were as radiant as stars against the night sky. Though I smiled boldly in return, I pressed myself against my father's thigh, felt his body shift and move as he rummaged through the belongings.

"Here," he said finally, pressing a tiny glass vial into my hands, "Hold this, Lizzie, and keep it safe." I gripped it tightly to my chest, this curious bottle full of white sand, sealed with a wad of red wax.

He locked the trunk again and, without bothering to replace the luggage he'd unbound and toppled, he took my arm and dragged me after him, elbowing his way through the close, crowded, swaying carriage.

When we returned, Violet looked at me but did not see me. Her blue eyes rolled back, her sluggish tongue and pink gums flashed as she drew back her lips in a snarl of agony. Her fingers dug themselves into the soft meat of her belly. Violet kicked out with weak legs and caught Molly on the knees, but the woman would not be dislodged from her daughter's side.

"She's dying," she said to John, "Oh, God, John! She's going to die on this train!"

I stood transfixed, mesmerized. I was not afraid. My curiosity burned in my gut like an ember as Violet cried out again, and my sister wrenched her limbs into impossible poses, like a contortionist in a gypsy circus. Violet was sick with a secret illness, and this fever would burn it out of her, purge her of whatever ailed her.

"She won't," he said, "Here, Lizzie, give the vial to me."

"Why does she move like that?"

"It is only the fever, contracting her muscles," he said to me in a calm voice.

"Could she die?"

"I hope not," said John. He withdrew a pearl-handled pocketknife and cut the wax away in little scarlet curls.

The crystals in the glass bottle were the same translucent white as moth wings. John measured a small portion into the hollow of his palm and, wrenching the fingers of his free hand between Violet's clenched teeth, poured the powder into Violet's maw. He clamped her lips shut and held her nose, forcing her to swallow as she thrashed in panic. When he released her, she gasped and screamed.

The crowd backed away as far as they could within the confines of the carriage, hearing the sounds of struggle.

Violet convulsed but did not vomit. She collapsed in a heap, mewling and retching. A slight pink hue returned to her cheeks.

"Give some quinine to Lizzie," said Molly.

He did not even take a moment to consider her request. "Not yet."

"BEFORE she gets ague, John!" Molly demanded. "I beg of you!"

I listened to my mother plead and my father refuse, but I paid them little attention. It was more interesting to watch Violet. The color percolated back into her face, her muscles relaxed, and tears leaked from the corners of her eyes. The touch of my fingers to Violet's brow proved that the fire still raged under her skin, but her fits had passed.

I touched my own forehead, too. There, I felt a similar dry heat, evaporating the layer of moisture imposed upon my bare skin by the jungle.

"No, Molly, I will not waste the quinine!" Father's voice was steely, confident.

"Waste!?" she screeched, "You would have us lose both our children?"

"We will lose neither," he replied, "Look, Violet sleeps, she is not dead! And Lizzie has not yet fallen ill -- perhaps she is immune."

My mother was on her knees, her hands clasping Violet's. "Oh, God, our Lord in Heaven—"

"I will not have you insult my art with one breath, then pray over these girls with the next!" he said, reserved but clearly angry. He shook the fist holding the vial of quinine. "THIS is what will save them, not some distant, uncaring Hebrew myth!"

"You're evil!" she screamed. The cords of her neck jumped, her cheeks flushed. "God has struck Violet down to test you! And He will find you wanting! You will be judged, John Saunders, you will be judged by He Who is Most High—"

Father slapped her. The sound was moist and blunt, like a mallet hitting a slab of beef.

I do believe that his violence frightened him more than her. He fell to his knees alongside Molly and they stared at one another, wide-eyed. He trembled and touched the crimson mark rising on her pale cheek. It would be the only time I saw him strike her, and his face contorted with guilt.

But he didn't apologize.

"Be quiet," he ordered.

She complied, biting her lips to keep from weeping.

"It is only a little fever," he said, "They will live, Molly, I promise you. And they will be stronger for it."

Molly held Violet's limp form close across her lap, humming a little nursery tune in the unresponsive girl's ear. My sister still shivered and lurched, but her skin was less like the color of putty, and more like the color of snow.

VIOLET and I spent most of the journey from Panama Bay to San Francisco in quarantine aboard ship, and while we both suffered high fevers, Violet's malady struck her with far greater intensity. She lost a fifth of her bodyweight, and the whites of her eyes adopted a golden tinge that took years to fade. We remained an extra month in California to let Violet rest, for she needed to muster her strength on shore before attempting the final leg of our sea voyage.

A position with the Colliery waited for the doctor, and we needed to reach Victoria before the end of summer. Understandably, John was eager to arrive, but he was patient, too, and knew that moving Violet might aggravate the ague in her blood. For five weeks, we lived in a hotel room with a view of the San Francisco docks. The fever had left me with no enthusiasm to do anything more active than observe the world outside: I watched the whaling ships leave for open waters, the paddle steamboats belch greasy clouds as they crossed the bay, and Chinese junks raise their lugsails as they fished for shrimp. I watched the Marin Headlands change from fiery orange to twilight blue with each setting sun. I watched Violet's strength return like a flower refreshed with rain.

Father wrote letters to his new employer to explain the situation, and they were accommodating, although perplexed why a man of good standing would choose the Panama route at the height of summer. Molly read their replies aloud, and even a little child like me understood the reason for her anger.

"How uncharitable!" she spat, "To insinuate that this malady is somehow your fault! Poor dear Violet lies in the arms of impending Death, yet Union Colliery has the gall to blame you, John? For taking us through Panama? Well!" She huffed and folded the letter sharply. "I shall not blame you in the least, my love. One mortal man can not understand the plans of God!"

"Violet does not lay in the arms of Death," John said to soothe her. He glanced at the cot by the window, where Violet lay like a sack of wet rags, revolving through cycles of sweating fever and weak sleep. "Another week more, and I'm sure she will be strong enough to travel again."

"I thank the angels that our little Amaryllis was spared the full sickness!" Molly exclaimed, and dragged me close in a rare show of affection. "And now God will deliver Violet back to us, too."

But I knew, it was not God who had infected us, nor was it God who saved us. I peered at my father over the crook of my mother's embrace, and I remained convinced that only my father's stash of quinine had saved Violet's life: a stash kept safe within the fortress of his traveling trunk. That lowly, battered and ugly piece of luggage adopted an epic symbolism. Our health and survival hinged on the trunk – in that trunk, he kept his surgical tools, his teaching collection, and his research, everything required for our salvation.

As a child, I fantasized that it might be bottomless, and whatever we needed would magically appear to save us from any fate. The trunk was mythic. It held secrets. Even though a decade had passed since our journey across the wretched isthmus of Panama, the trunk remained holy and sublime, a glorious and inspirational relic with the power to heal. Any threat could be repelled by its contents, and just as the vial of quinine had snatched Violet back from the precipice of a malarial death, I truly believed that the items inside the trunk could fend off dragons. John kept it in the corner of his hospital office, an old piece of furniture upon which he piled books, but I looked upon it with reverence. As I worked in my father's office, I would run my fingers over its battered surface and a shiver of delight would skitter up my spine.

16

May 13, 1898

I lay in bed, reading by candlelight, when the tiny tap of something small striking the window caused me to lower my book and scowl in the window's direction. What could possibly have disturbed my reading? It was far too dark for a bird; perhaps a bat? I'd never heard of a bat flying head-first into a house, but hundreds of bats lived in the trees on the hospital grounds, and maybe one of them wasn't quite as bright as its brothers. If the moon had disoriented the swarm, it wasn't impossible that—

Tap! Another sharp rapping, once and quick and light.

"Well," I thought, "I'd believe one idiot bat, but not two!"

I jumped to my feet and scurried across the room, tossing my book on the end of the bed. I shouldered the pane open and looked into the back yard.

At the corner of Father's surgery stood Shao, reeling back to toss another pebble at my window. He saw me, but too late to stay his hand, and I narrowly dodged the flying stone.

"Zao gao!" I exclaimed with a smile on my lips, and he covered his laugh with his hand.

"Can you come with me?" he whispered.

I aimed my ear towards the door, where I could hear Violet snoring delicately across the hall. "I think so," I replied.

"Wear trousers!" he added.

I pulled on my pants and an old wool jumper and left my room. I paused outside Father's bed chamber, and through his closed door I heard his rhythmic breath, the mutterings of a man dreaming, and the squeal of bedsprings when he turned. He slept deeply.

"They won't even know I've gone," I said to Shao as I joined him in the alley, and side by side, we rambled down the hill to town, keeping to the back roads and deep shadows. The din which rose from Dunsmuir Avenue -- men brawling, women screeching, mules braying, dogs baying -- was enough of a warning to stay far away and out of sight. "Where are we going?"

"It's a surprise."

"How did you know where I live?"

He cast me a sly grin. "Because it's my business to know where all the doctors live, and I've made deliveries to the hospital before. It's not that large a city, you know."

"True," I agreed, "Mr. Kelly didn't seem all that concerned that I was partisan to his habits. I suppose most people already know, and have the good manners not to mention it."

"I figure, as long as he does his job, he's helping to feed my sister's children," Shao replied.

"Can something really be bad if good comes of it?" I asked rhetorically as I followed Shao down the embankment towards the train tracks. "Do two wrongs really make a right?"

"I think so," he answered. "I have to think so. My survival demands it."

We made our way into Chinatown, and I noticed the streets were strangely empty here. No one sat on the porches. The gambling halls were eerily quiet. The cats had disappeared from the shadows under the boardwalks, and even the rats seemed less populous, as if they'd fled the place. I walked a little closer to Shao, my eyes wary. When he stopped abruptly, I almost bumped into him.

"Here we are," Shao interrupted.

We stood at the rear of a small shed, abutting a two story house, with a few big hogs sleeping in the dirt yard. One of the animals snored just as delicately as Violet.

"You got me out of bed to bring me to a pig sty?"

Using a barrel set against the side of the shed, Shao climbed up onto the roof. He beckoned for me to follow him, laying a finger to his lips to ensure I kept silent.

We crossed the sty roof to the house, and Shao scrambled onto a balcony, then up the handrail of the balcony and onto the house roof. I followed, picking my handholds with care. We followed the spine of the house to the next, and then stepped across a gap between the buildings. Shao's legs were longer and he crossed the gap with ease, but he paused and held out a hand to me, and helped me leap across.

Once more we followed this routine, up another balcony and onto a roof, balancing along the ridge, until we found ourselves on a three-story false-fronted building, almost as big as the hospital. This building was much broader than the houses, and the roof's angle was less steep. Looking over the false front, I saw that it looked onto Shan Gai, and we had slipped in from the back. Underneath our feet, I heard music and conversation.

"What's this building?" I whispered.

But he only smiled and led me, hand in hand, to the crest of the eaves at the rear of the building. Under the triangle made by the eaves was a small hatch, two feet by two feet. Shao reach over and tugged on its edge. It swung open.

"In there," he said. "I'll go first. Just don't look down."

He gripped the eaves and lowered himself over the side, reaching out with his feet until his foot found a solid step on the rim of the hatch. Then, letting go with one hand, he transferred its grip the to top of the hatch, and eased himself into the black hole. His hand appeared again, beckoning for me to follow.

A fall from this height *might* not kill me, I reflected. I held tightly to the eaves as I swung my legs over the edge and kicked out with my feet to find the bottom step of the hatch.

When my boot found firm footing, I mimicked his technique. As I slipped into the dark space under the roof spine, I found myself caught up in his arms.

And, I thought, it was a very enjoyable place to be.

But Shao flustered, and released me quickly, stepping away. "You made it!" he said, "I thought you might be afraid of heights."

"I'm not afraid of anything," I laughed, and looking around, asked, "What is this place?"

The air was thick with floral smoke, and a curious music filled the air, drifting up through the slats under their feet. Holding my hand, he led me through the dark attic, crouched over to avoid banging his head on the roof trestles. He guided me to a gap in the floor where one of the widest boards had been pried away. A nest of blankets, a few threadbare pillows, a wooden trencher of steamed buns and two green glass bottles of beer provided a cozy, intimate place for us to recline. A hazy shaft of light drifted up through the opening, and when I lay on my belly on the blankets, my face could peer through the hole to the grand room below.

Shao lay down beside me. "Be careful you aren't seen," he said, "But we can talk. They'll never hear us over the music."

I looked over the edge. My breath caught in my throat.

Directly below was a wide arena where men reclined on pillows and clustered in tight groups of ten, twelve, twenty. They smoked pipes and drank from tiny clay cups, and their conversations rang with celebratory excitement. A space remained clear at the front of the room, and I recognized it at once as a stage, devoid of props but hung with a painted backdrop of a pastoral countryside. I marveled at the talent of the artist, and then at the beauty of the landscape – with narrow pillared mountains and water buffalo in rice fields, it was unlike any farm I'd ever seen. Lanterns hung from brass hooks on the walls and ceiling, casting a gentle glow over the stage.

"Oh, Shao!" I whispered in awe, and felt, rather than saw, his happiness.

The conversation stilled. There was a polite pause, and then a man at the front right of the stage began a beautiful tune on an instrument which lay in his lap, his graceful fingers flying over the strings. A character emerged from the wings. The actor's face was painted stark white and eyes outlined with kohl, and he wore an austere brown costume with wooden sandals. He carried four or five scrolls under one arm, and a bag at his side held brushes and pots of ink.

"I'll explain, if you'd like," Shao offered.

I nodded.

"It's the Legend of Bai SuZhen, the White Serpent," he began. "Once upon a time, long ago, there was a young man who was a scholar, very bright and curious, but he was lonely. He prayed to the Gods for a companion, someone who would understand his love of knowledge. Someone who would give him delight, and learn about the joys of the world at his side...."

His narration became a beautiful layer to the music and story unfolding before us, and I watched, enraptured.

As the scholar traveled his path, studying the plants and flowers on the verge of the road, a tall woman dressed in long white robes began to follow him. The woman (who, I realized with a start, was actually a robust and bow-legged man) crept close, shied away, all the time lingering on the edge of the scholar's perception. She was curious, but dared not be seen.

"There was a snake," Shao whispered, "A devil in the form of a serpent, named Bai SuZhen, who came to earth because she was lonely. She noticed the scholar, and fell in love with him."

The white dress fluttered, and suddenly, the actor flipped his long gown over the opposite shoulder, a skillful and graceful move that magically changed the dress from white to red. "The serpent cast off her image and took the form of a beautiful young woman."

"She's still a bit chunky and bow-legged," I pointed out, "And she has stubble on her chin."

Shao chuckled and shoved me with his shoulder. "Shut-up. I'm trying to tell you a story. Now, the scholar noticed Bai SuZhen, and found her to be very pleasing to his eyes. Not only was she beautiful, but she seemed to enjoy all the things that he enjoyed, too, and he found himself in love with her."

The snake and scholar had begun to dance, gracefully criss-crossing over the stage, their hands touching for only a moment before a new item at the edge of the stage caught their eye. They were like butterflies, flitting back and forth, as the music rose and fell in magical waves. All the world was a delight to them.

A third character emerged from the wings: dressed in grey and silver, with a wig of long white hair. His face was painted in stripes of black. He had a noble bearing, and when the snake noticed him step onto the stage, her demeanor changed – she became furtive, sneaky, and sly.

The audience began to jeer. Men, with smiles upon their faces, began catcalling and cajoling. The snake responded in kind by raising her fists to the audience, flinging her arms around wildly, and running across the front of the stage with her finger to her lips. The third character took note, and began to approach the snake-woman.

"A monk, wandering along the road, recognizes that the serpent devil has enraptured the boy, and knows that the scholar's soul is in peril. Even if the snake loves him in return, such a match can never be allowed. It would surely bring the wrath of Heaven down upon the Earth..."

The monk rushed to the snake, and seized her about the waist, and began to drag her away. She kicked, screamed shrill curses, scratched at his face. The music took an ominous turn.

"...And the scholar, engrossed with his studies, does not notice her distress. When he runs to her aid, there is nothing he can do – he's only a simple scholar, and unable to defend his love."

"Surely a scholar would be better suited to combat than a monk," I said.

"Not in China," Shao replied. "Here, have a *cha siu baau*."

I took the steamed bun in hand and ate as I watched the play unfold, letting the savory pork filling linger on my tongue. The monk dragged the snake to the edge of the stage and, with an exaggerated toss, threw her out of the audience's view into the wings. A stagehand sloshed a bucket of water out.

"The monk throws Bai SuZhen down the well at the Leifeng Pagoda, which is so deep that it reaches the centre of the earth," Shao continues, "And there she is trapped forever. The scholar's soul is safe from harm, the Earth is saved from Heaven's wrath, and the monk lectures the boy on the perils of women's charms."

The audience roared its approval. Men held up their glasses and cheered at the outcome, and when the actor portraying the snake returned to the stage, he received a mix of groans and cheers. He began to dance in time to the music, and the man with the stringed instrument increased the tempo, until the snake woman was performing a lively and merry jig in his white and crimson dress.

I rolled onto my shoulder, rested on my elbow and propped my head in my hand. "What happens to the snake?"

"She's trapped in the well forever," Shao replied.

"All because she fell in love with the wrong boy?" I said, "That doesn't sound very fair."

"Life isn't fair," he reminded me.

"Well, yes, that's true, but this is just a story. Maybe the real world is cruel, but we can give every story a happy ending if we want." I ate the last bite of the pork bun and licked the sauce from my fingers. "Here, let me try -- Bai SuZhen escapes from the well, finds her beloved scholar, and together they begin a long and prosperous life together. Heaven doesn't notice, the meddlesome monk is busy beating up some other young couple he met on the road, and the snake and the scholar live happily ever after."

Shao grinned. "I don't think that's quite how the myth goes."

"Well, that's how I want it to go," I laughed. "Thanks, Shao, for bringing me. This really is amazing."

"You're welcome, Liz," he replied, rolling back onto his stomach to watch the next performance. "It's my pleasure."

17

JUNE 7, 1898

Miss Adele Kelly
136 Fort St.
Victoria, BC

MY DEAR FRIEND ADELE,

I RECEIVED your letter with great delight, and I am pleased to hear that both you and your mother are well. Your description of the Gorge Regatta to celebrate the Queen's birthday was so vibrant that I truly believed I had attended, and the O'Reilly family's picnic at Beacon Hill sounds delightful – oh, how I would have enjoyed your gentle company! Thank you, too, for the invitation to visit you this August, in time to attend the wedding of your cousin. I will certainly ask Father for his opinion, and if he gives his blessing, be assured that I shall accept your proposal. There are picnics and dances here every Saturday, but I lament that the company is rough and poorly hewn. Sweet Adele, I crave a decent conversation with a woman of good breeding, rather than some bumbling exchange of polite chatter with an uneducated drunkard!

The unseasonably dry May has transformed into a refreshingly damp June, and the woods have dressed themselves in a lush green foliage as vibrant and luminous as silk. Already, the cow's milk has adopted the same luscious yellow of buttercups, and when the dairy van delivered bricks of butter to our kitchen yesterday, they gleamed like gold! Agnes tells me that the farmers predict this summer to be hot and dry, which I feel is all the more reason for me to visit you in Victoria, where a fresh sea breeze makes each afternoon delightful.

Your advice regarding Amaryllis is well-considered and very astute, and I thank you for your wisdom. She wearies me, it's true. I suffer immeasurable embarrassment whenever my little sister opens her mouth and speaks her opinion because -- I can not believe her audacity – her opinions are so rarely correct! She was evicted from the school roster for fighting like a boy, and to my shame, Father did nothing to discipline her. In fact, he accepted her to his practice as his apprentice, and she has taken to his lessons like a duck to water. Have you heard of anything more absurd? A girl, which nature ought to have given a faint heart and delicate humor, cleaning medical tools and bedpans!

And she does not care that her clothes are bloodied! Only three days ago, Lizzie arrived home with her smock spattered with gore, as though she'd spent the morning in an abattoir. When I expressed shock at her appearance, she told me with smiles and laughter that she'd helped to save a miner's life, although they'd had to amputate the leg – have you ever heard anything more disgusting? The mere imagining of such horror makes me shiver. She is all eagerness to attend any surgery, and she confided in me that Father thinks it good practice for her to cut open the dead, so that she might study the internal organs with her own senses. Beastly! Most of the women in the church are horrified that a child would engage in such barbarous behavior, and I can scarce look at her without thinking of all the disgusting acts she has done. I fear she considers nothing sacred anymore. She has become as wild as a weasel!

And this, Adele, is the worst -- Father consents to Amaryllis running errands into Chinatown every Wednesday. Who knows what depravity she has witnessed there! Does she now accept their odd actions as rational behavior? I have been told that there are very few women there, and that those poor female specimens who dwell in the slums can be considered barely human. I lay awake at night, worried that my innocent sister will be corrupted by the Celestials' philosophies, and the fatigue has left me in a poor state each morning. Sickness and plague fester there, Adele, and nothing I say or do can sway Lizzie to abandon her visits. I have no idea what draws her there; she shows no natural fear and wanders naively into the jaws of the dragon.

Perhaps she is soft of mind, Adele. I dare not suggest it to my Father, for he gives Amaryllis all freedoms and he loves her too much to see her reckless ways. Never have I seen a man so blind to the faults of his daughter. But what if she is ill as our mother was ill? What if she is an imbecile, and no one has noticed but me?

As always, I hope you'll write me and share with me your opinions. You are a good friend, Adele, and I am blessed to have met you through your brother. Mr. Kelly continues to attend to his post with diligence and courage, and I look forward to regaling you with stories of his valor when next we meet. Please remember me to your dear mother and reply soon, for I desire your gentle conversation and good sense.

BEST REGARDS,
Violet

18

July 19, 1898

Alexander Kelly continued his pursuit of Violet, and she returned his affection, and with every passing week, it became more and more evident that she was considering his implied proposals.

On the third Tuesday of July, he came for afternoon tea. I sat with them around the dining room table, but Violet made it clear through her tone of voice and pinched mouth that I was an unwanted addition at the meal. I wished Father had come home for lunch, but he'd been unable – there was too much paperwork to complete before the afternoon's appointments. Agnes remained in the parlor, polishing the silver candlesticks, but Agnes approved of Mr. Kelly's company and felt little need to be a chaperone. So it was only us three: Violet, Lizzie and Alexander Kelly, who sat down to lunch upon cold ham, egg and leek sandwiches, and slices of radishes in vinegar.

Neither Violet nor Sandy were rude to me. In fact, they were cloyingly sweet, as if the abundant saccharine feelings shared between them had bubbled over the brim, and threatened to get everyone around them sticky, too. They fawned at each other, they made sweet silent promises with their eyes, but with a child sitting between them, the two adults were forced to make pleasant and bland conversation. No one was perfectly happy with the arrangement.

"Tell me, Lizzie, how have you been?" Mr. Kelly said. He flapped a linen napkin over his grey trousers. "Violet tells me you work very hard for your father."

"Yes, sir," I replied.

"It must be rather," he paused as he shook the salt mill twice, "Indelicate labor."

"Oh, but I'm learning a great deal!" I took a triangle of egg and leek sandwich from my plate. "Last week, I learned about the placement and function of the liver. Did you know it can regenerate if it's been badly damaged? And it's quite a big organ, in the human male. It's hard to hold, too. It's very slippery and gooey, about the size of a small cat—"

"God's teeth, Amaryllis!" Violet hissed, "Don't be so dreadfully gruesome!"

"I don't see what's so gruesome about a liver," I muttered, "We've all got one."

"You are very... enthusiastic," said Mr. Kelly.

"Morbid and vile!" Violet clucked her tongue in disapproval. "Learning things that no good lady ought to know!"

"We are all equal in death," I said around a bite of sandwich, "Male or female, it doesn't matter."

The constable's brow creased. "You attend to both men and women?"

"Sometimes," I replied, and sensing that he was uncomfortable with the thought, hastened to add, "I assist with the autopsies, mostly, but I help with the living, too."

"Oh, that is not right," he decided. "Your father does you no favors to expose you to the horrors of the grave at your tender age!" He nodded to Violet. "Wasn't I just saying, at the yesterday's picnic, that you ought to bring Amaryllis to church? Both of you ought to join me this Sunday." Mr. Kelly raised his sandwich, but before taking a bite, added, "I insist."

"That's a kind invitation, Constable," I replied, "But—'

"It is kind!" Violet interrupted with a smile, "We would be pleased to come with you, Sandy. I don't think Lizzie has stepped over the threshold of the church since Mother died."

"No, I haven't," I admitted. "But I really—"

"And Father McGill asks after you," Violet continued, "And wonders if you're well. There. It's settled. Lizzie and I will attend with you, Sandy, on this coming Sunday."

I felt there ought to be a particular sort of sound accompanying Violet's words, like the slam of a prison door. Boom! The finality of the decision was immovable.

As if on cue, the earth shuddered.

I felt the vibration through the soles of my stocking feet. The motion was not enough to make the dishes clatter, nor cause Agnes to look up from polishing the silver, nor break Violet from her prattling as she plucked at the sliced ham on her plate. At first, I thought I'd imagined the tremor, but I glanced at my glass of water. Concentric rings moved out from the centre, then faded into a flat, smooth surface.

There had been no sound, only a shiver of motion. A cold seed germinated in my stomach. In a mining town, the silence meant one thing.

An explosion, deep underground, gives no sound. No roar accompanies the shock that rolls up through the layers of rock and coal and earth and sand.

And only one mine was close enough to town to be felt through the soles of my feet: Number Five, where Shao worked with the mules.

A flock of sparrows took wing in my gut. I dropped my sandwich to the floor and clenched my hands to my stomach. I looked to the clock above the mantle, and forced down the fear that bubbled through me. What shift did he work? Sometimes it was night, sometimes day. Even I couldn't keep track of his schedule.

Maybe he's working in Mr. Tao's shop today, I thought desperately. I stood, my eyes still riveted on the clock face.

Violet's voice came from the end of a long corridor. "Lizzie? What's wrong?"

Horror percolated up in me, not soft or distant but loud and frantic. I fought down the rising panic with one hand clenched around the table's edge, and tore my eyes from the clock to look towards the housekeeper, polishing the silver. "Agnes?" I asked.

"Aye, me wee bairn?"

"Where is your husband working now?" I feared I already knew the answer before the question had left my lips.

"Down in the five," came the absent reply. "Why?"

Before I could say a word, the bells above the mine offices tolled. The first clang was musical and soft, an echo of brass mallet upon brass bowl, but almost instantly the peals rose to a frantic clatter. An echoing clang returned up the valley. A collective hush swept over the streets and the yards. Faces turned towards the sound; every ear knew what it meant.

Somewhere in the distance, a child began to keen. Horses bowed their heads, and stray cats crept, bellies to the dirt, into the cracks under the boardwalk. People poured from their yards and houses; there were shouts, calls to neighbors, cries of anguish. I glanced to Agnes and saw the woman frozen in mid-polish, her trembling hands the only indication of life, casting fractures of reflected sunlight off the filigree of the candlestick.

When it fell, end over end, time slowed. The mine bell sang out again, and the candlestick struck the wooden floor with a bang like a starter pistol.

Motion swept upon us like an ocean wave. Suddenly Agnes was flying out the door, her hands clasped to her throat and a strangled cry fighting to escape her chest. She ran, dropping bits of herself as she went: the rag, the apron, the jar of silver polish. Alexander cast aside his napkin and flew out the door. I grabbed Violet by the wrist and pulled her outside, and we joined the growing stream of people coursing through the narrow channels of the street, funneling ever closer to the head of No. 5. In the ditches, a few women and children had collapsed in little knots of despair. They were unable to carry on because their grief was too strong, or their fear of what they might find too overwhelming.

There was no question now, which mine had suffered an explosion. Black smoke poured out from the ventilation shaft. It flowed straight up like a beacon, up into the bright enamel-blue sky, cloudless from horizon to horizon.

When we arrived in the mine yard, we saw Agnes clinging to another miner's wife, both of them slumped against the side of the picking tables. The column of thick, greasy smoke billowed from the ventilation shafts. Some of the outbuildings had been knocked askew by the tremors, but the massive wooden tipple had not been damaged, and the screech of the winches cut through the cries of the women in the crowd. In a burst of dust and smoke, the cage appeared below the frame of the tipple. The iron doors banged open and the first flood of coughing, filthy men stumbled out, heaving for fresh air. Violet cried out, and released me to wrap her arms around Agnes' shoulders.

I studied the men who poured out of the bulkhead, choking and gasping from breath. Their entire bodies were black with soot, so I scanned for discerning characteristics – length of arms, breadth of shoulders, height or weight or way of walking, but they all looked the same. Shao could have been any of them, or none.

The cage door slammed and the winch screamed again. People jostled me back and forth. A knot of company officials arrived on horseback, each man dressed in a fine suit and polished riding boots, and they shouted directions to those on the ground without dismounting. Behind them came a wagon of draegermen, looking monstrous in their helmets and breathing apparatus -- strange alien creatures made of hoses and goggles and dun canvas overalls. The crowd surged forward and I found myself shunted towards the far fence of the picking yard. Violet and Agnes, clinging to each other, were swept out of my sight in the current. The winch screamed again. I was too small to see over heads, but the sound meant more men were coming up, and the draegers were going down to fight the fires. I saw nothing except the backs of men's shirts, frantic women tearing at their hair, and couples flinging themselves into relieved embraces.

And then, a hand on my shoulder made me turn.

Shao stood before me, his face smeared with coal dust, panting slightly.

"You're alright!" I gasped, gripping his arms. "I thought – I didn't know—"

"I took the day shift," he replied over the screech of the machinery. "There's been a cave-in. Bad. I don't know how many are dead."

I wanted to tell him I didn't care, all that mattered to me was that he was alive. But before I could find the words, Shao stepped back and shrugged off my grasp. A movement through the crowd had caught his eye. "Dr. Saunders," he said, and I turned to see my father pressing through the terror-stricken faces.

"I need your help, Liz," he said as he passed, his medical bag in one hand. He seized my wrist in the other. "Come with me."

He dragged me through the chaotic tempest of bodies, of men and women seeking each other out in the pandemonium. He nodded to an official on horseback as we broke free of the crowd. When we reached the edge of the yard, the mine operators let him pass through the perimeter to the head of the shaft and the returning cage. The deafening screech made my ears ache, the stench of acrid smoke burned my nose. I let him guide me under the tipple, which rose like a lattice of iron girders and wooden beans into the blazing sky.

"God help us, it's an ugly mess down there, sir," said one man as he fell into stride next to Father, "We've had one tunnel collapse and another left unstable with the blast. The draeger-men are gone down already, and they're draggin' every living man they can find out of the rubble, and bringing 'em into the mule stable." The cage coughed up another wad of soot-blackened men, hacking painfully into their sleeves.

"What's the count so far, Will?"

"At least ten dead," he replied. The man named Will rubbed soot from his eyes with the back of one filthy hand. "And I don't know how many injured, but with this blast? More dead than hurt, I wager."

John wheeled me onto the metal cage. It shivered and rattled under my feet. Looking down, the wire mesh showed nothing but a hundred feet of darkness under my boot soles.

Will balked. "You can't bring the girl down, sir," he said.

"I can, too," John replied, "She's my assistant."

"I have to insist—"

"Are we going to argue, or are you going to let us save who we can?" John bellowed. "Time is of the essence! Send us down!"

Will hesitated, then slammed the cage door on us, throwing the latch and hollering up to the winch men. The whole contraption screamed and shook as we began our descent into the sightless void.

I clung to Father's arm, blinded by smoke but sensing that we were plummeting fast, and I kept my mouth and nose hidden against the arm of my shirt. My eyes stung. Tears whipped off my cheeks. I wanted to yell to him, to question why he would need me, but I knew I would never hear a response over the roar of the fall and the banging of the chains.

I opened my eyes a mere crack to look between my feet. A tiny pinprick of golden dancing light in the distance rushed towards us. The cage slowed, and my stomach flipped twice, but I managed to keep my lunch down and my head up. The cage settled at the bottom of the shaft with a bang and a bone-shuddering crunch. A young man wearing a dented helmet held up a lantern, and two more unlatched the door and hauled it open, stepping aside to let us out.

The main foyer of the mine was a long, broad hall carved from the seam. Thick timbers supported the roof, each one as big as my waist, but all around me, I sensed the impending crush of weight -- tons and tons of stone pressing down upon us. The hot, moist, dusty air smelt like sweat and vinegar, a pungent fragrance that caught in the back of my throat and made me strain for breath. Broken lamps hung from hooks on the beams and the dirt floor sparkled with shattered glass. The explosion had rocked the area and destroyed anything fragile.

"They brought the wounded in here, sir," said the man in the helmet, his face striped with sweat and grime. If he was surprised to see a girl with the doctor, he said nothing to show it. He beckoned to us both, and I followed Father through a low-ceiling corridor, shored up with square beams that sagged in the middle. He led us into an antechamber, only slightly higher than Father's head. Here, chunks of rock from the roof littered the sandy floor. A line of stalls, strewn with hay, followed the bare rock walls. I could still see the chisel marks gouged into the stone.

Four mules shuffled at the farthest end of the stables. They jostled together, shoulder pressed to shoulder. Their eyes swiveled in their sockets, trying to process all the dangers that surrounded them, and their flared nostrils sucked in greedy gulps of air. Along a cleared space in the middle of the stable, the draegers had dumped the wounded, their only purpose to get the injured miners out of the way so that they might fight the flames that persisted in the rock. The air felt syrupy in my throat; there must still be fires burning in the maze of tunnels.

John knelt between two of the injured, and gave permission to move them up the shaft. The cage wasn't large enough to hold any more than two reclined men, so the wounded were loaded like sacks of flour onto the grate floor. The winch screamed, the chains pulled taut, and the whole contraption rattled upwards, leaving those below without a means of escape. I watched it vanish up the chute.

"Are you okay, Liz?" Father asked.

"Yes," I replied, "Just tell me what you need me to do."

Four wounded men remained on the stable floor. "See if there's anything to be done for these fellows, help to ease their discomfort," John ordered, "I'm going to see what can be done for the men still trapped in the fall. Keep your lamp low, understand? Any gas seeping out of the stone will rise and collect around the ceiling."

"Yes, sir," I answered.

With bag in hand, he vanished down the tunnel with the man in the dented helmet, swallowed up by the swirls of coal dust and smoke.

With the heel of my boot, I cleared the straw from the ground and set down my lamp. Its flame, starved for oxygen, was a mere nub of illumination and casting out a tiny, quavering circle of light. Three of the miners waved away my help; I was no nurse and they didn't trust my ministrations. I looked them over and a quick scan revealed bruises and lacerations, but nothing so dire that I could help them further. Maybe a broken arm, and certainly one dislocated shoulder, but their spirits were strong enough to refuse the assistance of a little girl in a dirty smock.

The last miner lay in a heap on the floor, silent. I struggled to roll the rotund man onto his back, and when he finally fell slack onto his spine, he let forth a groan. It was a lusty sound, strong and agonized, and it told me, better that words, that his ribs were whole and his lungs undamaged. And it told me more -- the timbre of his voice was familiar. For the first time, I looked at his face, and saw through the dirt and contortions of pain that this man was Hamish Gunn.

"Mr. Gunn!" I cried, shocked, "Where do you hurt?"

He slapped his leg. His face screwed into knots of ropy flesh, his white teeth exposed in a snarl.

"It's the leg, lassie," he wheezed. "I heard it snap."

I felt down the right thigh of his dungarees and found a brutal corner in the limb. The femur had broken clean. When the edges ground against one another, he screamed.

"I can't pull it straight – I don't have the strength," I said, but I gathered an armful of straw and wadded it under his head. His vision swam. "You'll be alright, Mr. Gunn. It isn't bad. Not crushed, just broke. You'll walk again."

His eyes cleared. He focused on my face and clung to my arms. His fingers became talons. "Oh, lassie, once I get topside, I'm no comin' doon ag'in!" Tears leaked from his eyes, cutting tracks of clean skin through the thick mask of dust. "God damn, they'll nae make me!" He shuddered, and a sob broke from his mouth, accompanied by a line of spittle.

"It's okay, Mr. Gunn. We'll get you up—"

"The walls groaned and Petey, he told us tae run like hell, and then the stones, they just rained upon us, right on top of all of us, the trip and the mule and the boys, and I saw one crush Petey's head like an egg, and I thought... I thought I...." He let out another stifled sob, and grabbed at my sleeves, and held me in shaking hands. "Oh, me Aggie! I want to see me Aggie ag'in!"

"Hush," I said, "You'll be fine."

For a while I let myself be held by him, but at length his grip relaxed and he let me go. His pain and fear subsided into embarrassment. I stood and gave him space, and taking my lantern, I walked as far as the mules at the back wall. Behind me, Mr. Gunn sobbed with his face in the ground, and I turned my back to him to give him privacy; no man wants a woman to see him cry.

Three of the mules shied away, but the largest pushed its soft, dun-colored nose into my hand. I ran my fingers over its neck, ruffled the stiff mane, clucked in the back of my throat.

A whistling groan came from the rear corner of the stable.

I peered around the edge of the stall and held out the lantern, though I took care to keep it low. A mule lay on the floor.

I saw at once that it was dying: this must have been the mule caught in the fall, dragged out of the way and forgotten by the draegermen. Its round barrel body was the wrong shape. It lay on its left side, and its ribs sloped upwards, not arched but flat over a field of crushed bones. In the low light, the muzzle was patterned with droplets of mucus and blood. Every breath was torture.

One long ear flopped to the sound of my approach. I knelt next to its side and the brown pupils, lolling in seas of white, rolled up to meet mine. The mule tried to struggle to its feet but gave up almost instantly. Three legs were straight and strong, but one was mangled beyond any recognition, and moved like marbles in a sack of donkey-hide.

I heard my name called out.

"I'm here!"

Father peered around the corner of the stall. "We're moving Mr. Gunn. Four dead, but the twelve injured will live. The one left in the tunnel is beyond my help."

"This mule," I said. "It's going to die."

"I suppose it is," he replied. "C'mon, Lizzie, we're needed topside."

"Give me your knife," I said.

"What?"

I looked up to Father and held out my hand. "Please, sir."

He reached into his pocket and pulled out his pearl-handled penknife, and tossed it to me. It was cold in my fingers but comfortingly heavy. I snapped out the blade, small and sharp as a fang, and ran my hand over the mule's graceful throat.

Under my palm, the carotid bulged with every frantic pulse.

My own heart began to beat, and every convulsion seemed to push aside ribs and lungs, growing fiercer and fiercer, squeezing against the restraints of my rib cage. Before this moment, had my heart never beat? It thrashed, it strained, it galloped, and my breath came faster now, a long steady parade of gasps; I couldn't get enough air to satisfy me. The world narrowed into a dark tunnel, containing only me and the mule. The beating of our hearts answered each other, a rhythm shared between the only two inhabitants of the universe, and I was falling forward into the stark beauty of this perfect moment.

Everything became crisp, defined. I saw the scene as if I were the member of an audience, and my body was that of an actor on the stage. The edges of the mule shone with a fiery aura, a pure light that radiated from within, and I stood at the side of myself, who had become a figure moving independently of my reason. I saw every hair on the mule's dun muzzle, every flicker of lamp light in its glistening brown eye, every speck of coal dust trapped in the pink froth at the corner of its gasping mouth. I saw myself and the mule as if we were the last two creatures on earth, and I drank in every detail, savored the eternal resonance of life's last spark.

The pearl-handled knife slipped effortlessly under the skin.

There was no shrill squeal of agony. The animal was in too much pain to feel the sharp sting of a blade sawing through muscle and tissue. My cut was a tiny wound compared to what the poor beast had already sustained. Jets of blood came rapidly at first, then lessened their arc as pressure diminished. A film fell across its eyes -- a curtain drawn on a stage, the closing petals of a flower in evening. Death was soft and welcome and merciful.

I heard the sound of wind in my ears, and I was suddenly cloaked in my own flesh again, rocking back on my knees. The energy no longer churned in my belly. Sluice gates opened and the reservoir of ecstasy drained out of me, and I became a husk of a girl again, a empty vessel. I hiccoughed, tried to recapture the easy, familiar rhythm of my breath. Every muscle melted downwards.

I stared down at the relaxed corpse. The death, the killing, the murder of the mule: it cried out for a memento. I reached down and nipped off the top inch of its grey ear, and for a heartbeat, fondled the warm, velvet-soft flesh between my fingertips. Then I slipped it in my pocket. I wiped the blade of the penknife on my sleeve and folded it back upon itself, and returned it to Father.

"Thank you, sir," I said as he took the knife, looking uncertain.

"No hesitation," he remarked.

"Why would I?" I replied, "It was clear what needed to be done."

I bowed my head as I passed him, alighting into the waiting cage next to Mr. Gunn. I wrapped my hands around the iron bars for the long ascent into daylight and the surface of the earth, and as we rose up from the belly of the black mine, I reflected that I had never before felt such sweet tranquility.

19

I SPENT the whole afternoon in the hospital, close to Father's elbow, swabbing wounds and stitching them closed. I fetched water for the injured and held lanterns up to shed light on emergency surgeries. By evening, I was spent. I dragged my weary feet home, eyes half-closed. Agnes had left a tin basin of warm water in the corner of the kitchen by the stove. I bathed, pulled on my nightgown, and dried my hair with a towel. My body was tired, but my mind was not.

I found Violet outside, sitting on the top step of the back porch.

As I sat beside her, I breathed in the sweet fresh scent of sun-warmed grass and apple blossoms. After the thick air of the mine, it flowed easily into my lungs. "Can't sleep?" I said to Vi.

"No," she replied, staring up at the stars.

We fell into an amiable silence. Dressed in our white cotton gowns, our hair loose around our shoulders, we sat silently in the coolness of the midnight hour and watched the crescent moon cross the sky. It was in moments like this that I felt we were the same sort of creature, rather than two divergent beings inhabiting the same landscape. Violet, without her pins and corsets and gloves, looked like a real human being, and less like an angel; as for me, with my bare feet freshly scrubbed and my hair combed, I was no longer a savage little wood mouse, but a mere girl.

Violet dropped her eyes from her star-gazing and said, "One of the chinamen came by this afternoon, and asked after you."

"He did?"

"I told him you were busy at the hospital, helping Father," she dismissed, "And I didn't think you had any errands for him today. You were far too busy."

I closed my eyes and sighed: Shao had worried for my safety, and knew I was okay. It sparked a little flutter of happiness in me, though it was difficult to feel anything more. The catastrophe had worn me out fully.

"And Agnes was inconsolable, all afternoon," Violet continued, oblivious to my relief.

"Mr. Gunn will be alright. His leg will take months to heal, but he'll live."

"Were you scared to go down into the mine?"

I closed my eyes to the moonlight and tried to remember the impenetrable darkness. Not scared of the mine, but scared of other things. Of losing a friend, when I'd only just found him. "No," I replied. "I wasn't afraid of the mine."

"I couldn't have gone down there, no matter how much Father pleaded."

"Did you see Mr. Kelly again?"

Violet nodded. "Sandy gave me thanks for our company and hospitality but he couldn't come back. His duty called. Everyone looks to him for guidance," she beamed.

"He's a good fellow."

"Sandy is quite wonderful," Violet agreed. "He's a man of strong reputation."

"More than just mere reputation," I said, "A reputation can be easily tarnished. No, I like his personality. He's very generous with people -- a politician if ever I saw one."

"God's teeth, Lizzie!"

"I mean it as a very good thing, Vi," I laughed, "He listens to people, and they do as he asks because they like him. It's an admirable quality." And with the way softened by my approval of Mr. Kelly's character, I added, "And he likes you, quite a bit. That's reason enough for me to like him."

"I like him quite a bit, too." Violet replied.

The mood between us lightened. I smiled and crossed my arms over my knees, and looked at Violet askance.

"How do you know when you're in love, Vi?"

Violet did not laugh, as I had feared, or dismiss the question with a wave of her hand. Instead, in a soft and vulnerable voice, she replied, "I'm not sure." She folded her arms over her bent knees, pulled close to her chest, and rested her chin on her wrists. "I think it's a mellow sort of feeling, like you know that you'll be safe and comforted, and he shall look upon you with adoration forever."

"Really?" I looked up at the moon, surrounded by pinpricks of light, an alabaster rowboat heaving its oars across a star-speckled sea. "It isn't a fiery sort of feeling? It doesn't start in your viscera, and rocket up through your heart, and leave you breathless? It doesn't make you dizzy, and feel a little sick, and maybe even a little scared?"

Violet shivered, "Oh, goodness, no! That's not how I feel about Sandy!" She giggled. "I don't think a woman should ever feel something so monstrous!"

"Oh," I said simply.

"Wherever did you get that idea?" she laughed, and then her eyes widened. She gave a little gasp, and with a conspiratorial grin, she pressed her shoulder to mine and said, "Who is he?"

"No one."

"What's his name?"

"He doesn't have one."

"God's teeth, Lizzie!" she said again, but this time, she laughed playfully, seizing a hank of my hair and tugging it, "Tell me!"

"Forget I said anything, Vi," I replied, and then, as the first crack in the dam gives way to a torrential flood, the words gushed out of me, and I couldn't stop myself from speaking. "Violet, it's so ridiculous! But I keep thinking about him, craving him, wanting the smallest peek at him! Every time I think of him – just the barest thought of him! -- I feel like my stomach has crawled up through my rib cage to wrap itself around my esophagus and strangle the life out of—"

"Oh, Lizzie, that just isn't romantic," Violet squirmed. "You've spent far too much time in the hospital."

"But it's true!" I replied, "It isn't mellow at all! It isn't a feeling of comfort! And if he ever looked at me with simpering, fawning adoration, I swear, I'd... I'd.... I'd claw his eyeballs out!'

Violet shook her head. "No, that is definitely NOT love."

"What else is it, then?"

"Hysteria, most likely."

I flopped back across the porch, arms outspread. "Oh, good Lord, Violet, I am most certainly not hysterical. Today, I was never so sure of any emotion in my entire life."

"Well, I have never felt like clawing out Sandy's eyeballs," she replied, "And I am fairly certain we are in love."

"Will you marry him?"

Violet was uncharacteristically thoughtful. After a minute or two of careful consideration, she said, "Maybe."

"That isn't very definitive."

"I've decided to bide my time, and wait."

I sat upright again and looked at Violet. Wisps of her loose blonde hair caught the breeze and floated freely, but her expression was fixed and stony, and her eyes gazed at the ground as she thought furiously. The expression was not joyful – which I would have expected for a woman in love and contemplating marriage. "Wait for what?"

Violet took my hand in hers. "I have heard from Father that—" She paused, biting her lower lip.

"Heard what?"

"Do not think poorly of me, Lizzie, but," She grinned and leaned forward a little, as if she might, at any moment, bound to her feet with unbridled enthusiasm. "Mason Briggs is coming to visit in a fortnight!"

"Dr. Briggs!"

"He's coming to give his condolences, and introduce Dr. Duncan's replacement to the hospital staff. Isn't that delightful?"

My heart sank. I'd grown rather fond of Alexander Kelly's constant adoration, and knew the constable would be wounded at the idea of a rival returning to town. But what hope did Kelly have, when Dr. Briggs, a fine surgeon from Victoria and an engaging, learned personality, was coming to visit?

"Does Mr. Kelly know?"

"Of course not." Violet scoffed. "My intentions are simple: I shall keep myself unavailable until any possibilities with Dr. Briggs are firmly extinguished."

But the soaring hope in her voice betrayed her high expectations. "Violet, you'll only be disappointed—"

"How can I be disappointed?" she replied, "I have two men who love me, and I shall be free to chose between them. What girl would not envy my position?"

'Me,' I thought, but said, "You have no evidence that Dr. Briggs has retained any fondness for you. Last summer, he came and went, and all he gave you were vague promises of fraternal affection, and a few spins around the dance floor."

"And in a fortnight, he returns to visit," Violet replied. The width and brilliance of her smile matched the luminous crescent moon. "For me, that's evidence enough."

20

August 3, 1898

And so, in a fortnight, Violet and I agreed that we would not pass by Kelly's office at the end of his shift, but would instead attend the arrival of the train, bringing passengers from the boat which docked at Union Bay. Wednesday was bright and sunny, warm but with a refreshingly pleasant breeze to whisk away the industrial vapors and smoke. Violet remarked that it was the most delightful combination of weather and temperature that one could hope for in the apex of summer. Not too hot, not too stifling, perfect for us to embark on an innocent stroll.

By the time I'd finished my weekly visit to the apothecary, I found Violet waiting for me outside Simon Leiser's Big Store, dressed in her finest black silk dress and cream overcoat. Black silk gloves protected her hands and her flaxen hair was braided and pinned underneath a broad black bonnet. She watched with pinched mouth as I arrived from the east, scuffed and dust-smeared, hatless and gloveless, wearing pants. "I trust your trip to Chinatown was uneventful," she said with a disapproving edge to her words.

"Absolutely," I replied, tucking the two copper pennies into her pocket.

"And where did you get that?"

"Sometimes I run errands for Mr. Tao's nephew."

"Amaryllis!" she exclaimed, as if the single word itself was a reproach.

"It's no bother—" I began, but Violet's eyes were fiery, and her voice was kept in a tight, restrained whisper, more powerful than a yell.

"It is highly improper," she interrupted, "For you to be running errands for some chinaman."

I scowled at her. "I was doing Shao a favor—"

"Do I need remind you at every turn, Lizzie, that you are a woman of upstanding breeding? It's disgusting."

"There is nothing disgusting in human charity or friendship," I replied, "Only in arrogance and pride."

Violet's eyes flashed open. "Are you saying I'm arrogant?"

"If the shoe fits," I sniffed.

"Well!" Violet spat, "I never! And that, coming from a stubborn little wastrel like you!"

"And judgmental, too," I added, "You have no right to tell me what to do, who to see, whose company to keep."

Our voices attracted the attention of passers-by; I caught the sidelong glances of women and the open staring of children. Even an old woman sitting on the opposite side of the street, swathed in brown shawl and ripped skirts, with her wiry black hair half-covering her smudged face and her bare calloused feet outstretched before her, stared at us. Her round white eyes, deep set in brick-red skin, peered from under the veil of hair like piercing marbles of quartz. Her face, pockmarked and smeared with grime, made those clear eyes appear even brighter. Even when our eyes met, the old woman didn't look away, but continued to appraise the Violet and I: one a prim lady and the other a girl in boy's clothing. She picked at her teeth and folded her scarred hands over her filthy knees, silently enjoying the entertainment.

I didn't mind the audience, but a flush rose up Violet's throat.

"Don't look at her."

"Why not?"

"It's not proper."

"I've never noticed her before."

"She's Alfio Perugino's wife," Violet said, turning her back to the dark, hunched shape in the gutter. "He brought her back with him last winter from his trapping. She begs for money, and worse." Violet weighed her next comment, and deeming me old enough for unpleasantries, added, "The boat arrives in Union Bay today, and that means new men, weary and worn out from travel. She'll make a few easy coins from their carnal desperation."

"Prostitution?"

"Bestial rutting," Violet sneered, looking down the street towards the store and the train platform. "She's probably simple."

But those quartz clear eyes were bright and cunning, not at all dull. Violet's broad, dismissive insult rose a flare of anger in me. At first, I wanted to punch her in the mouth, just like I had with Buster Gillingham. But then I thought of Father's disapproval – I'd managed to curb my temper in the last few months, but he might ban me from the hospital if I reverted to violence. Surely there's a better way to annoy Violet as much as her proud ways annoyed me?

I looked both ways to ensure no passing carriage and, before Violet could protest, I dropped off the boardwalk and onto the street. With a series of quick strides, I crossed the dusty road and came to an abrupt halt in front of the old woman.

Upon closer inspection, she was not old, but the world had not been kind to her. Her trials had left her as worn and thread-bare as her clothes. A thick sour-milk stench rose from her body. Her face was flat and scarred, but those unnaturally pale eyes examined me with candor.

"What's your name?" I asked.

I expected the voice which answered to be gravelly and worn. Instead, it resonated like the deep chime of a brass bell. From under the tangle of black hairs came a velvety answer, a surprising softness at odds with the woman's degraded appearance. "Nes'kweet," she sang. Then, as if remembering herself, said, "Nessie Perugino."

I reached into my pocket and withdrew my two pennies, and dropped them into Nessie's outstretched palm.

Nessie rolled the coins in her hand, and lifted those remarkable, arresting eyes again to me. "What's this for?"

"Whatever you wish."

The teeth that flashed were square and straight. Matched with her eyes, they created a trio of white brilliance amongst the darkness and grime. "Why are you kind to me?"

"Because it's better than not being kind," I replied. I turned on one heel and crossed the street, back to Violet's side.

Violet's pinched face gave a full account of her feelings. "She'll follow you, now," she hissed, tucking one little strand of blonde hair behind her delicate ear, "And she'll beg you for more. You've made yourself an easy mark, Amaryllis. I won't be surprised if you find your pockets empty."

Looking askance at my sister's haughty face, I replied, "I'll take my chances."

The rattle of wheels against axles chased the hiss of steam as it echoed up the valley. If Violet had planned to say more, she was quickly distracted by the piercing whistle of the train from Union Bay.

"It's almost here! Come on, Liz! Hurry!" she urged and hooked her arm around mine. At a brisk trot, we rounded the corner to the edge of Camp. We looked passed the Company Store to the flat expanse of the station platform, jutting off the back of the building like the bustle on the rump of a old lady's gown.

The tracks from Union Bay skirted the southern edge of town as they traveled towards the No. 4 mine site, out at the shores of Comox Lake, but just below the Company Store, a small branch jutted from the main line to create the short arm of a Y. This stopped in a dead-end alongside the platform at the back of the company store. The curious configuration allowed the train to race directly passed Cumberland, from dock to mine, when it had no need to pick up passengers or mail, but on Wednesdays, when the boat arrived, the passenger train was forced to back up the short arm slowly, with gears squealing and great huffs of smoke and embers belching from its stack.

A crush of people materialized out of the steam. Some came from the carriages, others arrived from the street or the stores. Burly young men in pinstripes and white aprons began moving freight from the last two cars. They tossed bales of jute, canvas bags of mail, and bundles of newspapers from Victoria to the platform. Wooden crates followed, then the baggage and personal effects of the passengers. Violet maneuvered us through this circus towards the engine, to the front of the platform, where the public carriages discharged a haggard cargo of women, men and children. It was easy to read on their drawn faces that these people had endured hard, long, and exhausting journeys from all corners of the world.

Violet laid one gloved hand on my forearm.

"Do you see him?" she asked. Her voice was taut like a violin string. "Is he there? Do you see?"

There was no need for a proper name. The reverence with which Violet whispered the pronoun was hint enough.

Before I could answer, three well-dressed men alighted from the first carriage, engrossed in an animated conversation. One face demanded Violet's attention – I could almost hear the sinews of Violet's neck snap as her gaze latched onto his handsome, well-trimmed face. He wore an expensive grey top hat and dashing grey coat, a purple silk scarf at his throat. When he caught sight of Violet, Mason Briggs raised one clean, white gloved hand to us in a crisp wave.

With a small squeal, Violet returned the wave, though she was barely conscious of the action.

"Oh, Lizzie! He's here!" she fluttered.

Dr. Briggs left his companions with a bow of the head and strode across the platform. He'd not changed much since I'd seen him last – still the same twinkling eyes, clipped moustache and narrow chin. Dr. Briggs moved like a marionette, and performed every action with deft enthusiasm. He held out his gloved hands. His smile was very merry.

"Miss Saunders and Miss Saunders!" he greeted us, and he gave a low, gentlemanly bow. "What a delight to see your fresh and smiling faces, immediately upon arrival!"

Violet curtseyed. "Dr. Briggs, we are so happy to see that you've come to visit!"

"I'm installing Dr. Gould," he said, "And I plan on being here for a month, at least. Last summer was such fun that, when I heard he had taken the Cumberland appointment, I was eager to join him and acquaint him with society here!"

"You and your companions must come for dinner tonight," Violet said, "I will not accept any refusal."

"I'm sure Dr. Briggs has suffered a long journey, and probably wants nothing more than a hot bath and an early night," I said, but my comment only made him laugh.

"Oh, Lizzie, you're just as I remember you! Unabashedly pragmatic! But I assure you, I'm not some frail and doddering aunt -- truly, I'm invigorated to see you both!" He nodded. "And I do accept, Violet, on condition that your father agrees."

"He will, I know it!" Violet replied, "He will be pleased for such jolly company."

"Then we shall attend," Dr. Briggs laughed, "I look forward to our conversations this evening!" He gave them both another crisp bow, and returned to his companions.

Violet watched the three men move to a waiting hack, where they waited until their baggage was secured before mounting the carriage. With a snap of the whip and a shout from the driver, they drove the short distance up the street to the mine office and Camp. We stood in silence on the platform, watching the vehicle depart. Violet's quietude was reverential, mine was merely polite, basking in the reflected glow of Violet's joy.

"He's so lovely!" Violet gushed, all previous disagreements forgotten with the flash of that masculine smile. We began to wander along the street, neither of us in any hurry to return home.

"I hope there's a dance this weekend," Violet said, crooking her arm over my elbow, "I should love a good opportunity to dance with him."

"It's not in good taste for you to dance, still in mourning for Mother." I replied, "I might get away with that kind of indiscretion, but not you."

"I would spurn etiquette for Mason Briggs."

This made me laugh. "So that's what it takes? A handsome face? Or perhaps the promise of financial security?" I sighed and shook my head. "Poor Mr. Kelly: he's already been forgotten!"

"Poor Mr. Kelly," she repeated, "You have simply no idea, Amaryllis." She leaned close to my ear. "He never has two pennies to rub together! The colliery must pay him a dreadful salary."

"Maybe he spends his money on personal pursuits," I replied.

At the preposterous thought as Kelly nurturing any sort of hobby, Violet laughed. "Personal pursuits! Hah! I can think of no hobby that could tear him away from his duties or gobble up his pay! He's all about work, work, work. At least, with Mason, I'll have someone to dance with!"

More wagons thundered passed, loaded down with crates, luggage and whole families. Pans banged, babies squealed, drivers shouted at willful mules as the axels squawked. The wheels cut deep ruts in the road and kicked up plumes of dust, even as they turned onto Dunsmuir Avenue and rattled towards the edge of town. One could barely think over the racket.

Once the wagons were gone, Violet continued. "It's been months since Mason's last visit," she said, "And he's looking well, even a little more robust than last autumn."

"He didn't look any different to me," I replied. We walked as far as the tinsmith shop, and I paused to look in the window. "Oh, he's handsome enough, I'll give you that. But still a bit frivolous, and too... too.... Pristine for my liking. I can hardly imagine him with his hands dirty."

"He's a gentleman! Why should he ever need to dirty his hands?" Violet asked.

"He's a doctor," I replied, "He should get a bit of blood on himself, now and again."

Violet shivered. "God's teeth, Lizzie! You've become positively ghastly!"

One more broad wagon came up behind us. Fresh miners hung off the sides, catching a ride to the hotels and lodging. I was only half-listening to Violet's prattling, and I noted the ragged coats and black caps, the travel-gaunt faces, the old clothes and battered gunny sacks. The wagon jostled to a halt across the street, outside the Waverley Hotel, and the driver set the brake. He laid the reins aside as the brawny dun-colored draft horses lowered their shaggy heads to converse together, chomping jaws and jingling bridles. Men grabbed their belongings and jumped from the back, eager to wash and sign up for work and rent a bed to sleep in. For many of them, it might be their first night as an employed man. The prospect of work could put a spring in a man's step, and install a sense of worth in his expression, before he came to understand the true, brutal nature of his new job. Tomorrow they would go below, into the black and byzantine tunnels, to scratch their sorry keep from the rock, but tonight they would rest and relax and imagine themselves as prosperous men.

Most of all, they were eager to buy rounds for one another in the Bucket of Blood. They wanted to toast their success at joining the company and acquaint themselves with their fellows over beer. The nights following the ship's arrival were always noisy, celebratory, gay. Once working, they would continue to spend their hard-earned coins in the Bucket of Blood, but by then, the hard drink would soothe their sore muscles and homesickness, and make them forget their obligations to the mine.

"...and he seemed so happy. I think he's done well for himself over winter!" Violet chatted, more to herself than to me. "And the other gentlemen with him, so very accomplished in appearance..."

The wagon was almost empty of men and luggage, the most enthusiastic and youthful passengers already in the bar. They were all eager to get to the business of slaking their thirst.

Except for one.

He wore a ragged grey-brown duster, a pair of patched denims and a battered black slouch hat over a tangled mess of unkempt hay-colored hair. His clothes were even more ragged than his fellow travelers, and I wondered how a character of such low means could afford passage from Victoria. His face was unshaven, his skin burnished brown by long days out-of-doors; I placed his age in his early thirties, certainly no younger. He spoke no friendly word to his companions, offered me no insight into his relation to them, and kept to himself. His smooth, wily confidence reminded me of a feral dog. His eyes were dark, blazing and full of cunning; they noted all who passed. He surveyed the boardwalk and the people before disembarking from the wagon, and as he leapt to the street, his scuffed boots kicked up a cloud of dust. He was taller than most men, and perhaps a little broader, but the shapeless coat hid his angles and would have made a skinny man look formidable.

Even as he mounted the steps to the boardwalk, he possessed a swaggering arrogance that made proper women frown and gentlemen step closer to their wives. A young lady on her afternoon's errands hurried by the Waverley's door; I recognized her as Miss Dell, the daughter of a colliery accountant, and a casual acquaintance of Violet's. The man cast a crooked grin to her, bowing his chin in a mockery of politeness. He took no pains to hide the lasciviousness of his lingering gaze.

Miss Dell turned her head to avoid meeting his stare and scurried passed. Those wolfish eyes lingered on the curve of her skirts, then turned to the opposite side of the street, where his gaze instantly latched upon the prim, clean figure of Violet.

I scowled. With a single step, I intercepted his line of sight, matched his intense glare, and silently dared him to look at my sister in so vile and base a manner.

He arched his eyebrows in surprise. That cunning smirk became a full grin, more amused than lustful. He grabbed his canvas sack from the wagon's hold and threw it lightly over his shoulder. He followed the last of the men into the Bucket of Blood, but not before looking once more over his shoulder at us, and casting a saucy wink directly to me.

Violet's grip increased, her prattling replaced with silence. She whispered, "Who is that?"

I faced her. She wore an expression of disapproval, the pretty mouth pulled down, the slight flush to the cheeks that forewarned an angry outburst at my improprieties.

"I may be mistaken, Vi," I began, "But I do believe that's the Devil himself."

21

THAT NIGHT, I once more found myself imprisoned in a corset and an evening dress and, like a child's doll receiving all of its owner's cruel attention, sat meekly before Violet at the mirror in my room. I gritted my teeth as Violet raked a comb through my messy tangles of ginger hair. The dress I wore had once belonged to Violet, and while the velvet insets were slightly worn and frayed, the silk had retained its vivid aqua color. The bright blue lace around my wrists and throat looked horrible against my sun-browned complexion. As she struggled with the tangles, Violet muttered to herself, knowing that words of admonishment would fall silent in my ears, but every now and again a comment rang out, perfectly audible.

"...and you will be pleasant, and say nothing directly to Dr. Briggs, and leave his company to carry the conversation, understand?"

"Yes, Vi."

"God's teeth, Amaryllis Saunders! Have you never used a comb in your life?" Violet stepped back to regard my head with her one hand on her hip. "I swear, it would be easier by far to shear the whole lot of it off and start afresh."

"Yes, Vi."

"And please, Lizzie, please..." She put aside the comb and bend down at my side, took my hands in both palms and implored me. "Please be decent and good and, above all, mercifully quiet. Won't you? For me?"

"You aren't a reflection of me," I said, "If Mason Briggs holds any fondness for you, his opinion of me won't change that."

"But they will, Lizzie!" she insisted, "They will! We shall spend our lives shaking off the shadow of our mother's insanity, and I don't think I could bear the burden of your indiscretions, too! These labels stay with a person, you know! They ruin you!" At the mention of our mother, Violet's eyes began to tear. She hurriedly wiped them away with the tips of her fingers. "As long as we stay here, where everyone knows of Molly Saunders and her mad notions, you and I will carry her reputation with us. Alexander Kelly is very kind to love me, but if Dr. Briggs is willing to take me away? I can cast off the gossip and the label and maybe I could be a woman of good society again."

"Why wait for Mason Briggs to save you?" I asked, "Violet, you could go yourself."

Violet's plucked brows drew together in a thunderous scowl.

"How do you propose I do something as ridiculous as that?" she said, "Utterly impossible, Lizzie! Utterly imposs-- where are you going?"

I knelt at the side of my bed. I dragged the tin box from its hiding spot, wiped off the dust with my palm and, returning to my chair, set the box on the boudoir. I was surprised by how heavy it had become. The lid creaked as it opened, revealing a cornucopia of trinkets, fabric scraps, papers, buttons, pebbles, the folded envelope, all the miniscule treasures of my short life.

"My goodness!" Violet whispered, her mouth agape, her eyes wide. She reached out to the contents of the box. "What are these—"

I slammed the lid down, almost taking off her fingertips. "Don't touch!" I ordered, wrapping my arms around it. "My collection is special to me."

"What's in there?" Violet said, "Rocks? Ribbons?"

I wriggled my hand under the lid and searched by feel for the marble bag. I pulled it out and shut the lid tightly. "There are lots of things in there, things that no one else would find special, except for me. But this," I held up the pouch. "This you can have."

My fingers plucked opened the drawstring. The motley mix of coins spilt into my palm.

Violet gave an audible gasp.

"If you need it, it is yours," I said to her look of astonishment, "There's over twenty dollars here. If you wish to buy passage on the steamer to Victoria, there's more than enough."

"But, how..."

"I run errands, and my clients pay me very, very well. No, don't say a word, listen to me," I said quickly, noticing the fluster rising up Violet's pale throat, "No one knows about this money, and I've been saving it so that I can travel the world, but I want you to have it."

"I can't take your money!"

"Yes, you can," I insisted. I poured the coins into the pouch again, satisfied by the sounds of substantial clinking. "Listen, I'll leave it on top of the tin box under my bed. If you ever need money, you can have it. It's your money now; I'm only keeping it safe for you." I took both of Violet's hands in my own. " And because I love you, I will be good and quiet and say nothing unless I'm spoken to. You have my solemn promise."

"In all my life, I don't think I've seen so much money all in one place!" she whispered in admiration. The look on her face reminded me of a robin that had flown full speed into a window.

"If you need it, take it." I repeated. "I know that we are very different creatures, and that I am a constant disappointment to you, and God knows you frustrate me to no end. But you're my sister and I love you, and your happiness is worth all the money in the world to me."

"Do you... do you really feel that way?" she whispered, wide-eyed.

"Of course. I love you very much."

Her brow furrowed. "No, I mean, do you really feel that I frustrate you?" Violet pressed a kiss to my cheek. "I ask much of you, Lizzie, because I know you are greater than some filthy little wood mouse, dressed in tatters."

I gaped. She leaned close and began, once more, to tie up my hair with ribbons, and arranging it in the best way possible.

"You ought to give that money to Father, so that he can keep it safe for you," she said, "Please don't think me ungrateful, but honestly, Liz – it is simply not proper for you to have such funds at your disposal!" She laid her hands on my shoulders. "I do appreciate your charity, truly I do, but a lady of good bearing has no need of money."

Oh, good Lord, would Violet never change?

A brisk knock from the front door echoed through the house. I returned the tin box under my bed, and by the time the we arrived downstairs, Agnes had already answered the door. Dr. Saunders stood in the library with three men. Mason Briggs smiled as we entered.

Father held out his hand. "And you remember my daughters, sir – my eldest, Violet, and my youngest, Amaryllis?" he said. He beckoned to us to sit and join them.

The lissome young doctor bowed. "How lovely to see you again," he said. His expensive pecan-colored suit, cut to the latest fashion, only accentuated his dapper manners. "Violet," he began, and he spoke her name with power and confidence, like a thespian beginning a scene, "You look more comely each time we meet! Our good Dr. Saunders tells me you've been practicing the piano?"

Violet delicately placed herself on the horsehide chair by the fireplace, the closest seat to Dr. Brigg's right elbow. I took my favorite seat at the window and spread my skirts around me, trying to find a balance between comfort and dignity.

"A little, but I do not yet have my mother's skill." she replied, demure, "It is good to see you again, sir."

"Please, call me Mason," he insisted. "Oh, I am so dreadfully sorry to hear of your mother's passing, but I am confident that she has found great happiness with God." He turned to me. "And Lizzie!" He threw up his arms as if confronting a happy surprise, "You've transformed into a lady since last I saw you! You look delightful – as merry as the first rose of springtime!"

"Thank you, sir," I said, grinning. He was so exuberant that I found it impossible to resist his charms.

"Please, let me introduce my colleagues," Mason said, gesturing to the other men, "This is Dr. William Gould, of Esquimalt, and this is Mr. Harris Fish, of Victoria."

Dr. Gould was a round, saggy fellow of middle age, and he nodded drowsily at the sound of his name. A sparse fringe of grey hair skirted the edge of his bald crown, like the sad tassels on the edge of a faded carpet. His bulbous purple nose and generous gut, along with the row of brass buttons threatening to pop from his dreary grey waistcoat, hinted at a boundless adoration of quality food and drink.

Slouched in the chair to Dr. Gould's left was Mr. Fish, a man of meager flesh by comparison, with sharp bones jutting from every angle. He gave a curt dip of his chin. His thick thatch of dark hair, shot through with streaks of silver, had been clipped short around a pair of kite-shaped ears, and his mutton chops were restrained and finely kept, giving his high cheekbones even greater definition in the low lamplight. Mr. Fish possessed a thin mouth, wrinkled around the edges and scowling slightly, but his eyes were watchful and clever. Even now, at our first meeting, he seemed to be scheming. I wondered if his personality tended towards perniciousness, mild wickedness, or mere schoolboy mischief.

Violet smiled politely and clasped her hands in her lap, but I could sense that this exchange of pleasantries was grating upon her. More guests to entertain left less opportunity for direct conversation with Dr. Briggs.

"Dr. Gould has come north to join the Company staff," Father explained, settling himself into his chair and taking up his glass of sherry from the side table. He turned his face to Dr. Gould. "And Lizzie hopes to follow in my occupation. I have taken her under my wing as my apprentice."

"A LADY doctor," Gould harrumphed, slapping the feminine title onto the profession with piqued interest and no small measure of doubt, "How do you find your lessons, my dear?"

"Engaging, sir," I answered, "And very enlightening."

"I've already brought with me a number of books from my library – it is abhorrent for a gentleman to travel without his books! Shall I lend you a few titles, to supplement your education?" His small eyes traveled up and down my figure. "I trust a girl like you would be good to them?"

Meaning, of course, that a girl is loathed to have dirty hands, or eat while reading, or do any of the nasty, brutish habits that a boy might dare. I tucked my hands, with their grimy fingernails, underneath my skirts.

"I would greatly enjoy reading any new books you've brought, sir," I replied, "I've almost exhausted the libraries of the other doctors here, and the hospital has very few volumes to choose." I turned to the second man, Mr. Fish. "And what do you do, sir? Are you a man of medicine, as well?"

"Mr. Fish is originally from Birmingham, by way of Australia," said John, "From a family a rail industrialists, yes?"

"Most correct," Mr. Fish agreed, "My father was instrumental in the construction of rail lines across Northern England, and my brother followed in his footsteps by participating in the construction of the Darwin to Pine Creek Line. I followed Emmet south but found the Australian landscape not to my liking. Have you ever been to Darwin, sir?"

"No, I'm afraid I have not," said John.

"Lovely city, and my brother is damned sure that the Darwin-Pine Creek will turn a good profit, but I could not stand the infernal heat. So I came to Canada for a spot of adventure, and simply have not left."

Dr. Gould chortled. "Harris has found himself mired in Victoria's society."

"Mr. Fish is a politician," Mason explained in a hushed tone.

"And here I am, many years later, as yet unable to escape." When he grinned, the length of his narrow smile fractured his face in two. "The landscape of Vancouver Island was not what I expected. Very lush, I must say. Very lush indeed." He tented his long fingers. "It has taken me years to acclimatize myself to the savage jungle with which I now find myself surrounded."

"Are you speaking geographically?" I said, "Or politically?"

Mr. Fish's grin stretched even wider.

"But you believe the train system will flourish here," Dr. Gould chuffed. This was obviously a long-standing point of humor with him.

"Indeed," said Mr. Fish, "And I have told my brother such. A rail line ought to stretch from Victoria all the way north, and connect Dunsmuir's coal fields with the ports southward."

"It does sound like a fine plan," said Violet. "We could travel to Victoria year-round, and never worry that the boat will run aground in the winter storms!"

"Precisely, my dear," Mr. Fish sniffled. "Rail will always be the most civilized way to travel."

"Then I wish you every success, sir." said Violet. "The winters here can be long and dreary; how I would love to visit the city during the Christmas season! The lights, the festivities, the displays and dances – wouldn't it be wonderful, Liz?" She turned her attention to Mr. Fish again. "We hardly ever go far in December."

"With a train system, the entire island would open up for you." Mr. Fish assured.

"It is Victoria that I would wish to visit. I can't imagine I would care to go anywhere else," said Violet, "Though I'm sure Lizzie would be eager to gallivant to the farthest edges of the known world, if you gave her a chance." She laughed. "Wouldn't you, Liz? With dirt up to your armpits and holes in your boots? I dare say, she'd be of the same kidney to a monkey, if we let her."

I hid my anger behind a terse smile. "Perhaps I'll see if Mrs. Gunn has any use of me in the kitchen."

"That's a grand idea," said John, and added to the guests, "I hope you'll enjoy our modest hospitality, gentlemen. I know you've had a long journey today, but surely a bit of company and hearty food will prove restorative."

I bowed out of further discussions and retreated to the kitchen.

"O, Dr. Briggs, he is verra fine!" said Agnes, standing by the stove where she had stoked the fire into a roaring blaze.

I sat by the kitchen window. It gave a wide view of the back yard and alley. The setting sun wove the sky into a tapestry of lavender and gold, and gilded the tops of the buildings and trees with the last rays of the day's light, but between the houses and trees, darkness had fallen. The dusk tinted all the shadows a deep purple, softening the world for its descent into night.

"He is very fine, indeed," I replied absently. My eyes ranged over the garden and orchard. Between the trees, the light was gone and the clusters of plump green apples had become a low-slung ceiling of black.

Agnes rattled the pans, rustled a bundle of dried mint, chopped the carcass of a chicken into juicy chunks. "Do ye think he'll eat my cooking? I'm nae well-trained."

"I find your cooking delicious," I replied, "If he is too stuffy to eat what's put before him—"

I stopped mid-sentence.

"Whae is it, m'lass?"

I squinted my eyes and peered more closely into the dark hollows between the apple trees. "I think... I think there's someone out there."

"Passing in the alley?" This would not be uncommon, for the alleys made lovely walking paths during warm summer evenings. They were the highways and byways for dogs, children and chickens, and for Chinese men with wooden buckets balanced on a shoulder yoke, which they would fill with outhouse soil to spread on their gardens.

I watched. The shape stepped a little closer to the house, and moved with stealth. It did not want to be seen.

"No," I said, "In our yard."

For a moment, as the figure moved between the trees, I saw the clear definition of a head and shoulders, and a hand reaching up to pluck fruit from the lowest branch.

Agnes paused at my side, peering out into the dark yard. "Are ye sure?"

"Positive."

"Well, I'll naught have them wee bairns trampling my beans!" Agnes growled, and grabbed the empty pan from the counter. She brandished it high like a cudgel, and rushed to the back door like a flustered hen, ready to beat sense into the youths stealing the apples. "Git oot, ye scampies! Git oot!"

I raced after her, and caught sight of the apparition leaping the fence effortlessly and bolting down the alley. By the time Agnes, with her rolling seaman's gait, and I, half-entangled in skirts, reached the gate, the alley was empty. Agnes leaned her bulk against the fence, scowling and panting for breath.

"And ye nae come back, ye boggin!" she roared.

I looked down the road. "Did you see get a clear sight of him?"

"I'm afraid I did not," she panted, "But if he comes back, he'll be in for a mighty terrible reception!" She thumped the pan down upon the fence's crossbeam with a merciless bang.

AFTER DINNER, the men retired to the drawing room for brandy and cigars. Violet and I returned to the kitchen to help Agnes. She was eager to get home, where she could attend to her own brood of boys and her recovering husband. Between the heat wafting out of the open stove, and the cinched corset snug against my skin, and the convection of the sun's rays now released from the hot earth to the cool evening air, the kitchen was unbearably hot. I flung the back door open to the night as Violet and Agnes fussed over the dishes, but almost at one, Agnes ordered me to close it again.

"Oh, why?" I moaned, "It's too warm!"

"There're all manner of beasties that'll come tae the smell o' cooking, and we nae need a raccoon or bear sniffing about the yard!" Agnes flapped the dish cloth at me. "Close the door! I've been in hotter kitchens than this!"

I tried to suck in a single breath of cool air before shutting the door. "This is torture!"

"This is proper," Agnes replied. "Now, get o're here and begin tae dry the plates, like a good lass. I want tae get awa tae the home; there's seven boys all waiting for a late supper, and one grumpy old husband who needs a kind ear tae listen tae his complaints."

"How is Mr. Gunn?" Violet asked.

Agnes clucked in the back of her throat. "As well as can be hoped, all things considered. He's nae the kind of man tae staying sitting for long, and I think being housebound is the hardest for him. But your father, he says it may be two months yet before the leg'll be trustworthy, so Hamish best be getting used tae being home."

"It was a clean break," I said, "And that's a blessing."

"My Hamish, he said kind about you, doon in the mine. He said you were his angel a-comin' oot o the nicht." Agnes looked at me with fondness, then she smiled at Violet, too, and threw her arms around our shoulders to hug us close. "Oh, you are fine girls, indeed, and I dinna ken what I'd do without ye! The closest thing I've got tae daughters, to be sure." Her voice warbled a little, and she pressed a moist kiss to the top of Violet's brow. "Yer mother was a fortunate woman, tae be blessed twice over!"

"I don't think I've ever heard anyone refer to mother as 'fortunate'," I said.

"But she was, no?" Agnes replied. "To marry a man as fine as yer father? She must've been a stunning beauty in her youth."

I considered this idea. Molly had always been a figure half-obscured by shadows, retreating from light and company. "She looked more like me than like Violet, and I'm no beauty, that's for sure."

"You're only plain," Violet assured. "Not loathsome."

"When I first met your mother," Agnes began, and she picked up a plate to dry it as she spoke, "I was taen by her grand presence. She haed the personality of a cat: graceful, pretty, but quick to lash oot, and she trusted no one. She was a woman tae be cautious aboot, and never friendly." She shook her head. "I nae mean this as any insult. She had a wee kindness in her, too, when the madness wuld lift. She had her guld days, and her bad, like any o' God's creatures."

"And more bad than good, near the end," said Violet.

"Well, she's safe in God's keeping," Agnes replied kindly. "But goodness, I dinna ken another who wuld keep me on my toes! I'm getting lax withoot her, always fussing around!"

"Maybe we could have canned pears this winter," I said, and laughed, "Or actually have a pomegranate or two at Christmas time!"

"And none of the catalogues will be cut to pieces," said Violet.

Agnes snorted in laughter, though she dabbed her sleeve against her eyes, too, to wipe away the tears that had formed there. "Oh, even with all her neep-heided notions, I miss your guld mother. She ken a fine way with keeping the house, she kept everything in good order."

"I miss her terribly," Violet admitted as she moved to the table in the window and took a chair. "It wasn't so sudden, but sometimes, when I wake in the morning, I believe for a second that she's still alive, and these last few months have only been a dream."

"I miss her voice," said Agnes, "I miss the way she haed of greeting the morning. She kent the value of patience and kindness, and she had a guld Christian soul."

I dried a dish absently, listening to the two women trade compliments back and forth, and finally said, "She was clever."

"I dinna ken if I'd say that of your fine mother," Agnes mused. "Well-versed, and with a bonny noggin for remembering figures, aye, but clever?"

"You mean to say, she was intelligent." Violet amended.

"No, I mean, she was clever." I insisted. "She planned, she schemed. She had an astounding talent for making others do as she wished."

Agnes gasped. "What a terrible thing tae say of your own dear ma!"

"It isn't terrible." I replied, "It's quite remarkable. We wouldn't be here, if it wasn't for her. She made it possible for Father to find employment here; she orchestrated this."

"To insinuate that our mother had the capability of manipulating—"

Agnes cut off Violet's comment. "To ken that your father had nae a word to say in the matter! That he's a pawn! Do you really believe that, girl?" Agnes pursed her lips and looked uncomfortable, but Violet openly scoffed.

"Mother had nothing to do with Father's position here, and I think it's terribly insulting for you to say so. To speak as if Father was some sort of puppet! To say he had no free will in the matter, that he could be so easily deceived!"

"I don't think he was deceived," I replied, "I only think—"

"Hush, girls," Agnes hissed, and stood slowly. Her small eyes stared at the dark crack of naked window where the lace curtains did not meet.

Violet and I clamped our mouths shut. After the bustle and noise of our disagreement, the abrupt silence had a palpable weight.

Footsteps pattered across the back porch.

"Mother of Jesus!" Agnes gasped. With surprising quickness, she grabbed the pan from the sink and rushed outside, dripping a long glittering line of water and chicken grease behind her. I ran close on her heels, Violet behind us both. We tumbled into the yard in time to see the dark shape glide over the fence again and sprint down the back lane, disappearing into the night.

"Goodness!" Violet exclaimed, lingering by the back porch, her eyes wide and her hands clasped to her throat, "Who was that!?"

"They were here before dinner, too." I said.

Agnes waited at the back gate, the pan raised like a cudgel over her shoulder, then ambled back through the garden. "Gone again, but mark me words, lassies, they'll be back now they've found easy pickings with our trees."

"It's that ugly woman!" Violet snapped, "You gave her money, and now she's marked you as easy. Didn't I say this would happen? Didn't I?"

"You don't know that it's Nessie," I replied, but the name caused Agnes to grab my arm and give me a solid shake.

"Perigino's bittock? Don't you be cavorting with her, lassie! She's nae right in the hied!" I was half-dragged up the steps by Agnes' unrelenting grip, and only released once we'd returned to the stifling heat of the kitchen. Agnes returned the pan to the sink. "That little strumpet has had the pox, she's got savage blood in her, and that's nae a combination for trusting. She wanders in Camp and all know to give her wide berth, for she'd just as soon rob you blind than look at ye!"

Massaging my upper arm, I muttered, "All I did was to give her a coin so she wouldn't sell herself—"

"My wee lassie!" Agnes said, horrified, "She wuld pocket your generosity and sell herself regardless! And now she's followed you home like a flea-ridden cur. Lord love ye, there's nae a scrap of good sense in that wee head of yours, is there!" She gave an open-palmed clout across my head, then turned to Violet, pointing sharply at her. "Nae a word of this breathed tae your father, ye ken? I'll talk to the men in Camp, and we'll have all straightened oot by the morrow."

I clamped my hand to my temple. "What do you mean by that?" I asked, but Agnes ignored me.

"Now, both of ye, bid your father and the gentlemen a fine evening, and I'll finish up me duties here and be awa home. Go on, go on." She waved her hands to shoo us away. "You're help is greatly appreciated, me doves, but I'll finish up. And not a word breathed to yer father. Not a word!"

22

August 5, 1898

The next night, I kept watch for hours at the upstairs window with the lights extinguished, but the only creature that visited our yard was a raccoon rooting in the compost bin by the outhouse. All was still. Nessie did not return.

On Friday morning, I worked in the garden, weeding between the rows of beans and layering rich, dark compost over the bare earth. Normally the house bustled with activity, but today, I'd been left home alone, and I couldn't have been more pleased with the arrangement. The first weekend of August brought a bank holiday, and Father had been kind to allow me a few days of freedom from the hospital, to do whatever I wished. He'd left at dawn to assist a miner who had been struck by a coal trip, and Violet had decided to attend the ladies' luncheon at the church, where she would serve tea, prepare scones, and trade gossip with other members of the ladies' auxiliary. As for the constant presence of Agnes, even that was gone. The Scotswoman dedicated her Friday mornings to visiting nearby farms, where she bought a week's worth of eggs and potatoes for the family.

All alone, I wrapped myself in my thoughts and my work. The dirt crumbled softly under the hoe, and a pair of starlings fluttered through the apple boughs above me. My contemplations kept me company – as I filled the wooden wheelbarrow with more soil from the bin by the privy, I absently daydreamed about the circulatory system, and the wonders of the brain, and how a man could have a teratoma growing inside him without ever sensing it. I mused that maybe, people had other things growing inside them, of which they were only vaguely aware. Maybe these things controlled their actions, and caused them to alter their decisions. A man with a benign tumor in his lungs would chose not to exercise, because his shallow breathing wouldn't allow it, and he would find any exertion uncomfortable– he might chose to become a clerk or a scholar, all because of a little knob of flesh restricting his breath. Were people able to change, or where they condemned to exhibit certain traits by the physical failings of their mortal flesh? Here was an interesting thought -- I'd have to ask Father for his opinion when he got home.

The silence perpetuated more silence. I felt perfectly comfortable to work with my head down, wrapped in drowsy quiet. I reached for a weed in the garden when a shape in the dirt caught my eye.

I rocked back on my heels, then swept my hand through the leaves, pushing aside the bean vines and creepers.

There, in the soft dry earth, was the clear impression of a naked foot.

'Nessie's footprint,' I thought. There had been no rain, and no one would have walked in the garden to disturb it – here was evidence that Nessie had lingered outside our home on Wednesday night. I stood and looked towards the house. The alignment and place offered a perfect view of the kitchen window, and the print had sunk deep into the soil. Nessie had stood here for a while.

Then, a thought occurred to me. I looked more closely, then shrugged my own foot out of my boot and held it along side the impression in the dirt.

The foot that had made this impression was 3 inches longer than my own, and more than an inch wider. The print was deep, too, and pressed into the earth by a very heavy body. My own slender foot fit neatly inside.

'Either Nessie has remarkably huge feet,' I thought, putting my boot back on, 'Or this was made by a man.'

I SPENT most of the afternoon searching for Nessie, whom I found at last in the alley behind the Eagle. The woman crouched amongst a few broken crates, chewing gingerly on a crust of bread, which she would dip between bites into a cup of warm ale. When she saw me advancing, she scrambled to her feet. Beer sloshed down her skirts.

The smudges of dirt on her broad, ruddy face couldn't hide the deep purple bruise on her right cheek.

"You wanted this?" she said in her melodious, rich voice. There was no blame or accusation, only a flat acceptance of the possibility, and perhaps a little fear that I had come to finish the job. The bruise, half-hidden underneath the bird's nest of wiry hairs, shone livid and swollen.

"No!" I said in horror, shaking my head. "No, I never!"

"The man said I stay away from your house."

"No," I insisted, "I never asked for anyone to hit you! Who hit you?"

Nessie shrugged. She raised her fingers to the bruise and winced at the touch. "I never go near your house. I never done before." She backed up a pace. "I swear, never!"

"You didn't steal our apples?"

Nessie shook her head. "Why do I need apples from town?"

Why, indeed – there were a hundred other trees between Cumberland and the lake, where Alfio Perugino had built his cabin. Why would his wife steal from three little trees in a fenced yard at the top of a hill in the middle of town, when there was a bounty of easier pickings so much closer to their home?

"I go no where near you," she insisted. "You're a nice girl. I wouldn't trouble you."

"I'm so sorry!"

The apology, unexpected, drew a piteous expression from Nessie. She tried to smile, but the expression caused her pain. "See? You nice."

"Let me look at your bruise," I offered. "My father's a doctor, maybe I can help."

"Nothing to be done."

"Maybe not, but let me see," I insisted, stepping closer. "This is my fault; let me make amends as best I can."

Nessie balked but consented, and let me examine the fierce contusion across her face. The skin was discolored with the reckless crazed pattern of broken capillaries and a greenish tinge to the surrounding flesh. There was slight swelling. The blunt impact had not been so strong as to injure the bones underneath, nor break the skin. "It's bad, but it'll heal in a week or two," I said, "And there isn't much I can do to help it. Do you know what a marigold is?"

Confused, Nessie nodded.

"Boil up some marigold flowers and, after it's cooled, wash the bruise with the extract," I said, "That will help it fade more quickly."

"You know medicines?"

"A little."

"My mother's father knew medicines. Not White medicine -- real medicine, forest medicine."

"He was an Indian doctor?"

Nessie sat down again, and gestured for me to join her. "He was not a doctor. Not like your father, a doctor. Not a white coat, top hat doctor." She laughed at the thought of it. "He spoke with the men of the mountain in his language, and they taught him to heal using the roots and leaves of the wilderness." She dipped her bread in her beer and took a bit, chewing slowly and painfully. "Like you, he used flowers and trees, but he used song, too."

"I've never heard of anyone healing with song."

"Mothers heal with song when their babies cry," she offered, "But

I think it is very sad, English people do not sing much," she said solemnly, "Unless very drunk at Christmas."

I smiled at her observation, and she smiled in return.

"Do you know any of your grandfather's techniques? The plants he used? I'd love to learn."

"I don't go in the woods," Nessie said. "Evil things live in the woods."

"Evil things?"

"Devils. Demons. They eat children and wait to possess your soul. I find the bones, you know." She shuddered.

"You find bones?" I said, "You mean, human bones?"

"Bones in the earth, in the swamp, sticking up, broken and chewed upon." She shuddered. "I do not dare go in the woods anymore. There are sinister things there, *diavolo*." She dropped her voice and whispered, "*Tsonakwa.*"

I leaned close and repeated, "Sun-ah-kwa?"

Nessie nodded, wide-eyed, but said nothing more. She took another hungry bite of bread.

"My sister says you're not to be trusted," I said, "Why should I believe you?"

Nessie shrugged. "Believe me, or don't. I still find 'em." She pointed one crooked finger at me. "Stay close to other people, Lizzie, because the evil things are afraid of towns. You must never go alone in the woods, or the devils will follow you, and eat you." She smiled slyly. "Your mama knew it. She knew to stay away."

I scowled, defensive. "What do you know about my mother?"

"She weren't as crazy as they say," Nessie said. "She knew well enough to warn us when the devils were on the hunt."

"I don't know what you mean."

"You don't know what I mean 'cause you ain't never seen the devil a-hunting through the woods." She nodded. "You run home, sweet little thing, and never you worry. The devil, he ain't after you."

A door opened behind us. A balding man lurched out.

"You still here, then?" he spat at Nessie. "Finish your beer and get, god damn it! And I better find that cup on the step when I get back!"

Nessie shuffled to her feet as he closed the door. Next time he looked out, he wouldn't be so charitable.

"Listen, Nessie," I said, standing. "There was someone in our yard two nights ago. A man, and from the size and depth of his footprint, a very large man. Have you seen anyone strange? Acting oddly?"

"All men act odd," she chuckled. "But I keep my eyes open for you."

"Thank you."

"And stay out of the woods, I tell you again." She jabbed one finger towards me. "Bad places, there. Old magic left to go rotten. My grandfather, he used to tend the woods, but without people like him, it grows wild, twisted, ugly. You hear me?"

I nodded solemnly.

"Good." Nessie gave a firm and final grunt. "You stay out of the woods and you will be safe." She hitched up her skirts and shuffled away on bare, calloused feet. Over her shoulder, she added, "I don't want to be finding your bones in the woods, too."

23

AFTER DINNER, Father daubed the last drops of stew from his moustache with his linen napkin, folded his hands over her stomach, and proclaimed loudly enough to be heard in the kitchen, "Mrs. Gunn had outdone herself once again!" Then, he lowered his voice to be heard only by his daughters, and added, "She still thinks I might dismiss her for speaking her mind. Must assure her I shan't, you know."

Violet set aside her fork. "I don't know what I'd do without her."

'Starve in a filthy house,' I thought.

"You've been very quiet tonight, Liz," said Father. "You've barely said two words all through dinner."

"I've had much to think about."

"Anything we can help you solve?" he asked pleasantly. "Your sister is very accomplished at sorting through gossip."

Violet gave an indignant huff, which made him grin.

"Nothing, really," I replied. I didn't want to recall the events of Wednesday night or Nessie's resulting bruises: the story would reflect badly on Agnes, whom my father was so determined to keep, and whom Violet didn't want to lose.

"You've been gloomy since I took you down in the mine. I ought not to have done that. The whole incident with the mule... you surprised me, Liz, and I fear it's been eating at you."

The mule? Oh, the mule! I hadn't thought about the mule since I'd killed the poor beast.

But John continued. "It's too much to expect a girl to bear, and you were so quick about it, I didn't have a moment to talk you out of such a brutal action. I regret it, my girl. I ought not to have put you in such a position, but I needed someone to help me with the men, and you were there in the yard—"

"I'm fine, sir," I assured, and I meant it honestly. "I haven't even thought about the animal since I slit its throat."

"God's teeth!" Violet exclaimed, "What are you talking about!"

I ignored Violet and continued. "The mule needed to die. It was in agony and nothing could be done to save it. I did what I thought best."

"Then what perplexes you?" said Father, "You look as though the weight of the world lies on your shoulders!"

I toyed with my fork and said, "I was thinking about the woods."

"About the woods? Well, that's a broad topic," he said, "What, specifically?"

"I suppose I was thinking that someone could very easily get lost in them, and die, and never be found."

Violet threw down her napkin. "Lizzie, you're positively horrid!"

But Father mused over this and said, "I suppose it's possible. But I would hope the town would search for them as soon as they were reported missing."

"Has anyone gone missing?"

"Not to my knowledge, no. Why would you ask?"

I considered my words carefully. "I heard some of the boys talking about old bones, found in the woods."

He smiled. "The forests are filled with bones, Liz. Anything that lives in the forest dies there, too. I really don't think you ought to fret about it – man isn't the only creature to die, but he is the only one to gather up his dead and put them in a graveyard. Everything else simply rots where it falls."

"You let your imagination get the better of you!" Violet admonished. "All this talk of death and bones – Father, you must cease with this ridiculous notion that Lizzie can help you in the hospital! She's a girl; she has not the constitution for gruesome tasks!"

"I've been pleased with her work thus far—"

"But listen to her!" Violet insisted, "I try to mould her into a fine young woman, but my efforts are thwarted at every turn by these macabre lessons of yours!"

"Violet, my dear, your sister has proven quite competent."

But she huffed and crossed her arms. "You are ruining her."

"Ruining! My Lord, I sincerely doubt—" He stopped abruptly and turned in his chair to read the clock on the mantle. "Good Lord, it's almost seven! All this talk of Lizzie's chores, and I almost forgot that I have an errand for her!" He grinned at me as he rose from the table and went into the hall, where he grabbed a small brown box from the table by the door. "Now, I know I gave you today as a holiday, but it's one small delivery that I dare not trust with anyone else. This is for Mrs. Faulks. I meant to take it to her myself this afternoon, but that poor fellow they pulled out of No. 4 needed all my attention." He passed the package to me. "Her medicaments, laudanum, for an easy sleep. I'd told her I'd deliver it by 7 o'clock, and here we are." As I stood, he added, "Be quick. Peggy's digestive system gives her pain in the evenings. I have wasted my breath in ordering her to abstain from her sherry, so by God, I hope this helps."

I grabbed my satchel from the coat hook on the wall and tucked the package inside. "I'll be back in no time," I replied.

I walked at a brisk paced down the hill towards the main street. The Faulks sisters lived in a narrow, two-story home at the corner of 4th Avenue and Penrith, which ran parallel to Dunsmuir Avenue. While I could walk from our house to theirs without ever touching boot to the boardwalks of Dunsmuir, I chose to make a short detour, and take this opportunity to stroll the length of the main street. As far as I figured, Peggy Faulks could stand to live a few minutes more without her precious dose of laudanum.

The reason for my detour was simple: with the bank holiday, the town was decorated gaily, and I wanted to see the flags, windows, and ornaments. There would be dances, sporting events, mule races and food, more food than could ever be imagined, of all types and nationalities, laid out on tables in sumptuous buffets – the halls were full of people, celebrating. Red banners and fine silk flags, the Red Ensign, hung in the shop windows, and in the slanted light of the early evening, it looked like every building was engulfed in flame. The red, white and blue patterns of the Union Jack entangled the lamp posts, too, and string suspended between upper windows held red triangular flags across the rutted streets. The town looked very merry and festive, a little less grimy and grey than normal, scrubbed clean and adorned with gaudy finery which made it awkwardly pretty.

The shops had been closed for the evening but the boardwalks were not empty. Couples strolled along the street, arm in arm, and enjoyed the twilight air. Little knots of friends gathered at the door of the Waverley Hotel, deciding what to do for the weekend. I recognized a few as familiar faces, and politely said hello as I passed. The doors of the drinking establishments had been propped open to the cool evening, and patrons with mugs in hand spilled out. The men sat on the edge of the boardwalk to drink, to converse, to sing bawdy songs in the warm air. My pace slowed because the festive atmosphere demanded to be savored.

The shop windows displayed a marvelous range of goods. Mrs. Frances, the milliner, had completed a suite of hats in red and gold, and I admired the fine workmanship and feathers from a distance. They were lovely pieces of art, but they spoke more to Violet's style than mine. Of greater interest to me were the books in the window of Simon Leiser's Big Store.

There were penny-dreadfuls about train robberies and cannibals, a few leather-bound classics of literature, and new publications which caught my fancy, too: a novel by a fellow named Bram Stoker, and a volume of Charles Darwin's "Origin of the Species". My heart fluttered. I briefly considered using my coins to buy them, then relented. I'd already promised the money to Violet – it didn't seem right to spend any of it, now that it was given freely away.

I admired the books for a few minutes, devising the best way to ask Father to buy them. The reflection of people in the glass, passing by me on the boardwalk, was like the endless flow of a river – broad movement, little definition, a faint backdrop to the concrete items in the window. But suddenly, with my own watery reflection staring back, I became aware of someone watching me.

On the other side of the street, resting his shoulder against the building, was the figure of a man in a tattered coat. Though the reflection was not clear, slightly warbled by the uneven glass, I recognized him at once: the miner whom I'd seen only a few days ago, jumping from the bed of the wagon, winking at me before disappearing into the hotel.

He might have been newly-expelled from the Bucket of Blood, or he might have been taking his leisure to admire the people strolling up and down the avenue, but my gut clenched. His eyes, riveted on my back, followed no one else.

I ambled to the next window pane. I never once looked behind myself. I kicked a few pebbles absently, then paused again as though casually viewing the candlesticks and tin cutlery on display.

And into the window reflection he sauntered into view. Again, he waited, watching.

I narrowed my eyes and, pretending to take great interest in the contents of the shop, I considered what to do next. The Faulks house was two blocks further east, located on the next street over. It was a short run.

I tightened my grip on my satchel. I took a deep breath.

Turning on my heel, I sprinted.

Full speed, I rounded from the busy main street onto Third Avenue, then turned right onto Penrith, and ran the length of the block to the Faulks' gate. I skidded to a stop and looked directly back, the way I'd come.

As he rounded the corner at a brisk pace, he halted. On empty Penrith Street, there was no crowd for him to hide behind, and it was obvious to both of us that I'd called his bluff. He was following me; there was no hiding it.

We appraised each other for a heartbeat. He was no longer a shadowy figure reflected in dark glass, half-obscured by twilight. I saw clearly that it was the man who had jumped from the wagon and brazenly stared at Violet.

I stuck out my tongue.

He startled. Then he raised one hand and, with two fingers, gave me a sarcastic salute.

I squarely turned my back to him as I slammed the gate shut. Without further words, I stomped up the steps to the Faulks' front door and rang the bell.

24

PEGGY FAULKS RECLINED along her chaise-lounge, the back of one hand pressed to her brow, the other hand clenching her generous belly. She panted, mewled, and clutched at the bottle I offered to her with a faint expression of gratitude, too weak with her malady to exert herself with joy. Surrounded by potted ferns and coal-oil lamps, swathed in a dressing gown of burgundy silk and her feet wrapped in matching slippers, the spinster Peggy reminded me of a swollen and bloated Cleopatra, barged down the moonlit Nile.

"Oh, dear girl, I am simply CHURNING inside!" she wailed. With trembling hands, she poured a generous dollop of laudanum into her glass of sherry, and mixed it well with a deft swirl of her hand. She downed the entire concoction in a single gulp. "I dare think, I may soon join the legions of the dead!"

"Nonsense," Kitty admonished. "You have an ulcer, Peggy, and nothing more." The smaller Faulks sister, austere and glum and thin compared to her sister-in-law's extravagance, gave me a respectful nod. "Thank you, my dear. As always, your father has been of great help to us. I am glad it is you who brought the medicaments; please, take this token for his troubles." She fished a brown envelope from the pocket of her dress and handed it to me. It was bad form to pay a physician, who was a gentleman and above the common practice of commerce, but it was widely understood that a messenger could accept payment and pass along the gratuity with no loss of face to either doctor or patient.

I took the envelope and tucked it in my satchel. "Do you mind, Miss Kitty, if I leave by your back door?" With one finger, I pushed open a mere crack between the curtains and looked out to the dark street. The quietude was deceptive – a figure in a duster coat and slouch hat rested his back against a shed on the other side of the street, two houses down. "I had some troubles on my way here tonight."

"Oh, dear girl, what sort of troubles?" Peggy gushed. The laudanum was working with a quickness that bordered on miraculous. She seemed almost back to her regular health.

"Nothing of great concern," I replied, "Only a bit of unwanted attention."

"So the men are deep in their cups tonight." Kitty shook her head.

"With the festivities tomorrow, I imagine they're getting a head-start on their drunken frolicking," Peggy sneered as she topped up her glass of sherry. "Might I offer a suggestion, Amaryllis? The best way to return home would be along the alleys and side-streets, avoiding all contact with the hotels. Surely the public houses will be dens of iniquity tonight, where the liquor flows with abandon, and leads men into temptation!"

"While it is always a great pleasure to see you, Lizzie," said Kitty, laying one skeletal hand on my wrist, "Perhaps it behooves Dr. Saunders to hire a young man for his evening deliveries? There are dangers lurking behind all doors for a woman of your fine visage." She leaned close. Her breath smelt of oysters. "Great sin, my dear. Great sin, indeed!" She gripped my arm. "What lustful demon would not quiver to get his claws into you, hmmm?"

"I am not nearly so fine as Violet," I laughed.

"Oh, but you are not nearly so coarse as you pretend," Kitty replied, "You might garb yourself in old kicksies and coat, girl, but there's still a pretty face hiding under all that tangled hair." She smiled at my discomfort, and what might be seen as welcoming or kindly on another woman's face was a wicked expression on Kitty. She did not grin easily; her face pinched and wrinkled and resisted the smile. "My sweet child, be easy. I shan't say a word to the doctor, nor will I try to clip your wings. I only look out for your safety, for it's a wicked world we inhabit, and incubi surround us."

"I was once very much like you," Peggy sighed, "A girl of such high spirits! Carefree and curious about the world!"

The thought that I might end up on a chaise-lounge, a beached whale half-pickled with cheap sherry and slurring with the first signs of laudanum inebriation, gave me a fright.

"But oh! The mortal world is hard upon a woman's frame and constitution," Peggy continued, her wistful nostalgia transforming into a bitter lament, "And it is only in the Wondrous Adventure of Death, returned to the bosom of God, that we find once more that carefree innocence and joy of youth!"

"I've never heard anyone refer to Death as a wondrous adventure."

"Of course not, Lizzie," Kitty said, "Our good Doctor Saunders and those of his ilk have dedicated their lives to repelling it. You have not been raised to understand that Death is a necessary progression of life! A step in the journey! It is not something to be resisted, but embraced at its natural time!"

"Foul, evil, wicked Science!" Peggy slurred. The empty glass fell to the carpet with a thump.

"You must forgive my sister-in-law," Kitty said, and cast a glance over her shoulder. Fully relaxed, with her head lolled back and her corpulent frame swathed in leagues of silks and linens, Peggy had taken on the appearance of a pile of laundry. Kitty clucked in her throat. "I believe she'll sleep the night through."

"She is a passionate woman." I said gingerly.

"Very much so." Kitty replied as we strolled down the hall, out of the parlor and to the kitchen at the rear of the house. "She draws ghosts to her like moths to a flame."

I looked at Kitty – the high cheekbones covered with thin flesh, the deep-set eyes that glittered like sapphires, the pronounced brow and vaulted forehead topped with wispy hair. Kitty had been beautiful in her youth, and had charmed her audiences all along the Eastern seaboard, but she was a faded blossom now, and knew it. There was no longer the unquestionable distraction of her beauty.

"Do you really see ghosts?"

"Oh, yes," was Kitty's instant reply. "I was very ill as a girl, and when I recovered, I found that I had stepped too close to the Afterworld, and had established a connection. I made the acquaintance of one who had gone before, and he would not let go of my company." She brought her hands together in reverence. "When I met Peggy, I knew that my spiritual guide had drawn us together. I saw instantly that her brilliance, her passion, could be a marvelous conduit for my séances. Together, we could establish a link between this world and the next." She did not smile again, but her expression warmed, and her mouth pursed into a little round o as she pondered her next statement – this puckish expression was far more endearing on her severe face than a grin. "You, dear girl, ought to join us for a séance. We hold them on Saturday evenings, you know."

"I doubt my father would agree to that."

"Oh, posh, it's only a séance! They're good fun, my dear, and a wonderful way to meet others! He lets you go to dances, doesn't he?"

"I don't like dances."

"Well, he lets you run about, free as a fawn, after dark! Surely, he'll let you come to our assembly, if only for the opportunity to socialize with your peers."

"But I don't think he would agree to it philosophically," I said, picking my words with care. "After all, he's a doctor."

"Well, that is neither here nor there," said Kitty, "Dr. Briggs attends, you know. He is deeply intrigued by the possibilities that lie in wait for us on the Other Side." She ushered me towards the kitchen door. "Tell your sister to join you. Our next assembly is tomorrow night, promptly at nine in the evening – please tell me that you and Violet shall join us. I know that Dr. Briggs will be thrilled to hear that two lovely young women of gentle bearing will be sitting along side him at the table. The spirits shall tell us their secrets and we shall delight in their ethereal wisdom. Who knows, we may be so lucky to have Caesar join us, or Boadicea, or King Solomon himself!"

In the front room, a great rattling moist snore broke the stillness, echoed closely by a rumbling fart. It was a very terrestrial sound, all things considered.

"I suppose," I replied. I glanced outside, along the cramped back yard and pert white fence to the alley, but saw no one. "Thank you for the invitation, Miss Kitty. I shall ask Violet if she's interested, and we shall do our best to attend."

VIOLET CLASPED both of my hands in own and gave a squeal of delight, so loud and piercing that it echoed around my bedchamber and bounced down the hall. "Do say it again!" she commanded with a laugh, "Please, Liz!"

As if by rote, I droned, "The Faulks sisters have asked us to attend their next scheduled gathering, on Saturday, at nine in the evening. They have asked that you and I join them," I paused, and Violet's grip on my hands tightened in anticipation, "For Dr. Briggs will be in attendance as well, and would greatly enjoy your company."

Violet let forth another piercing squeal.

"You're interested, then?"

My sister flopped back across my bed, her blonde hair flowing over her shoulders and down the edge of the mattress. We had both dressed for bed and retired for the night, but Violet would not let me sleep as long as she could prattle about Mason Briggs -- I made a reluctant audience, but I was the only one to whom she could discuss her thoughts and hopes and, dare I say it, obsessions about him. She released the soft and gentle sigh of an opium addict as she stared, dreamlike, at the ceiling. "Oh, Lizzie, this is too wonderful! You have done me such a service!"

"I had nothing to do with it," I replied as I laid down beside her, crosswise across the large bed. "I only asked Kitty about her supposed liaisons with," I opened my eyes wide and dropped my voice to a theatrical baritone, "The Denizens of the Nether Realms!"

"You'd best leech that skepticism from your voice, if you want to come," Violet warned.

"But I DON'T want to come!"

"You must!" Violet rolled onto her side to stare plainly into my face. "You can't let me go alone! That would be highly improper! You received the invitation, so I must come as your guest!"

I groaned. "Honestly, Vi—"

"Don't you believe in ghosts?"

"No."

"And what about heaven?"

I shrugged.

Violet gave a wrenching gasp. "I should know to expect less of you, Lizzie, than of other women, but to disregard God's Heaven? You shall burn for your paganism!"

"That's a cruel thing to say!"

"But true!" Violet rolled onto her back again and folded her hands under her head. "You suffer queer notions."

"I don't think I suffer at all."

"And where, then, do you think mother's soul is now?"

I pressed the heel of my palm to my forehead. "I'm sure I don't know, Violet. But the idea of a glorious man in the sky, watching us and waiting to punish us for the smallest exercise of our free will–well, I just think God must have other, more important things to do."

"God sees all, and takes notice."

"Then let me assure Him," I said, talking to the ceiling, "I am not worth His effort!"

Violet looked horrified. "You must come to church with Sandy and I. You must!" She grasped a lock of my hair and gave it a painful tug. "Such talk leads doubtlessly to damnation!"

I knocked her hand away from my hair. "I'm sure, as I burn in the fires of Hell, I'll be in entertaining company. I'll spend the first hundred years in conversation with Voltaire, and the second with

Galileo, and the third, seducing all the artists and poets of Paris. I shall start with Baudelaire."

Violet stared at me, stunned, and then began to laugh. "Oh, Lizzie! You're mocking me!" She reclined again, stretched her arms above her head, and shook her head at herself. "Sometimes, Liz, it's difficult to tell where your truth ends, and your jests begin! There's a reason, right there, for you to embrace a more pious life – I'll be able to tell when you're pulling my leg!" She chuckled again, and muttered, "Seducing the artists and poets.... Oh, goodness!"

We lay in silent thought for a moment, until Violet mused, half under her breath, "I wonder if Dr. Briggs asked Kitty to invite you. I wonder if this is his plan..."

"I doubt Mason Briggs is capable of such a scheme."

"Oh, I don't mean such a thing at all!" Violet replied, "Nothing evil or wicked! But we didn't have an opportunity to converse without Dr. Gould and Mr. Harris, and this would be a wonderful opportunity for him to foster our acquaintance." She shivered. "Mr. Harris: what an odd fellow! A man who prefers to spend his life alone, without a wife to nurture him, is certainly an abomination!"

"There are a lot of men without a wife here, Vi."

"Yes, but that's because there are so few women, Lizzie, and bachelorhood is thrust upon them! Unlike Mr. Harris, who has actively refused a woman's companionship to travel the world!"

"Well," I said, "Not everyone can achieve your exacting standards, Violet."

"Do you think he dreams of me?" she asked.

"Mr. Harris?"

Violet laughed. "No! Mason Briggs, of course!" She settled her folded hands under the back of her head. "I know Sandy dreams of me, for he's told me as such." Her eyes crinkled, her lips curved into a sly grin. "Do you think your nameless fellow dreams of you?"

The thought made me squirm. "Oh, no, I'm certain he doesn't," I said, "It wouldn't be in his nature."

"Do you dream of him?"

I felt the blood crawl across my cheeks. "Sometimes."

Violet pulled down the sheets and wriggled into the bed. "Tell me about him."

"There isn't much to tell," I said as I laid down next to Violet and we pulled the crisp sheet over us. The night was too warm for blankets, and the sheet was little more than a modest covering, to keep us feeling safe and secure. "He is kind, and thoughtful, and very intelligent."

"Is he older than you?"

"Yes," I answered, "He's never shown anything but friendship to me, Vi. There is nothing more between us, and he is utterly unremarkable. End of story."

"He must be extraordinary, to have turned your eye. Is it Buster Gillingham?"

I gagged, crossed my eyes, and laughed.

"Well, if you shan't tell me his name...." Violet began as she cranked down the coal oil gauge. The lamp fizzled and extinguished, and the room became a silent, secluded, dark confessional. "Tell me something more. One more bit of gossip, and I promise I won't pester you again."

I sorted through my description, careful to choose something that would give Violet no clues. It seemed that everything which made Shao so beautiful was also everything so dangerous – how could I possibly describe him without describing him?

At last, after cautious deliberation, I rolled onto my shoulder to face Violet in the gloom. "He is unconcerned by titles, class, and position," I said, "He does not define himself by the opinions of others. He just IS, and for that, I love him."

25

WHAT HOUR WAS IT, when my eyes fluttered open? I became aware of Violet lying next to me, breathing deeply and slowly. But behind the steady pattern of Violet quiet snoring came another sound, the whisper of movement in the corridor, like a great animal slinking on stealthy paws. It was a sound without definition, little more than the displacement of air and the gentle shush of a haunch brushing against the wall.

My eyes flashed open. I gripped the edge of the sheet, doubting my senses. Had I dreamt? Then my ears caught the tiny fragmented hush of a foot shuffling, along with the almost imperceptible rhythm of a person's breath. Someone lurked outside the door.

I rolled onto one shoulder to gain a clear view of the door, open fully and showing the yawning black hall. My fingers quivered, my throat constricted, but my heart continued in its steady, unfailing rhythm. I counted the beats as I listened, straining for any concrete sound to identify beyond Violet's puerile snores and mutters. Something was out there. Something advanced. I heard the faint shuffle again, no louder than a lion's paw set purposefully on the dust of the savannah. I bit my lip, wondering if I should wake Violet from her deep slumber or holler to Father for help.

I rose to my feet and stood with clenched fingers at my sides. My nightgown rasped against the sheets and fluttered around my legs but my feet were bare, and in three quick steps I was at the door, able to glean a clear view down the corridor toward Father's bedroom and the attic stairs. I pressed my shoulder to the threshold, listening, and peeked into the hall.

The corridor was still. Whatever had moved there was no longer advancing. I listened and heard my own breath like a tempest in the silence. The door to Father's room was firmly shut. The hall was deserted.

I turned to survey the other direction, down the hall to the stairs. I frowned: my view was blocked by what, in an instant of confusion, I took to be the outline of a solid oak wardrobe, square and impassible, stygian black against the gloom.

But the wardrobe moved so quickly, I had no time to utter a sound. As I inhaled for breath to power a scream, a massive hand clamped over my mouth and nose. An arm encircled me, clenched me fast to a broad body, and yanked me noiselessly out of the bedroom. I found myself borne aloft, bare toes grazing across the steps. His skin tasted of salt and horseflesh, and he carried me effortlessly down the stairs to the kitchen. When my face was released from the grip of a sweaty palm, I felt the thin, ice-cold line of a steel blade press against my throat.

"Say nothin'," his harsh voice hissed.

He stood behind me and pressed me close to his chest, but I knew him by the movement and shape of his frame: the man who had followed me to the Faulks' gate. His accent was unmistakably American, and his words were derisive and frustrated.

I remained as still as stone, made myself heavy and cumbersome in his arms, but it did little to deter him. He'd carried heavier cargo than the bony body of one small teenage girl. I glanced around the main floor and saw everything in disarray – papers scattered across the table, the pantry torn asunder, the bookshelves laid bare. I thought, with a pang of dismay, how upset Agnes would be to discover such a mess in the morning.

The thin edge of the bowie knife stung as he pressed it against my skin. I realized that he hesitated, unsure of what to do now that he'd been discovered.

"You can take anything you want," I offered in an even whisper, "There's an envelope of money in the drawer by the front door."

"Shut-up," he ordered. He dragged me a few steps to the back door, which swung open. "You say anything about me here, and I'll kill ya. Understand?"

Something in his voice, something deep and primal, sparked a change. At first, I didn't recognize the nature of the change -- I only knew that I felt odd, quivery, watery. My heart began to beat faster. It abandoned its calm and steady rhythm, and galloped within me. I had never felt such raw energy. I wanted to run.

This was fright! Real, honest terror! The fear flooded through me. I raised one palm to my sternum and I was rewarded with the pulse of a savagely-beating heart.

He yanked me off my feet and gave me a jolt. "You understand, kid? I'll kill ya."

"Yes," I whispered back, "I understand."

The man carried me to the back porch. The cool night air slipped under my hem like a cat and wound around my bare ankles.

"You scream, I'll kill ya."

"Oh, I won't scream," I said, "I promise."

He shoved me aside and nestled the point of his bowie knife against the base of my throat. From his arm's length, we regarded each other.

He was taller than six feet by maybe three or four inches, and perhaps the largest man I'd ever seen. He towered over me like a bear on its hind paws. He seemed as steadfast as a stone citadel, and his movements were silent and graceful in spite of his powerful size. I examined his face and decided that it was not unhandsome, and might even be considered becoming, if he bothered to scrape the stubble from his chin and wash the dirt from his skin. He had a strong jaw, a straight nose, and arresting eyes that, in the dim light of the half-moon, were the color of slate.

The knife in his right hand lowered. For the first time I noticed that he was missing a digit on his left hand. He had barely a nub of bone where the third finger should be.

He studied me with a perplexed and suspicious sneer. Rattled by my composure, he tilted his head to one side. "You ain't scared."

"Oh, I am." I replied truthfully. I couldn't keep from smiling.

"You sure the hell don't look it."

I rubbed the line along my neck where the blade's impression still prickled, but I remained calm and as still as a mouse. The delicious sensation of fear was retreating. Faded and distant but sweet and different, it left my skin tingling. All the world looked a little more crisp. "Why are you following me?" I asked.

His eyes narrowed, and the corner of his lips kinked up in a smirk. "Ain't that a good question," he said, "Why would I follow a little stick-limbed kid like you?" He advanced a step on naked feet and pressed the tip of the knife against my sternum. "You tell anyone I was here," he growled, "And I'll slice you right quick. Got it?"

I nodded.

He reeled around on his silent feet and vanished out the back door, and melted into the night to collect his boots from wherever he'd stashed them. I waited, counted to one hundred, considered his words. The fear was almost completely gone now, like little wisps of smoke dispersing through the air. I leaned my shoulder against the door frame and watched the darkness where he'd disappeared.

Then, when I was sure he was well and truly away, I turned to face the hall, the stairwell, the demolished parlor, the quiet interior of the sleeping house, and screamed my throat raw.

26

Alexander Kelly washed and dressed with miraculous speed once he'd learned who's house had been violated. By the time the parlor lamps were lit and a swooning Violet had been ushered downstairs on Father's arm, the constable appeared at the front door, appearing as dashing and composed as if we'd met him on the street in the afternoon. He nodded politely to Violet as she was arranged on the couch with a blanket and provided a glass of cordial to sooth her delicate constitution. Father gave her a kerchief to dab her watery eyes and, once all were assured that she would not faint from the horrors of the evening, Kelly returned his attention to me.

"Now then," he said, sitting opposite from me at the dining room table, "Tell me what you saw."

I took a sip of milk from the glass cradled in my hands and rearranged the high collar of my housecoat over the top of my neck. "When I came downstairs, I found everything in disarray and the back door left open. I was afraid the burglar might still be in the house, so I screamed and woke everyone."

"You didn't see anyone?"

"No, sir."

"Nothing?"

"Just the open door, and our house, ransacked."

"From what I can tell, nothing of value is gone," said Father, "The thief didn't come upstairs into the bedrooms, nor did he take Peggy's envelope of money."

Rufus McGregor, who had previously been studying the back exit, appeared in the hall between parlor and kitchen. "The lock was picked," he growled to Kelly. "Just like the other houses."

"Others?" said Father.

"Aye, sir," said Rufus, "Four homes on the street have been entered. When I went to ask your neighbors if they'd witnessed anything, we found their back doors picked open, too." He turned to Kelly. "There may yet be more that we'll only discover in the light of day."

"A career thief, then, who knows his craft! Surely he must have stolen something." Kelly said. "What manner of degenerate would come thus far, only to grow cowardly and not complete his thieving?"

"I know you'll find him, Mr. Kelly," Violet said from her installment on the sofa. Her voice quavered with strain and exhaustion. "He'll not be able to outrun your justice."

Sandy stood up straighter, became more brisk and businesslike, and stammered out a thank you for her confidence.

Through the windows of the parlor, lantern lights flickered outside as Kelly's men trampled the flower garden. They searched for a hint of the intruder but I was certain they'd find nothing – he'd known to remove his shoes to make his movement quiet, and he'd been able to pick the lock on the door. Over three days, he'd patiently watched our house for an opportune time; I suspected that this was not the first time he'd broken the law, and other than the faintest scent of his sweat on my night clothes, he was careful to leave no clues of his passage. He had taken nothing because he'd been interrupted, of this I was sure.

I wondered where he was now.

And I wondered what should I do with my knowledge, now hanging like a sword over his head.

27

August 6, 1898

"He threatened my life, ruined our belongings, ransacked the library --"

"Yes, so you've said! What I don't understand is: how can you sound so happy about it?" asked Shao, refilling my cup of tea. "And why.... WHY, Lizzie.... why didn't you give him up?"

He refilled his own cup and set the little clay teapot back on the edge of the brazier as we prepared to dissect the story for a third time. The apothecary shop was very quiet today, without even Mr. Tao to bother us, and Shao had been understandably upset with my tale when I'd first told it. He'd paced the full length of the room, fists clenched, looking at me with incredulity as I told him in a very calm and rational tone about a man holding a knife to my throat and threatening to (as I deepened my voice and mimicked the accent) 'slice me up right quick'. Finally, Shao sat next to me on the crates, shaking his head slightly at my disquieting scientific manner. I was prepared to study the man's words and actions, every nuance and syllable, with a sense of calm.

"Why didn't I give him up..." I mused. I rotated the teacup in my hands as I considered my answer. As I lifted it to my lips, the curls of steam wreathed my face. Truth be told, I wasn't completely sure, and had lain awake in my bed through the early morning hours, searching for a plausible reason. "Because," I finally said, "He made me afraid."

"That would seem, to me, to be a very good reason to report him!"

"Yes, I suppose, but I have something on him now," I said, "I know something about him that no one else knows. He followed me to the Faulk's home, but now he dare not go near me, in case I've revealed him to Kelly. And he can't be sure that I haven't reported him. And honestly, Shao, he probably assumes I HAVE described him in gory detail, for what girl in her right mind would not? Whoever he is, he dare not touch me, for should anything happen to me, the man I reported would be the first suspect."

"But you didn't report him," Shao pointed out, "And you aren't in your right mind."

"I feel like I am! For the very first time!" The thought made me laugh. I pressed my palm to my chest. "My heart beat faster and faster, and everything looked brighter and more crisp! It was breath-taking!"

Shao frowned in disapproval. "You're playing a dangerous game, Liz – you don't back a man into a corner."

"I know," I assured, "But..." I touched her throat, where the sensation of the knife could be resurrected by thought alone.

Shao waited for me to continue, and when I did not, be prompted, "But...?"

I stirred from my introspection. "But he could have easily left me dead, silenced the only witness to his crime, and he didn't. That surely must say something about the quality of his character."

"It says that a thief does not want to become a murderer," Shao warned, "Yet."

"He took nothing, so he's not technically a thief."

"Are you his legal council?!? Ai ye! Why would you defend him! And please, quit touching your neck; it's disturbing!"

"I'm not defending him! But," I searched for a reason, anything, to try and explain my actions, "He broke into all the doctors' houses, looking for something, and I want to know what! And I think the only way I'll ever know is to ask him myself." I leaned forward to look Shao directly in the eyes. "If I demand he must answer my question, or else I'll give him up to Kelly, he'll have to tell me!"

"Or he'll have to kill you," Shao replied. "He may still, if he feels threatened. For God's sake, Lizzie, be careful!"

A strange flutter rose through my veins; Shao was worried for me. It made me smile.

He mistook the expression for levity. "This is not a joke," he insisted. "Promise me, Liz, that there will be no more slipping out of doors after dark and no more excursions here to see me. Even on a Saturday afternoon! You ought to be at the sporting matches and the Bank Holiday picnic with your sister, not here with me. I beg you, tell your father to hire a boy to run his errands."

"You don't want me to come here any more?"

"Of course I want you to come here, but Liz," he implored, "I couldn't bear it if you were harmed or killed by this disgusting excuse of a human being! He's not trustworthy, he possesses no scruples, and you give him too much credit for decent behavior."

I lowered my teacup. "You know who he is!"

"I know he's hardly the kind of person you can trust." Shao looked greatly uncomfortable at the prospect of revealing anything. "A great filthy lout of a man in a grey duster and hat, with a finger missing on his left hand? There aren't many that match your description."

"What do you know of him?" I pried, leaning forward, "Who is he? C'mon, Shao, tell me!"

He refilled our cups and hesitated, weighing his answer to give me no more information than necessary. "He calls himself Jack. He came with other miners from California, but hasn't joined them on the mining crews. Instead, he hangs around the brothels and the gambling halls."

"He's a drunk, then?"

"He'll take a shot of whiskey if someone else is paying," Shao replied, "But I've never seen him with a bottle, and he doesn't spend a penny in the opium dens. He asks questions, but doesn't give up much information about himself, except to say that he's got a pistol under his coat and he's not afraid to use it." Shao slumped his back against the wall. "He's been roaming the back alleys of Chinatown for almost a week, and from all I've seen and heard, he doesn't yield to temptation."

"So why would he frequent such places, if not for a good time?"

"I have my suspicions." Shao looked to the empty doorway leading outside, and lowered his voice to a cautious volume. "Men let down their guard, talk a little more freely, when the drink is flowing. I think he looks for the faults and weaknesses in other men, and uses that against them. He's a swindler, Lizzie, and a thief, and not a man who can be trusted." Shao leaned his head close to mine. He whispered, as if the wind might pluck his words from the room and spread them far and wide. "Be careful, Liz. I can not warn you enough – stay away, as far away as you possibly can, from Jack."

28

At half-passed 8 o'clock, Kitty Faulks greeted us at the door. Both Violet and I had dressed in black skirts and white blouses for the occasion, and we found Miss Kitty dressed in a beautiful gown of emerald silk, trimmed with black feathers and gold brocade. Violet returned Kitty's greeting with enthusiasm and open arms. I stood to the side and silently wondered what the hell I was doing here, attending a séance, when the last thing I wanted to do was waste my time with spooks and boogey-men. There was a despicable and cunning thief out there who, only last night, had threatened to kill me. I wanted to be out looking for him, and setting him to task as to why he would dare insult me so.

Violet withdrew a silver coin from her clutch purse and dropped it in a glass jar, which had been set on a lace-covered table just inside the front door. When I looked at her with raised eyebrows, Violet explained, "It encourages the spirits to come, you know."

"I'm sure it does," I replied.

Kitty ushered us into the parlor. The curtains were drawn, and the lamps gave a low, gentle and intimate illumination. In the middle of the room sat a round table covered with a fine lace cloth, surrounded by six wooden chairs. On the table sat three items: a cream-colored candle in heavy silver candlestick, a small silver bowl brimming with clear water, and a painting in a silver frame of a noble Indian Brave, his head-dress made of red feathers and his buck-skin outfit immaculate, his hawk-beak nose set over a stern lipless mouth.

I looked at the idealistic portrait, and thought of Nessie, face beaten and despondent. The comparison between fiction and fact made my stomach clenched.

Four people had already assembled for tonight's entertainment: Mr. Fish sat on the chaise-lounge, nursing a glass of cordial. Dr. Briggs stood by the fireplace, conversing with Mrs. Jeanie Hughes, the plump and cheerful wife of Reginald Hughes, a mine manager for the Company. Mr. Hughes presently admired the landscape painting above the mantle, hands on hips and feet solidly placed, as if he were standing on a rocky crag of the Alps, surveying the actual mountains and valleys himself. He was a man of great travels and experience, short and squat but of a forthright and considerate nature, well-manicured and clean with a gravelly voice and brown, curly mutton-chops. At almost two decades older than his effervescent wife, he appeared worldly and worn; she, as fresh as a new daisy, and he, as wrinkled as an old oak, made a strange and yet jolly couple. The bubbly Jeanie giggled and held her gloved hand over her mouth at the witticisms of Dr. Briggs, but I saw by the genuine sparkle of Violet's smile that there was no jealousy hidden there, because the flighty Mrs. Hughes posed no great threat – she was safely married.

"Oh, Kitty," Violet exclaimed in a reverent whisper, clasping her hands at her chest, "The house looks positively mystical!"

"Doesn't it?" Jeanie agreed, "I said to Reggie, when we entered, I said, I've never seen anything so delightfully spooky!" She turned to her husband. "Didn't I say that very thing?"

He harrumphed in agreement and returned to his appraisal of the painting.

"May I interest you in a drink?" Kitty asked, and without waiting for an answer, brought two glasses of pale wine from the sideboard, already poured and prepared. "We must have libations, my dears, a splash of watered cordial to ease us into the evening," she explained, handing each of us a glass, "The phantoms prefer us to be relaxed and calm, and will not grace us with their presence if they feel we are bound by earthly worries and concerns!" She gave a little laugh that reminded me of a hacking cough.

"I don't know if I ought—" I said, but Violet shushed me.

"Be a good guest, Liz," she hissed out of the side of her mouth.

"Violet and Amaryllis!" greeted Dr. Briggs, leaving Jeanie with a polite nod and welcoming us with a candid grin. "Isn't this dreadfully exciting!"

"Indeed," droned Mr. Fish from his seat.

"I've never attended a séance!" Violet admitted, "Have you?"

"Yes, quite a few," said Mason, "I find them to be a most pleasant way of passing an evening and stimulating conversation. Here, do sit next to me, please." He held out his hand to an empty chair, and Violet fluffed her black skirts around her, and smiled as he took the seat at her right.

Mr. Fish propped himself in the chair on Violet's left, and waggled his hand at me to sit beside him. "Tradition dictates, the genders must alternate," he explained. "I suppose it ensures a man on either side, to protect you if the ghosts get randy."

"I have to admit, Mr. Fish," I said in a hushed whisper, "I don't really want to be here."

Seeing that Violet and Mason were tête-à-tête, he confided, "Neither do I, Miss Saunders. Here, let me stiffen that up for you." He rummaged in his coat pocket and brought out a silver flagon, and poured half of its contents into his own glass before emptying it in mine. It smelt medicinal, and a little like licorice. "A concoction to make our night pass more quickly. Let me be perfectly honest with you: I can't stand these beastly things. All a bunch of shrieking and squawking, if you ask me -- bloody mumbo-jumbo hocus-pocus horseshit, if you'll excuse the expression."

I could not keep from grinning.

The other four engaged in excited whispering, but Mr. Fish curled his lip and leaned his head to my ear. "I'm not one for these diversions, but Mason can not stay away from the Spiritualists and their ridiculous gatherings. He's bloody fascinated by them."

"Is he a Spiritualist, too?"

"I don't rightly think so – he'd lose his place with the company, if they ever suspected. It's not exactly a gentleman's pursuit, is it."

"No, sir."

"But Mason thinks it's practical, you know. Sitting here, in the presence of the spirits, he believes he is experiencing the divine with his own five senses. Feels it's bloody good science and all."

"And you?"

"Oh, good Lord, no!" Mr. Fish threw back his glass and the contents disappeared down his long throat. "My youngest sister was involved with the theatre in Birmingham -- I know how simple it is to dupe a rube. Masks and theatrics extend far beyond the stage, and it's very easy to hide the truth in plain sight."

My eyebrows arched. "Those are brazen words, sir!"

"People see what they wish to see." He grinned. "Every man has a mask to wear in polite company, Miss Saunders, behind which he hides his true nature."

I placed my elbows on the table and leaned towards him. "And what wicked nature do you hide from the world, Mr. Fish?"

"My dear girl," he began with a smile, "You are very bold to ask. Perhaps, one day, I shall tell you – but not today."

I wanted to continue the conversation further, but the lights dimmed as Kitty turned each lamp down. Only the single candle in the middle of the table remained. She pulled the curtains, one by one, shrouding the walls in thick, soft, red velvet. The fabric dampened the sound of our voices. With every sharp edge dulled, every flat surface now soft and crimson, the parlor had become as quiet and cloistered as a womb. Kitty stood and raised her hands, palm upwards. The light of the single candle threw her cheekbones into chiseled, half-starved relief. Her wispy hair surrounded her crown like a halo of silver wires.

"Now," she began in a theatrical whisper, "Let us begin."

. . .

A FIGURE EMERGED from behind a curtain, bold and confident, powerful as an rhinoceros. Its gold-edged robes glittered and sparkled in the faint illumination. Around its throat was a collar of pale blue topaz and glittering costume diamonds, sparkling in the low light. The figure's corpse-white face, with a pair of Etruscan eyes edged with kohl, swam into view from the pool of black shadows. Its expression was so immobile, so inhuman and so piercing that it became a doll's visage, an inanimate sculpture of fine porcelain clay, yet possessing a pair of living, glinting, piercing eyes.

I felt Mr. Fish press his shoulder against me. I couldn't tell if he was offering protection, or seeking it.

The voice that issued from that thick throat, from out of that round lightless cavern of a mouth, burst forth with such volume and baritone that that the crystal glasses shivered and candle flame danced. No hint of the simpering, cantankerous, melodramatic tone remained; this voice was epic, ancient, and volatile. This creature, who had once been Peggy, was transformed into a vessel of the Divine.

"WHO ATTENDS!" it demanded. The hands floated upwards, appealing to the heavens. The voice, around which the whole world now revolved, warbled with a strange accent.

Kitty spoke from behind my shoulder. "We, mere mortals, attend!"

"WHY DO YOU DISTURB ME FROM MY REST!" The topaz-blue eyes rolled themselves down until they were small half-circles of blue amid round glossy orbs of white. When they fixed their glare upon Violet, she squeezed herself into Mason's embrace and squeaked.

Kitty's voice was equally resolute, but it was still her own. "We call upon you for guidance! To whom do I speak?"

"I AM OF A THOUSAND THOUSAND NAMES!" the voice boomed, and the black-rimmed eyes snapped upwards to stare into the distance. It summoned forth a litany of titles, each one louder than the last. " ENOCH! ATROPOS! LEUCOTHEA!"

"And what must we call you tonight, oh Spirit of a Thousand Thousand Names?"

"TONIGHT, I AM MALAKH ELOHIM!"

Kitty stood with her fingers on Jeanie's shoulders. With Kitty's solid grip on Jeanie's sleeves, it was immediately evident that the poor, gleeful, blithe little woman trembled wildly before the spectral visitation. One loud noise, and poor Jeanie was liable to wet herself.

Kitty leaned forwards, her smile devilish. When she whispered in Jeanie's ear, her lips softly framed every sensual syllable.

"Do you have a question for Malakh?"

"I.... I..." Jeannie stammered, pressing herself back. "I don't..."

"I have a question," I said, taking a sip of my drink to moisten my lips. "May I speak?"

Violet aimed a dagger-sharp gaze at me. Mason looked thrilled.

"Ask your question!" Kitty prompted.

The sip of liquid burned in my mouth and throat, and turned into a fire in my belly. I set down my glass, rose my face to the looming figure, and asked, "Why does he follow me?"

A hush fell around the table as all craned forward to hear the answer.

"You must be specific," said Kitty, "Give the spirit a name."

I glanced at Kitty, then returned my eyes to Malakh and leveled my stare at the gold-swathed creature. "Oh all-seeing, all-knowing spirit," I said, and my voice dropped to a whisper. My field of vision drew in, focused like a beam of light. It seemed as if there were only the two of us in the room. "Dear spirit, there is no need for names. You, who can see into our hearts, surely already know the answer."

Silence, thick and tense, fell over the room. The kohl-rimmed eyes blinked; I saw Peggy fall out of her character as her expression faltered.

Then she drew her bulk up again, and the hands clenched at the sky, and the tendons leapt from her wrists like cords.

"HE IS IN ADORATION!" the figure screeched, "WHY DO ALL MEN FOLLOW WOMEN, BUT FOR LOVE?"

"I don't think so," I replied, and a sharp kick from under the table struck my shin.

Violet seethed. "Be! Quiet!" she hissed through clenched teeth, then to the room, cried, "Forgive my unbelieving sister, oh spirit! She is young and mistaken—"

"I'm pretty sure love has nothing to do with it," I muttered as I took another sip from my glass. To my right, the skeptical Mr. Fish stifled a guffaw.

"A certain urgency to your paramour's proposal, my dear?"

A frill of nervous laughter passed around the table, except for Kitty, who remained stoic and unemotional. The sound of mirth dipped and swayed in my ears. The shadows flickered, weaving back and forth, as if the entire scene had been immersed in green water.

"ENOUGH!" shouted the spirit, and with a frantic quality that sounded more like Peggy, "ENOUGH REVELRY!"

"Oh, forgiving spirit!" Kitty implored, and she strolled around the edge of the table to sink her talons into my shoulders, "The girl asks for his intentions, and does not believe them to be love – but the fullness of time will reveal your words to be correct, of that I'm certain!"

A knife to the throat is an odd way to show affection, I thought, and said aloud, "Where does he come from?"

"ACROSS THE SEA!" Malakh declared.

Which, I realized, was technically correct for almost everyone here – this was, after all, an island.

The hands on my shoulders gripped a fraction tighter. I braced myself for Kitty's voice, but there was a long and stagnant pause. It seemed that even Malakh waited for her line.

I turned in my seat and looked up into Kitty's face. The woman's expression was strange and distant.

"Mrs. Faulks?" I said, "Are you alright?"

Kitty stared straight ahead. "There is a girl. Thin, willowy. Long black hair. Dead for many years."

The quality of Kitty's voice stirred me from my seat. I shrugged from under her grip and took her spidery hands in my own. They trembled and felt clammy. "Kitty, do you need to sit? You look unwell."

The others strained forward in their seats, trying to catch Kitty's whispered reply.

"She is crying for you, Lizzie. She knows your name. She is afraid you will forget her, and she feels empty. Cold and empty." Kitty's hand drifted to her stomach. "Hollow. Pulled apart. She says to me," Kitty gently half-closed her eyes to listen, "Don't forget me. The devil ate me up, but I want to be remembered."

Then Kitty blinked twice, and the gentle quality to her face and voice vanished. "Lizzie," she said, confused, "Why are you standing up, child?"

Stunned, I studied her face. She seemed genuinely confused. She blinked slowly, like a sleeper who had been unkindly roused.

A polite clapping rose, and Mr. Fish guffawed.

"Oh, good show! Very good indeed!"

I eased back into my seat as Kitty continued her circumnavigation of the table, laying her hands on each person's shoulders, demanding that they ask a question of Malakh. I paid little attention.

I cast my mind back, but I knew of no young girl who had died, many years ago; Kitty must be mistaken. But the phrase, 'The devil ate me up' rang in my ears. Perhaps Nessie had spoken to Kitty – I looked at the silver-edged portrait on the table, of a patrician face and feathered headdress, and thought it not impossible that Kitty would seek out a woman of Nessie's ancestry, if only to dress her up like a noble savage and take her picture. What if Kitty gathered information from unlikely sources, and trotted out little tidbits when the situation demanded it? Maybe Nessie had told Kitty about our conversation in the alley behind the Eagle. Maybe Kitty's act was nothing more than a trick of memory and theatrics.

"You're right, Mr. Fish," I whispered, "It is a good show."

But the show was winding down. The candle had burned half-way.

"I IMPLORE YOU," Malakh boomed, "NO MORE QUERIES! I GROW WEARY OF MORTAL MATTERS!"

Which, I thought, meant it was better the leave the audience with more questions than answers.

"One last testament to your presence, oh spirit!" Kitty asked, "A physical example of your supernatural powers!"

I took a sip of my fiery drink, and watched with fascination as a gurgle issued from deep in Peggy's throat. The spectacular figure began to convulse. Each wave rippled up through the billowing reams of gold fabric. Peggy's eyes rolled back and became a pair of white marbles. All levity vanished.

"She's having a seizure!" Mason cried out.

Kitty silenced him with a thin finger pointed directly at him. "Do not touch her! Watch!"

The pale mouth opened, the clay mask contorted. Wet strands of white mucus belched forth from the slack jaw to land with a moist plop upon the table. A sour-milk stench filled the close air. Jeanie screamed and threw her hands over her mouth. The single point of light vanished as the candle extinguished, plunging the room into blind chaos. When at last Kitty lit a lamp from the kitchen, the only clue to the foul material's existence was a puddle of pale white liquid, as thin as buttermilk, in the centre of the tablecloth.

Peggy reclined over her empty chair, exhausted, no longer a vessel for any greater visitation. She looked disoriented. She slowly opened and closed her mouth like a carp. Mason and Mr. Hughes hurried to settle the frantic ladies, to silence their squawking and flapping, and Mr. Fish laughed at the circus.

A thin smile appeared, then vanished, on the lips of Kitty Faulks.

"Who witnessed it!" she cried out, "Who witnessed it!"

A torrent of voices erupted, a great swell of words that rose as the spectators clustered around the table again, picking up their fallen chairs, assembling their skirts and righting their glasses.

Peggy's face was wrung out like a wet rag, ashen under the smeared make-up. She gave a rattling groaned from the depths of her diaphragm. Her hair hung in disheveled, sweaty hanks over her forehead, and her grand costume hung awkwardly over her slumped shoulders. All the pompous rigors of decorum had been mercilessly wrenched out of her.

"Who witnessed it?" cried Kitty again.

A flurry of words answered her.

"Ectoplasm!"

"I saw a face in it!"

"I did, too!"

Now they squeezed close around the table to study the rank puddle with awe, and as they chattered, the experience grew and grew. What started as a hunk of cheesecloth, briefly seen by candlelight, became a face, then a mouth, that then trembled, then mouthed a single word, which everyone agreed looked very much like the word 'Violet'.

I listened objectively. I narrowed my eyes and noticed a number of places where, in the darkness, a sodden scrap of muslin could have been pushed aside – the porcelain pot holding a fern, a drawer in the table. Or perhaps a pocket under Kitty's crinoline? The little woman stood suspiciously erect, and the shadows cast over the floor by the furniture could effectively hide a growing damp spot on the carpet.

"He has made himself known!" Peggy gasped, and I had no doubts that her heaving breaths were legitimate; after all, she'd held a wad of fabric in her throat, spoken around it, and heaved it up at the most appropriate moment. All that took a bit of skill, albeit very earthly. "My spirit guide has shown you his face, and speaks to you as an acquaintance, Miss Violet!"

Violet paled and clutched Mason's wrist. "Oh, my!" she breathed in a mix of fear and exhilaration. "Did you hear that, Lizzie? I have been singled out by the spirits! Lizzie?" Violet scowled. "Lizzie, dear, you've gone terribly pale."

"Mr. Fish," I said, reaching out to him. The act of reaching seemed to go on forever, as if my arm was taffy, and he was sitting at the end of a long corridor. "Mr. Fish, what did you put in my—"

I crashed to the floor and took the tablecloth with me.

29

THE VOICES ROSE and fell like the tide. Pinpricks of light appeared in my field of vision. I heard the hiss of the lamps and the soft crinkle of crisp fabric, somewhere near my head: from the texture, a silk pillow case propped under my ear. I became aware, rather slowly, that I was lying down.

My eyes fluttered open. A line of drool had crusted at the corner of my mouth. I tried to rise to my elbows, but a steady hand on my shoulder kept me down.

"Be still."

The voice filled me with profound embarrassment and I flashed awake. I lay on the chaise-lounge by the windows, with a crocheted blanket over my legs and a porcelain bowl on the ground at my side. Father sat next to the chaise-longue, on a wooden chair taken from the séance table. The parlor was empty but lit to a blazing illumination with numerous lamps and candles. He released his hold on my shoulder and rested his wrists on his knees.

"Well," he said, "You've given Violet a scare."

I gulped.

"They told me someone named... Malakh?" He raised one mocking eyebrow. "...Malakh struck you down for disbelieving." He grinned, and sniffed my breath. "I would've said it was the absinthe, but what do I know."

"I came with Violet," I whispered. My throat burned and felt raw. "Dr. Brigg's was attending."

"Ah," he said simply. "I see." He grinned. "And did you learn anything?"

The contents of my stomach filled the bowl on the floor. I glanced at it, thought of the cheesecloth, and my guts lurched. "Do not accept drinks from Mr. Fish," I answered.

He chuckled and held out his hand to me. "Can you stand?"

"Give me a minute, please," I said, "I'm still a bit wobbly."

"And were the spirits in attendance?" he asked, and though he tried to remain objective, his words were playful. "Come now, you can speak plainly to me. The rest of your company has retired to the front verandah to discuss the evening's events. I promise, they can't hear a word you say."

I rested my head against the pillow. "Yes, sir, if by 'spirits', you mean Peggy's remarkable theatrics."

"As long as you were entertained, there's little harm done," he said, "Other than your 'fainting spell', I suppose."

"Did I break anything with my fall?"

"A picture frame and a candlestick, but I wouldn't be too concerned," he said. He took the skewed frame from the side table and handed it to me. "It looks expensive, but it's only cheap a bit of tin."

I flipped it over in my fingers, then held one palm to my forehead, which was slick with perspiration. "I think I want to go home to bed."

"Come along," he said, helping me rise to my unsteady feet. "I've arranged a hansom cab for us. It should arrive shortly."

Leaning heavily on his arm, we left the Faulk's parlor and made our way to the porch. Outside, the midnight air was refreshingly cool, and the stars above flickered and danced. The rest of the company sat on wicker chairs on the front verandah, just as Father had claimed. In excited, hushed whispers, they dissected the spirit's words and actions and, no less, my spectacular collapse at the close of the séance. A small table held a plate of cake slices and a pot of tea, and as Father and I exited the front door, Kitty gestured to the table.

"Please, take nourishment with us," she offered, and to me, said, "You gave us all quite a scare, my child!"

"I thought you'd been struck dead by the ghosts!" squealed Jeanie, and might have elaborated on the horrific nature of my spectacular demise, except that her husband gave her a sharp glance that caused her mouth to clamp firmly shut.

"Very glad to see you up and about," said Mr. Fish drolly.

I allowed myself to be helped into a wicker seat next to him. I smoothed my skirts over my knees and threw him a mischievous smirk. "I'm feeling much better, thank you." I took an offered slice of cake and bit into it with the ravenous hunger that comes from a suddenly emptied stomach. The bite was greedily welcomed by my belly, which growled with pleasure, and my viscera was happy for something to do instead of clench and convulse.

"Was it the excitement of the evening?" said Peggy. She was now dressed humbly in a black skirt and black blouse. Without make-up or robes, she appeared as mortal as the rest of us. "Did the presence of spirits cause you to swoon?"

I glanced sideways at Mr. Fish. "Yes, I suppose you could say so."

He laughed and took another bit of cake from the plate. "I say, after a display such as we've witnessed tonight, I'm surprised more of you ladies didn't vomit." He tore a hearty bite from the slice. "That ectoplasm is perishingly vile!"

"So we've turned your skepticism!" Kitty smiled.

"Harris will never abandon his skepticism," laughed Briggs.

"But you, Mason," said Father in a smooth voice, "You are a firm believer?"

"I've seen enough, John, to consider the possibilities," he replied. "Don't tell me you have no questions about what lies after death!"

"None, sir," Father replied. "None at all."

Kitty and Peggy swapped knowing, sly glances. Kitty offered Father a slice of cake as she asked, "Do share with us, then, your knowledge of the Eternal Beyond."

A spark flared in his eyes and the edge of his lip curled up in a smile. He opened his mouth to speak, then paused in a heartbeat, and changed his answer. “My dear ladies, I should not dare to ruin your fine evening with my dry and unimaginative beliefs.”

“But, John, we should dearly love to speak with you about matters of faith and divinity!” Kitty replied, “You, as a doctor, must have vast experience with the transubstantiation of the human soul from these frail, mortal remains!”

Father stood, for the cab and horse now rattled down Penrith Street towards us. “It is my vocation, dear Kitty, to keep those souls from transubstantiating, not to help them along.” He smiled. “But even I understand that death has its place, and is, in some instances, necessary. What lies beyond for us, is nothing for us to fear.”

“Well said, sir!” Mason cheered, raising a glass.

Father tipped his head to all in farewell, and set his silk hat upon his head as the cab rattled to a stop at the front gate. “Come, girls.”

I thanked all for the entertainment and rose on shaky knees to walk to the carriage, an open hansom pulled by one of the livery’s sleek chestnut mares. Violet lingered, only at the last moment bidding the party good night, and joined us as we climbed into the leather seats. With a crack of the driver’s whip, the springy vehicle pulled away. The fine horse tossed its head and trotted homeward.

“What do you believe?” I asked, as the carriage turned right on Fourth, bounced passed a block of miners houses, and then turned right onto Dunsmuir.

John, sitting with his back to the driver and facing us, gave an uncharacteristic shrug.

“Do you believe in ghosts?” said Violet, “Oh, I think I do. I nearly screamed when the ectoplasm leapt out of her throat!“

“Cheesecloth, Vi,” I amended, “Choked up by Peggy. It reeked of stomach acid, sherry and laudanum.”

“It did?”

I turned back to Father, who watched the world pass with a closed face, his mouth set in a hard line.

“Do you know,” he began slowly, “There was once a woman

named Mary Tofts, back in England, who claimed to give birth to rabbits?"

Violet's eyes widened. "Really?"

"The doctors, the surgeons, the midwives, the clergy, hundreds of people from miles around – they all witnessed her labor and the birth. With their own eyes they saw her push forth rabbits from her womb, though the babes were stillborn."

"Well, they would be, wouldn't they!" said Violet.

He raised one eyebrow to his eldest daughter. "Why would they be, Violet?" he asked.

"It's an affront to God. A rabbit, birthed of a woman? Such a monster couldn't survive."

"You test us," I said.

John blinked away from his appraisal of his eldest. "Sorry?"

"Mary Tofts may have pushed dead rabbits from her womb, but I wager they were dead when she pushed them in there, too."

Violet gave a horrified squeal.

"But they saw it! With their own eyes!" she insisted, "Father said that—"

"You can't trust what you see," I replied to her, "You rely so much on your sense of sight that you allow yourself to be tricked by charlatans and theatre props."

"Even the clergy said it was a miracle—"

"The clergy are flesh and blood, Violet, and just as gullible as anyone," I replied.

Father mused over my comment, neither agreeing nor disagreeing. "You don't believe in the eternal struggle between good and evil?"

I turned back to him. "People are capable of being cruel, deceitful or hateful all on their own – they don't need any god or devil to sway them. But they carry the banner of tradition to shelter themselves from the savage nature of their own actions." I looked askance at my sister. "When the miners beat up the Chinese men for making a paltry wage, or buy favors from an Indian woman only to knock her down when they're finished with her, Violet condones such behavior because it's the way it's always been. She sees it as the price of enlightenment and the mark of civilization. She doesn't recognize it as the innate nature of people to be cruel."

Violet, open-mouthed, took a minute to find her tongue, but when she did, it was laced with venom. "What?!?!" she cried, "How dare you! How dare you presume that I support–"

"Shush, Violet," said John, looking wholly amused with this turn in the conversation, "Lizzie—do explain, my girl. You assume that people are inherently cruel?"

I pouted and considered my position. "I think it's easiest for people to be cruel."

"And in those instances when a man makes an effort to be cruel?"

"Makes an effort? You mean, he understands what he does is immoral or wrong?" I shook my head. "I've never yet met a man who had not found a good reason, in his mind, to be cruel. Most create a sufficient excuse to support their actions." I shook my head. "But that doesn't make it right."

"Can a man ever amend for his cruel actions, then?" he asked, leaning forward, greatly intrigued by this conversation. "Can he ever bear out the balance of good and evil? Can he change his ways, and provide enough good to the world to make up for all the evil that he's done before?"

"I have to believe he can, if he truly wishes to," I replied, "Otherwise, there's no hope for us."

The carriage now bounced up the steep hill, passed the Presbyterian church. "And you believe all men are equal?" he asked.

"No," I replied, "I believe all people are equal. Not just men, but women, too."

Violet groaned. "Oh, Lizzie, not this argument."

"The pair of you confound me!" Father mused, still half-smiling, as he rested against the hard carriage seat and crossed his arms. "Nurtured in the same home, raised with the same circumstances, and yet, so varied in personality and position? It boggles the mind." He looked between our two faces: me, calm and thoughtful, and Violet, still flushed with anger and insult.

"Violet," he began, "You are a woman of your age. You are the paradigm of Victorian civilization, and you encapsulate everything to which we aspire in this generation. Etiquette, poise, beauty and perfection."

Violet smiled. She sat up a little straighter and gave me a haughty glance.

"And Lizzie," he continued, "You are not of this age at all. You, I think, belong to the next century."

"I do?"

"She does?" Violet's voice contained a little taint of helplessness.

The carriage eased to the verge in front of our home, and Father cast one more look into my eyes, probing there for evidence to support his theory. "We live on the cusp of a new era, girls: an age of reason and science, and the pursuit of new ideals, no longer steeped in blind tradition. It is women like you, Lizzie, who will give birth to the twentieth century."

"Thank you," I said cautiously. It was a fine statement, but something in the way he said it caused me to suspect, his assessment was not quite the compliment it seemed.

30

I'D HOPED to question my father further, but as the carriage drew up to the front gate, his face paled slightly. His eyes ranged over the front of our house with a sudden ferocity.

"God damn," he whispered between clenched teeth, and before the carriage had pulled to a complete stop, he flew from the seats to the front door.

Violet gave a sharp intake of breath, less theatrical than a gasp. It was genuine, heartfelt, horrified. "Oh, Lizzie! Look!"

The front door hung from its hinges, swinging slightly in the midnight breeze.

John rushed up the steps. I clamored out of the cab, pulling Violet after me, and looked up to the astonished face of the young man in the driver's seat. "Go, fetch the constable!" I demanded, and the driver snapped his reins and set off at a bold clip, down the hill towards Kelly's apartment.

Inside, the house was dark. I left Violet on the front porch and followed in Father's footsteps. I stumbled over papers, books, treasured belongings strewn across the carpets, and I heard his shifting movements as he made a cautious pass through the parlor and kitchen, no longer hissing damnations but silent, wary and watchful.

"Lizzie," he said, seeing my silhouette in the doorway, "Return outside and wait for help."

"He came back," I whispered, "He came back!"

John found two candles in the cupboard and lit them from the embers smoldering in the kitchen stove. He joined me in the front hall and, as he handed one to me, the pinpoint of light cast a circle of illumination over a devastated library, parlor, drawing room and pantry. He surveyed our ruined home with cold disdain, as emotionless as a snake.

"Vile coward," he hissed, "I see nothing missing, only broken —"

"My room!" I cried, I flew up the stairs to the second level. Upstairs, I was met with equal destruction – the bedrooms had been ransacked. Shards of porcelain from smashed pitchers and washing bowls crunched under my boot soles as I dashed into my room: the bedding had been stripped from the mattress and the cupboard thrown open, all its contents tossed aside. I fell to my knees beside my bed and found the tin box, open and in disarray.

My treasures! The bits and pieces of my life! Strange hands had touched them, knocked them aside, violated them, stolen them! My heart stuttered and my breath caught in my dry throat.

But the box was not empty. I rifled through it with shaking fingers. It was all there: the pebbles, ribbons, handkerchief, slips of paper. From my grandfather's letter, to the wizened scrap of mule's skin, to the glass quinine vial: nothing had been taken, only pawed through. Even the money remained, and I quickly counted out the coins.

Not a penny was missing.

From the hall came Father's voice. "Your clothes, your books—"

"It's all here," I said as he paced through my room. "It's a mess, and the thief searched through everything, but it's all here."

He paused at my window and glanced out into the yard. "For what purpose would he—"

Father's question turned into a strangled cry. Before I could ask him what was wrong, he flew down the stairs to the back door. I followed after him, and my candle extinguished as I ran, plunging the house once more into darkness.

We burst onto the back porch. The yard was a mess, with the flowers trampled, the wheelbarrow overturned and the garden tools scattered amongst the apple trees. But when Father noticed his surgery, he let forth a fierce howl of rage and indignation that echoed across the yard and down the hill. Glass from the smashed window glittered in the grass. The heavy door had been left wide open.

Inside, the surgery was destroyed. The medicine cabinet had been ravaged, the files thrown into piles of paper, the vials and jars broken. John stood in the doorway of the little brick building, his fingers of his left hand clenching the frame, his teeth bared. He held up his candle and the flame wavered, casting sinister shadows across the walls.

I drew up behind him and tried to peer around him. "God's teeth!" I exclaimed.

John stalked passed the shattered remains of the medicine cabinet. The acrid smell of herbs and potions, all mingled together in a dark stain across the blue Persian rug, brought tears to the corners of my eyes. "My walrus-hide bag is gone." He ran his hand over the empty square on the desk where he had left the portmanteau. "All my tools, my instruments, all of it."

"Are you sure?" I asked, "Perhaps you left them at your office or—'

"I'm sure," he replied.

A voice echoed from the kitchen door. "Hello?" shouted Alexander Kelly, "Are you out there, sir?"

John closed his eyes, took a deep breath and shook his shoulders as if shrugging off his anger like a cloak. It would be unbecoming to lose his temper, especially in the face of such destruction and insult; a gentleman fought his battles with a cool head, not with his fists or raised voice. "I shall deal with this, Lizzie," he said quietly, "Go back to Violet and ensure she is well. This is no place for a young lady – leave this for the men to solve." He raised the volume of his voice, and his words to Kelly were calm and collected, with just a modest hint of anger. "In the surgery here, Sandy. Do be careful. The intruder has left the place in a deplorable state."

Fury coursed through me – I was angry that a stranger would trespass against us, angry that he would dare steal from a good man like my Father, but most angry that I'd been shut out of any discussions between my father and Kelly. My father was always the first to defend my intelligence and curiosity! How dare he lump me in with Violet, as if I were a simpering example of the weaker sex!

"Good evening, Miss Saunders," said Kelly as I turned on one boot, "Please let your sister know that I'll soon attend to her health." He tipped his hat to me.

But I had no intention of returning to Violet. I raced upstairs to my ruined bedroom and swapped my dress and stockings for a pair of grey trousers and a white shirt. Then, plummeting down the stairs at a full gallop, I snagged my Father's wool cap from the peg in the hall and burst out the front door.

Violet huddled on the front verandah. With hands clasped to her breast and tears dripping off her chin, she looked like a porcelain doll, dropped and cracked. When I stomped out the door, Violet gave a little mewl of confusion.

"What's going on? Who would do such a thing?"

"I'll be back," I growled, pulling the hat onto my head.

"Where are you going?" She grabbed my hand, and her brow furrowed in concern. "Oh, Liz, stay here – we do not know what's happened yet!"

"I have my suspicions."

"What do I tell Father?" she implored.

"Tell him," I replied, wriggling my hand from Violet's fragile grip, "I need to satisfy my curiosity."

I pressed a kiss to my sister's cheek and ran down the road. Nosy neighbors gathered on their porches to wonder why, for the second night in a row, Alexander Kelly had galloped to the Saunders' house on his spirited, pale horse. None of them paid me any attention at all.

31

Though the midnight hour had come and gone, Cumberland's main street roiled with life. The steady chuh-chuh of No. 6 mine's bellows, coupled with the distant clanking of industry, provided a rhythmic beat to the merry-making of the Bank Holiday weekend. Men in filthy dungarees stumbled into the bars for a pint of bitter to slake their thirsts, work-calloused boys drove a new shift of mules along Dunsmuir, and women of questionable morals solicited company from drunken louts who loitered outside the flop houses and pool hall. Boisterous piano music, cat calls, wolf whistles, and the deafening sounds of nihilistic revelry filled the air.

I ran down the hill and reeled into the carnival atmosphere of Dunsmuir Avenue, and finally skidded to a stop outside the Waverley Hotel. The three-story building seethed with people. On the upper balcony, women and men sang songs and draped themselves over each other. Merriment seeped from every open window. Red Dominion flags fluttered from the balconies, and men raised glasses to toast the Queen, the company, their foreign homes, their mothers, their favorite horses, anything that warranted a solid swig from a bottle. The Waverley advertised itself as a temperance house, but on this holiday weekend, the guests seemed blissfully unaware of the definition. Tonight's celebration was in full swing.

Next door, a dull, drunken din came from behind the Bucket of Blood's double doors. Great bellowing cheers rose up at intervals; someone inside was buying rounds and making friends. Outside, two men stood at the edge of the boardwalk, engrossed in inebriated conversation and relieving themselves into the street – I recognized one as Hugh Donaldson, the blacksmith's son. I did not know the other.

"—and that goddamn constable doesn't let gambling in town," Hugh stammered. It was well known that he often took too much liquor, and that his disposition turned from charming to cantankerous with a third glass of whiskey. "And if he catches you rollin' the bones, and me with you? Well, I ain't about to take your side in things, got it?"

"I jus' asked if you wanted to take a wager on what's in Jack's bag," said the other man, shaking himself and fumbling with the buttons of his pants, "I didn't mean to get your pansy-ass in a knot—"

"You wanna make a bet, you go down Chinatown," Hugh continued, "You place your money with the goddamn heathens. Constable's too damn scared of 'em to throw 'em in gaol." The rest of the threat dissolved into slobbering mutters as Hugh turned on his noodle-weak legs and wobbled back into the Bucket. His pants remained undone.

I sidled up to the second man, who had slumped at the side of the boardwalk with his eyes closed. "You said something about Jack?"

"Goddamn pansy ass," he mumbled.

"Sure is," I agreed, "Now come on, man, tell me – what's this about a bag?"

He teetered on the edge of the abyss, and had only the strength to wave his hand in the general direction of the Bucket's door before he passed out.

Without thought or plan, I twisted my hair up and tucked it under my hat, and shouldered open the tavern door.

The Bucket of Blood smelt of rancid perspiration and spit and urine and coal dust, a noxious mixture that easily overpowered the warm waxy scent of the wooden floor. Here were all the perfumes of a night of masculine indulgences, distilled into a cramped chamber, hot and humid with sweaty, work-weary miners. At this late hour, most of the men were bleary-eyed and mellow and, to my benefit, no longer particularly observant of their surroundings. Ale turned their thoughts inward. They hunched over half-empty glasses, spinning loud tales of lost countries and fair maidens. A knot of young men played whist at a far table. A few others leaned against a pool table, but their game had dissolved into a good-natured dispute and drunken posturing. Scattered around the room, men lay propped in their chairs, or leaned heavily against the polished bar, behind which a mustachioed barman cleaned glasses in front of a wall of bottles.

The whole place appeared twice as big, reflected in a huge mirror behind the bar. Three mangy deer heads peered down from above the mirror, and a collection of dusty paintings hung at intervals around the room, giving my eyes a gentle respite from the screaming crimson-papered walls: a German landscape in a heavy gilt frame, a portrait of a melancholy woman, a Highland stag (looking far more robust than his decapitated cousins), and a smattering of photographs portraying sporting lads with balls, bats and bulging muscles. On the tables and the bar, and from sconces on the walls, the coal-oil lamps burned low to save fuel. They cast long shadows.

There, at the corner of the brass and hardwood bar, reflected in the mirror behind the barkeep, leaned a familiar figure in a patched grey coat.

"Another round, gents!" Jack yelled from the other side of the room. A cheer exploded.

A rough hand grabbed my arm and yanked me cruelly to the side, and I was wreathed in the ugly breath of a hulking man, a behemoth with one eye squinted closed and the other rolling, glassy orb studying my features. "Whacha doin' here, boy? Git home to yer mama."

"Let go of me," I snapped, and tried to wrench my shirt out of his palm.

Other bodies rose from their chairs and crowded close, roused out of their sorrow and introspection by this little flurry of activity at the door. Their shadows blocked out the feeble lamplight. The barman shouted, "Let the kid go, Winks – go on home, son."

"T'ain't no place fer you," Winks continued, swaying slightly. He sunk his fingers around my arm. His pupils rolled and dilated, in and out, and suddenly fixed upon my face with sharp recognition.

"Hey! You ain't no—"

A chair descended like a bolt from heaven and smashed itself into toothpicks across the back of Winks' thick neck. His painful grip suddenly vanished as his limp body completed the trajectory of the chair. The felled man dropped like a theatre curtain, revealing the figure of Jack behind him.

A wiry terrier of a man to my left lashed out, and the fist clipped Jack's chin. An arc of blood drops flashed like a string of garnets before splattering across the wall, window and floor. Jack grabbed at his mouth with a snarl and threw his own defensive punch, which landed squarely on the second man's nose. There was a moist crunch. The man wheeled back, clutching his face and howling. I ducked and narrowly avoided a somersaulting bottle aimed for Jack's head. The bottle smashed with an explosion of liquid and glass across the wall.

"Don't kill him!" someone yelled from the far side of the room, "He's payin'!"

But the fight had already begun, and there's no stopping a brawl once it's started. Another young man lunged at him, fists drawn back, ready for the punch.

Jack smeared the blood away from his mouth with the back of his sleeve and grabbed a shattered chair leg from the tangle of sticks under the unconscious Winks. He swung out, precise and calculating. The wood connected with the target's skull, creating a resonant thud and the sharp clatter of teeth. The man crashed to the floor like a marionette with severed strings.

I struggled to keep my footing. The shouts and howls of the fight rose up around me. Men barked orders to their friends and allies as they leapt gleefully into the fray. The crack of smashed wood and the high musical tinkle of broken glass came from all directions. A thick splash of liquid dampened my face, smelling of beer and copper, and a hand closed around my wrist and yanked me out of the melee in the general direction of the door. I was dragged backwards through the turbulent tide of fists and bottles, narrowly missing a punch or two, and it all occurred in a blur, so quickly that I barely had time to react.

Suddenly, the shelf of liquor collapsed. The great crash drowned out the cursing, screaming, raging, bacchanalian circus. A plume of spirits rose like a cloud and an antiseptic smell filled the air. The barman gave a shout of horror as his wares poured across the wooden floor in a tide of rum, whiskey and gin.

I tried to get my feet underneath me but the grip around my wrist tightened, dragged me faster out of the melee, and my shoulder howled.

Suddenly I tripped into the broad silent expanse of the warm summer's evening, out of the chaotic noise of the brawl. The door swung closed after us, cutting off the roar. I found myself swept up in two arms to keep me from tumbling off the boardwalk and onto the street.

"Well, now," said Jack, holding me as close as before, a sneer on his grizzled and blood-speckled face. "I guess this means I'm yer god-damn hero."

32

I WRENCHED free of his embrace and stumbled two steps away, wanting nothing more than to escape the fog of his beer-sour breath. I propped up against the side of the building to pull back the strands of hair from my face and wipe the beer and blood from my cheek with my sleeve. The walls of the Bucket of Blood heaved and churned, barely containing the explosions within. Every time a flying chair knocked the door open, loud bursts of noise leaked out, like spurts of water from a punctured canteen.

Jack stood straight, stretched his spine, and cracked his knuckles. His eyes wandered up and down my figure.

"Now, I'll admit, I don't normally find myself attracted to boys," he said, slapping the dust from his hands on the thighs of his workman's pants, "But I'm willing to make an exception for a dainty specimen like yerself."

I spat at his feet, and couldn't decide if I felt more disgusted or embarrassed.

"Hey, I wasn't the one tailing you!" he pointed out. "You followed me here, not the other way 'round!"

"But you did follow me!" I accused, "And you broke into my house and held a knife to my throat! Who the hell do you think you are?" I pushed away from the building to face him, hands clenched into fists. "What were you doing in my house?" I demanded, but the noise of the brawl had begun to spill into the street. Jack, barely repressing a laugh, grabbed my elbow and to propel me down the hill at a quick pace.

"C'mon, girl, before the fight catches up with us."

I had to run to keep up with his long strides. He dragged me over the tracks, to the mill yard at the edge of the new mine, and there he wheeled me around to plop me unceremoniously on a stack of hewn timber. Deposited thus, like a sack of rags, I watched as he surveyed the empty yard and dark buildings.

At last, scouting no one within earshot, he stood with arms crossed. "Jesus, yer a bit of a firecracker, ain't ya," he said, "Can't say I expected you to follow me!"

I bared my teeth to him.

"What were you doing in our house?" I demanded.

"Maybe I thought it was the wrong place," he replied, "Maybe I was too drunk to tell the difference. All the goddamn buildings look the same in this town."

"You're a liar."

"I'm a hell of a lot worse than a liar, sweetheart," he laughed.

I furrowed my brow and scowled. "Are you going to kill me?"

The arrow-straight question snipped his laughter short. Jack paused, his expression stripped of its bravado: for a heartbeat, he looked like a man who'd lost his footing, then, mustering his gregarious mask again, Jack threw me a lop-sided grin. "Aw, I couldn't murder a little guttersnipe like you, could I! You'd be missed!" He sat down next to me. "Besides, I want to make your acquaintance, like, and I can't bloody well do that if yer dead." He grabbed my hand in one massive paw and shook it. "The name's Jack Hunter."

I wrenched my fingers from his grip. "You're positively enchanting, Mr. Hunter," I sneered.

"So the ladies tell me," he replied, "And you might be?"

"Amaryllis Saunders."

"Well, that is a mouthful!" he laughed, showing square white teeth that flashed in the moonlight. "Pretty high and mighty title for a miner's daughter, ain't it?"

"I'm not a miner's daughter," I informed him. "But you already know that, I'm sure, having broken into our house, TWICE, rummaged through our belongings, and stolen my father's surgical bag!"

The smirk on his face left me feeling sticky, like he gleaned the greatest amusement from my prickly nature and would have been disappointed otherwise. "Well," he continued, "Miss Saunders. Amaryllis. May I call ya 'Amaryllis'?"

"No."

He counted on the fingers of his left hand, skipping over the nub. "Amaryllis, my girl, you've just accused me of breaking, entering, thievery, and threats to murder, all in one breath!" He leaned forward. "Pretty presumptuous of yeh, doncha think? Considering we just met and all?"

"Is it true?"

I expected a denial, and got a proud grin.

"Absolutely!" He laughed. "Now, see here, I'm just bein' enterprisin'! I don't got a lot of resources in this town, and your house is one of the nicer ones on the block, and it happened to be empty tonight. A hungry man'll do all sorts of things to fill his belly." He leaned close, dropped his voice to a conspiratorial whisper. "With you and your fine sister out, and your father following soon after, and no mother to keep the lanterns lit? It was easy pickings." He paused, weighing his words. "Is she dead? Or just run off?"

I drew in sharp breath, as if I'd stepped upon a pin. "What's that got to do with anything?"

"Most time I see yeh, you're dressed in black. Same with yer sister. Either you have a fondness for dark clothing, or yer still in mourning."

"My mother died in February."

"Well, it must be nice to ditch the weeds for a bit, hey?" He appraised me again and plucked at the shoulder of my shirt.

"Where'd you find your get-up? Far as I can tell, you don't got a brother."

"You're an insensitive bastard, you know that?"

"I truly am, both those things," he replied. "If you're mother died last winter, then your father must be the widower, Dr. Saunders."

"How many times do I have to tell you? I'm not a miner's daughter."

"I guess you ain't." He whistled low, and to himself, muttered, "Whaddaya know."

The row had spilled into the street above. We heard the first drifting cries for order and decency.

When he rose to his feet, I expected him to sprint down the hill to the dark, sheltering forests, where vengeful drunkards wouldn't be able to find a man on the run. Instead, Jack took two strides towards the road, back to the Bucket of Blood.

"If all you wanted was food, then why'd you take my father's surgery bag?" I demanded.

His eyes remained locked on the crowd spilling out of the bar. "It's a mighty fine piece of luggage. Good solid walrus-hide; them things don't never wear out."

"I want it back."

"Oh, you do!" he rounded on me, amused, "Well, I'll be sure and hop right to it, miss. I certainly wouldn't want to refuse the wishes of a fine, upstanding and proper lady like yerself." He looked over my beer-soaked and blood-speckled clothing, and laughed.

At the top of the road was a group of men, nursing bruised jaws and limping on battered legs. Two of Kelly's deputies on horseback cantered up the road to keep the peace, but the crowd was docile with drink and fatigue, and the fight fizzled into a bunch of lamely-thrown insults and one or two rude shoves. Men shifted the blame from one to the other. Most of all, they shifted it to Jack Hunter.

I looked between him and the distant crowd.

"You're going to let them catch you?"

"We both know I started the fight. I may as well face my punishment, doncha think?" He laughed. "I'll spend a night in jail, get a free meal and a free bed, and be out by morning. It ain't such a bad arrangement."

"If you don't return the bag," I threatened, "I'll tell the constable everything. And you'll spend more than a night in jail for holding a knife to a little girl's throat!"

He flashed wary eyes to me.

"Where is it?" I pressed.

"Stashed away safe enough, girl."

A voice called out from one of the mounted deputies. "Hey! Are you Hunter? The barkeep says you're responsible for this mess!"

He looked from me to the man on horseback. If he now harbored second thoughts about that free meal and bed, the time to slip away had passed. A rider would easily cut him off before he reached the trees.

"Alright, sweetheart," he began, "As soon as Kelly lets me out, you'll get your bag back. Don't you fret." He began to trudge up the hill, hailing the man on horseback with a raised hand.

"If my father doesn't have it back in his possession by tomorrow night," I demanded, "I'm telling Kelly everything!"

But Jack said nothing else, gave no nod or wave or any indication that he'd heard. With his hands shoved into the deep pockets of his coat, Jack strode towards the hotel, the boarding houses, and the colliery offices, and halfway up the hill, he lifted his head and began to whistle a jovial tune. He met the men as they descended the hill, forming a semi-circle around him.

"Yeah, I'm responsible," I heard him chuckle to them, "God-damn temper got the best of me."

A punch caught him in the stomach. He buckled to one knee, coughing. "Hey, buddy," he said with a pained chuckle, "Didn't I buy you a round or two? This is how you thank me?"

The men hauled him to his feet and dragged him towards the main street, where they could dump him in the Company jail to wait for justice. His boots left furrows in the dust, and he half-stumbled, spitting ropy webs of blood.

33

August 7, 1898

In the morning, when I rose from a bed still surrounded by the jumble of my belongings, I looked out my bedroom window to see Alexander Kelly, angry and determined, circumnavigating the house. He'd brought more men: Rufus at his side, the Moore boys, and Agnes' youngest son, Andy, who was a year or two younger than me and happy to be considered a man suitable for the work. They beat the flower beds back, looking for any clues, and my heart ached to see the bowers of marigolds and daisies flattened under Andy's stringent examination.

I still wore my pants from the night before, so I swapped them for a light cotton dress and descended the stairs to the main floor.

Agnes, on her knees in the kitchen, scrubbed at the floor furiously, thumbing her nose at the perpetrator with the only tools she had: mop, brush and rags. She glanced up and, with a smile, said, "If you're hungry, ye wee imp, there's a bowl of porridge in here, a-waiting for ye."

"Thank you," I replied, taking the bowl from the table.

"Did ye nae wash your face before bed?" Agnes said, "Ye've got a bit of jam or somethin' on your cheek."

I brushed the skin with the back of my hand and found spots of dried blood from the bar.

"I could nae believe it when I arrived this morning!" Agnes continued, bowing again to the floor, "Another great mess, and this one, worse than the first! And the constable, all a-flutter! Can you imagine the beast that would do such a thing to guld God-fearin' folk?"

"Surely, a beast," I agreed.

"And tae think, he's walkin' free amongst the townfolk!" Agnes shook her head. "I wager, all the doors will be locked tonight! I give thanks that I've got seven sons to guard the house, what with my Hamish laid up in bed and of nae guld use to anyone!"

"I see Andy's come to help. That's very kind of him."

"He's a fine lad, that one, and verra concerned for the safety of you girls," she confided. "I have hopes he'll be a man of law one day. The other boys are all working the mines, but if your Father requests it, I'm happy tae spare them tae help find the monster who did this."

The front door banged open. Constable Kelly strode directly into the library. I gathered up my bowl of porridge and followed him, and found Kelly standing opposite Violet, who reclined on the sofa with a slim volume in hand and a light blanket over her feet. He spoke to her gently but his face was grave.

"I do not wish to worry you, Violet, but we've found very little evidence in the yard to point to any suspect," he said, "And, this being the second time your house has been violated, I wish to install a guard at your door."

It was clear to me that this offer went much, much farther than collecting evidence against the trespasser. Kelly needed to make his presence known. With Dr. Briggs attracting Violet's attention, Kelly was a man in need of asserting his territory. Let Dr. Briggs continue with his parties and frivolities and séances -- Kelly was a man of the law, confident and well-prepared to stand between Violet and the harmful forces of the real world.

"Do you think that's necessary?" I said from the threshold.

Violet glanced towards me. "A dress today!" she said, "Will wonders never cease!"

"I'm working in the hospital this afternoon," I explained, then to Kelly, said, "I don't know if we need a man to stand guard over us."

"I'm afraid you do," he replied, "As I have reminded your sister, the perpetrator has trespassed twice, and for a reason which still evades me. Therefore, I shall do all in my power to ensure your security, and with your father's approval, I intend to post a man outside at all times, day and night."

"Goodness," said Violet, "I feel safer already!"

"Yes, but—"

"And you ought to curb your running about, Liz, or you put yourself in jeopardy!" Violet ordered, "I've already assured Sandy that you will stay within doors after sunset, and I shouldn't think you'd want to make a liar of me."

I frowned and said, "Well, you ought not put yourself in such a precarious position, then."

Mr. Kelly laughed, albeit nervously. "I must insist, Lizzie, that you remain safely inside. I'm sure your father will agree," he said, looking over my shoulder to Dr. Saunders, now entering the front door, "Under these circumstances, it is unwise for a young lady to run freely after dark."

I turned and looked imploringly at Father, but he nodded in agreement.

"With so many fine fellows keeping a watchful eye on our home, it behooves me to agree. Sorry, Liz."

"But--!"

"If you were injured, why, all these men would have sacrificed their time and energy for nothing!" said Violet, "Certainly someone means us harm, Liz. Do not be so daft as to think yourself impervious to injury!"

I scowled but said nothing.

"I'll tell Agnes to make lunch enough for everyone," said John as he continued along the hallway to the kitchen. He clapped Sandy on the shoulder as he passed. "Your help in this matter is whole-heartedly appreciated."

"Thank you, sir. Rest assured, even if I were not constable, I would keep your family safe because of your upstanding reputation and station, but it is my duty above all to protect this community, and I shall not fail." he replied, standing a little straighter. "I'll go out to examine the grounds again – Violet, do you feel well enough to accompany me?"

His invitation was eagerly accepted.

It seemed, to me at least, that even Violet understood the purpose behind Kelly's actions. He'd come to protect her, to be her champion, and she blossomed under the attention. They strolled along the edge of the lawn, conversing with heads bowed together as if they were on a leisurely Sunday walk. Instead of examining the ground for further clues, Kelly listened intently to her. He engaged her with stories of his daring exploits, and watched her reaction – to his satisfaction, Violet ooh'd, aah'd, and rewarded his valor with wide-eyed adoration.

"You're intruding, Liz," said Father from his desk in the corner of the parlor, where he busily sorted the papers. "Come and give me a hand. We need to make this place habitable again."

I took one end of the toppled chair and helped him set it back on all four legs. He picked books from the floor, I set the clock and photographs on the mantle. Most of the glass had been cracked, but the pictures were unharmed.

"Very little is broken," I said.

"That's some good fortune, at least," Father replied, setting his hands on his waist and surveying the room. "Your mother's taste in home décor tended to favor the sturdy."

In small paces, the house returned to normal. I fetched the broom to sweep the parlor and entrance hall. Father sat at his desk and recorded in his logbook the medications and tonics that had not been destroyed so that, by process of elimination, he'd have a clear idea of what he'd need to replace.

"I don't understand her," I admitted. "Do you think she honestly likes him?"

Saunders breathed across the ledger page to dry the ink. "She seems to."

"You have no objection?"

"Why would I?" he replied, "If she's fond of Sandy, and he of her, then I'm content."

I set the broom aside and flung myself across the horsehide chair, curling my legs under me and sitting backwards on it to face Father's desk. "Whom do you prefer: Mr. Kelly or Dr. Briggs?"

He cocked one eyebrow towards me. "What does Mason Briggs have to do with Violet?"

Father's expression clearly showed he knew nothing of her infatuations. "Violet is enamored of Dr. Briggs," I said, "Isn't it obvious?"

He gave a little huff of surprise as he sat up straight in his chair. He set his pen aside. "Goodness, not so obvious to me! Your mother was much better as picking up these sorts of things. Interpreting the subtleties of the female heart has never been my strong suit."

"Violet's conscious of her station. She thinks a marriage to Dr. Briggs would return her to polite society in civilized circles." I rested my chin on my hands, folded along the back of the chair. "She would happily marry Briggs to dodge the reputation that our mother has left us."

"Whereas you'll simply punch out the lights of anyone who breathes a word of it," he replied.

"I haven't hit anyone since leaving school," I reminded him, "I think I'm much improved."

"True, true."

"Violet wants to go back to London, and there's no man in this town capable of taking her so far. Kelly has reached the apex of his career, and can't climb any higher, and if she submits to an engagement with him, all she'll win is love."

"I may shake my head at her flurries of emotion, but underneath it all, Violet is a practical girl. She wants the best for her own future. A wealthy man is a simple route to contentment and security, and Violet knows it." He plucked up the pen again. "But there's no need to concern yourself, Lizzie. I'm quite certain Violet will find her efforts to secure Brigg's affection to be utterly useless."

"She will?"

"Absolutely." He scratched a few words in the catalogue. "Mason Briggs is already married."

I felt a great shudder go through the earth, as if the chair had been suddenly pulled backwards, or another explosion had rocked the mines, but I realized by her father's calm countenance that the jar was simply my own reaction to his sentence. "Married!" I gaped, then repeated, "He's married?"

"Lovely young woman, named Emma, last April." John said in small bites, "Already three months with child, he tells me."

My gaze dropped to the carpet.

"Damn," I said, and whistled low. "He ought to have told Violet, don't you think?"

John chuckled. "Mason Briggs is a young, flirtatious man who enjoys the attention of young, flirtatious women. Why would he breath a word to Violet about his marriage? That would deprive him of her charming attention." John returned his full attention to his list. "Mason Briggs is a bit of a cad, but harmless enough."

"Violet will be crushed," I said, "That isn't harmless."

"The heart is easily healed," he said, "Violet will spring back, and double her efforts to secure Mr. Kelly in cupid's clutches. You'll see, Lizzie – when she discovers that Briggs in unavailable, there might be a few tears and a bit of theatrical wailing, but she'll only be more resolved to secure a relationship with Mr. Kelly. Good will come out of it."

I puzzled over this as I glanced again to the window. Through lace curtains, framed by the bowers of roses and magnolias, Kelly and Violet stood arm in arm, speaking softly to each other. Violet clutched his hand. Her drawn face, the translucent pallor of a lily's petal, gave a hint to her temerity.

Would Violet's heart be so easily healed? I wasn't sure.

"I think you overestimate her resilience," I said.

"It isn't resilience, Lizzie; it's fickleness." He looked at me with pity. "Liz, you don't understand, I'm sure, that a key component of any woman's psychology is her fickle heart. Emotion is deep but fleeting for the female sex – Violet will feel deceived, but she'll soon move on, and forget she ever had affection for Dr. Briggs."

"How can you think such a thing?" I said, "Mother wasn't fickle! She may have been irrational at times, but her love for you was constant!"

John turned in his chair to face me. "Your mother was a rare woman, indeed, and I will never find another like her." He shook his head. "God knows, I wish I could have cured her of her ills, but they were too deeply rooted. She burned with her obsessions – you have no idea, Lizzie, how they tormented her." His voice lowered. "It starts as an itch that can not be quelled, and grows into a raging fire, until – oh, poor Molly. I miss her. God was cruel to inflict such trials upon her."

Because it seemed like the right thing to say, I added, "I'm sorry."

"It was impossible for Molly to find relief," he replied, "I did best I could to care for her." He bowed his head to his list again. "And, in her own way, she took good care of me, too."

34

After lunch, with the house returned to order, Dr. Saunders visited his office in the hospital; I followed close behind him. The day promised to be busy. Already, a small queue of patients waited on wooden chairs in the hall, and Dr. Gould was occupied with an emergency appendectomy.

The first patient, a boy who had slashed his hand open with a fish knife, sat patiently as Father stitched him together again. I cleaned the windows with a wad of newspaper splashed with vinegar, then polished the metal gurney in the centre of the room with a soft rag, and all the time, I fumed and seethed and clenched my jaw. It was heartily unfair, that my wings could be so easily clipped by the placement of a man standing watch at our house. In my opinion, a guard was utterly useless. Once the bag was returned to my keeping, I made a promise to myself that I'd no longer bother with the likes of Jack Hunter. He was too much trouble. 'And, considering the extent of the damage done to the Bucket of Blood,' I thought, 'He's bound to be enjoying his free bed for most of the day, if not longer.'

Of course, I couldn't rightly tell Constable Kelly that he already had the trespasser imprisoned, because that would own to the fact that I knew the identity of the guilty party. Still, if Hunter was locked away for one crime or another, it didn't matter to me. As long as he was incarcerated, our house was safe. And once the bag was returned, however he might choose to do so without letting slip his guilt, I was quite sure I'd never see Jack Hunter again.

So, I was more than a little surprised, shocked, and flabbergasted when I looked up from my chores to see Jack Hunter standing in the doorway.

In the harsh and revealing light of day, Hunter was just as large, daunting and scurrilous as he'd been in the middle of the night, but now he stood with shoulders hunched and hat in hand, attempting to present himself kindly. Compared to his previous chair-busting antics, he looked meek and mild-mannered, although it was not easy for him to keep up the facade. He didn't directly look at me -- it must've been difficult to ignore a girl in a black frock standing in the middle of a white tiled room.

He rapped the knuckles of his right hand on the doorframe.

Father looked up from the files on his desk. Seeing the man standing in the hall, he grinned amiably and said, "Good morning, sir."

"Mornin'," Jack said. He glanced quickly at me; did I see him almost smirk? He took a cautious step inside. "I was told you're the doctor on duty today?"

"Yes, yes I am," came the welcoming reply, "How can I help you?'

"I, uh..." He shuffled in, made humble by the clean clinical surroundings. His slate-grey eyes roved over every surface and noticed every gleam of metal – looking for something to steal, no doubt. "I think I busted my hand last night, Doc. I hoped you wouldn't mind takin' a look."

"Come here, then, and sit down," John invited warmly. He set the files aside on top of the travel trunk, and arranged a chair so that Jack could sit with his back to the windows and place his left hand in a patch of sunlight on the desk.

"I'm afraid I ain't a miner, sir," Jack admitted as he sat down and laid his left hand gingerly on the desk. The three fingers were bruised purple and gold. They had swollen into the gap where his ring finger ought to have been. "I haven't paid no dues to the Company, and I ain't got no insurance. But I can pay, whatever you're charging—"

"We do not talk of money in the clinic," came the perfunctory reply. "Now, hold still, and let me assess the damage."

Father took Jack's hand, laid it flat, and noticed when the man winced. "You seem to be missing a digit, sir," he said, studying the dirt-brown fingers, peering close to the ropy scar covering the nub of bone. "Not a bad job of closing up the stump, but a very old wound, indeed."

With Father's face trained downward and all attention on his missing finger, Jack took the liberty of glancing directly at me. I scowled at him as I continued to sweep the floor. "Yes, sir," he answered, "Been quite a few years since I lost it."

"May I ask how?"

"I'm not the sort to fall in with the gentle species of ladies, sir," he replied, "And when I ditched one of 'em, the jealous sort, she decided to make sure I never wore a ring."

"Goodness," Father said.

"I count myself lucky, Doc, that it was just the finger she didn't want me to use."

Father looked up and found Jack to be grinning with the joke of it. "You said you feared you'd broken the rest of your fingers, but not in an altercation with another vengeful lady, I hope."

"No, sir," was the reply. "This time, I was keeping a lady *outta* trouble."

"Good man, good man." John reached to the ground, and paused with hand in mid-air. "Damn." He sat upright, looking sheepish. "I've lost my case, and I'm not used to the empty space on the floor where it ought to be. Lizzie, would you run next door to Dr. Gould's office, and ask the nurse if I can borrow a length of gauze from his kit?"

I did so unwillingly, and hurried back to find Father and Jack chatting. Two more dissimilar men would be difficult to find: on one side of the table sat Father, clean and well-groomed, educated and scholarly, displaying an easy and confident manner as he examined the hand of his patient. On the other side of the table sat a roughshod brute, sweat-stained and dusty, with clothes that had suffered more patches and rips than one could count at a glance. His manners were awkward, strained, almost embarrassed. He might be accustomed to bars and brothels and gambling dens, but a centre of learning and medicine was not a place of comfort for him. Yet still, across the wide gulf of their lifestyles, these two men had discovered common ground to talk amiably. They appeared to get along with the ease and familiarity of school chums.

I found it unnerving.

"Here, Father," I interrupted, handing the roll of bandage to him.

Jack washed his hands in a bowl of water and gingerly dried his injured fingers, and as I dumped the bowl of grey water out the window, Father proceeded to examine the tendons and ligaments, taking note whenever Jack winced. Finally, Father bowed his head and began to wrap the gauze around Jack's hand, ensuring the bones were straight and unbroken with his fingertips as he worked.

Over Father's bowed shoulder, Jack stared at me, one corner of his mouth kinked upwards in a nefarious, wicked grin. The expression shifted effortlessly into the pleasant smile of a grateful patient as Father sat upright. "There you are, all bandaged," John said, "I can find no break in the bone, and I suspect you merely bruised the tendons with your chivalrous act. Give it a few days of rest, keep it clean, and it should be as good as new."

"Well, as good as it was," Jack corrected. "Unless yer claiming that a few days of rest'll help the finger grow back."

John laughed. "No, I'm afraid that's quite beyond my repertoire."

"Well, I woulda paid whatever ya asked, if it was within yer power," Jack replied, reaching into his pocket with his good hand. "So what's the bill, squire?"

But John shook his head. "No, no, it's quite alright. There's no need." He reclined in his chair. "It's been a busy day of tedious cases, but you've been good enough to break up the boredom with your tales of derring-do. No payment required."

"Are ya certain?"

"Use your hard-earned cash to rent yourself a room, have a good meal and a bath, and keep away from the fights. That will be payment enough for me."

"Very kind of ya, Doctor..."

"Saunders." Father held out his right hand. "John Saunders."

Jack took the hand and shook it firmly. "Mighty charitable, sir. The name's Jack Hunter."

"Good to meet you," said John, and he turned and held out one hand, "This is my daughter, Amaryllis. She helps me with the office."

I took the offered hand and matched the strength of the grip, and stared Jack in the eye. He gave me a clipped nod and mustered up his good manners, frayed and much patched but still there, hidden under the unshaven jaw and ragged hair. "Pleasure, miss," said Jack, "Must be nice, to have such a learned father to show you the ropes."

"It is, Mr. Hunter," I glowered, "Although until his medical bag is returned, I'm afraid my education has been hamstrung. It's difficult to be shown the ropes, as you put it, when the ropes have all been stolen."

"So it must be," he replied. "Well, good day to ya both, then. And thank you muchly, Dr. Saunders. I hope, next time we meet, it won't be under such nasty circumstances."

'THE NERVE!" I thought as I completed my chores. The unabashed, gutsy, deplorable, horrific nerve of the man! The mere thought of Father and Jack, chatting breezily and affably, left a sour taste in my mouth.

I decided that I ought to tell Father of my experience with Mr. Hunter, but I glanced over to the gurney where he examined the knee of Mr. Cage, a mule driver and part-time dog breeder. Mr. Cage had been thrown from a horse but, while the joint was certainly bruised, it didn't look bad enough to match his theatrical moans.

"Good Lord Almighty!" he groaned as Father massaged the kneepan and bent the limb. "Oh, mercy! Oh, sweet Jesus!"

"Deep breath, Clifford," Father encouraged, "It's not so bad."

"I promised the missus I'd bring her home a good pony," he

panted as beads of sweat appeared on his brow. "And Jimmy Ciprioni promised me there weren't nothing wrong with the animal—"

"And you already said it was spooked by a cat, Clifford," Father continued patiently. "Any horse can go funny in the head, if it's been spooked. Lizzie, can you fetch me some fresh linen?"

Mr. Cage continued. "I promised… I promised her…"

"There's nothing wrong with the horse; I'm certain you can give it to her with a clear conscious." Father rocked back in his chair and smiled. "A couple of days of ice and heat, and this knee will be mended."

"But…"

"Sell the horse, or take it back to Jimmy, or give it to her as you intended. But I'm sure this was an accident, Clifford, and not a breach of faith."

'A breach of faith.' The words rang in my ears as I left my father's office to fetch a length of fabric from the supply room.

Explaining to my father that I'd misled him from the beginning, that I'd seen the face of the intruder and followed him to the Bucket of Blood, that I'd presented Mr. Hunter with an ultimatum rather than put my faith in Mr. Kelly's justice – well, it rather smacked of collusion, at least in my mind.

'Besides,' I decided, 'I've given Hunter until tonight. It seems like a rum deal, to go back on my word. That would be something he might do, but not me.'

35

We locked up his office at four and left the hospital. "After such a poor night, it was a good day," said Father as we crossed the gardens. "I am terribly exhausted. You?"

"Yes, sir," I replied, "A little."

"Just a little?" He laughed. "Good Lord, my girl, you were up half the night, and woke early this morning to clean the house, and if I didn't know better, I'd say this whole event has barely left you with a cause for concern!"

"I know I don't look fretful, but —"

"Don't look fretful?" He laughed again. "Lizzie, your ability to understate the obvious is remarkable! If I didn't know better myself, I'd say you had not a care in the world! Most other girls your age would be utterly terrified, but you are untouched by worry."

"Not untouched," I corrected, "But honestly, what will fretting and worry accomplish?"

"How very pragmatic," he said as we mounted the steps to the front door. Agnes had propped it open with a brick to capture any drafts of cool air that might happen by. At the end of the porch, resting in one of the three wicker chairs, sat Rufus McGregor.

"Good day, Mr. McGregor," said Father as we reached the top step. "How does this afternoon find you?"

"All quiet, sir, and praise be for that."

"And Mr. Kelly? Is he here?"

"He's making a circuit of town," McGregor said. "He'll take up my post at midnight, and he hopes he might catch a snippet of news if he visits the pubs and the boarding houses."

"Well, do come in and join us for a meal," he offered. "If I'm not mistaken, I smell roast chicken coming from the kitchen, and I'm sure Agnes has made more than enough for all."

"Kind of you to offer," said McGregor, "But if you don't mind, my place is out here. I want whomever is watching to know that your house is under guard."

"Suit yourself, but I won't look unfavorably upon you if you join us, Rufus. A man's got to eat to keep up his strength for his duties!"

McGregor smiled his misshapen grin and began to speak when something behind us caught his eye. His grin vanished, his brows knit together in concern.

I turned.

Shaozhu stood at the gate. In one hand, he held Dr. Saunders' portmanteau.

"Good Lord, boy!" said Father, descending the stairs two at a time, "My case!"

Violet appeared at the door, and sidled next to me.

"Do you think he stole it?" she whispered.

"No!" I said in horror.

Oblivious to our whispering, Shao held out the bag. "I've been asked to return this, sir," he said, chin tipped down.

"Thank you!" Father exclaimed. A brilliant smile blazed across his face; he laughed out loud. "Where did you find it?"

"A man tried to sell it in Chinatown, and my uncle recognized it at once as yours. You are a valued customer, Dr. Saunders, and have brought this with you enough times to our shop."

Father held out both hands and took the walrus-hide bag from Shaozhu, who threw a fleeting glance over his shoulder to me. I smiled, and Shao could not hide a smile in reply, but quickly returned his attention to the doctor.

"I hope it's all in good order?" said Rufus, drawing close to John and seeing the case in his hands.

"Rufus, you know Chen Shaozhu already?" Father introduced absently as he peered through the belongings, finding nothing amiss. His fingers touched the instrument cases, the ophthalmoscope, and the pearl handles of the scalpels. He pulled out one and fondled it between his fingers, looking greatly relieved.

"Aye, I've seen you 'round town."

Shao pressed his palms together and gave a curt, polite bow in return.

"It looks to be here, all in good order," said Father, "Who did you say attempted to sell it?"

"I don't know, sir," Shao replied, "I never saw the man. But my wise uncle knew that you would be eager for its safe and quick return."

"And I am!" Father said, jubilant, "I'll fetch you a reward for your haste and your bother."

"There is no need, sir," Shao said, but Father would accept no refusal, and clasping his hand around the boy's arm, urged Shao onto the porch to take a seat. As Father whisked the bag inside, Violet stepped briskly out of his way. She looked peeved when I sat in the chair next to Shao.

"Hi," I said quietly.

"Hello," he replied, just as quick.

Rufus withdrew a small notebook from his pocket and, moistening the tip of a pencil on his tongue, leaned against the porch railing. "Now, Mr. Chen, if you don't mind answering a few questions..."

"I don't know what I can add," Shao said with a shrug, "Someone entered our shop this afternoon, just after the train from No. 4 passed town. The man offered the bag to my uncle. You might wish to speak with him -- my uncle will be better able to give a description than me, though his English is poor."

"I'll do just that," Rufus replied, curt. "I know my job, boy."

Shao lowered his gaze. "My gracious apologies, sir, I do not wish to presume."

"Did you hear his voice? Did you see anything?"

"No, sir. I was down by the old mine site, collecting bits of coal to use in our stove." He held out his hands to show the black smudges on his fingers. "As soon as I came home, my uncle told me to hurry here and return this promptly."

Rufus scribbled a few notes before hailing a spry boy who was running along the roadway. The burly man crouched down on stiff knees, and I heard him ask if the boy knew which man was Constable Kelly.

"Thank you for returning it, Shao," I said. "That's very kind of you."

"When I heard it was your house that had been ransacked, I wanted to make sure you were okay."

"I'm perfectly fine, thanks."

"You don't seem surprised to see me," he said, then added, "Or, rather, you don't seem surprised to see the bag."

Violet's voice stabbed in between our whispers. "You know each other?"

We both looked up to Violet. She studied us blackly.

"When I run errands to Chinatown, I go to the apothecary owned by Shao's uncle," I said.

Violet looked as if she'd sucked on an under-ripe plum. "It is very kind of you to think of my little sister's well-being," she directed to Shao, speaking slowly and clearly and a little loudly so that the foreigner could understand every word, "It is hardly necessary, of course. Mr. Kelly has all under control."

I felt a flush of annoyance rise across my cheeks, and was relieved to see Violet turn her attention indoors, and retreat to the cool interior of the house, leaving us alone on the porch.

"She's terrible," I muttered to Shao.

If he was angered by Violet's dismissal, he was aware, too, that time here was short, and other concerns nibbled at his mind. Shao rested his elbows on his knees and lowered his voice. "She's no worse than most, and better than some. Lizzie," he said, barely louder than a whisper so that the men in the garden would not detect the smallest word on the breeze, "I warned you: stay away from Jack Hunter."

"You know it was —?"

"Of course I do," he hissed, "He came in this afternoon with his hand all bandaged up, and gave this to me to return. Plus, he gave me a coin to pay for my troubles and asked that I not tell you anything more." His face was taut with worry. "Lizzie, he knows your habits. He knew to come to our apothecary, and no other." Shao looked darkly at me, and a thrill of foreboding skittered up from my gut. "Aren't you the slightest bit afraid?"

"I think I am," I said, unable to repress a smile. My heart pattered in my chest; it was a beautiful sensation. "Shao, I ordered him to return the bag, but I didn't think he would comply," I marveled. "At least, not so quickly!"

"You *ordered* him?"

"Last night, after we discovered the house was trespassed, I followed Jack to the Bucket of Blood, and I demanded that he—"

Shao grabbed my arm tightly. "You confronted him?!? Lizzie, you can't!"

"I was following things to their logical conclusion," I replied. I didn't shrug off his grip, as I would have for someone else – his concern for me blazed through the contact points of his fingers, and my heart beat a little faster at the feel of his skin.

"He's dangerous!"

"He's flesh and blood, like any man, and he has reasons and motivations." I leaned forward, "Can he be said to be following me, if I'm already following him?"

Shao took a breath to argue further, then thought better of it. His brown eyes flashed towards the roadway; into the boy's palm, Rufus had pressed a folded note and a coin. Shao looked at me with earnest. "I can't let you put yourself in peril, even if you're too daft to realize it."

I furrowed my brow in confusion, then raised my chin.

"And how do you intend to do to stop me?"

A light step on the threshold caught their attention and, as Father stepped outside, Shao released his grip on my arm to drop his hand to his lap.

Father held a small envelope in his hand. His face showed a shrouded grin of cautious bemusement, having stepped into a scene to which he was not welcome. Still, he retained his polite dignity and drew no attention to the closeness of our chairs.

"Here you go, Mr. Chen," he said, "For your troubles. I can not express how much it means to have that bag back in my keeping."

Shao stood and took the envelope, and gave a polite bow. "Thank you," he replied, and turned to me, bowing again. "Good day, Miss Saunders."

I stood, clasped my hands to my chest and returned the bow. "Zai jian, Mr. Chen," I said, studying his face for any hint of his intention.

He stepped down from the verandah and walked directly towards Rufus. My heart stuttered as his course became clear. He was going to tell on me, I just knew it. He was going to clip my wings the best way possible: hand Jack to the authorities and reveal me to be a fluff-headed, meddlesome, little girl.

But instead, Shao kept walking, only giving Rufus a nod in passing.

My breath left my lungs in a huff.

"A pleasant fellow," said Father.

"He's been a good friend," I replied, confused. He'd been enough of a good friend that I could read his concern, and I knew that a good friend such as Shao would endeavor to tell Kelly everything if it meant keeping me out of harm's way.

"I have no objections to whom you keep as friends, but do be careful, Liz." He crossed his arms. "They're very different from you."

I reeled on him. Seeing insult in my expression, Father disarmed me with a cool laugh.

"Oh, I don't mean the Chinese, Liz. I mean, men. I haven't yet determined if you take after me or your mother, but either way, friendship is a difficult ship for you to sail."

"Explain, sir," I demanded.

He laughed and held out one hand to me, and together we sat on the porch. "Your mother was consumed by her desires and directed them poorly. I'm far more rational and analytical, and given to seeking love in cold ways. Molly and I are two ends of a spectrum. Violet seems to have landed somewhere in the middle. I haven't figured which way your personality leans, but I know you are nothing like Violet, so you're bound to take strongly after your mother, or strongly after me. And either way, love will not come easily to you."

"You don't mind my friendship with Shao?"

He shook his head. "No. Why would I?"

"I just assumed you would. It isn't proper."

"You've been very clear, ever since Westbury, that you don't care much for propriety. I blame your grandfather, taking you on tomboy foolish rambles through the hills." He reclined in the chair and folded his hands behind his head, and surveyed the flattened flower beds at the edges of the yard. "You view the world differently, and given that you're the offspring of Molly and me, how can I fault you? We haven't exactly raised you to be conventional."

"Then perhaps I take after mother. She was far more unconventional than you."

"No," he said, "I'm beginning to think you're more like me." He smiled. "It was, at your age, that I began to understand my place in this world. I see in you a reflection of myself, Liz. You're much more observant about the world than most girls your age, and you notice things that others don't. It is a very handy skill. It can keep you out of all sorts of scrapes and trouble."

I pondered this for a moment. "You checked your medical bag for its contents, and seemed most relieved to find your scalpels."

Father's eyebrows arched. "My, you are observant, indeed." The chair squeaked as he leaned forward. "You have a biscuit tin upstairs, into which you put all sorts of detritus."

I sat up straight. "You know about it?"

"I do. And I know it's sacred to you, and I would never trespass there." He smiled to reassure me. "If I were to have a box of treasures, my scalpels would hold a place of honor."

"Why?"

"Well," he began slowly, "My father gave me these tools – they were his. And I hope to pass them along to you, when your training is complete. When I look at them, I remember my father and all that he taught me, and I am relieved to have them back in my keeping."

"I think you're right," I replied. "I do take after you."

He grinned, and in a loving gesture, scrubbed his palm over my crown. "I hope so, my girl. I dearly hope so."

36

As Father reclined, I glanced to the street and saw that Shao had disappeared around the corner. This did not bode well. I stood and, hesitating a moment, said, "I promise to be back for dinner."

Father looked bemused but asked no further questions. Instead, he waved his hand in the direction of Shao's departure. "Go on, catch up with Mr. Chen," he urged good-naturedly. "Where you get your boundless energy, girl, I'll never know!"

I flew from the house at a run but Shao was already far ahead. By the time I'd reached Dunsmuir Avenue, he was striding up the stairs to the boardwalk in front of the constabulary. The shaggy pale mare was tethered to the post: a clear indication that the constable was inside. I was about to call Shao's name, to stop him and convince him to keep my secret, when the door to the office opened.

Alexander Kelly greeted Shao with a look of puzzlement.

I skidded to a stop on the other side of the street. They chatted briefly, and before I could interrupt, Mr. Kelly held out one hand and invited Shao inside. Both looked gravely concerned.

The door swung closed after them.

"Damn," I muttered.

I sat down on the dusty boardwalk directly across the street from Kelly's building, crossed my arms, and waited for Shao to emerge.

And waited.

And waited.

The bells of the church rang out to call the Roman Catholics to evening mass; the hour must've been close to five. A couple of hansom cabs rattled passed, and a crowd of people in finery obscured my view. The constabulary door disappeared and appeared again between the shifting forest of horse legs, cart wheels and cotton dresses, but I paid no attention to the moving sea of people. Instead, I kept my eyes riveted on the still and silent door, like a cat at a mouse hole.

It was only when a body thumped down next to me, hanging its mud-spackled trouser legs over the side of the boardwalk, that I broke my gaze.

"Whatcha doing, girl?" said Jack.

"Waiting for my friend," I replied tartly.

"The constable's a friend of yours, is he?"

"No," I said, then, "Well, yes, but it's not him I wait for." I threw an acidic glance at Jack. "I was most certain that Mr. Kelly would have kept you in jail, rather than let you free."

"Well, now," said Jack, plucking at the bandages around his left fingers, "I was injured, and I told him I ought to see a doctor, elsewise I might end up with a lame hand. He figured, since all I'd done was start a ruckus, that ain't no good reason to keep a man from getting the proper medical attention."

"How kind of Mr. Kelly."

"Yes, ma'am, it was."

"And how is the hand?" I asked coldly.

"Fine and dandy, thanks for inquirin'." He flexed the fingers. "Yer father seems like the sort who can work miracles."

"My father is a man of science, sir. If it's miracles your looking for, you'll find a full selection of denominations along Penrith Street."

"I'm not much of a religious man," he admitted.

"Frankly, I'm not surprised."

"And what about you, kid? I thought for sure your family, all prim and upstanding-like, would have their own goddamn pew reserved at the front."

"I'm sorry to disappoint you, Mr. Hunter," I replied, "But my father rarely attends church, now that my mother is dead."

"Let me guess: he lost his lovely wife, and with her, he lost his faith in God."

For the first time, I turned from my vigil and stared openly at him, appraised the square face and the hanks of brown-blonde hair hanging from under the slouch hat. He wasn't smirking, he wasn't joking. His grimy face appeared earnest and open.

"My father has never had faith in God. My mother made him go, and when she died—" I frowned, caught myself. I sat upright to make myself taller, more imposing, even though I was still a head shorter than him and my eyes only reached his shoulder. "What do you care, Mr. Hunter?"

Jack shrugged. "Most London doctors I ever met were godless heathens, drunk on their own god-damn power. I wondered if yer pa was cut from the same cloth, religiously speakin'."

"London doctors? Oh, I'm sure you've met a few," I sneered. "I imagine you're well-versed in the physicians' circles. By God," I whispered, my eyes widening, "You might even be a fellow of the Royal College! How silly of me, not to notice!"

"Well, I suppose yer right," he replied, "It seems a fella of my calibre would be speakin' out of turn, wouldn't it."

I sighed. "I apologize, Mr. Hunter. That was rude of me. You were kind enough to return my father's medical bag, and I ought not belittle you because you're poor."

One side of his mouth kinked in a grin. "Poor?"

"I suppose a man in your situation must stoop to steal, to put food in his belly. No man is evil, but good men do evil things when the situation warrants it."

"No man is evil?" He laughed. "Now who would put such a crazy notion in your head, girl?"

I lifted my chin. "My mother." Then, shifting uncomfortably, I withdrew from the friendly, if superficial and sarcastic, camaraderie that had developed between us. I returned my gaze to the door. "I don't think you're evil, but Shao is not so certain of your alignment, and is in the constabulary at this very minute, telling Mr. Kelly that you stole my father's medical bag."

"Damn, is he?" Jack didn't seem alarmed, only surprised. "I thought that Chinaman had a good head on his shoulders."

"Shao does have a good head on his shoulders," I replied, "He's concerned for my safety, and is quite certain that you will kill me, if you aren't stopped by the law." I couldn't suppress a warm smile at the thought of Shao's protection. "He puts his own reputation on the line for me. If you say anything to prove him wrong, or if I deny what I told him in confidence, they'll punish him mercilessly for lying." I looked back at Jack. "So I won't deny it, if they ask. Which means, Mr. Hunter, that Mr. Kelly will be looking for you when he comes out that door, fully armed with the knowledge that you threatened to kill me, and when he asks me if it is true, I shall heartily agree." I folded my hands on my lap and swung my legs over the boardwalk. "I suggest you ought to run."

Jack pursed his lips, furrowed his brow. "You think so, hey?"

"I do."

"Mighty chivalrous of you, Amaryllis, giving me a head start and all." Then he guffawed, so loudly that it bounced off the storefronts and echoed down the street. The people loitering outside the Waverly looked up at his mirth. A cat scurried from under the boardwalk, further down by the livery.

"You'd laugh at my charity?"

He pushed himself off the boardwalk and stood in the street, and took off his cap to run his hand through his mess of hair. "The thing is, Amaryllis, I didn't come all this way to sit and chat with you on the side of the street. I saw ya here, and thought I'd give ya my regards, seeing as how it's Sunday and you're a fine lady and all, but you ain't my purpose." He tipped his chin to me. "I came this way to meet Mr. Kelly, and have a little chat with him myself, man to man."

Across the street, the door to the constabulary opened. Kelly and

Shao stepped into the doorstep, talking with animated gestures, both men wearing somber expressions. In one hand, Kelly carried his rifle, but this didn't deter Hunter at all.

"So if you'll be so kind as to excuse me," Hunter continued, tipping his hat, "I'll be on my way to turn myself in, like the law-abiding citizen I am." He reeled around and took two steps into the street.

Then he paused. Hunter turned back to me.

"It's Sunday, girl, which means you ought to go home and study yer bible." He grinned, and said, "I'd suggest John 8:44."

I leaned forward, sure that I'd misheard. "What?"

But Hunter was already striding across the ruts, maneuvering his way nimbly around humps of manure and divots torn out of the dirt by oxen hooves. He slapped the pale mare's rump in a friendly greeting as he passed, then hopped onto the other side of the boardwalk. Without care or concern, Jack blithely strode straight towards Alexander Kelly.

Shao fell back a step as his jaw dropped in surprise. Kelly immediately raised his gun to his shoulder, but Hunter held up his hands to show that he was unarmed and hailed both men with a merry "Good evening, gents!" And when he and Kelly retired into the building, leaving Shao outside, Hunter made sure to cast a crafty sneer in my direction.

SHAO OFFERED to walk me home, but the route we took was circuitous, rambling and slow, so that when I finally reached the end of my tale -- from following Jack to the Bucket of Blood to his visit to Father's office to our amicable chat on the boardwalk before surrendering himself to Kelly -- we had traveled no farther than the apple trees at the edge of my yard. The sun hung a hand span above the western horizon, lazing about the glassy blue sky and reluctant to set.

Even under the shade of the trees, the penetrating heat of the August sun rose up from the baked earth, suffusing everything with a sticky heat. A bucket under the water pump held the drips and drabbles that leaked from the pipe. I splashed a handful of water over my face to scrub the sweat and dust from my brow.

"What does he mean, John 8:44?" Shao asked.

"I don't know," I replied, shaking the water from my hands, "But Mr. Hunter doesn't strike me as the kind of man who studies the scripture."

"Maybe he has the whole thing memorized, so he knows the exact passages to ignore," Shao replied, leaning his back against the wall of the surgery.

"My mother's bible is in the library – come inside, and I'll fetch it."

"I'll stay out here, thanks."

I squinted at him, wrinkling my nose. "Don't be ridiculous; it's cooler inside."

"I ought to stay out here," he reminded me.

An awkward silence descended over us. Shao spoke first.

"I don't want to get you in trouble, Lizzie. Your father is a kind man, but even he knows some things are improper." Through the kitchen window, Agnes hurried back and forth, preparing dinner, and Shao dipped his head in her direction. "I can assure you, your housekeeper won't abide it."

"Agnes needs to keep her nose out of my business," I snarled.

Shao shrugged. "Maybe, but I shouldn't be here at all. If I go inside, your neighbors will see."

"Oh, sod it," I huffed, "Well, at least sit on the back porch." I grabbed his hand. "The neighbors can't accuse you of anything indecent if you're in full view."

Reluctant, he let me drag him to the top step, and at my insisting, sat down. I dashed down the hall, into the library, and returned almost instantly with a thick, leather-bound tome carried under one bony arm. I plopped it down on the porch with a solid thump, summoning up a faint miasma of white dust from between the boards, and flipped open the covers to reveal pages so thin and fragile that they were translucent.

"Gospel of John," I muttered to myself, expertly flopping a chunk of pages open and running my index finger down the columns of words.

"Ah, it's you out here, is it, miss?"

Both Shao and I looked up to see Rufus McGregor's lumpy, lopsided face appear around the corner of the house. His body strolled into view after it.

"Yes, sir," I replied.

He grinned, a frightful expression that showed too many teeth on the left, and not quite enough on the right. "If you should need any help," And he looked pointedly at Shao, "You be sure to let me know."

"I will, Mr. McGregor, I will," I replied, and held up the book, "But there's nothing to fear here – we're only studying the Good Book."

"Ah! Carry on, then, carry on." He smiled again, this time at Shao, before continuing on his rounds, peering behind the surgery and circumnavigating the privy with its decorative bed of smashed marigolds.

"Ah, here we are," I said, once Rufus was out of sight, "John 8:44."

"And?"

I couldn't suppress an incredulous laugh as I read the passage aloud.

"Ye are of your father the devil, and the lusts of your father ye will do."

I thumped the book closed, crossing my arms over my knees, and gazed towards the hazy blue mountains.

"What the hell does that mean, do you think?"

"I think it's pretty obvious," I replied.

Shao looked at me for an explanation.

"Now that Jack has met my father face-to-face," I said, "It's only polite to introduce me to his own."

37

Day slowly lost to the relentless, languid advance of night. By the time Agnes served supper, the stars had appeared, but no one complained; the day had been far too hot for an early meal and only after the sun began to set did anyone feel much like eating. Besides, Mrs. Gunn had spent the whole afternoon cleaning the house, tidying the rooms and picking up broken pottery, instead of caring for her own family as she often did on Sundays. Dr. Saunders gave her leave to go home as soon as she wished, but she insisted on making dinner for us, too. "I must be making sure ye chicks are nourished," she said to me as I helped her in the kitchen, "All skin and bones on yeh, ye wee little boggin! My own boys are hearty enough to look after themselves, an' if I take an extra night to make sure you're well-fed, too, nae a one will miss me."

"But what about Mr. Gunn?" I asked as I chopped the string beans into little bite-sized pieces.

"Oh, he ocht tae be fine wi'oot me," Agnes waffled, "He's a wee bit cranky, with his leg a bittock sore, an' he limps about the house, snarling at all that moves." Her cheeks drew up into rosy apples. She took the chopping board and dumped the beans into a broad pan of boiling water. "Let him chastise the cat for the nicht. I'm needed here, more than there."

Agnes had prepared a fine dinner, indeed: fresh vegetables from the garden, pan-fried chicken, and gravy so thick that it flowed as slow as treacle on the plate. Conversation was relaxed and easy -- we were all exhausted from a very long day, and no one felt much like talking. The only thing to mark the dinner as odd was the constant presence of Rufus McGregor on the front porch, sitting and smoking his pipe. Though Father offered once more for him to join us at the table, McGregor steadfastly refused every invitation to leave his post.

"A cool bath and bed for me," said Violet, "That's all I'm looking forward to!"

"I barely slept last night," I said around a mouthful of chicken, "Tonight, I doubt I'll feel my head hit the pillow."

Violet glanced to the front door. "I shall sleep better, knowing Mr. McGregor's there, but I don't think I'll sleep well."

"I'm sure we're all quite safe," Father assured, "Your Mr. Kelly has been very kind to us."

"He has, hasn't he," Violet replied, looking smug. "I believe his affection for me has ensured our safety from whatever monster lurks in the night."

I tried very hard to blanche the sigh from my voice. "Yes, Violet, this is all your doing."

"Well, there is a certain security in having a man of law and justice at your side," agreed Father as he set his knife and fork upon the side of his empty plate. He might have said more, but we heard Rufus hail someone from the porch. Father trained his ear towards the open door. "Speak of the devil!" he said, standing, "I believe that may be our good constable now!"

"Bit early to take over Mr. McGregor's post, isn't he?" I said, looking at the clock on the mantle. The hour read 10:13pm.

But Father had already gone to the front door.

Alexander Kelly stood there, dressed in full uniform. Rufus McGregor was leaving by the front gate, shaking his head slightly: he had been promptly and fully relieved from his duty. Kelly watched him go, looking undecided. He had dismissed Rufus, and now stood alone on the porch. Every jitter spoke of his nervousness, but he was too sharp and too professional, too well-trimmed and well-heeled to change his course of action.

"Good evening, sir," Father greeted. He held out his hand and shook Kelly's palm warmly. "Please, join us! We're just about to begin our pudding, and I'm sure there is more than enough to share – Agnes, another plate, please?"

"Thank you, sir, thank you very much," said Kelly, taking the empty seat at the opposite end of the table, "Good evening, Lizzie, Violet."

"Good evening," Violet replied, "How are you tonight?"

Kelly hesitated. "Oh, quite well," he replied, but his mouth was downcast and his eyes wide. I noticed miniscule beads of perspiration on his neck, which caught the lamplight and glittered like a sheen of gold dust on his skin. He gave Violet no second look.

"Have you sent Rufus home?" said Father, looking perplexed.

Kelly nodded briskly. "I need to speak with you on a grave matter, John. And," He glanced at Violet, "Privately."

"What's wrong?" Father said, his brows drawing together, his fingers tenting over his plate as he leaned forward in his seat.

But Kelly pulled at his collar, and gave Agnes an absent thank-you as she set a china bowl before him, piled high with blackberries, cream and cake. "I fear it is not for the ears of young ladies, sir."

"Is there a great hurry?" John asked, "I dare not take a pudding away from Lizzie – she is quite territorial about such things, and bound to feel greatly wronged if dinner is cut short." He threw a teasing grin to me as I crammed a spoonful of plump berries into my mouth. "Allow us to finish our supper before you and I retire to the library to discuss this grave matter."

Kelly considered this request, and at last, said, "I do believe it can wait a few minutes more."

But Violet leaned forward with eyes glittering. Here was a bit of gossip to tempt her, and she would worry it from the bone if required. "What is it, Sandy? You look greatly vexed! Is it news of the intruder?" She laid her hand on him. "Do you know who the burglar is?"

"I must insist that I speak with your father first," Kelly said, but his eyes snapped magnetically to me. It took him a visible effort to tear them away, and he didn't know where to aim them, so he stared at his pudding. His skin greyed.

Father's mirth dropped away. "Is it something to do with Lizzie?"

"Not specifically, sir," said Kelly, but the answer was too vague, too ephemeral, for John's comfort. It was not an emphatic 'No'.

Violet rounded on me. "What have you done now?"

"Nothing!" I said. "I swear!"

But Kelly must know all about Jack, now, along with my hesitance to put faith in the law. I searched Kelly's face for a hint of why he'd come: what had Jack told him? Had the man openly admitted to holding a knife to my throat? I gulped. Did this make me a willing accomplice to the theft and ransack of my own home? Could I be arrested for causing an obstruction of justice?

Father took the linen napkin from his throat and set it aside. "We'll discuss this now. Immediately. Girls, do feel free to continue with your dinner, and I expect you to help Mrs. Gunn with the dishes afterwards. How long will this take, Kelly?"

"I really don't know," he stammered.

"Ought Lizzie to come with us?" said Father as he stood, "If this matter concerns her?"

"No, this isn't for a lady's ears," Kelly repeated, and as he stood, I now saw that he trembled. He pushed his fingertips against the tabletop to keep his hands from shaking. Sweat trickled from under the cuffs of his sleeves. "I must insist, sir, that you and I clear this matter up between us."

Father scowled. "Come, then. Let's have it." Grabbing two glasses and the decanter of brandy from the sideboard, he escorted Kelly into the library, and closed the door behind them.

38

Both Violet and I, under the guise of assisting Agnes with the dishes, devoured our dessert and hurried into the kitchen, but instead of washing the china and cutlery, we left the woman at the sink to press our cupped hands and ears to the door that separated the library from and kitchen. At a casual glance, it looked as if Violet was attempting to squeeze herself through the cracks in the wood. "What are they saying?" she whispered, "What?"

"I'm sure I don't know," I said, "But if you could stop asking for a moment, I might be able to hear them!"

The conversation in the library remained a muted hum of masculine voices, barely audible through the thick door. The clink of glass to glass as John portioned out the brandy was louder than their words.

"If Mother had been in there, she would have been shrill enough to hear, clear as a bell," Violet complained.

"Oh, do shut-up!" I insisted, then said, "Did Father just say 'horrific'?"

Violet pressed her ear closer. Her eyes circulated thoughtfully to the left. "I think he said 'terrific'," she replied.

The tense and restrained cadence of their sentences could be interpreted in many ways, none of which were particularly positive.

"It doesn't sound as if their conversation is terrific."

"What do you think they're speaking of?" said Violet.

I closed my eyes to concentrate, but heard nothing distinct.

Then, I considered my next words very carefully -- I hadn't wanted to bring up my own part in this falderal, least of all to Violet, but this seemed increasingly unavoidable. "I think," I began slowly, cautiously, "I think I may know."

Prying her ear from the door, Violet said, "What?"

"This afternoon, when I followed Mr. Kelly back to his office," I whispered, swallowing, "I saw the constable catch the man who broke into our house."

"Really!" Violet stood upright. "Why didn't you say something earlier? God's teeth, Lizzie, that's wonderful news!" And she pressed her cheek to the door again, eyes gently shut, like lovers conspiring. "Maybe Father did say 'terrific'!"

Agnes levered herself away from the sink, and pulled up from the hot water a pair of pudgy bare arms, fiery red and swathed in a lace of soap bubbles. "Git awa from the door, lassies," she shooed with great disapproval, "Leave the men tae their discussion! 'Tis nae a fitting habit for lassies of your station, twittering and eavesdropping like a couple of shameless scullery maids!"

"Who was the man?" said Violet, looking at me just long enough to frame the question.

"One of the vagrants," I replied, "I know on good authority that he's been caught. I saw it with my own two eyes. I wager he'll be spending more than just tonight in jail."

For someone who so loudly scorned eavesdropping, Agnes had remarkably sharp ears. "Well, that IS a spot of bonny news!" she clucked, sloshing her hands in the sink again, searching for the last spoon to be scrubbed, "I haed been afraid that the roustabout who trespassed against such guld, God-fearing men was wandering free! Well, ship him tae Nanaimo, I say, and let the guld judge have at him!"

A deep, cutting laugh stabbed out of the dull din of conversation. Violet's eyebrows arched.

"Oh, that do not sound exactly celebratory," she whispered.

"Justice, the law, the apprehension of cruel men – oh, it's nae fit business for lassies," Agnes continued, frothing herself into a self-righteous boil. "And long have I been worried about your salvation, both in body and in spirit, but I ocht tae think that a guld and moral man like our dear constable would be equally disturbed by these dark goings-on! Maybe e'en more so! I hiv me only the heart of a mother beating in my chest, but he has the whole town tae shepherd, and I shuld think any fracture of the law wuld burn in his belly, and cause him physical pain!" She withdrew her hands from the water and dried them on her apron. "The shame of failure does nae sit well on the shoulders of moral men!"

Violet rose her chin and glanced over her shoulder to Agnes. "What are you getting at?"

"He's come tae tell your father aboot the capture, I ken, but there're other reasons, too, for think: ye hae been imperiled by forces unknown, trespassing against the sanctity of your home!" She jabbed one thick finger in Violet's direction. "Aye, I wager he's come to ask your hand, using the prowess of the capture tae prove himself tae your father!"

"This is no time for a marriage proposal," I said.

But Agnes clucked in her throat as she took a small shovel from the coal scuttle and threw a few small stones behind the stove's grate. She waited until the flames licked around their edges before shutting the iron hatch. "He's come tae save ye, Violet. All men are the same. Now, come away from the door, girls, and let all work itself oot in the fullness of time," Agnes cooed, and tossed a dishcloth to each of us. "Dry the pots and pans, and do me a good turn. The sooner the kitchen is clean, the sooner I can go awa home tae tend tae me own lads."

The front door slammed. Both girls turned sharply. Violet drew her hands over her mouth to cover her surprise as Father appeared in the doorway between front hall and kitchen. He scowled and deep lines etched his face. His gaze, which blazed like the coals in the grate, pierced Violet. She fell back a step at the force of its intensity.

"What has he said to you?"

Violet, affronted by the sharpness of such an interrogation when she had clearly expected matrimony, braced her slippered feet. "Said to me?" she repeated, affronted. "He's said nothing to me!"

Father took the bold statement as an affirmation that something, indeed, had passed between them. "Whatever he's told you," he said in a low, measured tone, "It's not true."

Violet stuttered. "I'm sorry?"

"He is mistaken," Father claimed. He paced across the kitchen, chewing on his lower lip in thought, greatly agitated. "Mr. Kelly has been sadly misinformed."

We three women traded looked of confusion.

"Sir, if you don't mind," said Agnes delicately, "Can I make you a cuppa tea?"

He nodded briskly, stroking his chin with his fingers, thinking. His expression smoldered.

"Mr. Kelly has come into misinformation concerning your mother, and I do not yet know by what channel it has reached him, for he would not say. But it reflects poorly upon my character, and he came to ask if the stories were true."

"Your character, in question!" Agnes blustered, setting a kettle of water onto the hot stove. "Good Lord, sir! You're a fine man, upstanding in the community, and kind to all! I ken I've been harsh in the past, and warned ye of the rumors that fly about the city, but I can nae imagine why Mr. Kelly, of all people, would put stock in vicious gossip!"

"Nor I, Agnes," he replied.

"What gossip?" I asked.

"Nasty things, foul things," he spat, "Rumors which dogged us for a horribly long time. I thought we had managed to slip its chains upon arriving on Vancouver Island. God damn!" The exclamation burst from his white-edged lips, the frustration echoed through the room. John pressed his palm to his brow.

"But these rumors," said Violet, "They aren't true?"

"Not a lick of it," he said, "But I can't ignore that these idle stories have had power in the past to tear apart our lives, and they may again. It's the reason why we left London, girls, and why we left Wiltshire. Both your mother and I thought that, with the entire British Empire between ourselves and England, we might reclaim a spot of peace. I thank God your mother is dead and buried, now that it has caught up to us again. If she'd been alive, this would have certainly destroyed her."

I sat at the kitchen table and folded my hands. "I know these stories aren't true, you've said as much. But what lies could have such impact?"

Father took a seat across from me as Agnes brought a pot of tea and set it between us on the table. "It concerns a woman your mother knew in London." The bile rose in his words, and he struggled to add, "A woman named Hannah Pibbs."

At this, Violet sat next to me. Her face turned pale with worry. "Our maid?"

He bowed his head. "It pains me to repeat the terrible libel spread by those who endeavored to destroy me. But, the facts are these: your mother was a lonely woman, living in a house of servants with two young girls, and she struck up an unnatural friendship with the maid. Hannah was of an age with your mother. And your mother was never one to hold to social customs! So it fell to pass that the two of them became confidents, although their friendship did not sit well with the other servants."

"I can imagine not!" Violet huffed.

"Molly gave Hannah liberties that a mistress ought not to give. She allowed Hannah to abandon her uniform, which the cook and the kitchen girl resented, and she even went so far as to give a dress or two from her own wardrobe to Hannah. A lovely mauve one, in particular, was her favorite. Can you imagine? A maid dressed in purple? Your mother was the laughing stock of her circle." He glanced at Agnes. "A housekeeper may wear her own austere clothes in the colonies, such is not frowned upon, but in England, house staff is expected to keep proper dress! And with the other women in their blacks and whites, and this merry little parakeet garbed in aubergine silk! It was ridiculous!"

I could feel the warmth of shame radiating from Violet.

"Which, I imagine, caused your friends and acquaintances great discomfort."

"It did, Liz. Fewer and fewer called on your mother for social visits. And your mother made no effort to leave her card at other doors, and finally, no one came by anymore. She'd been lonely before, but she became a pariah."

"Surely Mother must have seen what her actions wrought—"

"Of course she did, Violet, but did she care?" His voice cracked with frustration. "Molly had found friendship elsewhere and needed no one else. She and Hannah were thick as thieves, the two of them!

"We were seen as fools; my practice began to suffer. So I evicted Hannah from our house, with much protestations from your mother. It was for the best!"

"Of course it was, sir," Agnes cooed, "I dinna ken what else ye could do!"

"I don't see how this reflects badly on your character," Violet said, "You did what a husband should do, when his wife fails in her duties to manage a house."

His expression grew distant. For many minutes, he pondered his next words, knowing that the worse was yet to come.

"We decided to start again with a fresh retinue," he began, his voice quiet, "I dismissed all the staff. We didn't even have a butler to open the door. I felt it was for the best: your mother, grief-stricken, needed no reminding of her failure. We would rebuild our household. I began to advertise for new help, beginning with a cook, but I had sorely misjudged the characters of the three women I had fired. And I learned, all too well, to never underestimate the strength of the lowest class."

"They did nae speak poorly of ye, did they?" Agnes whispered, clutching her hands to her bosom.

"They did. They spread falsehoods far and wide, told everyone with a willing ear about Molly Saunders and her curious notions, labeled me to be a poor father and a charlatan. The worse of the three was Hannah herself, for she believed Molly to have been a false friend, and she told ugly, ugly tales. Too ugly for me to divulge; the mere though turns my stomach!"

"How dreadful!" Violet consoled, "That a woman whom you'd hired, whom you trusted with the duties of your family, would so abuse your trust and household! Appalling!"

His face contorted. "If only others felt as you do, Violet!" He swallowed; the memory cause him obvious pain. "Hannah's brother, a Spitalfields butcher by the name of George Pibbs, took up her case and pled for her to be reinstated, but of course I refused! Nor would I agree to give her a good reference – I could not, in good faith, recommend her for any decent house! Her nature had been revealed to us: a foul harpy, a mean-spirited shrew, worthy of no good person's trust."

"But surely the gossip of a few coarse drunkards could nae carry so much weight against you, sir!" Agnes exclaimed. "The lowest class from the slums – who would believe them?"

"One would think their lies would fall on deaf ears," he replied. "But they were eager to take vengeance upon me. The tales began to spin out of control. Any death that happened under my care transformed into shameful failures -- no longer were they the limitations of one man trying to save another. They became exhibits of my complacency, incompetence, and ineptitude. It seemed as though every patient I took became another test, another trial to be passed, and if my care faltered, it was seen in the public eye as evidence of my neglect. Your mother faltered under the strain of it. Her weakness of mind only compounded the problem. Here was concrete proof that I was a quack, for I could not even save the one I loved the most."

His voice cracked with anguish.

"Now, not only was I disgraced, but I was married to a mad woman. Hannah Pibbs and her cronies, too numerous to count, saw fuel to feed the fires in which my hard-earned career was burning. Their gossip spread upwards, through the maid-of-all-work to the gentleman's butler, to the upper classes, until it didn't matter to whom I was recommended: they'd heard the claims of my inability, and none were willing to risk my care. At last, I was dismissed from the gentleman's club, which was more of a blow to our lives than I care to admit -- a public declaration to all that I was ostracized by my peers. We no longer had a social circle or the support of friends and colleagues. Your inconsolable mother, overcome by guilt for her role in the whole charade, locked herself away from the world. We were financially, socially and psychologically bereft."

Violet held her head in her hands and watched Father with moist eyes. "That's when we moved to Wiltshire?"

"Your grandmother was generous to take us in," he said quietly, "It has pained me, all these years, that Molly brought such shame to her parents' household. I tried to be a country doctor, but the gossip followed. Your grandfather, Captain Worthington, was good enough to enlist the help of his friends, and Mr. Diggle made our connection to Mr. Dunsmuir, who was in such need of medical staff for his company that he cared little for my resume. He needed no recommendations other than Diggle's, and he was willing to take my credentials as they stood, issued by the Royal College, and untainted with the scandal that dogged us. To him, I am forever grateful." As Agnes set a cup of tea before him, he said, "We severed all ties with England, vowing never to look back at the dark hell that the country had become to us, and start afresh here."

"How does Mr. Kelly know of this?" said Violet.

My gut clenched, then flipped over on itself, and tied itself into a tight knot. How, indeed? What might have opened this Pandora's box? Perhaps a letter, waiting in my own Pandora's box, upstairs?

"I don't know, he would not divulge his connection," John replied. "I have told him it is all lies, all of it. He believes me, and has promised to do his best to silence such rumors as he has heard."

"And it is a wee tale, easily squashed," said Agnes. "Your dear Molly is safe in the grave from the sting of her own reputation, and you can nae be blamed for your wife's poor judgment." Agnes' eyes drifted to me. "Do ye see what wickedness comes of a woman's curious behavior? Take this tae heart, girl."

"I think you ought to have told us this before," Violet said, "And it might have spared Lizzie from her own bad habits." She laid her hand supportively on his arm. "Mother's death, the house ransacked, and now this! It is too much!"

Agnes returned to the sink and began putting away the dishes. "You've been nae but a good doctor here, and helped all, and for all I've said in the past to ye, sir, I dinna ken your character is in question. These lies will find no guld soil to root here."

"Thank you, Agnes," he said.

He looked terribly tired, I thought. Slouched over the table, his collar undone and sweat on his brow, he looked as wrung out as an old rag.

"Do you think Captain Worthington might have told him?" I said. My guts churned. I clenched my hands as a tide of guilt rose in me. "Do you think he might have written a letter to the constable?"

John considered this. "I don't know why, after so long, he'd bother," he said at last, laying his own palm supportively on Violet's hand. "We're dead to him, and with luck, forgotten." He shook his head. "No, I promised him -- I swore on my love for your mother -- that I would never return to England, nor contact anyone from our sad life there, nor do anything to reflect badly upon him. I gave him my word, he would never hear from us again! There is simply no reason whatsoever for him to contact us, or Kelly, or anyone!"

"Father," I started, softly and slowly, "Please don't be mad..."

He rose his eyes to meet mine. A tension crossed the muscles of his face, and his body stiffened. "Amaryllis," he warned, "What do you know of Mr. Kelly's assertions?"

I felt a moment's stab of panic, like an ice pick dipping into the hot meat of my heart. I clenched my teeth and stomped it down, pushed it into the dark cellar of my soul, until the panic was nothing but a distant ache in my belly. If this was my doing, I would own to it.

"I wrote to our grandfather," I said.

Father's hand struck forward and seized my wrist. Both Violet and Agnes shrieked.

"What?!?!" He yanked me close. His voice hissed. "When? When did you do this, Amaryllis? WHEN?"

As his grip jerked me forward and his fingertips buried into my flesh, I saw the way in which his face contorted. He was normally such a reserved man. Only a moment ago, he'd been too exhausted and worn to look any of us in the eye, yet my solitary sentence had shocked him into life, sent a bolt of action ricocheting through him. If he had, indeed, seemed to me like a wrung-out rag, it was a rag infused with coal oil. With the tiny spark of my words, it burst into violent flame.

I ignored the pain and surprise, and regarded him steadily. "February."

"I told you – I BEGGED you – to leave well enough alone!"

The cords of his neck bulged, his teeth flashed. The fingers of his hand bit into my wrist. Livid purple bruises appeared on the surface of my skin, but I remained impassionate. I watched him clinically and heard the low grinding of his teeth between his clenched jaw. Violet and Agnes clung to one another, terrified by his temper, but I remained unmoved. Maybe my calm nature calmed him -- he slowly, carefully, unfurled his fingers from my wrist. They left deep impressions in my skin.

"I apologize," I said as I massaged my wrist.

"You don't know what you've done," he threatened.

Violet wrung her small hands. She dropped her voice to a modest whisper, and returned to her seat next to me, wrapping her arms around me. "I'm sure it will all blow away," she cooed, although I needed no comforting, "I'm sure Lizzie didn't mean any harm, Father. It's all been a dreadful mistake."

John studied me, and I gazed back at him with equal strength. My heart pulsed steady and even. Even the distant ache of my guilt was gone.

"You could stare down a train, my girl," he said, "If ever I doubted, I know you are my child."

"I did what I did because I thought it was right," I replied. Then, almost absently, I added, "You've hurt my wrist, I think."

Agnes grabbed a dishtowel, dampened it with cool water from the bucket by the door, and knelt at my side. The limb was already a patchwork quilt of contusions, yellow and purple and gold. She wrapped the dishtowel around it, watching my face for any sign of pain, finding only a blank slate. "I think Violet's the only one of ye that feels any pain by this," she said quietly, and turned to John. "Shame on ye, sir, for harming a wee girl!"

"If you dismiss her as a 'wee girl', you're a fool," John said. He returned his attention to me. "You did what you thought was right, Lizzie, but that does not negate the problems that will come of it – your grandfather has suffered a change of conscience, and now fears that I will ruin his good name without your mother to keep me in line." He dropped his head into his hands, and his shoulders shook as he whispered to himself, "Oh, Molly, you would have known what to do."

"Sandy will remain prudent," Violet replied, "I can convince him. He'll swear on his love for me, he will not sully your reputation." She stood. "I'll ask him to return the letter to me, and we can destroy it, and all be done with this."

I looked to my sister's hopeful face, and thought of the little packages dutifully delivered to Mr. Kelly's doorstep. 'And if Violet's pledges of love fail,' I thought, 'There are other secrets that Mr. Kelly keeps, which will work just as well.'

But John sat upright and shook his head. "No. You will stay as far from him as you can, Violet, if only for a few days. You will say nothing more to Kelly. I will sort this out. Understand?"

She looked as if he'd struck her instead of me. "But why?"

"Trust me, I will take care of this. Go home, Mrs. Gunn, and tend to your own family. All of this will be sorted out in due course. As for you, Lizzie," He glared at me. "You've already done enough harm. Leave well enough alone."

39

FATHER THREW on his light tweed coat and rushed from the door, and Agnes left soon after, once she had provided us with tea and cookies. She pressed a kiss to our crowns. "Be strong, gurls," she encouraged as she shuffled out into the night, "This will all come tae naught, I'm sure."

Once they were gone, Violet paced back and forth across the library, wringing her hands and fretting with enough animation to fuel both of us together. "We must talk about this! I'll explode if we don't!" she hissed, traversing the library floor for the fifth or sixth time.

I chose to remain inert. It was a better place to be. Look at Violet, an utter whirlwind of unfocused emotion, blustering around the room with one hand tracing her course on the bookshelves, her breath rising in stuttered huffs and her heart practically hammering out of her shivering body. I placed one palm on my own chest and felt the calm, easy, familiar rhythm. I wondered if I could resurrect that delicious gallop that Jack's fear had instilled in me, but I was hesitant to turn on the switch again, open up the door to the cellar. I made a conscious decision to not feel, not now. If I opened myself up to feeling emotions, who knows what would burst out?

"How can you be so bloody CALM!" Violet said.

I glanced sidelong at Violet.

"Fretting won't solve anything," I said.

"But how can you not fret about THIS!" Violet raved. Tendrils of her blonde hair escaped from her braid and wisped around her head. Standing in front of the lamp, illuminated from behind, they billowed like golden clouds at sunset. "This is OVERWHELMING!"

"How can you live with so much feeling coursing through you?" I asked. "You're all twittering and brooding and—"

"God damn it, Lizzie!" Violet shrieked. "Don't you even feel the slightest smattering of guilt? You did this!"

Violet began to cry. I recognized her sobbing as an outlet for her rage rather than an expression of sorrow, and I warmed to her, seeing how much she hurt.

"I'm sorry that I've upset you," I began, "It wasn't my intention. I only thought Grandfather would want to know that his daughter was dead; it seemed proper. I was only trying to be good."

"Mason Briggs won't look at me twice now!" she wailed.

"That would be best," I said, "Because Mason Briggs is already married."

The sentence arrested the sobs bubbling from Violet's throat. She jerked to a sudden stop, open-mouthed. Her lips framed the question but had no breath to propel the word forward. "What?"

"I meant to tell you," I said, "But Father says Dr. Briggs married last winter, to a girl named Emma, and —"

Violet's shriek tore through the still air. I imagined flocks of ravens in the surrounding hills startled from their perches by the scream, rising like a black tempest of flapping wings. The lantern glass shivered in its stand, the fronds of the potted ferns rustled, the barometric pressure in the room fell. Violet howled and pitched and wailed in a growling, growing revolution of sound, round and round, louder and louder, increasing in shrillness and volume with every exhalation, until I clapped my hands over my ears and cowered into the crook of the couch. Feral cats in the garden ran for their lives. Angels in the highest nooks of Heaven likely did the same.

Violet only stopped when her lungs were completely empty. The great rattling inhalation to refill them took ages. Her lips darkened, or perhaps the edges whitened.

She fell upon me with brandished fists, and attempted to pummel me into a paste, grunting with the exertion of every wild blow. I rose my arms to cover my face and submitted to the thrashing. Violet had as much strength as a sparrow, and the shock of being attacked by her held far more impact than any of her jabbing, ill-aimed limbs. After a few limp punches to my shoulders and chin, Violet collapsed at the end of the couch like an empty puppet, heaving for breath against the bindings of her dress.

"I'm a fool!" she wheezed. Tears leaked out of her eyes, the air leaked out of her lungs. "Oh, I'm a fool! A fool!"

I rolled onto my shoulder to face the morose lump of flesh which had once been my proud sister. "No, you aren't."

"But I am!" she wailed, "How Sandy must hate me! He's been so good to me, and I've held him at arm's length, waiting for something better." Violet's hitching gasps dissolved into hitching sobs.

"He hasn't abandoned his courting of you," I said. "Sandy still shows great favor to you – he still loves you, even if you've been a silly duck. Look," I clamored for an example. "When he came to the house after we'd been robbed, he came for you. He didn't want to speak in front of you tonight because he didn't want to embarrass you." I enfolded Violet's hand in my own. "He really does love you, Violet! He really does!"

But Violet raised her eyes to the ceiling. The tears that crossed her cheeks reflected in the lamplight.

"He'll never wish to marry me, now," she wailed, "I'll have to take your money and flee this place, and build a life of my own as a solitary maid, and I'll die alone. No man will ever want me, especially a man of law, when our family has such a shameful shadow hanging over us!"

I grinned. "Never fear, Violet. There are ways to make all things happen." I leaned forward and whispered, "Mr. Kelly has a shadow of his own."

Violet perked up. "He does?"

"He's addicted to opium, Vi."

Her blue eyes, which had darkened to indigo in the low light, opened wide. "God's teeth!" she hissed, and with a few minor adjustments, her expression of despair became revulsion. "This is a poor joke, Lizzie!"

"It's not a joke, Vi. He takes a little with his tea, every now and again, and he's the sort of man that feels the sting of guilt for the smallest indiscretion." I scowled. "Just a minute ago, you were horrified that Mr. Kelly would look down upon you, and now you look as if I've presented you with a cockroach."

"But I thought Sandy was a good man—"

"Stuff and nonsense, Vi!" I interrupted. "Mr. Kelly is as good a man as one can hope for! So he partakes of opium to calm his mind, in small doses and on rare occasions; wouldn't you, if you were faced day after day with the rigors of fights, drunken imbeciles, domestic disputes, explosions, death, and all the rest? In case you haven't noticed, Vi, this town was built on the cusp of Hell's gate, and there are times when Mr. Kelly is the only man standing between order and chaos!"

Violet's revulsion melted into stunned bewilderment. "You think so?"

"I do!" I replied. "I have nothing but high regard for Mr. Kelly's character."

"I love him," Violet said, and there was a genuine quality to the statement that I'd never heard there before. Violet produced a crisp linen hanky from one of the folds of her black dress and wiped the tracks of moisture from her face. "Do you think he'd still marry me? God only knows what Grandfather told him in the letter."

"If you tell him you know he chases the dragon, and that you'll proclaim his addiction publicly if he dares repeat the letter's contents to anyone, he's sure to do whatever you wish!"

"Oh, Lizzie! That's despicable!'

"But it would work."

Violet considered it. She slumped down in the crook of the couch and smoothed the black skirts of her crinoline. "I suppose it would."

"It's only a little bit of evil, in pursuit of the good."

Violet set her jaw and pound one fist against her knee. "Then I'll go now," she determined. "I'll confront Sandy with his own addiction and tell him we must both, together, keep our secrets from the world."

But I held up my hand. "Wait until tomorrow."

"Why?"

"I fear that the revelation of Mr. Kelly's addiction will have dire effects on more than just the constable. Give me one night, Violet, to smooth the way for you and Mr. Kelly to speak about his habits."

"I think you've done quite enough to bring this situation about," Violet said sternly, "If you hadn't written that letter to Grandfather—"

"For that, I apologize, but humor me, Vi." I grabbed my boots and my coat. "Mr. Kelly will know I told you, and I don't want his anger to reach any farther than me."

"Who are you protecting?" Then her eyes widened. "Oh, Liz! You haven't been entangled in – oh!" She stood. "You can't think to go into Chinatown at this hour!"

"I've been before, later than this." I tugged on my coat. "I'm not afraid."

Violet looked exasperated. "You don't fear anything, Liz, and one of these days, it's bound to get you in serious trouble!"

"Wait until the morning before you speak with Mr. Kelly," I repeated, and pressed a kiss to Violet's cheek. "Don't go anywhere. I promise, Violet, I won't be long."

"I do love you, Lizzie," she said, smiling through the sniffles and tears. "I love you so very much." Then she gave me a little shove on my shoulder, and said, "Go on, do what you must. I'll see you when you return."

40

THE STREETS of Chinatown were dark and empty. I fetched a pebble from the gutter and, with a sharp snap of my wrist, tossed it against the window directly above the apothecary door.

A face peered out and muttered something in a language I didn't understand.

"Chen Shaozhu!" I whispered, "Chen Shaozhu!"

Men's voices, angry and fuzzy with sleep, grumbled from behind the curtains. I heard Shao's voice and, soon after, his face popped out of the window. The light was too low to see his expression clearly, but his body jerked with surprise. Instantly, he disappeared inside, only to rematerialize a moment later from the apothecary door.

"What the hell are you doing here!" he hissed in a half-whisper, seizing my elbow. "You can't be here!"

I found myself boldly pushed along the alleyway. When I glanced up, I saw round, shadowy faces at every window.

"I need to talk to you—"

"You can't just show up here in the middle of the night good lord Liz you'll get us both in horrible trouble!" The whole sentence was delivered in a rush of breath. We hurried along Shan Gai toward the train tracks. "You can't be here after dark! Don't you realize what they'll do to us—"

I wrenched my arm free. "Shut-up and listen to me," I said. "I told Violet about Mr. Kelly's opium addiction."

"What!"

"I had to," I began.

He jabbed his finger down the length of Shan Gai, to the train tracks and the little cabins of Camp.

"You are leaving Chinatown right now, before anyone sees us together," he demanded, "And if my uncle finds out you've told your sister about Kelly, ai ye! I don't even want to think what he'll do to us!"

"But I needed—"

"No, Liz! Out!" Shao seized my arm again, to start walking.

But his hand clenched my wrist, directly over the pattern of bruises, and I cried out so sharply that he dropped my arm as if I were on fire. I hugged my arm to my chest, wincing.

"What did I do?" he asked, bewildered.

I choked back the pain, set my teeth, and tried to form a reasonable explanation.

But Shao didn't wait for an answer. Instead, he took my hand gingerly in his own and peeled back the sleeve. Underneath, the pale skin revealed a mottled mess of black and blue.

"Ai, Lizzie!" he gasped, "What happened?"

"I had a... disagreement with my father."

Shao looked at me with questioning pity. Then, softly, he said, "Come back with me, we need to treat this right away."

I followed him silently to the apothecary and sat on a stool at the counter as he lit the candles from a coal in the brazier. Then he put the kettle on to boil, and pulled a glass jar from the shelves.

"Tell me what happened," he urged as he worked, scooping a spoonful of paste into a mortar. "Your father is a good man; he'd never hurt a soul."

I took a deep breath and spoke quietly. "My family was chased from London by rumors of my mother's madness, and now, the sordid details of my father's ruin have followed us here." I rolled back my sleeve as Shao poured a bit of warmed water into the mortar, then a dash of oil from a flask, and began to grind the ingredients into a fragrant paste. "He's terrified that these lies will dog us out of town and destroy him. I suspect that my grandfather, spurred by my letter, has written to Mr. Kelly and told him that my father is here without good references, and my mother was utterly insane. So, to keep him quiet," I said with a sigh, "I told Violet that Mr. Kelly has a secret of his own."

"You'd blackmail the constable?"

"I'm desperate to right the wrong I've done," I replied. "But I fear I'm only going to make everything worse."

With gentle fingers, Shao began to smooth the paste over my skin. His touch traced long, graceful lines over the narrowest point of my wrist, then circled around the hollow of my palm with motions that were patient and elegant. As he worked, the friction of his skin released the perfume of dried flowers and sweet oils. The bruise sang under his ministration, but the poultice was warm, too, and caused my skin to tingle.

"Other people have made their own choices, Liz. They've acted of their own accord," he said, "You can't take the blame for what your father or mother did years ago, nor can you blame yourself for Mr. Kelly's weaknesses."

"But I may have hurt you, too," I said. My throat constricted. "If Mr. Kelly's opium habit becomes public knowledge—"

"I'll be fine."

He sounded so certain, but I didn't share his confidence. "If this becomes public knowledge, Mr. Kelly won't keep your name a secret; he'll be the first to reveal his sources. You and your uncle will be arrested for smuggling."

But Shao shook his head. "I pay my dues to the Guan Yu tong. My benevolent society will help me, if I need it." He lowered his head to his work, feeling the delicate bones under the contusions. "The opium trade goes much deeper than jiu fu and me, and there are people in both communities, yours and mine, who would rather not disrupt the flow of trade." When he glanced up, his eyes were calm. "Coal isn't the only commodity that fuels the economy here, and Mr. Kelly isn't the only one in town with a habit."

"Still," I said, "I'm sorry."

"For what it's worth, I forgive you, though jiu fu won't be pleased to lose a valuable customer." He took a rag from the shelf and wiped his hands clean. Examining my wrist from a distance, he whistled low. "Honestly, Liz, I wouldn't have thought your father capable of such brutality."

"He was angry and quick," I said. "This caught him by surprise, and he's never been fond of surprises."

"Keep it wrapped in cool cloths, and elevated, and--" He smiled at himself. "Of course, you know this."

"But I don't know this!" I replied, holding the wrist to my nose. The poultice appeared glossy and sleek in the candlelight. "What did you smear on my skin? It smells like... like... is that honey?"

"A little. It's called *di da jiu*, fall wine. Not fall, as in "autumn", but fall, as in "tumbled down the stairs". I've had to change the recipe a bit – we don't have all the traditional ingredients here -- but it still works to heal bruised tendons and muscles."

"You made it yourself?"

He nodded as he wrapped a clean rag around my wrist.

"Thank you." Then I remembered my manners, and said, "*Xie xie.*"

He leaned his elbows on the counter and chuckled. "Any time. *Bu yong xie.*"

"Shao!"

We both leapt to our feet. Mr. Tao stood in the doorway to the rear of the building, his face black with rage. He jabbed his finger in my direction, and when he spoke, I couldn't pluck individual words from his sentence: to my ears, he spouted a great gushing flood of angry sounds from behind clenched teeth.

"I don't mean to intrude," I said to him, then turned to Shao again, and said, "I'm sorry. I'll go. And... and thank you."

I gave Mr. Tao a respectful bow and backed out of the apothecary, and returned home at a run.

THE HOUSE WAS dark and silent.

I entered through the front door. A thick stillness filled in the air. No lamps were lit, and the rooms smelt stagnant and abandoned.

I went upstairs and looked into Violet's room, expecting to find her asleep. The bed was empty.

"Vi?" I called, but only my voice echoed back.

I shouldn't have left Violet alone. My sister had been a bundle of nerves, excitable and flustered. 'Of course Violet would leave,' I thought, 'She could barely sit still!'

I looked out my window to the back yard. A dim lamp illuminated the surgery, causing a hazy amber glow to emanate from the window, and I recognized the shape of my father as he paced the narrow floor of the building. Every motion spoke of anger. The door had drifted open a mere crack, releasing a hair's breadth of light and casting a thin line of gold over the garden, but as I watched, his hand appeared from within. He seized the handle, slammed it firmly shut.

I wondered if I should disturb him and let him know that Violet had run out to find Mr. Kelly.

But no, I decided, that wouldn't be fair. Hadn't I crept away to meet with Shao? Give Violet and Mr. Kelly an evening to sort out the problems between them. By morning, cooler heads would prevail.

I watched the closed surgery door for a long, long time but saw no more movement from within. Father had locked himself away from the world and taken sanctuary in his private den. Eventually, I went into Violet's room, closed the door and crawled in to my sister's bed. 'As soon as Vi returns,' I thought, 'She'll wake me and tell me her news, and all will be well in the morning.'

And feeling secure, I relinquished myself to a dreamless sleep.

41

August 8, 1898

But in the morning, when I woke, Violet had not returned. Her nightgown still hung in the closet, the door was still closed. Everything in the room remained as I had left it.

I heard the sound of sobbing in the kitchen, and descended the stairs on bare feet to find Agnes crying, hunched over the table.

"Mrs. Gunn?"

The woman looked up, her eyes swollen. "Oh, me wee bairn!" She sprung to her feet and enveloped me in a suffocating embrace.

I shrugged free of Agnes. "I was asleep, in Violet's bedroom—"

"Yer dear sister is missing!" Agnes cried, "Do ye ken where she's gone?"

"No, I don't," I said, shaking my head. "I last saw her in the library, around eleven or so."

"Yer father says she snuck out in the wee hours and disappeared, and he's gone to find her," Agnes cried, "And you, a-sleeping through it all! I dinna ken what to do!"

"We'll have a cup of tea, and sit together and wait," I said, confused by this turn of events. "And I'm sure Violet will be back in no time at all. Perhaps she's gone to speak with Mr. Kelly, and give her own perspective on last night's conversation."

"I dear hope you're right!" Agnes wept, dabbing at her eyes with the sleeve of her brown smock.

But when Father returned, mid-morning, he was furious. "Gone," he said, "I've been looking for her for hours, but I can't find a sign of her." He collapsed at the table, his head hung low. He wore his sleeves primly buttoned, but his collar was loosened and his armpits were stained with sweat, and he dragged in a tired breath. "I haven't felt such exhaustion in years! When I was a younger man, I'd be at the hospital for days on end, but now?" He gave a bark of a laugh. "I'm too old to be running about all day and night after wayward daughters! I've lost my stamina. Draw a bath for me, Agnes, I need sleep before I can keep going." He looked to me. "When did you see her last?"

"Just before midnight, in the library."

"And after that, she left?"

I balked. "I don't know."

"How can you not know?" he replied, "When did Violet leave the house, Liz?"

"She's gone to speak with Kelly," I blurted. "I don't know when she left, but I know that's where she's gone."

Father's brows drew together thunderously. "Why? I ordered her to stay here, and let me deal with him!"

"Because I told her a secret, something to buy the constable's silence. It's the only place she would have gone – she was desperate to save your good name." I set my jaw. "Mr. Kelly is embarrassed that he takes opium."

"Oh, mighty God!" wailed Agnes, her hands wringing in the folds of her apron like a pair of nesting piglets.

Father slouched in the kitchen chair and chewed over this bit of information.

"At the moment, I will ignore how you know that, Liz," he growled.

"If you find Kelly, you'll find Violet," I said, "Of that, I'm certain."

"I've been all through the town and didn't see the man," Father spat, "But when I do..."

He let the threat hang in the air as he heaved himself to his weary feet. "Agnes, warm a bath for me. I can not continue in this state."

"I'm sure Violet will come home," said Agnes, "It's nae in her character to be out all hours! I'd expect such beastly behavior of this one," Her gaze speared me, "But nae your eldest! She's a guld girl!"

"Where ever she and Kelly have gone, I hope they work out their difficulties, and come back with their mouths firmly shut," Father snarled. He pointed one long finger at me. "And the same goes for you, too. Let this whole ugly affair end here."

"Yes, sir."

"Do I have your promise, Liz, that you will not breathe another word about opium, or your grandfather, or your mother's ridiculous notions, or any of it?"

"Yes, sir."

"Good." He slammed the flat of his palm on the kitchen table. "Finished." He stood. "I'm off to wash and sleep, and Agnes? As soon as Violet comes through the door, I want you to wake me. She and I will have a long chat about her place in this house and the importance of following my rules."

Agnes looked relieved. This, in her mind, was how a wayward daughter ought to be treated. "Yes, Dr. Saunders. I'll see to it."

"Good." His eyes met mine. "How's your wrist this morning?"

"Better."

He nodded. "I've already informed the nurses that I shan't be in the office today, but I expect you to finish your reading. We'll do our rounds tomorrow morning, and I want you well-versed on the symptoms of black lung. Yes?"

I nodded. Without another word, he dragged his weary limbs up the stairs to his bedroom.

But as soon as Agnes had gone out the back door to draw water from the pump, I grabbed my boots and slipped them on in a great hurry, making a knotted mess of the laces. I ran out the front door and down the hill to the constabulary, unsure of what to say in Kelly's presence. I was determined to find him, for he would know exactly where Violet had gone. He may have even hidden her himself.

But as I jumped onto the boardwalk and reached the front door of the building, a broad, purposeful figure pulled out of the morning crowds. We stopped short at the sight of each other. Jack Hunter looked even more worn and grizzled than normal, which before today, I would have thought impossible. Dust smeared his face, his hat was missing, and he'd obviously spent the night in his clothes. From the wisps of hay trapped in the hem of his coat, he'd slept in a barn somewhere.

"What the hell are you doin' here?" he said, confused. He pulled his hand to the hip of his grey coat -- a small gesture and easily missed, but the parting of the coat revealed a flash of metal on a pistol grip, and I knew the bowie knife lay flat against his leg underneath, within easy grasp.

"I could say the same about you!" I replied sharply, "I thought Mr. Kelly would have the good sense to put you behind bars, and ship you off to Nanaimo at first chance to face justice for threatening me with a knife!"

"If you don't get out of my way, I'll damn well do it again," he snarled, "I gotta speak with the constable, and I've got no time to waste with a meddlesome bag-o-bones like you!"

"I've come to speak with Sandy, too, and good company dictates that ladies go first." I turned my shoulder to him and reached for the door. "I'm looking for Violet."

"Yer sister's gone missing?"

"Yes, and I should think—"

But without waiting for my answer, Jack barged passed me, shoving me into the doorframe in his haste. He burst into the constabulary, shouting, "Kelly!" as he entered.

Rufus McGregor, crouched over the stove in the corner and feeding chunks of coal to the morning flames, bolted back at the intrusion.

"Damn!" he exclaimed. Then, seeing Jack and clearly unimpressed with the bold entrance, he scowled. "A knock would've been better form, mate."

"Where's the constable?"

"You've got a problem to report? I'll do just as well—"

"No, you won't," Jack replied.

McGregor's expression clearly showed that this dismissal was an insult to his abilities. "Now see here—"

"I gotta to speak with Alexander Kelly, and him alone," Jack insisted. "Where is he?"

McGregor huffed, tossed the last bits of coal into the stove and slammed the iron door. He shook his head. "Kelly's not here."

"I can goddamn SEE that!" Jack roared. "Where the HELL is he?!?!"

"Hey, now! There ain't no reason for that tone!" Rufus replied, pulling himself up to his burly height and giving an implied threat; he was fit, and hale, and not beneath subduing a man by force. "Kelly just hasn't come down this morning from his bed. He was out half the night, and I thought I'd give him time to catch his sleep before I go drag him out of his cot. Though with all your racket, I'd be surprised if he isn't already awake." He caught sight of the slight figure behind Jack, and tipped his chin. "Well, we've got a lady present! Good morning, Miss Saunders! I didn't see you there!"

"I've come to report, Mr. McGregor," I asked, stepping forward, "That Violet never came home last night."

Rufus' smile became a concerned frown. "Never came home?" He glanced upstairs. A sly smile crossed his face. "Now, I don't think you've got much to worry about, miss. She was in good keeping." He leaned forward to impart a secret. "When I saw Kelly last, he was rushing off to meet with your Violet."

"When?"

"Oh, let me think," he said, rubbing his chin with his index finger. "I came to water the horses 'round eleven o'clock; the moon was up when I was finished, so close to midnight? No, it must've been passed midnight, now that I think of it, by half an hour or so."

Jack spoke before I had a chance. "And you saw Kelly?"

"Spoke with him, in fact," Rufus said, "He'd come to fetch his pale pony." He crossed his arms. "It's a constant, that one. Good horse-flesh, reliable."

"Where was he going?" Jack demanded.

"He said he wouldn't be back soon, that he was going to speak with Miss Violet." Rufus nodded towards me. "I thought he must be making his way up to your house, and wanting to go as a gentleman does – not on foot, but in the saddle."

"I never saw any indication of a horse in our yard," I said to Jack, now that our quarry was the same.

Jack turned to Rufus. "When did Kelly get back?"

"I don't know," Rufus replied, "When I came into the office this morning, the shutters were drawn."

"But the horse was back." Jack prompted.

McGregor faltered. "I don't know. I was planning on checking the horses after I got the office running."

Jack was first out the door, as driven as a hound after its prey, with me close on his heels. We circled the building to the stable in the rear yard, where the colliery kept three good horses for the law's use. Jack threw the bolt and slid the door open. Inside, the stalls were hazy with shafts of morning sun, slanting in through gaps in the boards. Dust motes swirled on the still air. A brassy chestnut and a dappled grey stood side-by-side, shifting and snorting at the intrusion. The third stable was empty.

"Gone," I said as Rufus caught up with us at the stable door.

"Or never returned," Jack replied.

Along the side of the constabulary, a long flight of wooden steps rose to the second floor, where a small door led into the constable's private dwelling. Rufus rushed up the stairs and pounded on the door. No sound came from within. He cupped his hands and peered in the window. "God damn," he muttered to himself, then turned to Jack, crowding behind him on the landing. "Stand back." He grabbed the banister, braced himself against the wooden railing, and kicked out with one leather boot. The door gave way and banged open.

The two men pushed their way in first, and by the time I was inside, they had already fanned out to look through the three rooms; kitchen, bedroom, parlor. I waited in the kitchen and set my palm on the side of the stove. The iron was stone cold. They rushed back and forth, calling Kelly's name, but I could tell by the stillness and the smell of the air that a space had gone the night without a fire. The apartment had sat for hours, empty.

"He didn't come back," Rufus said, confused, as he returned to the kitchen. "Well, I'll be damned. Where the hell—"

But Jack barreled out the door and was already halfway down the back stairs. I dashed to catch him, gripping his coat sleeve to stop him at the bottom step.

"Where are they, Jack?"

He reeled on me. His eyes were cunning and calculating, the mind behind them turning franticly, but his voice remained low and strong and even. "I hope they're far, far away from here."

"What's that supposed to mean?"

"Kelly's got himself mixed up in some nasty business, that's what I mean," he said, "And if you value your hide, you'll keep quiet about it, and don't say a word to no one about what you know."

"But I don't know anything!"

"And that'll keep yer skin in one piece, girl," he replied, yanking his coat sleeve from my grasp. "Go home, Amaryllis. You can't do nothing for either of 'em."

"But if they've run off—"

"Then they got a head-start," he said. "God speed to 'em!"

He headed east at a brisk walk, which had increased to a run by the end of the block.

When I returned home, bewildered and confused, Agnes threw her meaty arms around me and squeezed me to her formidable bosom, proclaiming loudly to the kitchen and house that one of the lost lambs had returned.

Violet did not return in the afternoon. By evening, I felt mad with worry, but Father refused to let me leave the house, and with Agnes prowling the rooms like a protective mastiff, one bright black eye forever trained upon the door, I was bound to remain inside. Father walked the streets again, looking for his eldest daughter, and when he returned, the half moon had risen behind a bank of snowy clouds, heralding the first hint of a storm on the horizon.

"No one has seen the constable all day. McGregor believes Kelly has fled," he said as he shrugged off his coat, "They've eloped, the two of them."

"It canna be!" Agnes said.

But he nodded as he hung his hat on a peg by the door.

"They've quit the place, Agnes. The rumors have scared them both, and they've left us, lest Violet's life be dogged by the same shame as my own." He shook his head violently. "I knew he did not believe me! I knew it! There was a look in his face, as if the rumors he'd heard were too pervasive to be anything but truth!"

"Violet wouldn't have left us!" I insisted, but John dismissed my comment with a shake of his head as he grabbed a glass from the sideboard. He poured himself a generous dose of brandy.

"We do not know what she'll do," he said between swigs, "She's overcome with emotion. She's prone to rash decisions. She lets her heart lead her, and not her head. Briggs won't have her, so she'll take Kelly, and she's made more desperate by the notion that no one will have her, once our soured past is revealed."

"Violet wouldn't leave, all for a rumor," I insisted.

"But Kelly would, knowing his life to be left in ruins if his addiction was made public," Father said, "She knew as well as any that, if the company found out, they would be shamed." He glared out the window to the growing cloudbank flowing over the mountains. "I spoke with Father McGill, and he says that Kelly has, for a few weeks now, considered taking his employ to Victoria. He's made inquiries. I suspect he'd go to Victoria, where there is no fear of being discovered as an addict and he'll be but one of many men in the force. No, I'm quite sure of it," and he shook his head, "They've quit this place. Violet has weighed her family and past with her husband and future, and we've come up lacking."

"If they're going tae Victoria, then they'll take the boat south," said Agnes. "I can nae imagine Violet traveling overland."

The SS Joan made trips weekly, and I counted back the days to the last influx of new men to the company. "The boat leaves from Union Bay in two days," I determined, "They'll have hidden somewhere nearby. We could still find them, catch them."

"So I suspect. I've already sent word to the pier, and Rufus is gathering his deputies to hunt along the rail tracks and road to Union Bay, in case they've decided to ride that way tonight and stay in the inn at the bay." He slammed the empty glass down. "Agnes, fetch me a bite of dinner, before I join the men."

"I want to come," I said, but he gave a derisive laugh.

"I'll have no such nonsense," Father replied. "Perish the thought."

"She's my sister, I can't leave her to ruin herself!" I insisted.

"No." He downed the last dregs of brandy in the glass, and slamming it down to accentuate his point. "I do not want you involved in this affair. It's bad enough that I have one daughter, running wild with a man, besmirching herself and my tattered reputation with her ridiculous, childish, impulsive hysteria!"

"But—"

"That is enough, Amaryllis! Enough!" A flush of crimson crossed his face, anger seethed below his collected countenance. "Agnes, please ensure that Lizzie stays indoors this evening and attends to her reading. This is no time for me to worry about her, as well!"

42

STORM CLOUDS GATHERED along the ridges of the Beaufort mountains and rolled between the peaks like dove-grey skeins of wool, sopping wet, blocking out the starry sky. A crowd of volunteers, hastily assembled by Rufus McGregor in Kelly's absence, gathered outside the Saunders' home. As I watched from the window, I recognized faces in the crowd, illuminated by the flickering lights of torches and miner's lamps. Mason Briggs was there, and Mr. Fish, looking dour at the prospect of a wet, rainy evening stroll. Mr. McGill arrived, too, dressed in wool pants and white shirt, the long Presbyterian robes in which he was normally garbed being entirely unsuitable to search for wayward lambs. Agnes' seven sons clustered together on the porch, a small battalion of red-headed ruffians who looked as exuberant as puppies at the prospect of a hunt. Thirty men congregated in the front yard to join the search for the fleeing pair, and they milled aimlessly like cattle, awaiting direction, trampling the flowers.

A few of the neighboring women, too, arrived to lend Agnes their support. The housekeeper made them welcome, ushered them into the parlor to serve them tea and scones, and to co-miserate on the ills of youthful impetuousness. I accepted their hugs and words of condolence, and sat in the window seat to watch the men outside.

Peggy Faulks swept into the house in a gaudy array of furs and silk scarves, and gave passionate apologies that her sister-in-law had not come; Kitty had sequestered herself in their parlor and was presently consulting the angels for any clues to Violet's location. Esther McGill commented that, without a mother in the home to guide them, John's girls were bound to lose their way.

"In my opinion," she began in a scandalized hush, "This whole tragedy could have been avoided if John had attended church like a good Christian and put the spiritual care of his children in my capable hands."

This comment met with grave agreement from all. A few of the guests stole surreptitious and pious glances at me.

I said nothing in reply, but returned my attention to the men outside.

John stood on the porch to address the crowd. He supported himself with a hand against the railing and drew strength from the solid beams of the house. The rain had not begun to fall, but trembles of thunder growled in the distance. An oppressive tension filled the air.

He thanked them for coming. He encouraged them to look in every barn and stall, house and shed. Then, his speech finished, the crowd of men flowed out and along the street, holding their torches and lanterns aloft. A few had borrowed horses and mules but most were on foot. Every man in the crowd was well-acquainted with Violet's beauty -- I could not help but think the majority of them were there, not out of kindness, but out of a desire to act as a knight in shining armor to a princess in peril. They stormed down the hill towards town, breaking into groups and clusters. The light of the torches whirled away like bursts of sparks from a raging fire, borne aloft on columns of billowing smoke. The house fell morbidly serene without the shouts of the men outside; only by the buzz of chatter from the women in the parlor disturbed the silence.

I moved from the window seat to the couch and struggled to remain calm against the chaotic mess of emotions that stormed inside me: fear, rage, hurt, abandonment, rejection. It took all of my concentration to lock them away, to control them and assert dominance over them. How could Violet leave, in such haste and without a word to me? I closed my eyes and listened to the steady rise and fall of the wind in the eaves.

I cast my thoughts back to the mule, dying by my hand, down in the guts of the earth. I thought of the sad, soft rhythm of its breath, the way it gently slipped into the void without protest or struggle.

My pulse began to slow.

The women chattered as tea was served, but I left them on the main floor and climbed the stairs to my room. I reached under the bed and dragged out the tin box, and set it on the dressing table. The hinges squealed as the lid opened. The soft cold fur of the mule's ear tickled my fingers as I took it from its reliquary. The memory of that eerie tranquility trickled through me. I sat on the edge of the bed as I fondled the soft, desiccated flesh, a solid *memento mori* to accompany the sense of calm.

My shoulders relaxed.

I breathed a sigh of relief. In the empty room, the sound reminded me of the last exhalation of the mule, a release of air flecked with blood. My fingers slackened, my body lightened. My eyes opened and I lost myself in thought, daydreamed freely, and recalled the sweetness of an intimate moment shared between me and the liberated soul.

My gaze rested for a moment upon the contents of the open tin box.

I sat upright. My eyes widened.

"Zao gao," I whispered.

Nothing inside the box had been disturbed. Nothing had been taken. I realized, with a start, that I'd half-hoped to find the contents ravaged and all the money gone. But there, between the slip of Hannah's handkerchief and the pebble from the graveyard, was the little sack of my savings. I spilled the bag of coins onto the bed and counted them. Every penny I'd made, every penny saved, every penny I'd freely insisted Violet use to purchase of passage on the ship, remained.

All the money -- all twenty three dollars and fifty-two cents, a mishmash of sovereigns and queen's heads and copper half-pennies and even a guinea or two, carefully collected, jealously horded and meticulously accounted – all the money was there. I counted it three times in rapid succession, but I knew even as I piled the coins into towers that tallying it was unnecessary. Either the money would've been taken in its entirety, or it would still be in the tin box. No one would take half the money, not when the entire amount was needed.

But it was all here. All of it. Every last copper penny.

I rocked back on the chair and looked at the glittering pile of coins on my quilt. I wanted to tally the treasure for a fourth time, but that wouldn't change the result.

Violet had disappeared without a penny to her name. And Kelly didn't have any finances to call his own – he spent his earnings on opium. Violet knew where my money was squirreled, and knew she had my blessing to take it, and yet it all remained, every last bit.

Twenty-three fifty-two would buy them each a ticket on the steamer to Victoria, and pay for lodging and food until they could find their own way in the world. That amount could have given them the security to get clean away. I couldn't imagine a scenario in which Violet would leave without the money, so desperately needed and so easily accessible, and so perfectly placed to give an eloped couple the boost they'd require to start a life together.

Unless, I thought, where Violet had gone, money was of no use.

"You're counting pennies? At a time like this?"

I bolted back in surprise.

Agnes stood in the bedroom door, holding a tray of scones, a tea cup and teapot. How long she had been standing there, watching, I did not know.

"You're a queer one, lass," she accused.

"Do you think," I began, and I allowed my voice to crack, "Do you think Violet will come back?"

This first, tiny hint of despair gave Agnes an excuse to join me, and she set the tray down on the dressing table and enfolded me into a motherly embrace. "Och, dear," she crooned, "All will be well, I'm sure."

"I'm not so certain." I whispered.

Agnes sat down beside me on the bed. "Where ever they wuld be, my girl, your father will find them." She smoothed her fingers over my cheek. "Come, now. You and I, we'll pray together for their safe return. God will listen, my wee lamb. You'll see."

43

THE STORM BEGAN AFTER MIDNIGHT. Lightning fractured the black sky and cast the dark forests into stark relief. Rain slashed against the window pane as the howling winds ripped the world apart. I huddled in the wooden chair at my bedroom window, dressed in my nightgown and wrapped in a quilt. I clenched the blanket tightly around my shoulders to ward off the unseasonable chill, watching the wind whip through the trees. The landscape became a torrential maelstrom of dark, light, water, earth, as if the elements themselves were willing to uproot all of man's constructions in a desperate bid to reveal Violet's whereabouts.

Agnes, dedicated to caring for me in Father's absence, had decided to sleep in her day clothes on Violet's bed, and through two layers of shut doors, I could hear the woman's rattling, bovine snores shake the floorboards and reverberate down the hall.

A movement in the yard, underneath the thrashing apple branches, caught my eye, but I had to wait for a flash of blazing light to illuminate the slender figure there. My breath caught in my throat. I discarded the blanket across the chair to run on silent, naked feet, down the stairs and into the kitchen.

By the time I flipped the iron locks on the back door, Shao had reached the porch. He cowered under the eaves, his arms wrapped around himself in a futile attempt to stay warm and dry. His clothes hung from his frame, sopping wet, making a little puddle where he stood.

"What are you doing here?" I asked. Without waiting for an answer, I grabbed his sleeve and tugged at him. "Come in! Come in! You'll catch your death!"

He shuffled inside, shivering, his teeth chattering. A bitter wind, more of November than August, gusted through the yard like a stampede of horses. Questions rushed through my head, passing each other at a frantic gallop. "If you're caught – what are you doing here?"

He shivered violently. Cold rain plastered his blue-black hair to his scalp, and his grey shirt clung to his frame. I shoved him onto a chair at the kitchen table, then promptly turned and stoked the glowing embers in the stove, adding coal until blue flames licked at the black stones. I fetched a scone from the pantry, a spoonful of butter from the pottery crock, and a few loose leaves of tea; by the time the water in the kettle boiled, the tea thrown into a mug and smothered with steaming water, and the mug placed alongside the buttered scone on the table, Shao had warmed up enough to move his tongue.

"Thank you!"

But I was not yet done. I ran to the linen cupboard and found the softest towel, and when I brought it back to him, he'd already removed his soaked shirt. I handed him the towel, wrung out his shirt in the sink before hanging it to dry by the stove, and finally plopped into a chair. "What are you doing here?" I asked at last, and added, "You'll catch hell if they see you!"

"Don't care," he said around a mouthful of scone.

"Why not?'

"I had a visitor tonight," he began, but the scone was almost finished, so he opted to devour it wholly and wash it down with a swig of hot tea before continuing. "A man's voice called up from the apothecary, so jiu fu woke me up, gave me the knife for cutting paper, and told me to see who was calling at such an ungodly hour. When I got downstairs, I found Jack Hunter at the door."

"What?!"

"Looking awful, I'll tell you. Muddy as a sow, right up to his armpits, and soaked through with rain. Sticks and twigs in his hair. He ordered me," and here, Shao raised one eyebrow suspiciously, "To come here immediately, and stay with you."

"What?!" I repeated, with even more amazement.

"He said," Shao dropped his voice, "He didn't want you staying alone while the men in town were out, roaming the tracks. He said it wasn't safe."

"I'm perfectly safe," I replied. I looked up to the ceiling, where the rumbling snores of our sleeping housemaid could be heard, and added, "I'm hardly alone. Agnes makes enough noise for a company of three." I reached out and pressed my hand to Shao's. "You're in more danger than me, running through the streets in a storm after nightfall. If anyone sees you—"

"There's no one to see me," he replied, "They've closed the shift at the mine and all the men within a ten-mile radius are looking for your sister. Anyone without a good reason to go abroad is tucked into their houses, next to their stoves. The streets are deserted."

"You might not risk detection, then, but you certainly risk being struck by lightning!"

As if to punctuate my point, a rending boom rolled over the town, simultaneously accompanied by a flash of cold, purple-white light. Shao jumped, and we both looked to each other. He laughed.

"All this time, I've called you 'Lizzie', but you're actually Lei Zi."

"I'm lazy!"

Shao smiled and shook his head, sending a few glassy drips of water flying from his drenched hair. "Lei Zi is the goddess of lightning." He glanced outside, where the apple boughs danced and whipped under the onslaught of wind. "She's married to Lei Kung, the god of thunder, and when they argue --"

Another rending boom and flash cracked over the valley as the Lei family's domestic dispute raged across the heavens.

The thunder echoed up the valley, rolling in waves against the mountains, and an easy peace fell across the kitchen. For the first time in almost a day, I felt safe, and wholly composed, and perhaps even a little hopeful that the men would return with good news. Shao sipped at the tea. A healthy color had returned to his skin, and I reclined in the chair and pondered our situation. "I thought you didn't trust Jack."

"I don't, my little Zi-zi," he replied, "But when he suggested you were in danger, I couldn't ignore him."

"I'm in no danger. I'm in a locked house," and I pointed directly up. "With a genuine Scottish dragon to guard me."

I WOKE an hour before dawn to the absence of sound against the window pane. The rain had stopped. A pale lambent shaft of moonlight gilded the library floor with a square of silver, perfectly quartered by the wooden cross of the window pane.

"Shao," I whispered.

He stirred next to me, propped against the end of the sofa, muttered something too quietly to hear. I hesitated to pry myself from the curve of his body, for he was deliciously warm and the air in the library felt cold enough to see my breath, but as I rose higher and higher into that state of wakefulness, I became increasingly aware of the precarious nature of our situation.

"You have to wake up," I whispered against his earlobe. Then I nipped it, hard, and he startled into full alertness with a stifled gasp.

"Zao gao!" he said, at first due to the pain, clutching at the bitten lobe, and then again, realizing his surroundings. "I didn't mean to sleep—!"

"They aren't here yet, but they will be." I slipped my bare feet from under the hem of my nightgown and touched my toes to the cold wooden floorboards. "You have to go home."

"I promised Jack I'd keep you safe."

"Difficult to do, though, if you're hung from a tree for stealing my virginity."

"True," he replied. "Very true."

"And I doubt they'd listen to me, if I assured them our friendship was platonic," I continued, hauling him to his feet and hurrying him to the back door. "I'm not known for my adherence to rules, and the old gossips of this town would have a bloody field day if they even caught a whisper that my innocence was imperiled."

"You have my word, Lizzie, I would never dare to lay a finger on you—"

"Oh, please, you wouldn't?" I scolded, "Then I'm forced to think you find me repulsive." I took his dry shirt from beside the stove, tossed it to him, and he caught it in a fluid, easy motion. "At least do me the courtesy of telling me you would, if given the chance."

"Oh, I definitely would," he answered, quick enough to make me laugh.

I led him to the back porch and, for a moment, we stood in the brisk grey air before dawn. The storm had scrubbed the sky clean. I noticed the stars flashing and sparkling a little brighter than before.

"They'll find Violet," he assured. "You'll see. She'll have second thoughts, realize her mistake, and come home."

"I hope so," I replied, and took his hand in mine. "I miss her."

When our lips met, I wasn't surprised. Our connection came as naturally as the surf caressing the sand. He cradled the back of my head in his hand, and we fit together as comfortably as we had on the sofa, where our easy conversation had melted into unintended sleep. I brushed my palm over his hip, felt the valley of his spine at the small of his back, savored the warmth of his skin against my own. The chill of the air vanished.

Then Shao was gone, disengaged so suddenly that the cold temperature left in his wake was a slap across my face, and I became achingly aware of only an absent space in front of me.

We said nothing more to each other, in case the sound of our voices scarred the pristine, perfect, post-storm silence. I watched him pull his shirt over his head as he vanished between the apple trees, his body tiger-stripped with shadows. Shao passed without any hesitation through the back gate, never looking back nor showing any hint of leaving anything behind.

44

August 9, 1898

Exhausted, filthy, and rain-soaked, the search party returned as dawn light seeped over the eastern horizon, less than an hour after I sent Shao home. From the way they hunched in their saddles, from their tired and ghastly faces, it was clear without words that they'd found no trace of the couple between Cumberland and Union Bay. The crowd fractured into smaller groups, then broke apart as each man went his separate way home, to beds and wives and families, on horses so tired they could barely lift their hooves.

Father did not, immediately, come inside. He lingered for a while on the porch, watching the first streaks of cold daylight in the east. At last, shuffling through the front door and trailing a line of water after him, he faced Agnes and me in the kitchen.

"Nothing," he said, "No sign of them."

Agnes' chin trembled. Tears spilled down her cheeks. "They nae took shelter in the inn, then?"

"There's no sign of their names on the register and no one in

Union Bay has seen them." He sighed and collapsed in the chair. "I am at a loss as to where they could be."

I felt ill, cold, empty.

"It's clear to all that Kelly has decided to forgo his position. He has abandoned his post, true to form, in the vile method of an addict and a coward," spat Father, exhausted and bone-weary, "Such is the opinion of all: he's taken Violet with him. His horse is gone. They have fled, and fled completely."

But I shook my head. "She wouldn't have abandoned us. Do you think Kelly took her against her will?"

"No," said Father, "I dare not imagine Mr. Kelly forcing himself upon her."

"But we dinna kent him to be an addict, neither!" Agnes huffed, "He hid his evil soul well!"

Father remained unconvinced. "My only thought is this: she has decided to live with him as his wife, in a place where no one knows their past, and they have together left without us. How can I fault her for running? I did the same thing, in my attempt to escape our poor fall from polite society." He collapsed in the chair at the kitchen table, drawn and shivering from long hours out of doors, soaked to the skin. "He nurtures poor habits, and is given to temptation and impulsive decisions. Perhaps this flight, without taking responsibility for his addictions, is merely one more clue to the weakness of his character."

But, I reflected silently, Violet had left the money in the tin box untouched. How could she have moved on without money? The contents of that little marble bag would go a long, long way to securing their new life together, wherever that might be.

The kitchen fell quiet.

At last, Father spoke. "I can not accept the thought of Kelly spiriting Violet away without her consent -- he has never treated her with anything but fawning kindness, and the act of force against a lady is not in Kelly's character."

But something, a tiny mite of doubt, gnawed at my intellect. It was too small to categorize and too elusive to crush. I could accept Father's suspicion that Violet and Alexander had eloped, hoping to dodge the shame that would befall them if these two rumors, one true and one false, were to become publicly known, and all things pointed to that rational outcome.

But I could not shake the thought that something far more sinister had happened.

In the morning, while Father slept and Agnes was elbows-deep in the washing tub on the back porch, I went for a walk. When I announced to Agnes that I was going to look for my sister, the woman gave me a cloying look of sympathy. A wee girl, after all, was hardly equipped to find clues when twenty men on horseback had proven useless.

"Stay home, my girl," said Agnes, "You can do no good, and it's unseemly for ye to be wandering so."

But I slipped out the front door, my mind set. The men on horseback had focused their attention on the railway tracks, and in all the hotels and inns and barns and haylofts between here and the docks in Union Bay.

I didn't need to go so far. I had other plans.

In my crisp black cotton frock and stockings, my ginger hair back from my face, I hurried from the house. I was eager to feel the touch of warm sun on my skin. The streets were strangely still. After a full night of searching, the men had taken to their beds, and instead of the regular bustle of a Tuesday morning, most of the shops on Dunsmuir Avenue remained shut with little paper notes taped to the doors saying things like "Closed Due To Recent Tragedy", or "Closed Until Further Notice". I even noticed one that read "Closed For Disaster", although this was less a premonition, and due more to thrift on the part of the proprietor. Why waste a clean sheet of paper to make a new sign, when the old sign used for mine explosions works perfectly well?

The day was not yet hot, but a humid warmth rose from the rain-soaked earth and promised a sticky afternoon heat. Women tended to their gardens and scattered grain to their chickens before the sun forced a slowness on the day. I noticed Miss Marsh standing in the door of the empty Cottage School, surveying the street with arms primly crossed. She kept the school house open through the summer to tutor the slower children, but most students were loathed to attend on such a beautiful day, and they would certainly play truant during July and August. The crack and hue of a baseball game, played on the field at the other end of town, was evidence enough of their whereabouts. Miss Marsh listened to the cries and laughter with a look of displeasure on her face, steeling herself for the excuses tomorrow: I didn't feel well, our cat gave birth to kittens, my pa needed me to collect coal shards for the stove. If she marked them on creativity, they'd all receive passing grades.

When Miss Marsh noticed me at the distant corner, she perked up. A student dedicated to her lessons? But when Miss Marsh recognized the skinny little elf as a child that she, herself, had banished from the building, she slumped again, useless, and gave me a half-hearted wave.

I waved back. Then, sure that my next action would cause a little tremor of saintly self-congratulation in Miss Marsh, that she had chosen wisely to root such a vile influence from the innocent lambs in her care, I walked briskly to the front steps of the Bucket of Blood, pushed open the door and stepped inside.

The saloon was almost deserted. A thick, sweaty, dog-kennel smell lingered in the air, but the sweet beeswax scent of freshly polished wood added a gentle ambiance to the room. The stuffed deer heads watched me enter with three pairs of glassy eyes. Without the mirror behind the bar, the Bucket of Blood seemed cramped and small. Hanging from the bare wall in its place was an absurdly long rifle with powder horn, succinctly performing a double function as both curious decoration and a bold warning to the belligerent. A neat checkerboard of small square tables filled most of the open space. Two elderly men nursed their morning glasses of ale by the window.

A young woman swept up the sawdust on the floor, peppered here and there with wads of chew and discarded chicken bones. Her long brown hair was coiled in a braid on her crown and she wore a plain, honest smock.

When I entered, she paused in her work and held the broom aside.

"Good morning, duckling," she said warmly with a broad and open smile. She possessed a oval face that ended in a tiny pointed chin. Her sparkling hazel eyes, flecked with yellow, flashed and danced like the Welsh lilt of her voice. "How might I help you this morning?"

"I need to leave a message for Mr. Hunter," I said, "And I believe he's staying here or in the Waverley next door."

Her dark brows drew together. "Hunter," she mused, measuring the name against an internal list of patrons filed in her memory, "No, I don't think so."

"I'm almost certain he is," I replied, "He came off the steamer a fortnight ago, and arrived with a group of miners from Victoria. The wagon brought them here."

"Aye, I know the group," she said, "But I'm sure there's no Mr. Hunter amongst them. We did have a whole host of new miners arrive with the ship, but they were mostly Eastern European – queer names on them. I'd have remembered a good, solid name like Hunter."

I frowned in thought. "Are you positive? A tall man, broad shoulders, brown-blonde hair...." I tipped my head to the bare wall behind the bar. "He started a fight that broke the mirror."

"Oh! You mean Jack!"

"Yes," I said, nodding, "Jack Hunter."

"Oh, I know Jack," she replied, and the way she said the word 'know' seemed deeper and more meaningful – she didn't just recognize the name. She knew him quite well. Her expression disapproved, but her eyes sparkled. "Aye, I'm well aware of ... what did you call him?... Mr. Hunter, and he's been kicked out of here, I can assure you that!"

"Do you know where I might find him?"

"No I do not," she huffed, "And he can go a-scuttling back to wherever he came from, for all I care!"

I furrowed my brow. "Certainly someone must know where he is, to hold him accountable for the damage to the bar."

"He paid the account," she assured, "Paid it in full, in cash. And good riddance!" She jabbed one finger against the centre of my chest. "And if you know what's good for you, you'll give him a wide berth! He's got a silver tongue, that one, and enough bob in the wallet to dazzle a girl, but don't you be fooled! He'll break your heart sooner than spit on you!"

"Yes, that sounds like the fellow I'm looking for," I replied.

"Well, if you're so determined, ask at the Union, or the Vendrome. He's American, so you might try the Eagle first." She took up her broom again. "And when you see him, you tell him that Rhianna says he can burn in Satan's fire, for all she cares, and to Hell with him!"

She spat on the ground, in the sawdust, and stamped her boot.

I left Rhianna and went first, as suggested, to the Eagle Hotel, but discovered that Jack had not been seen by any of his countrymen there. I went back up the street to the Union, then along to the Vendrome, again without success. A description of him might bring dawning recollection, but his full name was always a mystery. No one knew much about him, except that he was free and easy with buying the liquor, thereby securing himself many fond and fleeting acquaintances. I stood on the corner outside the barber shop, across the street from the Company Store, and puzzled over the enigmatic figure of Mr. Hunter.

By noon, I found myself knocking politely before entering the door of the constabulary. There I found Rufus McGregor, sitting before a pile of papers on Kelly's desk, tearing off great hunks of a sandwich between his crooked teeth.

He grabbed a napkin and dabbed at his concrete jaw. "G'afternoon, Miss Saunders," he blustered, putting down his lunch.

"Hello," I replied, "Please, don't stand. I don't wish to interrupt your meal."

"Oh, a man's got to eat some time," he chortled, "And now, with

Sandy gone, there's only me to do the tallying, so I catch a bite when I can. I'm sorry about the state of things with your sister and Kelly – I wish I could have brought her home yesterday, but Kelly, he's a sharp fella." He tapped the side of his brow with one calloused finger. "He knows all the hiding spots where the criminals hole up, though I never thought he'd be one to use 'em. Still, we'll find 'em, I promise." His smile was a admirable attempt at enthusiasm, but I saw it falter. "How might I help you?"

"I'm looking for a particular gentleman," I began, although my tongue tripped over the word, "And I'm hoping you can help me. Would you know where I might find Jack Hunter?"

The accommodating grin dropped off McGregor's face. "The brute looking for Kelly yesterday morn? Dear God, girl, why would you be looking for trouble like that?" McGregor began to shuffle through a stack of pages there. "I've had more complaints about him in the last two weeks – fighting, brawling, drunk, propositioning the ladies, married and otherwise— I have my suspicions that he's a pick-pocket, too, and given to thievery."

My ears pricked up. "You *think* he might be a thief?"

"And as soon as I have a scrap of evidence against him, I'll be running him out faster than a cat with its tail on fire!"

McGregor, it seemed, was unaware of Shao's accusation, and knew nothing of Hunter's part in my father's missing portmanteau bag. I considered the implications: Kelly had not told McGregor of his discussions with Hunter, not left any record of Hunter's arrest in all the piles of paperwork. Why not?

"Well," I said, "Mr. Hunter has been less than gentlemanly in his conduct with me, and it was my understanding that Mr. Kelly spoke with him on Sunday concerning a spot of trouble I'd had with him. In fact, I had hoped he'd spend a few nights with your hospitality," I gestured toward the empty cell, "But he walks free, and I wish to know why."

"I'm afraid I can't tell ya," he said, looking perplexed. "I was guarding your house all of Sunday afternoon, and Sandy said nothing to me about taking Hunter into custody. I know the man's a curly wolf, that's clear enough from his conduct, but he's done nothing in my presence that warrants anything more than a stern warning." McGregor continued to shuffle through the files. "Do you think he's the one that broke into your house? I wouldn't put it passed him."

I clenched my fists and weighed my answer: I didn't want to lie to Mr. McGregor, whom I'd come to respect.

"I'd hoped that he and Mr. Kelly would've discussed such a possibility when they spoke on Sunday."

Rufus paused and scowled in thought. "Aye, you said it was last Sunday that Kelly spoke with him."

"Yes."

"And you're sure it was Sunday?"

"Positive." To assure him my information was sound, I added, "I spoke with Mr. Hunter myself on the late afternoon, and the Roman Catholic church bells were tolling for evening mass as he turned himself in."

McGregor, finding nothing amongst the papers, rubbed his palm in thought over his heavy chin, causing a rasp of stubble. His eyes ranged upwards as he considered. "Well, if he turned himself in, Kelly set him loose without writing anything down."

My hopes sank.

"So where did Mr. Hunter spend his Sunday evening?"

"Can't say," said McGregor. "Do you think he's mixed up in this business with Sandy?"

"I don't know," I replied honestly. "When we saw him on Monday morning, he looked as though he'd slept the night in a straw pile."

"That could've been any barn from here to Union Bay," McGregor replied. "And all that says about him is, he's too poor to afford a room for rent. Or, he got too drunk celebrating his liberty to make it back to a decent bed." The deputy eased his bulk back in the wooden chair, causing the wooden slats to creak and groan. "It's possible, Miss Saunders, that if Sandy was considering abandoning his post, he might not have seen fit to bother taking a prisoner into the jail. It would have been one more responsibility to leave behind."

"Possible," I mused. "I last saw Mr. Kelly after he dismissed you from our porch on Sunday night. He came to speak with my father." I cocked my head to one side, thinking. "You claimed to have seen Mr. Kelly later that evening, yes? Around midnight? He was fetching his horse to visit Violet?"

"That I did," McGregor replied. "Close to midnight. He claimed Violet had summoned him, and he was going to meet her."

"Summoned him?"

"Aye, that's right," he said. "With a note and a lock of her hair." McGregor smiled at the girlish romance of it. "He found a locket of her blonde hair, tied with a black ribbon and a wee note, wedged in the doorframe of the constabulary. When I asked him where he was going, he said that I ought to keep my nose to myself, for he was going to meet Violet and he wanted no interruption. They had much to work out between them." He chuckled. "If I'd known he was planning to elope, I might have tried to dissuade him. But I thought the two of them were meeting for a tryst, and I was wishing him all the luck in the world."

I pondered this. "Where did she go, at that late an hour, if not directly here?"

"I don't know," Rufus said, "Like I said to you before, I thought Sandy was riding to your house to meet Miss Violet, as a gentleman might, on horseback. If she wasn't there—"

"—Then where did they meet?"

The two of us sat in quiet contemplation.

"I should like very much to speak with Mr. Hunter," McGregor mused, "For if he spent the Sunday in conversation with Sandy, I'd like to know what was said between them, and why Hunter was in such a hurry to continue their conversation on Monday morning. There's a chance he might help us find the constable, or know if he planned to leave. Thank you, Miss Saunders." He stood up and tipped his chin in gratitude, and made a gesture to the door; our conversation had reached its end. "I'll be sure to let you know what I find about this fellow, if you like. I can't for the life of me determine why Sandy would be so eager to go," and he swept his open palm towards the files, "With all his paperwork unfinished and a half-drunk cup of coffee on his desk? He wasn't the kind of fellow to be taken to fancies, and even with his affection for Violet, he had a duty to Queen, country, and company. Maybe Mr. Hunter saw or heard something through the night. Maybe he holds the key to Sandy's curious departure, and he doesn't even know it."

'Or maybe he does know it,' I thought as I left, 'And is keeping it very much to himself.'

45

"Mr. W.H. Ireland, secretary of the Trades and Labor Council, thought it was time to do something in regard to the Chinese. They entered into competition at less wages than the white man, while they occupied the best part of the city, and lived in dirt and filth, and sent all their money home... Mr. Forster, MPP, said that regarding the employment of Chinese in the mines, the miners said that they were fatalistic in their religion, and were therefore dangerous." - *The Chinese Question*, Victoria Daily Colonist newspaper, Thursday, Jan. 29, 1891

When I returned home, I found Agnes on the back porch. She had hung the rugs from the hall over the back banister, some with their patterns facing up and some with their patterns facing down. With a bamboo cane, Agnes reeled back and whacked them, sending plumes of dust from both the carpet pile and the canvas backings into the garden air.

"You have a visitor, waiting for you in the front," she said grimly, and reeled back to whip the dust from the rugs again.

Shao sat on the top step of the porch, looking grave. A small parcel was tucked under one arm.

I sat next to him, in the shade of the clematis. He asked, "How are you?"

"I'm very worried about Violet."

"Has there been any news?"

"None," I replied, "And I think something terrible has happened. I don't know what, but the pieces don't fit together." I looked at him askance. "But I'm very glad you're here."

"I think—" He paused, seeking the best words to explain, his dark brows drawn together and his calloused, scarred hands clasped in his lap. "Jiu fu suspects I broke curfew."

"You could have been anywhere."

"He's not an unintelligent man," Shao said, "He knows exactly where I'd go, and whom I'd seek."

"Well, what can he do?" I replied, affronted.

Shao took a breath. "He has respectfully asked that I join the mine crew at the coal face."

"He respectfully asked, you can respectfully refuse."

"No, I can't," Shao explained. "I don't have that luxury."

"Why not?"

I felt waves of frustration rise off of him, saw him clench his hands around his knees. "He is my uncle, and my benefactor, and he is the head of my house. If I go against his request, he will have me ejected from the benevolent society, and I will lose any security they give me." He glanced at me. "You can't possibly understand."

"What sort of security is worth risking your life at the coal face? Do you know anything about explosives?" I tried to keep my voice down. "You could be crushed, or asphyxiated, or caught in a flash fire –"

"Without the benevolent society, I have no one. No family, no station, no place. No money, no one to represent me, no hope for a job." He hunched his shoulders against the thought of a dire future. "It's better money than working with the mules, and jiu fu knows, if

I'm exhausted at the end of the day, I'm less likely to sneak out. And that means less trouble for him."

"You can't—'

"I have to." Shao looked uncomfortable as he admitted, "I have no choice."

I plucked at the hem of my skirt. "You'll be careful?"

"Absolutely."

"You're supposed to protect me, you know," I said, without malice or bitterness. The comment was a fact, like the sun rising or the endless churning of the tide. Shao had promised.

"I can't protect you when I'm in danger myself," he replied.

I pressed my palms to the top step. He put his hand next to mine and, very lightly, brushed the tip of his little finger against my finger. An impossibly small gesture, but my entire body disappeared, and the only part of me to remain was the point of our connection.

"I'm sorry I've put you in this position," I whispered. "I never meant to make things worse than they already were."

"Don't be sorry," he replied, equally soft. "I'm not sorry at all."

"If there's an explosion," I began, but the pressure of his finger's touch strengthened, and it stopped the words in my throat. He had worked with the mules at No. 5, and seen the misshapen, scorched bodies brought up from the black tunnels. He knew to the marrow of his bones what dangers lurked in the lightless, gassy labyrinth.

"I'll come back and visit you, as soon as I can," he promised. "You have your father and Agnes here. Make sure you stay with one of them, at all times, okay?"

If I didn't agree, concern for my safety would dominate his thoughts. The only way to insure his security was to know he suffered no distractions, and was free to listen to the subtle hissing of the stones without thinking of me.

"Okay," I agreed.

He visibly relaxed: his shoulders dropped and his mouth came close to smiling. "I have a gift for you." He placed the parcel on the porch as he stood. "If I'm down in the mines, I won't need it anymore. Hopefully, it will keep you safe while I can't."

When Shao stood and walked away, his steps were brisk and decisive.

I did not unwrap the parcel immediately. I sat on the porch, drenched in summer warmth, and focused on my smallest finger. It continued to sparkle with the fading memory of his touch.

At last, I set the box on my lap and untied the white string, unwrapping the brown paper, and found a narrow wooden box, roughly hewn from a single block of cedar. The lid popped off easily.

Inside, set on a bed of crisp straw, was Shao's curved apothecary knife.

When Agnes came to the door, she found me sitting alone on the top step, hugging the box in my lap, staring at the azure sky.

"What are ye doing, girl?"

"Trying to decide how I feel," came my solemn reply.

"Well, I best suggest you feel penitent," said Agnes, "For your father is awake and taking his tea, and you owe him an apology. Were ye nae meant to help in the office today? Instead, you spirit around the town, consorting with heathens, causing me to suffer great worry!"

I came cautiously into the dining room and found Father, reading his papers, eating a boiled egg and brown toast slathered in butter. When he looked up, he smiled.

"Agnes tells me you were out all morning." He tipped his triangle of toast in my direction. "I'm happy to see you home."

Waves of frustration and rage bubbled off of Agnes, like little puffs of steam escaping from under the lid of a boiling pot. The woman had anticipated a noble, parental display of fireworks, a great reining-in of a wayward daughter who had taken to gallivanting around the streets without a chaperone or permission. Instead, Agnes witnessed a jolly morning greeting between John and Amaryllis, with John even going so far as to invite the girl to sit with him, and eat the rest of breakfast together, as if nothing improper had happened. No switching! No paddling! Not even the barest threat of hard labor with demands to reflect on what she'd done! Just toast, and tea, and a welcome greeting! Denied the joy of witnessing a proper punishment which, it was evident by her irritated snort, she so desperately wished to inflict herself, Agnes promptly stormed off towards the kitchen, wiping her robust hands on her apron. As soon as the door closed, I heard the rugs once more sustain a sound and solid thrashing.

"Are you mad at me?" I asked Father as I approached the table.

"Not in the slightest," he replied, "I'm thrilled to see you well, and hale, and back to your old self, rambling through the hills and getting up to mischief." He set aside the papers, neatly tapped them into a pile. As he offered me a piece of buttered toast, he noticed the box under my arm. "What have you there?"

I set it on the table. "A present from a friend."

"Well, he has some skill, then, to have carved such a clever item for you." He rapped his knuckles on the top of it, and the wood gave a pleasing, solid sound. "Tell me, where have you been this morning?"

I sat in the chair at his right. "I was looking for Violet."

"And?"

"I found nothing."

"Well," he replied, "We can hope that Violet will still return to us of her own volition." He dipped the corner of his toast into the yolk of his boiled egg.

"Tomorrow the steamer leaves for Victoria. Can we be on the dock, to cross paths with them? Maybe the sight of us will spark compassion in Violet's heart, and we can persuade her to come home."

He finished chewing his toast and dabbed at the corner of his mouth with his napkin. "It's not a bad idea, Liz." He thought for a moment, then said, "But the sight of a father who has caused her shame might only make her more determined to leave. What if you went, alone?"

"You'd let me go by myself?"

John considered this carefully and nodded. "I can't see what could possibly happen between here and Union Bay. You'll take the passenger train directly there, find Violet, and return on the afternoon line. I have no doubt that, if Violet saw me, she'd run and hide." He gave a weak smile. "But you, Liz, can persuade her. I know you can."

I was heartened by the idea, and Father seemed rejuvenated, too. He almost looked merry at the prospect. He had every confidence that I'd find Violet and Kelly at the dock tomorrow, and his aplomb was infectious – I began to believe that yes, it was not only feasible, but destined to be so. I'd find Violet boarding the SS Joan. No other outcome was possible.

"I can't guarantee that I'll return Mr. Kelly," I said. "I doubt he'll listen to reason, and he'll know he's in for trouble if he comes back."

"Try your best, Liz," he replied. "I know you always do." Father dabbed away a bit of yolk which had caught in his moustache.

A fracture appeared in my happy mien.

He sighed and looked at me with pity. "Oh, Lizzie, what is it now?"

"It's just that...well...." I leaned my elbows on the table and dropped the volume of my voice. "What if something's happened to Violet? I can't believe she'd leave without saying goodbye to me."

He shook his head.

"Be rational, Liz. If Kelly asked Violet to elope with him, he wouldn't have given her time to come home and pack. He couldn't risk that she'd change her mind. Don't you think, at the sight of you, she might very well do so?"

"Maybe," I replied, unconvinced.

"She loved you very much," he continued, "And I'm sure a glimpse of you, and a tearful goodbye, would have been enough to cause her to reconsider."

"Maybe," I said again.

Father took a deep breath, and chuckled low, assured. He pushed his chair back and set the balled napkin on the table. "I had a long night of walking and I tell you, Lizzie: I'm not used to it! My legs have not felt so stiff in years!" He stood with slow and purposeful movements, wincing as the muscles ached, giving a laugh at the resistance in his joints. "I have rounds in at the hospital today, and I know I asked you to join me, but I'm giving you the day off. From your expression, I think you need it more than me! I'll be home for dinner. We'll have an early night and you'll take the first train in the morning to Union Bay. How does that sound?"

I balked.

"Listen," he said with a smile, "I bet that Violet and Sandy are spending their day at the seaside, enjoying the sunshine, and eager to start on their journey together. There's no reason you have to spend the day fretting. It's beautiful outside. Go, sit in the garden, read and relax. And I promise," he added, "Once our lives have returned to normal again, we'll resume your lessons."

I SPENT the day in the garden, reading the books which I'd borrowed from Dr. Gould under the shade of the apple trees. I tried not to think of Shao, working underground in the darkness, scraping at the coal. I also tried not to think of Mother, disregarding propriety and throwing her entire family into chaos, sacrificing her station in life for the friendship of a paltry maid. Instead, I tried to imagine Violet and Kelly wandering arm-in-arm along the beach at Union Bay, excitedly discussing their plans for their grand adventure, eager to start their lives together as man and wife.

I failed on all accounts.

But fretting made me tired, and the drowsy bees filled the air with a gentle, sleepy hum. I laid my head against the tree and drowsed, too.

My ears caught the sound of a second hum, a lower thrumming sound, that flowed underneath the familiar droning of the bees.

Setting my book aside, I followed the sound, so soft that it was almost imperceptible, to the door of the surgery. Something hummed within: softly, gently, but constant.

I tried the latch but the door would not open. Father had

slammed it shut, and he must've locked it and taken the key. Even when I pressed my shoulder to it, the door would not budge.

I prowled around the perimeter and held my ear to the window and the walls.

The relentless drone came from all angles. 'It must be a wasps nest,' I decided, and thought it best to leave it alone.

46

AUGUST 10TH, 1898

THE TRAINS DID NOT RUN at night, but the mines never stopped producing. The morning shift at No. 4 mine began by loading the night's haul onto the first train, and the endeavor could take an hour or so to complete, depending on the enthusiasm of the morning laborers. The train then departed No. 4 and arrived at the Cumberland station to pick up passengers and freight before continuing to the docks at Union Bay, rocketing as fast as possible to make the best use of time. Most mornings, the ships that waited at Union Bay's long pier were transport ships, and took heaping loads of coal to be sent around the world, but on Wednesday mornings, the SS Joan arrived to take all other items, both living and inert: people, sacks of mail, livestock, and cargo, bound for the southern harbors of Nanaimo and Victoria.

This meant, then, that the first train on a Wednesday morning carried a host of living, shuffling, breathing creatures on its back, instead of its familiar load of undemanding coal. The station behind the Company store became a shifting, heaving mass of life, with most faces pointed west, looking for the first hint of light and steam as the engine rounded the bend from No. 4.

We heard it first: growling, grinding, chuffing, belching clouds of steam over the trees. Then it rounded into sight, a massive serpent of steel and glass, painted green with gold trim. Most of the engines used by the Colliery, like *The Duchess* or *The Queen Anne*, were steel-grey and heavily dented, but the company had recently acquired *The Victoria* from the mines at Wellington, and she was not yet battered with hard labor.

The engine slowed, then paused at the junction while the bulls pulled the pin on the coal cars. Then, dragging only its passenger cars, *The Victoria* shunted up the high arm of the Y and jostled alongside the station platform. The bell clanged as it lurched to a stop.

Dressed in a black frock, I let the noise and clatter of the train wash over me. Father bought a ticket and drew next to me on the platform.

"Come along, Liz, you'd best find a seat," he said, holding out his hand. He looked doubtful. "I do wish I was going with you."

"Don't worry -- I'll bring Violet home," I promised as I took the ticket.

"Good luck, my girl. I'll look forward to seeing you, and Violet, at dinnertime."

As he turned to go, I snagged his sleeve. "If you're in your surgery today, you ought to be careful! I heard a nest of wasps in the eaves."

He gave me a clipped nod. "Thank you for the warning -- I shall. Ah, look! It's Mrs. Hughes!"

The effervescently plump and giggly Jeanie Hughes hurried along the platform to the train, holding up a hem which seemed determined to trip her.

"Good morning!" Father greeted as she joined us. "I'm heartened to see someone on the train that knows my daughter!"

"Hello, Dr. Saunders! Hello, Lizzie!" Her little elfin face was pinched and strained. "I haven't run so far since grade school! I've lost all my breath!" Her laughter bubbled up and capered in the air. "Are you going to the bay, too? I visit my sister there every fortnight. Oh, this shall be a lovely ride today!"

The whistle blew again.

"On you get, Liz. There you are, Mrs. Hughes." Father stood back as we climbed the steps onto the carriage. "Good journey to both of you!"

There was little time for passengers to settle or secure their baggage, and before I'd taken my seat and looked out the window to my right, the cars were backing down the Y and nudged onto the main tracks, fastened once more to the bulging open cars of greasy black coal. The whistle blew twice. The whole serpent of cars and cargo shifted, shuddered, shimmied, and began to slide along the southern perimeter of town.

Mrs. Hughes sat to my left. "What fun, Lizzie!" she said, "I do love train rides! I go whenever Reginald allows me, and my sister -- perhaps you know her? Enid Princely? – well, my sister lives in a lovely cottage by the shore, and I do enjoy spending a day or two with her! Are you going to intercept Violet? Oh, this is a dreadful business, isn't it!"

'It didn't take Jeanie long to get her breath back,' I thought. I smiled and nodded politely.

Impenetrable walls of green soon eclipsed the buildings. As Jeanie continued to talk, I watched the world flash by in a blur of verdant motion. The trees knit their branches as a barrier against civilization. The train galloped down the easy switchback grade, through brakes of ferns and copses of slender maple trees, where their broad leaves filtered the golden sunlight and cast an lush radiance over the forest floor. Back and forth, back and forth we went, through slopes of virginal evergreen forest that seemed to stretch forever. Jeanie chattered absently beside me, but I watched the trees dash by, and felt sure there existed more shades of green in this landscape than the human eye could ever perceive: bright silky greens, drab olive greens, and a green so dark it was almost black. I took a deep breath of fresh air, and the breeze from the open windows smelt of loam and sap.

"—then I said to Reginald, I do love the bay, and I fair think I could live many happy days at the shore! It's a lovely little place, when were you there last?" Jeanie asked, and without waiting for an answer, she continued, "As I said, I told Reginald we ought to move to the sea, because it's so much better for my complexion than all this coal dust floating about in the air, but he'll have none of it! This is where a man makes his money, he says, and not sitting in a little shack by the water, tying fishing lures! Besides, he says he doesn't think I'd make a very good fishwife because I can't stand the smell of fish. And I can't! Any of them! They all smell perfectly dreadful!"

For a split second, the foliage parted and the train thundered over a trestle. Far below, I caught a silvery glimpse of the Trent River, little more than a thread of water during the days of summer.

The trestle was a minor feat of engineering, built of wood and iron, almost a hundred feet high from tracks to water. The meager expanse of the Trent River was no major obstacle -- in summer one could cross it by jumping from exposed stone to exposed stone without wetting one's toes -- but the ravine itself made a deep cleft in the landscape. Crossing the trestle was bound to draw a fearful breath from those of weaker constitutions. I looked down into the narrow canyon, but before I could snag a clear view of the water, the train had rumbled over the span and the trees slammed closed around us, like curtains promptly shut.

"—but my sister is very happy indeed with her husband, and they have three fine children, two girls and a boy, and she's bound to have another soon, and do you think Violet will be happy in her new life?" Jeanie paused. For the last half hour, it had taken only a nod from me to keep the woman chattering, but at this question, the conversation fell silent. A simple nod would not do. Jeanie wanted more.

"I'm… I'm sorry?" I stammered, turning from the window.

"Do you think Violet will be happy?" Jeanie repeated, "Or do you think she has made a dreadful mistake? Reginald says Mr. Kelly is a horrible embarrassment to the company now, and he should hang his head in shame for abandoning his post without so much as a word to his employer, and I only wondered if you think Violet will be happy, to have eloped with a fellow whose character is so irreparably smeared?" She took a quick breath. "It really is quite a shame, but it's all frightfully romantic, too. What do you think?"

"Oh," I said; I hadn't thought I'd need to say a word at all. "I think Violet would be happy, if she and Kelly married."

"But not eloped," Jeanie inferred, "Well, I do think that makes good sense. I'm sure Mr. Kelly will be able to rebuild his reputation and find himself solid employment eventually, as long as he doesn't try to return to these parts, for gossip can be quite cruel, can't it? I doubt a man would hire him to muck a stall, now, with such a dreadful misstep as he has taken in his professional life, but if he has no need of references, he can perhaps start fresh and new in a distant city and no one would be the wiser to his horrid fall from grace. And it doesn't reflect well on your sister if they were to be living in a sinful partnership, but Violet is a bright and bonny girl, and I imagine she'll hustle him to the doorstep of the nearest church as soon as they reach Victoria, and reclaim her dignity, and all will be well—"

The train chugged, the whistle tooted at a herd of deer milling on the tracks. The wheels held an ongoing chattering conversation with the tracks. I felt the first pangs of a headache.

"We're almost there," said Jeanie, interrupting herself, and pointed to the little plank houses peeking between trees and footpaths converging at the sides of the railway grade, eventually wearing into a track wide enough for a wheelbarrow or mule cart. Signs of habitation materialized out of the wilderness: a little stone bridge crossing a muddy creek, then an outhouse half-hidden behind a cluster of salal bushes, followed by neat stacks of wood drying in preparation for winter. The smell of sea salt drifted on the air.

The train eased into the station of Union Bay, jostled like a nervous horse, and finally screeched to a complete stop upon great billowing rafts of steam. The whistle wailed, the bell clang, the steel doors clattered opened. Passengers discharged onto the platform. There were squeals of delight, women hugging one another, men greeting friends with a tip of their bowler hats. Chinese workers unloaded luggage and replaced it with cargo freshly plucked from the bowels of the SS. Joan, which rode high at the end of the pier.

"Now, will you be okay on your lonesome?" Jeanie said as we dismounted. "You can come along with me for lunch with Enid if you like, I'm sure she'd greatly enjoy an opportunity to chat."

"No, thank you, though I do appreciate the invitation."

"Quite alright, I'll tell Enid you say hello, though, shall I?" She smiled kindly and pointed one hand along the platform "The pier is down that way, Lizzie, you can see it from here, and if you find your sister, do give her my best regards."

"I shall, Jeanie."

A woman with the same plump face and glittering eyes waved from the roadway, and Jeanie waved back. "Good luck, then!" she said, pressing a kiss to each cheek, "Good luck!"

I drifted through the crowds of people, letting the flow of bodies guide me towards the pier. The arrival of the boat was a cause for jubilation. It brought friends, fresh fruit and goods, and news from far-flung countries. In every direction, I saw smiling faces.

Except for one. At the end of the pier, Rufus McGregor stood at the head of the ship's gangplank, speaking with the captain. As I approached, he looked up with a hooded, somber expression.

"This is a surprise, to see you here," the deputy said.

"I hoped to intercept my sister," I replied.

He shrugged his ox-broad shoulders in a gesture of helpless surrender. The fibers of his shirt creaked under the strain.

"I've been here since last evening, but I've heard nothing, seen no hint of them. I thought they might've stayed at the inn," and he pointed to the two-story, plaster and timber building, next to the new post office and school house, "I'm sorry to report, Miss Saunders, that there's been no sign of them."

The captain of the Joan was a rotund, salt-encrusted man with thick curly black hair and a thick black beard that encircled his face. He wore a dark felt coat and held a clay pipe tightly clenched between his teeth, and his diminutive stature required him to reach up in order to clap Rufus on the shoulder, a gesture performed with ease and familiarity. "And yon good fella here has informed me of the likes of girl and beau," he chuffed, "And I can assure ye, I've seen no sign of 'em, though I'll be sure to note any I might gather up at points south." He turned to Rufus. "They might've hired a canoe and Indian, ye know, but I doubt they'd hire one to take 'em as far as Victoria – mightly expensive, that would be, specially if the Indian sees 'em to be desperate." He gave a hacking belly laugh around the stem of the pipe. "No, I wager they'll be catching the Joan at the next point south, from the docks in Nanaimo."

"I suspected that myself," said Rufus to the captain. "I've sent word to the constabulary there, and considered a letter to the force in Esquimalt, but I know that won't make me any friends." He crossed his arms. "I don't want to shame Kelly with the involvement of the Dominions, but I'm starting to think I have no choice. As it is, the company will strip him of his livelihood and good name, but if I involve the Dominion Police in this mess—"

The captain nodded.

"T'would be a shame even to the community, if the government gets in the muddle," he said.

Even I knew, it would disrupt the delicate balance between workers and company. And worst of all, it would require the pubs to close on Sundays, the opium dens to shut, and the wayward pleasures on which the working force required to be wiped from public view. A regiment of Dominion police was of no good to anyone.

The men swapped farewells, shook hands, and the captain returned on board. Rufus and I began to stroll back to the main street of Union Bay, which followed the curve of the shore.

"Mr. McGregor, answer me truthfully," I said. "Do you have any hope of finding them?"

He thrust his hands in his pocket and watched a knot of passengers hurry by, struggling with their luggage. When he spoke, his words were quiet and thoughtful, carefully chosen. "I thought today I might be lucky, Miss Saunders, but honestly...." He shook his head. "I've found no hint in Kelly's belongings to explain his rapid departure, and I'm losing hope that I'll ever see either one again. They've made themselves damn near invisible."

No letter, then, I thought. Kelly has taken it with him, to keep himself secure against the threat of being revealed as an opium eater and routed by Father. A stalemate, of sorts.

"I, too, am losing hope," I replied, looking along the busy street and the little cluster of buildings: post office, school, inn. "I'd thought I might—"

I stopped.

There, leaning in the doorway of the roadhouse, stood Jack Hunter. His narrowed eyes followed me.

"Mr. McGregor," I said, "We are being watched."

But as the deputy rose his head to follow my gaze, a group of passengers hurried by. With shawls and parasols and luggage, they obscured the doorway of the inn. When the crowd cleared, with many hats doffed in apologies, the door to the inn stood empty.

"I don't see anyone, Miss Saunders," he said, scanning the people along the street. "Are you sure?"

"Quite."

He harrumphed. "I shall accompany you back, then, to the train and home." He offered me his elbow. "I've already misplaced one Saunders girl, and I'm loathed to lose another."

For a moment, I considered running after Hunter, but he'd seen me first. He was sure, now, to stay out of my way. So, resigned to return, I grinned up at Mr. McGregor. I slipped my hand over the crook of his arm. "May God keep Violet and Sandy safe, and grant them a long and joyful life together, wherever they may be."

47

AUGUST 14, 1898

THE MACHINE of industry refused to stop for two eloped lovers. Miners with families to feed could no longer afford to range through the farms or woodland, looking for a pair of star-crossed paramours who had, so perfectly, vanished, It was obvious to all that Kelly and Violet did not want to be found. They had covered their tracks impeccably.

Life returned to the normal routine of work and play, and wherever Violet and Kelly were bound, no one wished them ill, though people grumbled a bit when their names were mentioned. All the hard work of looking for them had interrupted the schedule of public life. The elder ladies said it was a shame, what Violet had done. The younger men who had looked favorably upon Violet themselves agreed, but couldn't fault Kelly for wanting to sweep away such a beauty for himself.

For four days, I buried my nose in my studies to avoid walking in public. Normally, people rarely paid attention to me, but now, it seemed as if every woman in town wanted to offer condolences, then slyly ask if I had received any word or hint of Violet's whereabouts. Before the scandal, I'd only been a curious little girl in a pair of boys' trousers. Now, in a single morning, I had received invitations for tea at the Ladies Auxiliary Luncheon, a picnic in the village park, and an informal social at the house of Esther McGill.

"I don't want to go to any of these," I said to Agnes, who clucked and flustered at the sight of so many cards: dresses would need to be washed, and boots shone, and gifts procured.

"Tis rude not to go!"

"Then let me be rude!" I replied, tossing the cards on the table by the door. "They didn't want me at their tea and picnics before! And I was certainly happier with that arrangement!"

"Och, you're a neip-heeded chick!" Agnes said, "What kind of odd child dislikes a party or two?"

I threw my hands in the air and grunted in frustration. "If Father needs me, let him know I've taken my books, and I'm studying down by the swamp."

"Tis an unseemly place for a girl to go alone!"

I slung my satchel of books over my shoulder, and yelled, "Has that ever mattered to me before?" I slammed the door as I left.

I kept my head down, my eyes on the dirt road; I didn't care to speak with anyone. I walked briskly, but suddenly I heard the pattern of footsteps following close behind me, and when I looked up, I discovered that I'd been accompanied by Jack Hunter. How long he'd followed me, I wasn't completely sure, and the sight of him rose a quick and savage anger in me.

"You!" I exclaimed.

He drew up alongside me and shoved his hands in his pockets. "So yer sister's gone and run off, has she?"

"And what have you got to do with it, Mr. Hunter?" I repositioned the heavy bag on my shoulder and jabbed one small finger into the middle of his chest. "I looked for you everywhere, and when I finally saw you in Union Bay, you vanished!"

"Well, I weren't all that eager to talk to the deputy," he admitted, "I figured on catching Kelly before he left town."

"As were we all," I snapped.

"Well," he said, looking momentarily amused by my rage, "At least I was tryin' to be discreet about it."

I scowled up at him. "It doesn't matter how discreet I try to be: aside from the sporting matches and the garden parties, gossip is the main form of entertainment here." I shifted the bag against my hip. "It may be a city, but it's a very small one."

"Gossip also tells me, they ain't found a sign of your Violet."

"No."

When he bent down to stare me in the eye, I noticed the swing of his coat fell heavy on his left side, where the folds hid the weight of the pistol on his hip. "I don't know no one else in this town but you, Amaryllis Saunders, so I s'pose that counts you as a friend. I wanted to tell yeh, I'm mighty sorry for your loss."

"My loss?" I started to walk along the boardwalk. He fell into step next to me as I said, "Some people say she'll reconsider and come back, and I know she'll write me eventually. She isn't lost, Mr. Hunter."

But Hunter shook his head. "I won't tell ya she's comin' back, 'cause I don't believe it." He reached out for the strap of my bag. "Goddammit, give that to me. Yer gonna crush yerself, under so many god damn books."

"I'm quite alright—"

"No, you ain't." he said. He wrenched the bag from my grip and swung it easily over his shoulder. "You weigh what, 50 lbs? I've seen horse turds bigger'n you."

"Charming."

"Whatcha got in here?" He looked over the book spines, sticking at odd angles from the top of the satchel, and read the title from the thickest. "'The Principles and Practice of Medicine'. This Osler fella, he writes a ripping yarn, does he?"

"Yes, actually, he does write a good book," I replied caustically, "And what do you mean, you don't believe it? You don't think Violet will send me a letter to tell me she's alright? You underestimate my sister, sir. She doesn't want to hurt us. She might've left, but she'll let us know when she's well-installed, safe and happy."

Jack caught my elbow and stopped me in front of Simon Leiser's Big Store. "Other people might sweeten their words to you 'cause they think you're just an innocent kid, Amaryllis, but I won't lie to yeh. You may be a kid, but yer far from innocent." He leaned close. His breath smelt of coffee and bacon. "You're in danger of disappearing, too, sweetheart, if you ain't careful."

I wrenched my elbow from his grip. "Is that a warning or a threat, Mr. Hunter?"

When he grinned, there was a hint of wolfish cunning to it, a carnivorous salaciousness, that gave me shivers. "I told yer celestial buddy to keep one of his beady little eyes on ya, and I can see," he drawled, casting a sarcastic glance over my shoulder, "That he's doing a damn fine job of it. Leaving you alone, to wander the streets, all loaded down with a pile of reading? I woulda thought he'd be more vigilant, seeing how much I paid him."

"Shaozhu's been put to work in the mine," I snarled, "And I can keep myself safe enough, thank you."

"Really, now?" he replied. "Maybe the malaria didn't getcha in Panama, and you managed to talk your way out from under my knife, but do you think you can dodge Death forever, Liz?"

I ceased struggling from his grip and let him hold my wrist in his sweaty paw. My anger vanished, replaced with a feeling of cold dread. In a whisper, I said, "How do you know about Panama?"

"Your father kept you in Aspinwall just long enough to get infected," he said, "I hear it knocked your sister for a wallop, but you seem to have come through the fevers just fine."

"How do you know –"

"Ask your father why he'd risk takin' two girls through the hell of the French project, rather than by train through Chicago." Jack leaned closer. "Ask him what the hell he was thinkin'. He's a doctor – he knew how many men died of ague down in them swamps."

"Hey!" a voice cried out, and I looked up the street to see Mason Briggs hurrying towards us, shaking the silver head of his walking cane in our direction. "Get your hands off of her! She's got nothing for you!"

Jack released my arm sharply. He backed away, hands raised. "Ain't no problem here," he assured with a greasy smile, "Just givin' my condolences, squire."

Before I could say a word, Briggs positioned himself between me and Jack, and people along the boardwalk and in the windows of the Big Store turned to the gathering confrontation. Briggs, slight and sprightly and well-heeled, did not touch Jack, who was twice the size and twice as filthy. Instead, he stepped forward with the walking stick held tightly like a cricket bat in one hand, emboldened by gallantry and a gentleman's right to rule his immediate surroundings. "She's got nothing to give you, you miserable vagrant. Go beg elsewhere. There's no need for you to sully this fine lady with your presence."

"Ah, she's a fine lady now, is she?" said Jack, smirking.

"And if you don't move along quickly, I'll find some way for you to spend the night in the local cell, understand? We may be short of a constable, but this is still a law-abiding town! Get along."

Jack dropped the bag of books and nodded to me. "Good day to ya, then, Miss Saunders."

"Wait!" I said, and pushed around Briggs to snatch Jack's sleeve in my hand. "How do you know about Panama?"

"A lucky guess," he replied.

"That was no god-damned guess," I replied.

He grinned. "Have I rattled ya, Liz?" Then he snapped the collar of his coat up, nodded crisply to Mason Briggs in a show of ironic deference, and strode down the hill towards the new mine site and the mill yard, where groups of unsavory ruffians gathered to seek a day of labor to pay for a night's entertainment.

Briggs gave an aristocratic bow and offered me his arm. I wrenched the heavy bag over my shoulder again and took his elbow out of politeness. My head spun; I held tightly to his elbow to keep from running after Jack and assaulting him with questions, or the walking cane, or both.

"Please," said Briggs, "Allow me to escort you as far as the Willard

Block." As we continued along the street, he added, "Your father is a brave fellow, raising two daughters in a place such as this. There are too many poor influences, and such dangers that can scarce be believed! I would much rather raise a family in Victoria, where there are social teas, and fine peers, and a greater chance of prospects. I will speak to your father about it, as soon as I am able." He looked down the street, noting the character of people who clustered outside of the establishments. "Mostly men, hardly any women, never mind a selection of young ladies like yourself with whom you can be acquainted! It must surely be lonesome at times for you, Amaryllis."

"Violet and I have always watched out for one another." I said. I lowered my chin. "I feel I may have failed her."

"Oh, no! You mustn't think so!" he replied, "She's made her own decision!"

"You're of the opinion that she's eloped with Kelly?"

"Is there any other explanation?" he asked. "I myself have felt the sting of this nasty set of affairs, for people say my own marriage was that which drove Violet to such desperate measures – I never meant to give her false hope. She is a cheerful girl, and brimming with humor, and I found her a delight to engage in conversation!" He looked dejected. "I feared that, if I told her of Emma, your dear Violet would spend less time with me, and see me as a fruitless waste of effort."

"She's given to flights of fantasy," I explained, "Especially in matters of the heart."

"Well, I have spoken with the Faulks sisters and arranged for a séance tonight, and hope that mysticism may prove triumphant where science and brute effort has failed. Would you attend?"

"I'm not certain that would be a good idea, Dr. Briggs."

We stopped outside the Willard Block, his destination. He shook my hand, and held my palm in his warm embrace for a long moment. If I looked bewildered, he stammered to explain. "I know, after our last encounter with the Great Beyond, you are less than convinced, but I would not think to continue in a venture of this nature without the assistance of our spiritual guides. Mr. Fish tells me he will attend only if you are there – he says you are a shining beacon of light, by which the spirits can find their way to our table, and he could not bear a session without you by his side."

I could almost hear Mr. Fish's cynicism percolating through Brigg's faithful, if naïve, message. "I suppose I could," I agreed.

"Perhaps you could bring an item of Violet's, something personal and unique, to give the spirits assistance?"

"If it would help."

"Then tonight! It's set. The Faulks sisters are quite eager to gather a table for a séance, and I know they'll be pleased, and perhaps even a bit relieved, to have you in attendance. Your endorsement will be heartily welcomed." Briggs released my hand. "Come at eight, bring your father if he wishes. We shall attempt to discern dear Violet's present location with the help of our guardian angels."

48

I FOUND Father at the hospital, pouring over a stack of paperwork with a china cup of tea steaming on the corner of his desk. I closed the door behind me as I entered, unsure of what to say.

"Good afternoon," he said, glancing up for only a moment. "I'm afraid I have no patients for the rest of the day, Liz, and little need for your hands; the Board of Directors requires a report, and I find myself mired in paperwork –"

"One quick question, if you don't mind."

"Is it about your studies? I expect you to have read about the pulmonary system—"

"No, sir."

He set his pen aside the ink well and folded his hands in his lap. "What is it, Liz?"

"I wanted to ask you about Panama."

He gave an audible sigh. "Why this fascination with long-ago days? You have enough to keep you occupied in the present."

"Was the trip though Panama your idea?"

He pursed his lips. "Yes. I suppose we could have gone through Montreal, and overland by train, but I thought it best that we go the full distance by ship."

"Why?" I asked, "If we'd gone by train—"

"Neither you nor Violet wouldn't have become ill, I know." he replied. "It is a burden of grief I have carried in my heart for many years." He returned his gaze to his papers.

I looked at him sidelong, and said in a quiet voice, "Are you sorry? Really?"

"Of course I'm sorry," he said without meeting my eyes, "Why wouldn't I feel remorse?"

I measured his careful reaction, and said, "I remember you saying that, sometimes, one sickness can cancel out another."

John gave a small laugh, deep in his chest. "Are you accusing me of orchestrating your sickness, Lizzie? For you were ill, too."

"You do very little without great forethought," I said.

"So, you wonder if I planned for us to visit Panama, so that you and Violet would contract ague? I shouldn't want you to think I'd risk your lives, if not for a very good reason."

I cast my mind back to Panama – the humid stench, the painful fever, the sweating and boils. I thought of the quarantine we'd endured on the ship, and recalled with startling clarity the vision of Violet clinging to life, wrapped in bed sheets soaked through with sweat.

"What reason would be good enough, I wonder."

Father looked uncomfortable. He chose his words with care. "My dear Molly was ill in the mind. If my daughters had contracted the same illness, I would never have forgiven myself." He sat back in his chair, and the words flowed more easily from his lips – it was easier to speak the truth than keep it from me any longer. "Your mother was so very, very sick. I didn't know if you were ill, too, but I could not bear for you and Violet to have contracted her disease." He took a sip of tea to moisten his lips before continuing. "It was my good fortune to discover the works of Julius Wagner-Jauregg, an Austrian physician, who has done extraordinary work in the treatment of mental aberrations at the University of Graz. In one of his essays, he proposed the use of a deliberate introduction of an infectious disease to cure madness, and suggesting malaria or erisipila as most suitable to the purpose. So when I recognized the signs in Molly, it seemed prudent to expose you and Violet to the jungles of Panama, and hope that you would suffer a cure before the disease weakened your mind, too." He breathed deeply, and his smile contained a measure of relief. "I believe Wagner-Jauregg's cure has proven sound. If we'd stayed in England, you'd most likely be dead."

"What is the disease?"

"An unnatural obsession," he replied, "Of which I was unable to cure your mother." He reached out and ran his hand affectionately over my crown. "But you, Liz, are as healthy as a horse, and Violet is far better than she would have been, had she never suffered from malaria. Panama burned the madness out of you. And so, to answer your original question – no, I am not truly sorry. It's not in my nature to waste my time with regret."

I LEFT his office and said nothing to him of Mr. Brigg's invitation, afraid that he would see my curiosity as a sliding descent into mysticism, but when I returned home, I told Agnes that I wished to attend a gathering with Mr. Briggs and Mr. Fish as my chaperones. The woman cocked one eyebrow in curious contempt.

"Well, at least you've dressed seemingly," she mused, glancing over my demure grey dress and black stockings, "And that's a blessing itself. I can nae find fault with your chosen company. Both are guld, decent gentlemen." She pursed her lips and thought about it, and finally said, "Your father has sent word that he'll work late in his office tonight, so I'll have no occasion to speak with him."

"He won't mind, I'm certain," I replied as I pulled a dark woolen cloak over my shoulders.

"But he oocht tae," Agnes declared, "And if I do see him," she added, waggling a finger, "I'll be sure tae tell him where you are."

"As you must," I replied, "I'll be home as quick as I can. I don't enjoy these beastly things."

"Aye, I've heard you've nae got the stomach for 'em," Agnes

teased, then released me into the evening and closed the door behind me.

By the time I arrived, a small but dense crowd of admirers had gathered in the Faulks' parlor. The intimate and quiet flicker of pillar candles had already replaced the hissing light of the gas lamps. The excitement of the week had stirred up a dash of mysticism in even the most reticent individuals, and the Faulks had fanned the flames of this fervor into a raging livelihood for themselves. They'd held a séance every night since the eloped couple had left town, and even tonight, five women and three men crowded around table in the centre of the room, spread with a patterned scarf to give it an exotic, Egyptian flair. The jar by the door was already half full of glittering coins. Mason Briggs rose to his feet as I entered, and extended a hand, to offer the empty chair at his side.

"Miss Saunders!" he chirped, "We saved a chair especially for you!"

"Good evening, my dear," droned Mr. Fish, and flashed a toothy grin that might been deemed, in more discerning company, as hideously gruesome. "We find ourselves propped beside each other again."

"I'm not so thirsty tonight," I confided, and he laughed.

"And Mrs. Miller and Mrs. Cray," said Dr. Briggs, sweeping one manicured hand at the women across the table, "You've met them before, have you not?"

"Yes, thank you, hello," I said to each in turn, and the two ladies nodded and smiled. Both were wives of mine managers, middle-aged and gathering their weight about the hips and thighs. The other women were of lower status and warranted no introduction, but I said 'Hello' to them nonetheless, and they looked uncomfortable but returned my greeting.

I reached into the leather satchel slung over my shoulder. "I've brought these, which Violet likes." I set a pair of silk, peach-colored gloves in the centre of the table, were they lay deflated and dejected, empty skins, casting long dancing shadows in the candlelight. "She bought them last year and wore them frequently before Mother's death."

Kitty drew alongside my chair and regarded the gloves with awe. "Oh, the spirits!" said the woman in her dulcet voice which, in its depth, held a quiet sort of power. "Already they muster about the table! I see them!" She admired the gloves, and whispered, "We begin!"

A reverential hush fell across the room. The shadows seemed to grow darker, thicker, and the room became a confessional. I leaned a little toward Mr. Fish, who patted the curve of my knee in comradery.

"Rise up, o spirits!" ordered Kitty as her hands stretched towards the ceiling, "Rise up and hear our cries! We implore upon you, guide us!"

The anticipation that settled over the room dampened all sounds. I held my breath and strained the limits of my hearing for some sound, any sound, to break the tension.

From behind the curtain came a rustling of fabric, the whispering swish of glass beads, and the tinkle of little metal bells. Peggy emerged, dressed in a sumptuous purple robe so decadent that it would have made the emperors of Rome jealous -- a thousand Tyrian whelks must have given their lives for the hyacinth hue of that fabric, which by flickering shifts of candle-light and shadow became the shimmering color of clotted blood. "THOTH, GOD OF KNOWLEDGE, HATH ARRIVED!" she shrieked, flinging her arms heavenward.

The flames flared and Peggy's face loomed over the table, wide and white. Mr. Fish scrambled backwards, startled.

"I HAVE COME!" she screeched in her unearthly, high-pitched, warbling falsetto, "I WALK AMONG YOU! YOU SEEK A WOMAN, A FRAIL BLOSSOM, THE FIRST VIOLET OF SPRING!"

Fish leapt into the conversation. "Yes, the elder Miss Saunders!"

"SHE IS HAPPY! OH! SO HAPPY!" continued Peggy, "SHE SIPS THE SWEET NECTAR OF TRUE LOVE AND RESTS IN THE SAFE BOWER OF HER LOVER'S ARMS."

Kitty prompted her sister-in-law. "But where, o great spirit?"

"I SEE, I SEE, A SHIP ON THE SEA." Peggy continued, "A MAN OF JUSTICE, THEY SAIL TOGETHER INTO A GLORIOUS HORIZON, ABLAZE WITH THE FLAMES OF THEIR AFFECTIONS."

I leaned forward. "What are they running from?"

Peggy faltered, then rolled her eyes into her head and tipped her chin back. "THEY RUN FROM A GREAT DISAPPOINTMENT, A DISSATISFACTION. THEY POSSESS A DESIRE FOR ADVENTURE."

"What does Panama have to do with any of this? Is that where they've gone?"

"UH...I DO NOT SEE SO CLEARLY—"

"How does he know about Panama? How does he know we got sick there?" My voice rose in impatient anger. If the rest of the company had questions, I paid no attention. I aimed every query at Peggy like a flaming arrow. "C'mon, Thoth, answer me clearly. Who is he, and how does he know about Panama?"

"THE MAN OF LAW AND JUSTICE—"

"Not Kelly!" I demanded, "I'm not talking about Kelly!"

"Lizzie, my dear," Kitty said, laying one hand on my forearm. "Please sit down and calm yourself, child."

I shrugged off the woman's soothing hand. "Answer me this, Thoth: why didn't Violet take the money?"

"Money?" said Kitty.

I leaned forward. "Yes, the money! It was more than enough – why didn't she take it?"

"Goodness!" said Peggy, her face ablaze with curiosity. "There's been no mention of any riches.... Did you say money?"

"How much money?" said one of the managers' wives.

"The spirits speak in riddles; perhaps the reason is there, amongst the tidbits they share... perhaps, with some financial incentive....." Kitty explained.

"The spirits ought to speak plainly, if they're going to speak at all," I demanded. "Or don't they know what I'm talking about?"

Peggy and Kitty traded a look of urgency, and Peggy's warbling voice boomed, "THOUGH DIFFICULT TO SEE THROUGH THE

SHIFTING VEILS OF THE FUTURE, I SHALL REVEAL THE PRECISE LOCATION —"

"Horseshit!" I shouted.

A gasp of horror rose from the ladies. Mrs. Miller and Mrs. Cray rolled their eyes at such a vulgar display of poor, provincial manners. Kitty stepped back as if struck.

Rage flared up inside me, so fast and dizzying that the room around me dissolved, and my entire focus fell upon the wide, pasty face of Peggy Faulks. I leapt up from the table, knocking back my chair with a bang, and snatched the silk gloves from the centre of the table.

"How dare you profit off of Violet's disappearance?' I demanded, shaking the gloves at the woman, "How dare you have the audacity to squeeze money out of these poor rubes? You're shameless!"

"Please, child, sit down and—"

"I will not!" I raged at Kitty, "I refuse to listen to any more of your tripe! My sister is missing!"

"She's in love—" Mason said, laying a soothing hand on my arm.

I bared my teeth at him. "She's gone!" I shrugged off Mason's hand. "I'm sorry, sir, to disappoint you, but I'm afraid I can no longer stay and listen to this ridiculous fable. There are no spirits, there are no empyrean angels leading Kitty and Peggy, and there is certainly no great cache of wealth waiting to be given to these batty old swindlers." I shouldered through the door and into the night.

But at the gate, a voice calling out made me stop. When I turned, Kitty ran towards me, looking fragile and spindly.

"Wait, Lizzie! Wait!"

Over my shoulder, I cried, "I have nothing else to give you!"

"I don't want your money!" Kitty insisted, grabbing my hand. "When you were here before, I spoke to you, a woman called out to you—"

"No, I won't listen to it!" I refused, "It's all a ugly trick!"

Kitty's eyes were wide. "But it wasn't, my girl! I mean, yes, Peggy's spirits are an act, I'll own to it – but that night, my words... they weren't scripted, I swear!"

"Then do it again!" I commanded, my words knife-sharp with sarcasm, "Ask the dead woman calling out to you, where is Violet? Where's my sister?"

"I can't do it again, not at a whim!" Kitty pleaded. "Oh God, I wish I could! I wish I could tell you where your precious sister is, but I can't! Maybe if you ask the dead woman, or give me her name—"

"Or drop another coin in the jar," I spat. "Go on, Kitty, you have a room full of suckers to rob." I turned on my heel and ran.

Even the cool evening air couldn't dampen the fury that boiled within me. I clutched at my chest as I ran westward, head down, panting to catch my breath and contain my temper. I could hardly bear it. My anger flamed through my core like a windstorm, burned my throat, ripped at my gut.

At last, I collapsed against the corner of Simon Leiser's Big Store, heaving for breath. The moon moved a hand's span in the sky as I tried, unsuccessfully, to wrestle my emotions under control. At last, when my breath slowed and my pulse returned to its familiar rhythm, I pressed the palm of my hand to my brow, only to find it peppered with beads of sweat.

People were not meant to feel so blindingly, I thought. They're not meant to be filled with such power – given time, this sort of rage could tear a girl apart.

I BURST through the ragged curtain into the apothecary, seething with an ungainly anger that made my fingers spasm and my teeth gnash. I barely remembered running the whole distance between Simon Leiser's store and Chinatown, and paid no attention whatsoever to all the polite society and businesses sandwiched in between. My full focus drove me headlong through the door, my braid loosed and my hair now unbound, my black frock gathered between my knees. "Where can I find him?" I screamed. "God damn it, Shao, where is Jack—"

The hushed discussions in Cantonese abruptly ceased. Ten or fifteen men milled in the apothecary shop, and they had been trained to fall silent at the first hint of English – their own experiences had taught them, English was the language of brutal and cruel men, and an Englishman had every legal right to beat them for the smallest indiscretion. A few even bowed their heads. But when they realized it was a girl, a very slight girl, red-faced and clench-fisted but no bigger than a twig, that had blundered into the midst of their convocation by mistake, they parted a clear path to Mr. Tao.

Pale tallow candles slumped along the counter, casting light over the rows of gleaming glass jars. The air was hazy with smoke. He advanced two steps, shocked and stunned, and the smoke in the air curled in his wake. Almost instantly, he recognized me and regained his composure. This was his shop -- he would suffer no trespass.

"You interrupt!" Mr. Tao accused. He jabbed his index finger to the door. "Get out!"

His thunderous expression might have struck terror into most girls, but I was far too angry to notice. I planted my feet. "I want Shaozhu!" I demanded, "Where is he?"

The two rows of owlish faces watched me like a deliberating jury. Most were older, grey and wrinkled like Mr. Tao, but one familiar face appeared in the far doorway, young and smooth, strong and open.

And ablaze with embarrassment.

Shao pushed himself to the front of the men, and bowed to his uncle, saying something in hushed and hurried Cantonese.

Mr. Tao raged back at him, stabbing his finger into the middle of Shao's chest, then pointing rapidly between me and the door. I might not understand a word of Cantonese, but my grasp of body language was fairly comprehensive.

"I'm not getting out!" I replied. Mr. Tao's jaw gaped at either my insolence or the misperception that I understood Cantonese. "I need to talk to Chen Shaozhu!" I stamped my foot. "Right! Now!"

Shao stammered, then pushed his way through the crowd, bowing his head and making a point to apologize directly to each elder as he passed, until he could seize my forearm and boldly commandeer me out the door. In the alley, he towered over me, standing closer that he might have dared otherwise. He scuttled me away from the building, down the steps, across the street, and into a narrow yard squeezed between shacks.

Without any apology, he pushed me up against the rough wall. "Damn it, Liz," he hissed, "That was the council to the benevolent society! And now, you've barged in, paying no attention to good manners--" His statement came to an abrupt stop. He suddenly noticed that I stood with fists clenched and shoulders trembling, and a dark ferocity blazing in my eyes. He clutched my forearms. "Ai ye, Lizzie! Are you okay?"

"No, goddamn it!" The loudness of my own voice startled me; it bounced off the sheds and along the alley, and I heard echoes of my yell resound along the rising valley walls. I dropped my voice and said, "No, I'm not okay! My sister is missing! And the bloody Faulks sisters are profiting off of it, and no one seems to listen when I say: there's something very, very wrong!"

"They've eloped – there's nothing we can do—"

"They haven't eloped!"

Shao examined my face, looking for some hint of what to say. "This isn't like you—"

I started to shake, my heart pounded in my chest. Frustration welled up inside until I feared I might burst. Through clenched teeth, I said, "Jack claims she's gone, and I'm in danger, too, but I can't pin him down long enough to wrestle a decent answer out of him! He knows what's happened to Violet!"

"She left with Kelly—"

"She didn't!" I screamed, "Tell me where Jack is! I need to ask the bastard myself – what happened to Violet!"

"I don't know where he is!"

"You do, too!" I accused as I thumped my fist against his chest. "Where is he, Shao?!?!"

"Keep your voice down!" he replied, and looked across the street, up to the windows on the second levels. He grabbed my arms and held them close to my sides. "I don't trust him—"

"I don't trust him, either, god damn it!" I replied, "But don't try to shelter me from him!"

A burning rage sweep through me like a wildfire across a hill of dry grasses: a galloping cavalry of flames, swift and unstoppable, leaving dark dead earth behind. A swell of noise burst up from my throat in a roar of rage, and I closed my eyes, let myself be towed under by this vast ocean of feeling, bared my teeth and screamed with head tilted back to the sky. My heart pounded, and I was sure that the muscle of love and life was set to beat its way up through my throat, shove aside my tongue, and spring out of my mouth like a mountain lion. God, it hurt. It HURT! Rage wracked my body. That sweet fire burned through my fingernails and coursed like a river of molten gold down my spine, that sense of unity with all the fires that burned in the universe and urged the stars to wheel through the cosmos. I felt the rushing of air in my ears, as if falling through a tunnel, and I feared that I would split in two again. If I submerged myself in this white hot furnace of anger, if I released my hold upon myself as I had done down in the mine, I knew it would consume me.

I gasped for a breath and dug my fingernails into my palms, creating little crescent moons of pain.

The temptation ebbed, slowly at first, then faster. I fell back a step to lean against the wall of the shack.

Shao released my arms. He stood at arm's length. His eyes were impossibly wide.

"Are you.....," he began, cautious, already aware of the answer, and asking a question that seemed ridiculously flimsy compared to the howling demon I'd become, "...Okay?"

My knees collapsed. I slumped against the wooden shed. All the rage left me, poured out and dissolved into the ether. I became a husk of a girl with nothing inside. I reflected, as if from a far distant place, that it felt cold to be so full of nothing again.

"You look ill, Liz," he said softly, carefully, and held out his hand. Every joint wobbled, from my ankles to my neck, so he wrapped an arm around me and half-carried me into the apothecary shop, passed the circle of elderly men.

Mr. Tao said something to Shao in Cantonese, then looked directly at me and hissed, "Bai SuZhen".

I felt Shao tense. His reply to jiu fu was respectful and submissive, but containing a low tense resonance, a sub-sonic growl of warning, that caused jiu fu to hold his tongue and let both of us pass.

Shao escorted me up a crooked set of stairs, each one set at a different angle than its brothers. The doors leading off the second story landing were as cock-eyed and jumbled as the steps, set into walls that sloped to the ceiling and flared at the bottom; the combined elements of the structure gave the impression that the building contractor was cross-eyed, one-armed and mildly insane. Shao booted open one door. It squealed in protest against a tight door jam, and he ushered me into a room which I mistook, at first, for a broom closet.

It was crowded with items, not because there were hundreds of objects inside, but because the space was too small to contain very much of anything at all. It reminded me of the cabins on board the ship to Panama: a treasure trove of ragged possessions, crammed deck to rafter with boxes and crates and jute sacks and pallets and straw bedding and patched blankets hung from cords strung over the ceiling. This, I realized, was the entire length and breadth of Shao's home, most likely shared between he and jiu fu and, from the presence of two additional pallets, a pair of other men as well. At the far end of the room, smeared with dust, a single square window gave a view of the neighbor's wall across the alleyway.

He levered me down onto a corner pallet and pulled the curtains of blankets closed, shutting me off from the world. The sound of his feet on the creaking boards retreated into the stairwell, vanishing through another door into the warren of rooms and corridors that honeycombed the building – if four men lived in this tiny space, how many called this single building home? I floated for a while on the waves of adrenaline left behind by my anger, and listened to the sounds of talking and movement through the thin walls: up, down, to the left and the right, the voices created a constant murmur from all directions, too low to pluck individual words from conversations, and most likely in a language I didn't understand. My eyes drifted over the unpainted grey walls, speckled with black mildew, and the brindled, yellowed water stains across the ceiling. My fingers reached out to caress the fringe of the grey wool blanket, which hung from rusted nails pounded at irregular angles into the support beams. The room smelt close, sweaty, swampy, but a broken pane in the window allowed a wisp of cool evening air to seep in. The cargo chest at the end of Shao's pallet seemed new: like the walls, it was constructed of unpainted wood, but freshly hewn and yellow, hairy with straw still trapped between its cracks. Where the crowbar had bit between lid and box to pry up the top, an explosion of slivers as long as my fingers splayed out from the planks. A few beads and stones sat on the top, along with a small cracked cup full of sand, where the burnt ends of little sticks stuck out like porcupine needles.

The curtain moved aside. Shao sat at the end of the straw mattress, and took my satchel. He dropped it next to his bed.

He held a cup of tea. Silvery shawls of steam encircled his hands as he passed it to me. Between us, he set a small wooden trencher carrying thin wedges of baked fish, pink ginger slices, a pale white lump of steamed dough. I took the lump in hand, broke it in half to reveal an interior of shredded pork drizzled in a sweet red sauce. The flavor lingered on my tongue, overwhelmed my sense of taste and smell, and I recalled eating one before, at the opera house.

He watched me eat, never once interrupting.

At last, I asked, "What did your uncle say to you?"

"He told me to be careful," Shao replied. "I told him I always am. With greatest respect, of course."

"But he called me Bai SuZhen," I said.

Shao blushed, which made me grin.

"He believes we are insulting the gods," I inferred, "And that I'm a demon sent to tempt you."

"Something like that."

I took a sip of tea, and the taste was strange – not unpleasant, but reminiscent of soil and roots. It had the perfume of dark things recently dug out of the earth and exposed to the light.

"What is this?"

"I thought it might calm you," he said, "You were very.... upset."

"Upset?" I asked, and laughed weakly, "An understatement, Shao."

He curved his spine against the wall and hugged his knees, and the corner of his mouth kinked up in a grin. "Is that what English doctors call 'hysteria'?"

"Hysteria? No, 'hysteria' is a doctor's way of saying he doesn't understand women," I replied. "That was not hysteria. That was something else."

"Is it your mother's illness?" He looked gravely concerned.

I pondered his question. "My mother never got angry, not like I do. She was afraid of everything and everyone, but she hid herself away and kept distant from people." I thought back to what Father had told me this afternoon, said without regret. "Father wanted Violet and I to catch malaria in Panama, to burn our mother's sickness out of us, and he says we were healed. We've never shown any symptoms."

"A brutal remedy," Shao said, "Risky, too."

"But worth it, in his estimation." I wrung my hands in my lap, considering my own poor temper. "No, this isn't my mother's illness. This is frustration, Shao, and I've never dealt well with other people."

I sipped at the tea again. I could almost feel my muscles relax, one by one.

"I can't put my finger on it, Shao, but I know that Violet didn't elope."

"But everyone has said--"

"I know what everyone has said," I replied, "Everyone is wrong."

Another sip of tea slid easily down my throat and unfurled tentacles of warmth and relaxation through my limbs.

"Then what do you propose to do?" he asked.

"If I could just talk to Jack--"

"No."

"Why not?"

He shuffled closer, so that we sat side by side on the bed. "You are too innocent, Lizzie. You don't understand how cruel people can be." His smile held pity. "This isn't your fault, and you should be joyful –

you've been born into a life of privilege. But Jack is a *huaidan*, a bad egg, the kind of man who will use your innocence against you."

"You underestimate me, Shao."

"Lizzie, you're only a girl—"

"I am a girl," I said, "That is true. But *only* a girl? Has no one ever said you were *only* Chinese?"

His dark brows drew together. "All the time."

"And we both know, Shao, you are more than *only* one thing."

A sly smile flickered across his face. "I still don't trust Jack."

"How much did he pay you, to protect me?"

Shao blinked at the question. "What?"

"I just wondered," I replied, taking a bite of the steamed pork bun, "How much I'm worth to Mr. Hunter."

"A lot." Shao hesitated. "A month's wages. Almost enough to pay my debts."

I rocked back on my bum, hugging my knees to my chest. "He holds a knife to my throat, threatens to kill me, steals from my father. Then suddenly, he's paying you to protect me, giving me condolences on the disappearance of my sister, and carrying my book bag for me. He knows we went to Panama. He claims my sister won't come back." I considered this for a moment, then said, "Shao, I don't think Mr. Hunter is *only* a huaidan, either."

"Close," he said, nodding slightly in appreciation. "More emphasis on the first syllable, but almost perfect."

"*Xie xie*." I licked the last of the sauce from my fingertips. "Mr. Hunter broke into every doctor's house, but he only stole from my father."

"You think Jack targeted your father? But, why? What would anyone have against your father?" said Shao, "He's a good man, well-respected, helpful—'

"Who fled from his wife's poor reputation in England."

"But how would Jack know your mother?" Shao asked. "She was dead before he ever arrived." He took a slice of ginger from the plate and ate it, thinking. "Do you think Jack and your father have met before?"

"I don't believe so," I admitted. "Jack visited my father for medical assistance, and my father didn't recognize him. I'd swear, they'd never seen the other."

"Appearances change—"

"But not so drastically." I pondered this, then said, "Mr. Kelly recently came into mistaken information regarding my family, and on Sunday night, he and Violet fled. The last person to speak privately with Mr. Kelly was Mr. Hunter. What, pray tell, did they discuss?" I sipped the tea. "If I can't find Mr. Kelly to speak with him myself, the only other person I can ask is Jack."

We sat for a while in silence as Shao considered my words. "And if Kelly has shared his fears with Violet, she may have fled of her own choice."

"But not without me." I replied. "I know I disappoint her, but she still loves me."

Shao nodded at this. "I agree."

"I've spent hours, trying to find Jack, and I've had no luck." I chuckled. "I even wore a dress, figuring I might be more persuasive if I looked less tomboyish. Batting her eyelashes and wearing frilly things seems to work miracles for Violet, but I feel stupid." I plucked at the dress. "I feel like one of those simpering cherubs on the cover of Lady's Home Journal."

"I think you look lovely," he said, "And very persuasive, indeed."

A blush rose up my skin, and my heart beat a little faster, but there was no rage or fire accompanying it. I reached out one hand, ran my palm along his cheek and chin, and with the lightest touch of my fingertips, drew his head close to mine.

His lips tasted savory.

The wooden trencher, empty, clattered to the floor. My dress soon joined it, his clothes following after. I felt the smooth, lean length of his body next to me, noticed the small white scars on his hands and his arms, smelt the sweet fragrance of dried herbs and wood smoke in his blue-black hair. Neither of us hesitated, neither asked for permission from the other. We melted together with as much resistance as two beads of water. Deft hands sought out the curves and lines of each other's body, exploring in the falling twilight, and when he rolled on top and arched his body into mine, a bright punch exploded up through my torso.

I did not cry out. My mind had split again; one side drowned under waves of ecstasy and pain, and the other watched it sink below the surface, ready to reach across the divide and catch it and drag it back up into the dry safety of reason. The rational portion of my soul catalogued the uncontrolled reactions of my body: tense arms, fingers clinging to the mattress, heels digging into the straw. Like an anthropologist crouched at the edge of a tribal village, I logged notes regarding this curious ritual of "sex" and deemed it, after thoughtful consideration, to be a fascinating and wondrous reaction to the reproductive element of "lust".

Suddenly, the divide narrowed. For a single gasping breath, I felt frantic – I had been too busy to notice that a threshold had been crossed. Pain and Ecstasy had sunk claws into passive Reason and were surely dragging it under, and poor Reason no longer wished to fight, to hold onto itself, to understand itself as an individual entity. I let myself go, and suddenly there was no sense of self, no division between them. There was only the white, intense illumination of perfection, so overpowering that every other sensation vanished, swallowed up by the starburst magnitude of my rapture.

Bliss faded. The mold-speckled walls and brindled ceiling swam into focus. Self-awareness rose like an island out of the euphoric ocean.

I became aware that Shao had collapsed next to me, and now nuzzled his face lazily in the hollow under my chin, whispering melodic secrets to my flesh in a pidjin of harmonic languages. From the side of the mattress, I pulled the thin blanket over our sweat-slick bodies. I caressed his hair, half-listening to him as he fell asleep in my embrace. I wondered if the world would see the difference in my face, now that I was party to the thaumaturgic mysteries of copulation; I had been made aware, I *knew*, I had touched the grandeur of creation, I was open to sin. It was not quite triumph I felt, but something close, blended with tranquility.

This made me smile.

I'd felt the same sort of honey-soaked, gentle, mellow tranquility once before, last June, on my trip into the mine with Father. I nestled myself into Shao's embrace and mused that maybe this tranquility was a little better, because this time, nothing had needed to die.

49

A SOOTHING HAND on my shoulder interrupted my satisfied sleep.

When I pried open my reluctant eyelids, the first thing I noticed was that Shao had already dressed, covered his lean and muscular body in his shapeless flannels. He had splashed his face with handfuls of water taken from a leather bucket in the corner. The second thing I noticed was a consuming silence, thick as treacle, which stood at complete odds to the persistent whisper of voices I'd heard before. The building had fallen silent. That seemed to have put Shao on edge, for he jumped at the tiniest creak in the floorboards.

"You have to go," he urged, and when I hesitated, more out of sleepiness than reticence, he added, "The association meeting has finished, the men have gone. I can't let jiu fu find you here." He handed my dress to me, then turned his back to give me privacy while I dressed.

"What time is it?"

"Almost midnight."

"Oh!" The need for quickness turned my fingers into clumsy sausages. "I've been gone too long!"

I jerked to a stop at the sound of my own prattling. A scolding from Agnes for coming home late would pale in comparison to what would befall Shao if his uncle found a naked white girl in the boy's bed. And, to take it one step further, Mr. Tao's fury would be nothing, compared to the fate that would materialize over their humble Chinese apothecary, should the Company discover the horrific affront to all that was good and decent in Victorian society which had occurred in this tiny room on the second floor.

Dexterity returned to my hands. Never in the history of illicit dalliances had a row of pearl buttons been so hastily closed.

"I'll walk you home," he offered, "Come on, hurry, we'll go out the back door and avoid the porch and street." He helped me to my feet, but before I let go of his fingers, I drew him close and kissed him again, long and languid. He melted into the kiss, then pushed me away.

"No," he refused, "Not again."

He led me down the stairs, through the warren of rooms and corridors, to the front porch, and we ran along the street to the edge of Chinatown. Here, I reached out once more to him, and in the shadows of the plum trees, held his fingers in mine. He dared not draw any closer to me. A slight touch was all he allowed.

We parted, and I ran along the tracks towards Cumberland, alone.

When I tumbled into my own bed, with white sheets as clean and crisp as freshly fallen snow, I thought of that sublime tranquility he'd driven into me, that singular moment in which reason had given way to felicity, and marveled at it.

And fell deeply, unabashedly, consummately asleep.

50

August 15, 1898

In the morning, I woke to the distant cacophonic music of the mines: metal grinding against metal, the rhythmic squawking of cogs and sprockets in need of oil, and the churning noise of the cars hauled up and down. I heard rattling trips dumping piles of stones, the back-and-forth hiss of boys raking dross and slag, the shouts of the mine boss keeping lazy help in line. Laying in bed, almost a mile away from No. 5, I could tell the contents of each lift's cargo: the elevator car moved slow and steady when it carried men or timbers down into the lightless shafts, and sounded like a giant grinding his teeth. It rocketed furiously fast when hauling up coal, and the grinding became a growl.

I heard other sounds, too – in the kitchen, Agnes hummed to herself and pounded the wooden table for every third note, which meant she was kneading bread. A bevy of sparrows gathered in the apple trees and chattered to each other. A horse cart clip-clopped up the hill. The driver gave a whistle. A woman in a garden laughed lightly at a flippant joke. I rose from bed and surveyed the back yard.

The garden tools leaned in neat rows along the surgery wall, and the flat-bottomed wheelbarrow with its wooden wheel sat next to the bucket at the pump in the back corner of the yard. It seemed like any other summer morning.

My concerns from the night before had not disappeared, but they held less power in the daylight. I questioned my suspicions – yes, Violet was gone, but maybe she had chosen to go, and maybe she was satisfied with her decision. My anger at the Faulks sisters had mellowed and, without that fire, I began to think that maybe my fears were unfounded. The scant evidence did pointed to an elopement. Perhaps Violet and Alexander Kelly were enjoying the sunlight and planning a future together, and I was worried needlessly.

I wondered if I ought to feel more, or if I ought to feel differently. Violet had abandoned us and left an empty void in my life, yet the world continued to turn. Even our mother's death had little impact on the constant mechanisms of the world -- the sun still rose and set, the birds still sang, the tides still ebbed and flowed. The mundane pattern of daily responsibilities swept in and filled all the cracks where Molly Saunders once existed.

And now, the same was happening with Violet and Mr. Kelly. People noted their absence, then moved on. I wondered if the world would continue to turn so easily when I, myself, had moved away. I turned from the window, felt the stiff ache between my thighs, and wiped the blood from between my legs with the hem of yesterday's skirt. As I dressed, I pondered the thought of a world without me in it, and realized that yes, I was just as expendable as every other human being that had existed before me, and every human being that would come after me.

'How can a life have so little impact?' I thought. 'How can we continue to do anything with a sense of urgency or importance, when time will erase our names from the annals of history, and everything we do amounts to precisely nothing? No one will remember me when I am dead. No one will remember my mother, my sister, my father. All we have done will be forgotten.'

When I thumped downstairs, I was in a sour mood.

Nor was Agnes in a pleasant state of mind, and she rounded on me as I entered the kitchen. The woman's face had gone red with the exertion of pounding the life out of the bread dough.

"Where were you last evening, me love?" she asked, "Your father ate his dinner alone, then spent hours looking for you!"

"He did?"

"Aye, that he did! Would ye expect less?" She reeled one hefty arm back and plowed a fist into the dough again, to remind it who was boss. "He's already lost one daughter tae her foolish fancies, and here he was, thinking himself tae be left alone, and you gone on some merry goose chase, and up in hills, eaten by wolves! Lord help us!" The bread suffered another blow. "He sent me home, rented a horse from the livery, and rode all over the valley looking for ye!"

"He did?" I said again. I wisely assumed that, if I said anything out of turn, I'd suffer the same fate as the bread.

"Aye, and the poor man is in his bed still, all worn oot with worry and exertion! And oot a pretty pocket for the rental of a horse!" Her fist vanished into the dough with a bang. "I wager you be on your best behavior from now until Kingdom Come, you hear me? Running off like that? May our Lord have mercy on your soul for such wickedness!" Pow! "Such thoughtlessness!" Pow! "Such horrid, horrid behavior!" Pow! "I would tell you tae apologize straight away, except that the merciful thing tae do is let your poor father sleep!" Pow!

"When he wakes, a fervent apology will be the first thing I do," I promised, and this soothed Agnes Gunn a bit, and caused the red in her cheeks and forehead to fade into a healthier color.

"If you were one of my brood, awa all the nicht tae the wee hours, I'd have strung you up by your ankles from the weather vane and left the ravens tae pick your bones." She waggled one flour-white finger at me. "And you wouldn't be in those ridiculous pants, my girl, or running freely hither and yon all over God's green earth. I'd have given you a solid education, none of this unrestrained freedom tae read whatever you wish, and do whatever you fancy!" The bread suffered a series of knock-down, drag-out assaults. Bits of flour and dough hit the walls. "Your father is a guld man and a gentleman and it's nae my place tae tell him how you ought tae be raised, but if ye were my wee bairn—"

A knock on the door cut Agnes' intentions short, and I almost ran to the front porch, desperate for escape from the thought of life as a Gunn.

51

On summer mornings, as the first rays of the crisp sun kissed the wide grey waters of Comox Lake, Alfio Perugino pushed his skiff from the beach below his cabin and paddling along the eastern shoreline to fish. Sometimes he went out far into the lake, and other times he stayed close to the cabins that clung to the south-east shore, but there was a small cove, a secret cove, the location of which he guarded jealously, that he loved the best.

The last fragments of a glacier, nestled high in the Beaufort Mountains, fed the lake with melted water, and while the cold water made for uncomfortable swimming, it produced fat, healthy, and succulent trout. In Perugino's special cove, underneath cliffs garbed in a plush cloak of coniferous forest, a rim of muddy flats plunged down into the bottomless depths. Mosquitoes, black flies, damsel flies, dragonflies, all skittered on the surface of the water, performing an intricate aeronautical dance in their pursuit of microscopic prey, and up from the abyss came trout, silver-bellied and speckled, as big as a man's arm.

He did not come here often for he was afraid that he might lead a watchful competitor to his beloved spot, or scare the fish with his habit and cause the trout to abandon the place. However, he'd avoided his cove for almost a week, and on this summer's morning, he judged it safe to return to his cherished fishing hole. His boat slipped noiselessly over the glassy water, coasting to a gentle stop in the middle of the cove, and Perugino laid aside his paddle, took up his old cane pole, and baited the hook with a juicy, plump, pink worm. He loved the feel of the worm's cold flesh wriggling against his hand, and the way it would switchback around his finger in a brainless reaction to the hook piercing its girth. Then, over the side went the hook and the worm and the line, into the frigid water which, even in August, remained as bracing as freshly-melted ice.

Perugino kicked back, rested his heels on the side of his boat, and watched the cumulonimbus clouds surge by. He wasn't thinking anything in particular, only ruminating on the blueness of the sky and the whiteness of the clouds and the perfection of a prospective trout dinner, when the skiff gently, and strangely, bumped.

It wasn't uncommon for the skiff to nudge against a submerged log, but a log makes a solid sound against the bow, wood against wood. This made a thump, but a soft thump, a gentle thump. He grabbed the oar as he sat up and peered over the side.

The glacial waters, normally clear and clean, appeared clouded with strange waves of black reeds. Perugino dipped his fingers below the surface to the depth of his wrist and felt the softness of silk, and let his eyes follow along the tangles of black until they fixed upon reams of long gold threads, glinting pale from deep under the surface, gently waving back and forth with the lazy current. He thought at first that this was a stump swept down by the autumn rains, hung up with garlands of dead weeds and tangles of gold summer grass.

The current parted the gold to reveal a face, round and pale with eyes open, staring up through three feet of water.

Perugino's breath caught in a strangled choke. He scrambled back in his little skiff so quickly that the boat bucked and almost threw him in the water.

Unable to pull her out, he returned to the cabins and brought back two other men, Bruno Gallo and Felice Moretti. They left Perugino's skiff at the dock and took Moretti's larger rowboat. Perugino felt a ping of regret that his secret cove would be a secret no longer, but consoled himself that it would no longer contain a dead woman, either, and that was worth the sharing.

After half-an-hour of searching, they found her again, floating like a mermaid under the surface. Only her billowing skirts broke the surface of the water. Gallo muttered in Latin, crossed himself, and closed his eye in reverential prayer. Moretti only stared down into the dark water, shivering slightly. With Gallo to act as a counterweight, Moretti and Perugino gripped the skirts and hauled her up, and she came easily, effortlessly, sliding from her watery cradle into the hot summer sun, leaving behind her graceful aquatic dance and becoming sodden and heavy in the dry world above.

Rivulets of ice-cold water streamed from the remains of her clothes. Her black skirts were torn to ribbons, and the corset seams had burst from the swelling flesh bound within.

They paddled back, speaking low in their mother tongue, for Italian was easy and fluid for them, and the beautiful words much more suited to the contemplation of death. It was only when they bumped and shimmied against the dock that Alfio Perugino switched back to English, and called for his wife.

Nessie ran into town on her bare feet, straight to the door of Dr. Saunders.

I, desperate for escape from thought of life as a Gunn, flew to the door and opened it wide. On the porch, I found the frantic, panting, sobbing figure of Nessie. Her throat heaved for breath, her bare feet were scabbed and bloodied.

"Agnes!" I shouted over my shoulder, "Bring water!"

Agnes pressed a cup of water into the woman's hand, but we could scarce get a word from her. Breathless and frantic, Nessie sobbed wildly, and tried to cling to Agnes for support. Agnes was loathed to let the woman touch her, but I reached out and hugged her, and Nessie covered her face with her hands and trembled all over, struggling with words that she did not want to say. When her watery eyes fixed upon me, her mouth contorted with renewed grief.

A great rushing sound filled my ears. A freight train sudden bore down upon me, its massive headlamp illuminating all in front of me and throwing Agnes and Nessie into sharp relief. I reached out a hand to steady myself against the doorframe. Already, the hand trembled.

"You've found Violet..." I whispered.

Nessie, unable to form words, only nodded.

Agnes staggered against the wall and wailed. She stumbled into the parlor and collapsed in the chair by the fireplace and sobbed, holding her hands over her face and drawing her legs in. I eased Nessie onto the wooden chair by the front door. I was reluctant to leave, but there was no one else to fetch Father. I pulled on my boots, and with Nessie installed in the hallway and Agnes hunched on the chair in the parlor, I ran across the street and over the garden grounds.

I found him in his office, attending to a nine-year-old boy with a rattling cough. A woman sat in the hall, engrossed in the latest Hudson's Bay catalogue, and by virtue of their shared chestnut hair and bone-rack frames, I discerned that she must be the boy's mother.

I entered the office without knocking. "Father?"

John glanced up to my stony expression.

"They've found Violet," I said.

The mother in the hall lowered the catalogue and leaned forward in her seat.

Father stood as still as a cat, digesting the words. He blinked twice, then bundled up his stethoscope and tapped the boy on the knee.

"I'm sorry, Tommy, but I'll have to ask you to run next door to Dr. Gould's office." He stood and helped the boy to his feet; the child's enthusiasm had been squashed by congestion in the chest, and I heard the wheezing in his breath that suggested the earliest symptoms of whooping cough. "Hurry along, now," John urged, "Dr. Gould is a fine fellow, and tell him I've sent you. He may favor you with a barley sweet, if you do as he asks." He tucked the stethoscope in his medical bag and grabbed his coat from the back of his chair. As the boy and mother shifted down the hall to the next office, John followed me down the corridor and out the main doors.

"Where?"

"She's at Alfio Perugino's house."

"Take this," he said, handing me the bag. "Tell Agnes I'll be home, then, as soon as I can." His path peeled away from mine, and he began walking down the hill to Dunsmuir Avenue.

"You haven't asked if she's alive or dead."

He turned, held one hand up to shield his eyes from the sun.

"I don't need to." he answered. "You're not smiling."

Without waiting for my reply, he turned on his heel and began to walk briskly down the hill.

When I entered the front door, I found the women exactly where I'd left them: Agnes still in the parlor and Nessie seated on the wooden chair in the hall. Nessie pulled her hands from her face and wrapped her arms around her torso, but said nothing. She was aware that this small kindness of an invitation indoors was my doing, and any further motion or sound would strain the hospitality which Agnes, distracted by her grief, had begrudgingly allowed.

Only when I pressed a cup of tea into Agnes' hand did the woman take stock of her surroundings, and she calmed down enough to keep from spilling the hot liquid over her fingers. I kneeled on the floor at her feet, and appraised the flickering eyelids, the quivering lips, the blotched complexion under the curls of grey hair. Consumed by the first waves of grief, Agnes looked old, but as her breathing slowed and she sipped her tea for comfort, her color returned in patches.

"Oh, my poor girl," she crooned, reaching out to caress my face. Her mouth twisted down again into an ugly reflection of a smile, a reverse emotion, a mask of tragedy. "I can nae believe she's dead!"

I held the woman's pudgy hand and tried to comfort Agnes, but I wasn't very good at this sort of thing – it was the role Violet had played.

With her mouth half-hidden behind her hands, Nessie

hiccoughed. "I am sorry. So sorry to bring bad news." Tear tracks latticed her face, but her breath had returned to its normal pattern. Her weeping was quietly dignified.

"But how did she die?" I asked, and a sharp, stabbing pain pricked my heart.

Both women looked to me, expecting tears, but I had none to give. Even this wrenching of grief felt more like heartburn: a physical manifestation to fill the void, when I lacked anything more consuming.

"Obsessed with love for a shamed man? And her own father, shamed? And all prospects for a happy life slipping away? How do you think she died, you fool girl!" Agnes cried, her voice soaring to a fevered pitch, "She took her own life!" She aimed her fury at Nessie. "Is that nae right!"

Nessie hesitated, afraid to find herself under Agnes' vicious scrutiny, aware that she would always fall short of the woman's standards. "It's hard to tell," she stammered, "They pulled her from the lake—"

"You see?" Agnes shouted at me, "Dear God, girl! Do ye no understand? She threw herself in the waters and lost all, including her eternal soul!"

I startled. "No!" I replied, "I refuse to believe—"

"It nae matters what you, with your cold heart, believe!" Agnes pleaded, "God sees all, girl! He knows all! And he knows that Violet has committed self-murder, and that you feel nothing for the loss!" She put down the tea and gripped my hands tightly, and her hand connected with the bruises left on my wrist, now a faded purple and gold. The stabs of pain made me flinch. Agnes saw me wince, and she sought any further hint of a reaction, but remained unsatisfied. "Is that all ye can feel? A little twitch for the death of your beloved kin? You'll not shed even a tear for her?"

I floundered, struggled for some way to deal with the frenetic misery in which Agnes drowned. "She wouldn't have killed herself—"

"Ye are a beast, girl! A wicked parody of a child, with nae soul tae call your own! It ought tae have been you that died, and not your bonnie sister – she was the one with a guld heart!" Agnes released me and clamped her hands over her face, curling over and keening into her own lap. "Your dear father has gone tae collect the body, and all ye can do is sit here with your empty soul, caring not at all!"

I took a single step back and wrapped my arms around my shoulders, trembling. Already, Violet's name had been replaced by an anonymous title, The Body, without identity or personality. She had been transformed, becoming a thing instead of a person. All that had made Violet was gone. Only a sopping rag of flesh remained.

I fled upstairs, to my box of trinkets, desperate to find something to hold.

52

THE MEN and the mule and the rattletrap wagon threaded slowly through the streets, and for a while I lingered at the bedroom window, watching them vanish and reappear through the houses from my hill-top vantage. Then I returned downstairs, ignoring Agnes and Nessie, and stepping outside into the afternoon warmth. The wagon was coming, and I'd rather meet it, head-on, than cower inside with the women.

When Nessie drew next to my elbow, no words passed between us. We stood side by side in the door. Despite the sticky summer heat, Nessie pulled her ragged shawl tighter over her broad shoulders. The moment of silence that passed between us was not uncomfortable. We shared a sense of relief.

At last, I asked, "How did Alfio find her?"

And Nessie told me, about the fishing spot and the boat, and the three men pulling the graceful body from the water.

"Will you tell Chen Shaozhu?"

"Yes."

"Thank you. I'll pay you for your time."

"No money," Nessie replied. "If you give me money for this errand, I will be offended."

The casket drew closer, the axles and wheels creaking wood-against-wood. The weary mule put one hoof before the other, the men barely lifted their boots. A few had already removed their caps, though more likely due to the heat than to any sense of condolence.

"Lizzie," whispered Nessie, "I gotta tell you something."

I looked to the woman beside me.

"Your sister," Nessie continued, and her eyes were filled with sadness, "She did not kill herself."

"You've seen the body?"

Nessie nodded discretely. "I was there when Alfie brought her from the lake." The woman swallowed. "But she did not drown neither."

"How, then, did Violet die?"

Nessie's face contorted with sorrow as she considered her words.

"There are spirits in these mountains that feed upon human flesh, Miss Saunders. They eat the soft bits, the liver and guts, the places where the soul resides." Nessie looked out to the foothills, which rose in successively higher ridges until they ended with snow-capped mountains. "The Reverend McGill, he tells us that God keeps us safe in towns and houses, but God can not see the devils that live under the roots of the trees."

"Reverend McGill tells us that God sees all."

"God sees all He made," Nessie corrected. "But He didn't make Tsonakwa, the cannibal woman, who eats innocent children who are lost in the woods. I tell you, Tsonakwa has stolen your Violet from you."

The wagon halted at the gate. The driver kicked the brake in place before grabbing the mule's bridle. He fondled the animal's ears and cooed at it while the others began to unload the cargo, pulling back the wool blanket to reveal the casket underneath.

"A devil didn't do this," I said, shaking my head. "I don't believe in devils."

"Believe whatever you want," Nessie replied, "You may not believe in devils, Miss Saunders, but that don't keep the devils from believing in you."

The bearers passed through the gate with grim, wordless greetings; a nod of the head, a tip of the cap, downcast eyes and sullen frowns. Nessie and I stood aside as the men shouldered the simple pine casket and brought it up the stairs, onto the porch, and through the open door. We watched as it was brought into the parlor and installed on the table, in the exact spot where, only a short time ago, our mother had lain.

With a light touch on my elbow, John pulled me aside.

"You do not need to be here for this, Lizzie," he urged, "Agnes can assist me."

But my eyes burned and my chin was solid, stoic. "Right now, Agnes is in no fit state to fetch water, never mind this grim task," I replied. "You ought to send her home."

John considered this, then nodded. "I suppose yes, you're right."

"I've attended my fair share of autopsies with you, I'm capable of helping you." My eyes drifted to the casket on the table. "I'm needed here more than anywhere."

"Violet has been in the lake too long."

"This isn't Violet any more." I replied.

John was clearly uncomfortable with my proposal, but he clapped a hand on my shoulder, which I took as a begrudging agreement. He embraced Agnes and asked the men to escort our maid home, and gave them words of gratitude for their service. I watched them go, filing silently away. I noticed Alfio Perugino pull Nessie close to his hip and hold her tightly, pressing a kiss to her crown; the small gesture spoke of thankfulness, and love, and a humbling reminder of mortality.

53

"You do not have to be here," Father said once more.

"Open the box," I replied.

He took the poker from the hearth, for the casket lid had been banged tightly into place. "You are not at all like your mother," he said. "She ran from death."

I raised cold eyes to him.

"This needs to be done," I said, "There's no reason to hesitate. Waiting will only make our duty worse."

He took a deep breath and shunted the metal bar into the crack between the lid and casket. With an undignified grunt, he pried it open.

A moist, muddy, earthy stench flowed out. The scent brought forth memories of the lake's low ebb, when the algae that blankets the exposed beach dries in the sun.

The creature inside was no longer the lissome, lithe beauty that Violet had been in life, but a swollen and bloated mockery of beauty. Her eyes were half-closed and her parted lips had been dragged open by the weight of a slack jaw. She lay on a bed of folded white linen with the ruins of the mourning dress wrapped around her bared, fish-white limbs. The arms were veined with purple lines as thick and graceful as earthworms, and she looked soft and pillowy to the touch. Her feet formed a V at the terminus of blunt legs, grotesque with their enormous burden of fluid. My breath stuck in my dry throat, but the blind face gazing up at the ceiling was no longer my sister's; this face was fat, and homely, and piggish. The nose, once pretty and pert, was now dwarfed by thick cheeks and almost swallowed up by the surrounding flesh. The fair blonde hair looked vaguely familiar, but even it was matted with twigs and dead leaves, and in a messy tangle that Violet would never have allowed.

A speck of mud dotted the white of the right eye. John wiped it away with the tip of his finger. "Go, fetch water from the pump," he said, his voice flat and quiet, "Gather cloths, too."

I did as I was asked, and when I returned, Father had smoothed the tattered dress down over the pale, cold legs, and tucked the hem tightly around the ankles.

"Shall I fetch a new dress for her?"

He shook his head. "The bloating," he said in a whisper, "I doubt we'd fit her in it."

"Then we'll bury her in these clothes?"

He nodded and said nothing more.

We worked in silence. I washed the strangely fat forearms, the wrists, the purple-white hands, all the while breathing through my mouth in light, shallow breaths to avoid the taste of drowning. I finished the left arm and moved to the right, working methodically, ignoring the whole and focusing only on the small inches of skin in my field of view. When I reached the fingers of the right hand, I unfurled them, straightened them.

The lamplight caught the fingers and I paused.

Violet's fingers nails were cracked, crooked, wrenched free of their beds with extreme force. Underneath each was a half-moon of crimson: torn skin, black blood, and fine dark hairs.

"Father," I said, "Look."

He drew close. "Her nails have separated from her fingers. Sometimes it happens, when the flesh swells."

"But blood, and hair--" I insisted, "This was no suicide. She fought."

"Kelly will have wounds, then," he replied.

I jerked my head back to stare at him and saw a man utterly unsurprised. "You think Kelly killed her?"

"Doubtlessly."

"You haven't said anything—"

"What needs to be said?" he asked in a low, conspiratorial tone, "Everyone assumed Kelly to be a good man. He was hand-picked by management to uphold law and justice in this town. There are those would believe he could be an addict, but this? No, the Company will not listen to it. Their choice of a murderer for a constable will not reflect well on their judgment."

"But, if he killed Violet, and is free, he might—"

"Rufus is arranging a hunt, but holds no hope of finding him." Father took a linen rag and wiped his hands. "We've already looked once for Alexander Kelly, without success. He's silenced the only one who dared hold his addiction against him, and he's fled for a new life elsewhere." He took Violet's hand in his own, and shook his head sadly. His shoulders trembled. "They'll want us to bury her and put this whole ugly situation behind us."

"I won't!"

"Lizzie, be reasonable—"

"It's not fair!"

"Rufus will do what he can, but he hasn't the man power to search endlessly." A glimmer of moisture in the corner of his eye caught the lamplight, and he wiped it away with the cuff of his sleeve. "He certainly will not find Kelly."

"You can't be certain."

"No," he agreed, bending again to the grim task of preparing his eldest daughter for the grave, "But of what can we be certain in this life, Liz, except for this?" He rapped his knuckles against the side of the casket.

I watched him wash Violet's face. He struggled to pull a comb through the tattered remains of hair. When a knot of blonde hairs pulled free from the sodden scalp, he stopped and lowered his head, closed his eyes. His face remained soft with grief. A few tears rolled down his cheeks.

"Did Mother ever cry?"

Father set the comb aside and ran his palm over Violet's swollen cheek. "Once," he said, "But never again, after we left London."

"Agnes felt so much – so much! – and I have only a dull ache in my heart," I said, "And I can't help but think something is horribly, horribly wrong with me."

"No, Lizzie, nothing is wrong with you," he assured. He held Violet's dead hand again and stared into the filmy eyes. "Emotion makes us weak, distracts us from our duties." Father lowered his head and began to silently weep.

WHEN WE WERE FINISHED, Father sought refuge in his surgery. I didn't chase after him or pester him. It was clear he desired privacy.

Instead I sat for a long time next to the casket, now closed , and held my hands folded as if in prayer. I wasn't praying – if God hadn't listened to Violet's cries for help, why would He bother with mine? – but the gesture seemed appropriate.

Torn skin and dark brown hairs under the nails on Violet's hands. A woman defending herself would lash out at her attacker, rake her fingers over the murderer's skin, and take away little bits of it with her. She would aim for the nearest patch of exposed skin, the face, perhaps, or the arms which held her. I tried to remember how Sandy's arms looked. His hair and moustache were decidedly auburn, but I couldn't recall the color of his body hair. He wore a jacket and sleeves, even on the hottest days of summer, as a man befitting his respectable station. Those hairs may have been his, trapped under Violet's nails.

Maybe.

I couldn't be sure.

Of what I could be sure, I ran through like a checklist. I weighed each fact against the others.

(1) Violet had been missing for a week.

(2) Rigor had passed. The eyes were filmy. From the state of Violet's body, it was safe to assume that she'd been dead almost as long.

(3) Whoever killed her would still have scratches on his arms and hands.

(4) If they found Kelly, it would be easy to link him to Violet, for he would be marked by her hands.

If they found him.

With every successive thought, my teeth clenched a little more tightly, and my hands looked less like folded in prayer, and more like a pugilist's fists, ready to fight at the first hint of a bell. A thought bubbled to the surface of my mind. Jack had given every indication that he knew why Kelly had run, but when we bumped into each other on Monday morning, Violet's disappearance had surprised him. He assumed Kelly had taken Violet with him, alive and whole.

'Ergo,' I thought, 'Kelly had reasons to leave other than Violet's death. He may have killed Violet, but her murder was incidental.'

Jack had expected Kelly to leave, even without blood on the constable's hands.

But Kelly, with blood on his hands, had left as quick as he could.

If Kelly was found and brought to justice for Violet's murder, what would he do? I had no doubt that he would try to buy his innocence with the story of what transpired: he would bring forward my grandfather's letter, reveal my mother's fall from polite society, shame my father with his cowardice and poor reputation, and tell the magistrate of Violet's threats to blackmail a constable into silence. Yes, I thought, capture would end poorly for Kelly, but it would also end poorly for John Saunders, too, no matter what the truth.

No wonder Father was reluctant to chase after him. If Kelly were made to stand before a jury and regale the Crown with his reasons for flight, it was Violet's memory that would suffer, and our family's reputation that would be dragged through the mud. Father's intentions were clear: let Violet remain the silent victim in all of this.

Shao's knife lay on the mantle in its carved box. My gaze fell upon it, and my mind seized on one possible solution.

Violet's memory could remain untarnished and justice could be served without the meddling of the law. My method was simple: find Kelly before Rufus and his men.

Find Kelly, and make him pay for Violet's death in blood.

54

I CONSIDERED the best course of action.

To find Kelly, the logical step would be to think like Kelly, and the only way I could do that with any accuracy was to determine why the constable had fled.

And that, I thought with a grimace, meant tracking down the only man in town who seemed to have any idea why Kelly would run.

But visiting the boarding houses and hotels had already proven fruitless, and Shao refused to co-operate. I wasn't prepared to waste my time with respectable establishments again. The answers would all be the same: Jack wouldn't waste good money on a hotel bed, if he even had the funds to pay for such luxuries in the first place.

'So', I considered, 'What would a man like Jack waste good money on?'

The answer hit me like a fist.

I paused at the door of my home, wondering if I dared. A glance over my shoulder at the casket on the table spurred me on. Violet would be horrified, but then again, it was on Violet's behalf that I went. Wasn't that reason enough?

Yes, I decided. It was plenty.

The afternoon had slipped away and the sun cast long shadows pointing east. I moved through the early evening crowds like a somnambulist, barely noticing the miners arriving at the boarding houses from their shifts, or boys running home for dinner, or crows returning to their nests for the night.

At the farthest eastern edge of town sat a fine new house, fronting onto the sleepy goat track road leading to Union Bay, and painted stark white to set it apart from the shacks, mule sheds, and shanties that dotted the surrounding pastures. The house boasted a generous porch, where a row of ten or twelve wicker chairs had been set for the inhabitants and their guests to enjoy the lazy summer's evenings.

But this evening, all was quiet and still. I loitered for a while at the gate. Like a soldier planning his advance across a very large, very daunting mine field, I surveyed the lush flower beds, the bushy ivy that crawled along the fence, and the stone walkway curving with grace and aplomb to the front door. It all looked so clean, so innocent, so well-tended. And, at this evening hour, so strangely quiet. Someone had taken care to draw the shutters over every window, and of windows, this house had many: at least eight along the top floor, and four large windows on the main story. I mustered my courage and was about to push the white picket gate open when the wooden shutter covering one upper window clattered open.

A puzzled face appeared.

And almost as soon as it popped into my view, it vanished again.

I heard the snap as the slide bolt on the front door was drawn open.

A gargantuan woman flung the door open wide. She flew out the door onto the porch, her red silk kimono billowing with the force of her passage. Her bare feet thrummed on the wooden boards. The long waves of black hair, unbound, framed a stern, square face: handsome but formidable, and not the sort of woman to deal patiently with strangers. "Who are ya, and whatdaya want," she demanded. It was not quite a question, but rather more of a command.

"My name is Lizzie. I'm looking for someone."

"I doubt you'll find him here tonight," said the woman, "Most of the men have been rounded up for a posse." She cast baleful eyes westward, along the dirt track to town. "And even if you did, we don't care to wake up our clients and give them any trouble."

"I'm not here to give anyone trouble," I insisted, "I'm looking for Jack Hunter, and I was with him on Sunday when—"

"Jesus! You said yer name was Lizzie?" she gasped, and her square face blossomed into a gregarious smile, missing three teeth.

"Yes..." I replied, suddenly unsure of myself.

The woman whistled and set her hands on her solid hips. "You're mite bit younger than I thought you'd be – there ain't no accounting for taste in a man, is there!" She laughed. "Why didn't you say you were a friend of Jack's! Come in, come in."

With gigantic hands, the woman ushered me into a spacious parlor and shut the door behind me. The bawdy house held the sounds and smells of many people, hidden away in upstairs rooms, snoring peacefully. The furniture was as fine as any found in the upper class homes of Victoria. A lacquered piano in the corner was as nice, if not nicer, than the instrument in my own parlor. This was a place of entertainment, where men were made comfortable, a haven from the cramped squalor of their boarding house beds. No expense had been spared to give the illusion of grandeur and wealth, and to help them forget their poverty with a bit of wine and song.

"Come on through to the kitchen, girl," urged the woman, and I followed her to a sunny, spacious kitchen. A small plank table by the window had a view of the backyard, and a light dinner of toast and tea had been set for one. The woman took another plate and cup from the cupboard and brought them to the table, and set a place opposite her chair.

I took the offered seat and didn't bother to hide the bewilderment in my face. "I'm sorry – did I hear you right? You referred to me as 'Jack's friend'?"

"Lord Almighty, he chatters about you all the time! Lizzie this, Lizzie that..." said the woman as she poured a cup of tea from a blue-

and-white china pot. She peered a little closer at my face, and her eyes opened wide. "You're the doctor's girl, aren't you?"

"Yes, ma'am."

"So it was your sister... oh, I'm sorry. I heard the news from one of the girls – it's a crying shame what Kelly's done." She set the teapot down and sat again, smoothing the lines of her kimono along a pair of strong, lean legs. "Call me Mercy," she offered as she set the china cup of tea in front of my hands.

"Thanks."

"Jack said you'd come by. He's a wily one, he is."

"I looked everywhere, and I was starting to think no one knew him," I said with a relieved grin, "I checked all the hotels, the jail, down Chinatown, everywhere!"

"Well," said Mercy, "He's been staying here with us. Rather nice to have a man around the house, to do the heavy lifting and such."

"So he wasn't here to....um...."

"To grab himself a feast of oysters?" She laughed as a blush raced up my cheeks. "How old are you?"

"Fifteen."

"Old enough to know what we do, but still young enough to get all flustered by it. You're a cute girl, Lizzie, especially when you're embarrassed. Men pay triple for that expression alone." Mercy took a savage bite from a triangle of buttered toast. "Jack may have spent a bit of money on some of the girls, but no, that's not why he's here. He needed a place to stay, and he pays well, and it's good to have a trustworthy fella around, in case a few of the newer patrons need putting in their place."

"You think he's trustworthy?"

"As much as any man can be," she replied.

"Jack told you I'd come?"

"He did," she agreed, "He said you were dreadful curious about the world, and there wasn't much that prevented you from finding the answers to your questions – not decorum, not public opinion, not even good sense. He seems to think he knows you quite well. So tell me, Lizzie my sweet, how do you know him?"

"I...I don't," I stammered, "I've met him a few times, he..." And I furrowed my brow. "Look, to be perfectly honest, he broke into my house and threatened to kill me." The look of surprise that crossed Mercy's face was almost comical. I scrambled to find something redeeming about Jack's character, just to soften the blow. "But he saved me from a barfight, too, and he's been following me, and I think he knows something about my sister's murder."

"Hell," Mercy spat, "If half of what you've said about Jack is true, I've got a few questions for him, myself!" She plopped her half-eaten toast on her plate and stood up to her full, imposing height. "I told you, I don't want any trouble brought into my house, and if he's breaking into houses and threatening young girls? Well, I want none of it." But the idea clearly confused her; she'd trusted her instinct and it had never led her wrong before. "We'll go wake him up, you and I, and put the screws to his thumbs, as it were."

Upstairs, a long gauntlet of closed doors hid the sounds of snoring and low conversations in each tiny room. I followed Mercy along the straight hallway, and young women dipped quietly out of each chamber, withdrawing from their clients with practiced stealth and heading downstairs to the back yard, to the washing house. They gave me shy smiles. Perhaps they would have been more brazen if I was a man with a fat wallet, but a strange new girl in the house was an odd sight. They defaulted to polite greetings, like words muttered to passing strangers while stepping off a train.

At the far end of the hall, a narrow staircase twisted up onto a landing and led to an attic or loft, but instead of mounting the steps to this unseen third floor, Mercy stepped alongside the flight, to a door leading into a space under the landing. She gave a brisk rapping on the narrow door.

"Jack?" she asked through the keyhole, "Jack, ya goddamn bastard, are ya awake?"

A moment of silence passed.

Mercy tried the door and found it unlocked. It swung open on a tiny, austere, windowless room holding only a single bed and a small bedside table. The stump of a candle on the table was the only other furnishing, next to a few leaves of paper, scribbled with words; there simply was room for no more. The hook on the back of the door was empty of a coat. Mercy studied it for a moment as the anger rose in her face.

"Well, god damn! God damn him! He's up and gone!" she hissed, and she reeled around to look over my head and down the corridor, her lips pressed tightly together, her eyes darting from door to door. Perhaps alerted by the sound of women talking in the hall, a slight, olive-complexioned girl peeked out of a far room, and backed quietly out it, shutting the door softly behind her.

"Yvette," Mercy called in a half-whisper, unwilling to wake anyone but too angry to cloak her voice with sweetness, "Did you see Jack leave today?"

The girl, only a few years older than Violet had been, shook her head. "No, ma'am, I ain't seen him at all."

"Well, I've been up since noon," Mercy mused, rubbing her hands together, "And I never saw him come or go." She rapped her knuckles against the side of the stairwell, the same sort of thoughtful twitching as an angry cat's tail. "He owes me for room and board, the miserable scut!"

"Maybe he'll come back," I said, " See? His belongings are still here."

"That don't mean nothing," Mercy muttered, "Even my own girls disappear if I ain't watching 'em! They take up with some miner, leave their stuff and never come back – it ain't like folks are courteous in this line of work!"

"Yes, but—" I took the letters from the table, and was in the process of flourishing them to Mercy when my gaze locked on the first letter in the pile.

One side of the thin, oft-folded paper carried neat, precise lines of my own handwriting. I read the words as if seeing them through a lens of water, washy and finger worn, stained with grease and time.

"Dear Grandfather,

No doubt but that you are questioning the identity of this strange woman, who is so bold to write you and so brazen to call you 'grandfather', but though many years separate our acquaintance, our ties by blood can not be so easily forgotten, and I hope you will forgive me for my forthright greeting...."

55

THE LETTER in my hands was a link, a physical connection, between myself and Jack. It turned my insides cold.

How many times did I read and re-read my own words as I stumbled home, barely noticing the squadron of men on horseback trotting down the main street? I heard my name called out, and looked across the horses and the men, each with a rifle slung from his saddle. I raised my hand absently to Rufus as he hailed me again.

He nudged his horse, a broad chestnut gelding, close to the boardwalk. "Good Lord, girl, what are you doing out? You ought to be home with your father, don't you think?"

"People seem to be fond of telling me where I ought to be," I replied.

"Without Mr. Kelly, it's been a rough bit to keep this town together," he warned, "The place is like a damn pressure cooker, excuse my cursing. I don't need to remind you, there's a murderer abroad, and with most of the law-abiding folk hunting for Kelly, it would be a good night for ladies like yourself to stay safely locked indoors."

I looked to the faces of men riding passed; I doubted there'd be a single horse left in Cumberland tonight.

"We're heading down the road to Courtenay, to see if anyone has heard or seen him there," he said. His horse shifted and snorted, tossed its black mane, chomped at the bit. It pulled at the reins to join the flow of men and beasts.

"Do you think you'll find him?"

Rufus tipped his felt cap back on his head, then crossed his arms and leaned down over the pommel of the saddle. His voice lowered, although under the sound of two hundred hooves striking the dirt and men yelling one-to-the-other from their saddles, the noise alone hid his voice from any eavesdropping.

"Miss Saunders, I won't lie to you. Kelly isn't here any more – he's killed your sister and run, and whether it's south or north or into the woods, who can say. But he'll hang if we find him, that he knows. So," Rufus tipped his hat to me, "I wager we won't find him."

"Do you mean that he is too wily to be caught?" I asked, "Or that you don't wish to hang him?"

Rufus only smiled. "I only catch the man, Miss Saunders, I don't mete out the justice. That's for the representatives of the Crown to do. I'll do my best to locate him, but it'll be damn hard for me to put Kelly on the boat to Nanaimo, to stand trial and then dangle. It's the God's honest truth, and I hope you don't think less of me."

"I do not think less of a man who speaks the truth," I replied. "You are an honorable fellow, Mr. McGregor, and you do the town credit."

It struck me, as I was saying it, that I had once thought the same of Mr. Kelly.

Rufus McGregor tipped his cap to me in appreciation, and with a click of his tongue, urged the gelding back into the stream of movement.

"Lizzie, is that you?"

I closed the front door and kicked off my boots. When I glanced into the library, four faces looked back: Father, Mason Briggs, Dr. Gould and Mr. Fish. They each held a glass of amber brandy, and the scent of cigar smoke drifted lazily through the air.

"Good to see you home, Liz," said Father, gesturing with his glass to the kitchen. "I've left you a cold dinner in the pantry; it isn't much, compared to what Agnes would make you. My skill in the kitchen is rather lacking, but it's the best I could do. When you've eaten, would you join us?"

This gave me pause for consideration – not that I had a choice in the matter. If Father asked me to join the men in their conversation in the library, who was I to refuse? But it was odd form, and something about it caused me to dread the reason. So I collected the plate he'd prepared: sliced jellied tongue, boiled carrots and bread smeared with butter, and returned to the library to sit in the horsehide chair. Dr. Gould was the only gentleman currently with the stub of a cigar in hand, and Mr. Fish was setting his empty glass on the side table. They had obviously been talking for a while.

"I passed the deputy-constable and fifty men on horseback," I said as I settled into the chair, "They're following the road to Courtenay, to see if Kelly's run that way."

"Let's hope they find the scoundrel, and bring him back hog-tied on the back of his little white pony," said Dr. Gould. His words had their corners rounded off of them; he was already slumped heavily to one side in his chair.

Father's eyes were sharp and bright. He had not drunk much of his brandy, if any at all. The level in his glass was higher than the other three. "Lizzie, the gentlemen and I were discussing our future – your's and mine."

"Our future?"

He nodded. "How would you feel about relocating?"

Mason Briggs leaned forward in his chair and patted one hand on my knee. "There is an opening in my practice for a man of your father's talents, and we would be happy to welcome you into Victoria's polite society." He gave a wide, merry grin, but his eyes were suitably melancholy. "The loss of both your mother and sister, in less than a year... this wretched, filthy outpost can hardly hold many happy memories for you."

I looked from Mason's invitation to Father. "You can't be serious? Leave?"

"Why not?" he replied, "It's as good a time as any." He and Mason exchanged glances, and I saw that it had all been decided without me. Like the trunk and the medical bag and the furniture, I was about to be packed up and bundled away, and I didn't have a word to say about it.

"My wife Emma will be thrilled to have a new friend to entertain," Mason added, "And we've planned a lovely garden party for late September, which would be an ideal time to formally introduce you."

"But I – this—" I thought of Shao, and my heart ached. "I can't leave." I clenched my hands and added, "I won't!"

"You can't stay here forever, my dear," the corpulent Dr. Gould slurred.

"Of course I can't," I snapped at him, "But I can't go now, either. I can't just—" My voice caught in my throat. "I can't leave Violet. For the love of God, she isn't even in the grave yet, and we're leaving her behind?"

Dr. Gould shook his head. "Poor girl."

"Save your pity for someone who wants it," I seethed at him, then took up my plate and fled to the porch, slamming the door behind me.

I had picked at the slices of meat and the carrots, and eaten only a few, when the door opened and Mr. Fish sat beside me, unfolding his bony legs with creaking joints. He gave a low, depreciating chuckle at his own crotchetiness. "I rather like you, Lizzie," he began, "I'd hoped you come to the capital and inject a bit of spice in its admittedly bland society."

"You aren't enticing me to change my mind, Mr. Fish."

"Oh, how I'd love to see you stand up and proclaim a bold 'Horse-shit!' at every hint of swindling and pomposity in Victoria's social scene!" he laughed, "And trust me, in a city full of government officials? You'd be shouting on every street corner, at every dinner, at every function!"

I smirked.

"But I can understand your reluctance, too," he continued. "It is too soon. Please forgive me for suggesting it to your father."

"This was your idea?"

"I'm a ragged old bachelor, with half my family in Australia, and the other half in Birmingham," he confided, "I don't keep many friends, and it's rare for me to find someone I actually like. But you, Lizzie," He grinned. "I like."

We watched the birds in the neighbors' plum tree, twittering and frolicking from branch to branch, as the sun sank slowly in the west; neither of us said much for a few moments, and I offered Mr. Fish a bit of my dinner, which he politely refused. The air was cool and quiet, and even the constant rhythm of the mine bellows had stilled.

"So," he said quietly, "There's a lad here who's caught your fancy, hey?" He laughed as my eyebrows arched. "Why else would a girl want to stay here, hmm? Some ruggedly handsome miner, no doubt, all muscles and grit and untamable, indomitable spirit." He gave a winsome sigh.

"There is a boy, yes."

"Well, listen," Mr. Fish confided, "When you decide to leave, with or without your beautiful young Adonis in tow, you will always have a place to stay in Victoria. My house is large, and my eyesight is poor. I hardly notice anything impolite that happens on my grounds."

We traded mischievous grins.

"That's very kind of you."

"Isn't it?" he agreed. "The city can do with a little bit of a shake-up, and you seem to me the type of girl who can do it. The Faulks sisters, all aflutter by your proclamation, have created a roaring campaign based on your upset – oh, you haven't heard? They say the spirits possessed you and caused you to yell in tongues." He harrumphed. "I was unaware that the angels were so vulgar." He patted me on the shoulder as he stood, and said, "You've given me a smattering of hope, dear Lizzie, that heaven may not be as dull as I feared."

56

MR. FISH RETURNED to the men, and closed the door quietly behind him.

I pulled the letter from my pocket and read it again, but the sunlight was almost gone and the words were illegible. I picked at my food, thinking. How did Jack get this letter? The paper was soft and felted with wear, and the folds were well-creased; it had been folded and unfolded a hundred times. The black edges of the paper were scratched, torn, and grey. When I lifted the edge of the page to my nose, I smelt Jack's sweaty fingerprints.

He did know me, before I ever had a sense of him.

But the words, my own handwriting, told me nothing more. Eventually I folded it in three and returned it to my pocket, and contented myself by watching the bats flit through the upper branches of the trees, catching damselflies.

By now, most of the people here knew that a dead girl had been dredged from the lake, and that the girl was Violet Saunders, and that this whole sordid affair had taken a brutal, dark turn, from illicit romance -- despicable to the older ladies, titillating to the younger -- to suicide or murder. No one populated the streets. Honorable, hard-working men were riding to Courtenay and back, asking at every hamlet and farm if Kelly had been seen. Women and children had locked themselves indoors. Most summer nights on Cumberland's streets were lively and personable, but this one was reserved, furtive, and empty.

In the library, I heard low conversations. The men continued to drink and smoke, and discuss the politics of the day, but eventually the visitors took their leave, and the three men bid me a good night as they took to the streets and sauntered home.

Father sat next to me on the porch and watched them depart.

"Dr. Gould looks very unsteady," I commented.

"He has a miraculous talent for consuming," John replied, "The man must have a stomach the size of a barrel, and just as impervious to hard knocks. Next time he visits, remind me to break open the inferior brandy – I doubt he'd notice the difference."

"Mr. Fish tells me that the invitation to move to Victoria was his idea."

"Yes, it was, but they came, too, to give condolences," John replied, "It was an honorable visit."

"But neither they, nor you, have joined the hunt to look for Violet's murderer."

John weighed my comment and took his time to reply. "Tracking and hunting is not where our talents lie," he admitted, then tipped his chin towards the three figures, now vanishing over a swell in the road. "Can you imagine hoisting Dr. Gould onto a horse, arming him with a rifle, and sending him off to look for Kelly? The town is much safer with him, passed out on his own couch." John reclined against the banister post and folded his hands over his stomach. "Besides, I'm needed here. I intend to sit with the body and let you sleep."

"Are you sure? You look tired."

He yawned. "I am tired, but I'm sure." He tipped his head. "Go to bed, Liz, and enjoy an hour's rest. You can take watch at midnight."

"I'm not sleepy," I replied, "And I'm enjoying the outdoors. If you don't mind, I'll stay out here a little longer."

He ruffled his hand over my hair and retreated to the parlor. When he closed the door after him, it cut off the flow of light spilling from the lamps in the hall.

I turned back to rest my elbows on my knees, and took a deep, contented sigh. It was so peaceful, so quiet, and--

Pop!

I slapped my hand to the sharp pain on my brow. Something had struck me on the forehead, and now rolled across the porch. I snatched it up.

A chestnut conker.

Pop!

This one shot wide, and struck me in the shoulder. I leapt to my feet and pressed close to the clematis bush before a third could strike me, and I peered into the dark shadows across the street.

In the hospital yard, the gardens and lawns were empty, but a movement at the corner of a shed caught my attention. I grabbed the chestnut that had rolled across the porch, fondled its glossy surface between my fingers, and waited. A figure stepped away from the wall, cautious and quiet.

I reeled back and whipped the chestnut towards him. There was a satisfying 'thunk', followed by a grunt, as the chestnut struck my target in the stomach.

On bare feet, I crossed the road and raced over the lawn, and flew into Chen Shaozhu's welcoming embrace.

"I heard they found your sister," he said. There was no need for a greeting to soften the comment.

"Yes."

"I'm sorry to hear it."

I let him enfold me in his arms and hug me, and I pretended to weep, if only to soothe him.

"Will you walk with me?"

"I need my shoes," I said, "Wait here, and I'll be back."

When I returned to him, we held hands and walked in silence for almost a block. Our path turned east to follow Penrith Street passed the row of churches: United, Presbyterian, Catholic. I found myself both comforted and annoyed by his presence. He exhibited a chivalrous need to consol me, but it was a waste of breath and effort. I wanted to talk to him about other things. There were more pressing topics than how terribly melancholy the whole event was, and how much I was going to miss my sister, and how well my father was taking it all, considering the loss of a beloved daughter.

Yes, yes, I thought, it's all very sad. Mourning lasts a year, and grief follows a person forever, but Alexander Kelly is still out there, free, and if Shao hoped to help me catch him, we ought to muster our forces as soon as possible.

So I said as much to him, which shut him up for a while.

At last, he gave his head a little shake, as if a bug crawled in his ear.

"Are you heartless?" he asked, and I couldn't tell if he was repulsed by me, or only asking for a fact.

"I suspect so," I finally replied.

We walked another block, keeping to the darker side of the street, but seeing no one.

At last, to break the uncomfortable quiet, I said, "Jack is involved in this. I need to talk to him."

Shao tensed his jaw, but said nothing.

"I know you think you're protecting me," I began, "But I need to speak with him, and if you have any idea where he might be—"

"I already told you, I don't trust him."

"Nor do I! Believe me, if I could avoid him, I would!"

He pulled away from me and put distance between us, stopping at the corner with his back turned to me.

"He said I was in danger of disappearing, too," I continued, "He knows that Violet caught malaria in Panama." I withdrew the letter from my pocket. "And today, I tracked him as a far as the brothel at the edge of town, and I found this in his belongings."

I offered the paper up into his hands. Shao took the letter, although in the dim light of the crescent moon, he couldn't read the words.

"What is it?" he asked.

"The letter I sent to my grandfather."

His eyes snapped back to it again. "What?"

"My letter, Shao!" I tapped my finger against the paper. "Jack brought my letter with him! The letter I sent to my grandfather! In England!" I watched with satisfaction as his brows drew together. He tried again to hold the letter up to the moonlight, to catch enough illumination from its weak beams to read my handwriting. "And I received a reply from the captain," I added, "Which means my letter reached its destination in Wiltshire, and wasn't intercepted between here and there! Tell me, Shao, how did Jack get his hands on it?"

"I don't know!" He sounded genuinely bewildered.

"Have you seen him since Violet was found?" I pressed, "Has Jack spoken with you since I saw him last?"

He lowered the letter and looked blackly at me. "I spent yesterday on the face of No. 5, chipping blast holes into the coal," Shao curtly replied, "And all last night asleep, exhausted. So, no, I did not see him."

"But you know where he is?"

"It's dangerous, Liz—"

"He hired you to follow me, he used you to bring the medical case back—"

Shao's answer possessed the sharp edge of offense. "He didn't *use* me."

I ignored his anger. "I think Jack Hunter knows my grandfather," I said. I seized his wrists in my hands. "I need to know how he's entangled in this, because I think this might be my fault. I sent that letter to the captain, and my actions have set in motion a series of events which resulted in Violet's death, and I need to understand *why*."

"You can't feel guilty about Violet's death," he said as his eyes searched my face for any hint of emotion. I realized that, in fact, he hoped I did feel guilt, because it would be better than nothing at all.

"Let me talk to Jack and I'll come to that decision myself," I urged.

He gave a ragged sigh, hunched his shoulders, and weighed his options. Finally, he gave a resigned nod. "Alright, fine. I'll take you to him, but I'm not leaving you with him. The man has no moral compass, and I'd be a fool to trust him alone with you." He grabbed my hand. "He paid me to protect you, so I damn well will."

57

SHAO LED me through the alleys of Cumberland, into the swampy lowlands, and onto the railway tracks. We walked along the raised bed with only the moon to light our way. Camp passed on our right, then Chinatown on our left. We skirted the orchards and gardens of the Japanese township, and passed the cabins where eight or nine families of black Americans lived. I wondered if we'd follow the tracks as far as No. 4 mine and the shores of Comox Lake but Shao stopped at a low point in the swamp, then turned onto a narrow deer track, heading directly south.

Even amongst the trees, the moon provided enough illumination for me to see my way. The scent of the bog, thick and pungent, surrounded us. Wild rose bushes, lush with leaves and rosehips, created a tunnel of growth through the lowest reaches of the wetlands, and through gaps in the bushes, the moon glinted on the surface of a pond, almost level with the trail on either side. Spears of bulrushes and reeds stabbed up through the foreboding, mercurial surface of the water. I picked my way carefully along, testing each footstep, not wanting to stumble into the shallow pools which flanked us.

Then the path began to slope gently upwards.

Single-file, we pushed through the underbrush until we passed the bog. The path curved sharply and began to rise. It followed the banks of a percolating creek, passing through cleared land before entering a cedar forest. I reached forward and Shao took my hand. The tall straight trunks rose like cathedral pillars around us.

Chinatown was far behind us now. When I looked back, all I could discern of civilization were a few faint lights through the trees, like faerie lanterns dancing, which vanished as the river took us up out of the swamp lands. The path climbed in steps through pools carved in the sandstone river bed.

The relentless, patient flow of clear water had, over millennia, carved the stone into pulled-taffy formations. Where the bedrock had proven impervious to erosion, the creek flattened and the water trickled along banks of gravel, but where the land rose up again, the sensual curves of sandstone created another necklace of silvery pools, connected by cascading waterfalls. Some pools were large enough for a refreshing swim, others were no bigger than a stewpot.

The path cut deeply into the forest loam, crisscrossed with exposed cedar roots, then rose over a hump in the land. On either side, the banks vaulted in mossy slopes fringed with overhanging ferns, and the cedar branches knit above our heads into a ceiling of green and black, sprinkled with stars. The branches blocked out the moonlight, but ahead, emanating from a deep hollow carved by a waterfall, a flickering sphere of illumination glowed in the darkness. The sweet, comfortable smell of wood smoke tickled my nose.

I listened and heard the crackle of flames, but nothing else.

This had once been a pool at the side of the creek, but the winter had brought debris from higher reaches and blocked the channel. The re-routed water drained away and left behind a dry bubble in the exposed rock, large enough for a man and a fire and a place to lay his head, but little else. The rain storm might have soaked the ground but the hot weather and sun of the last few days had evaporated any moisture, and Jack had found himself a secure, hidden nest that, while it would never shelter him from the rain above, certainly hid the light of his fire from any distance. I looked down, five feet or so to the floor, and saw the imprint of a man's body in the gravel. The tiny fire had been quickly banked.

I stood and surveyed the shadow-ribbed forest. A breeze, high in the canopy, capered between the branches. "Mr. Hunter!" I called out, loud and brazen. "I know you're here."

The name bounced around between the sandstone banks, and threw itself back at me three times, each one successively softer.

"I've come to speak with you, Mr. Hunter," I continued, "If you would be so kind as to show yourself, I would appreciate your presence."

My voice echoed back. It faded, leaving a thick silence.

Then,

"You unarmed?"

Hunter's voice rang out clear and crisp. I reeled around and looked up to the top of the bank, seeking the source, seeing only shadows. "I am," I confessed.

Jack's disembodied voice continued. "Now, that ain't smart, is it?" I caught a hint of movement amongst the darkness, a prowling body moving silently and slowly that was nothing more than black against black. "There's a lotta things that would eat a little girl like you, out here in the woods."

"I'm not afraid of you, Mr. Hunter," I proclaimed. "I would appreciate if we could speak face-to-face. I do not enjoy talking to phantoms."

To my left, higher on the creek bed, he slid into view between the trees, moving into the dim light cast by the small fire. The light reflected off the blade of the knife in his hand. He lowered and sheathed it as he approached. "And why wouldn't you be afraid of me, Amaryllis? You don't know me from Adam."

"But you know me," I said, "In fact, you've known me since before setting foot in Cumberland." I brandished the letter. "Isn't that right?"

His look of surprise lasted only a second. "So you've been to see Mercy, have ya?"

"I believe I've left her with a few questions regarding the quality of your character," I replied. "You might wish to avoid her for a few days – she's none too pleased to learn she harbored a thief."

His eyes flickered to Shao. "Our deal was, you'd keep my location a secret, Jim boy. You ain't getting a dime from me now."

Shao's face, stony and closed, gave nothing back. If he was angry or insulted, he wasn't about to give Jack the satisfaction of knowing so.

"As for you, kid," Jack said, once more returning his gaze to me, "I ain't never met a girl with less sense. I coulda sliced you up right quick, and no one would ever be none the wiser." He brushed passed me and jumped into the hollow, and snatched up the charred stick from the ground to stoke the banked fire into life again. "Well, you came all this way to talk to me, so," He jabbed the stick into the gravel. "Take a seat and we'll talk."

I leapt lightly down into the hollow and sat across from him. Shao dangled his legs over the side and sat above and to my right, a guardian angel hovering behind me.

Without hesitation, I said, "My sister is dead, Mr. Hunter."

He bowed his head. After a pause, he said, "I'm sorry to hear it."

"Did you know she was dead?"

"No, but I had my suspicions."

"They fished her out of the lake today," I said. "And the gossip says it was suicide, but I know for a fact it was murder."

"And who do you think done it, Liz?"

"Mr. Kelly is the logical suspect."

"Logical suspect?" He laughed.

I glared at him. "Violet eloped with Alexander Kelly. I surmise that she regretted her decision, and he killed her before she could return to town to shame him. Everyone assumed him to be a man of high morals."

"High morals?" He gave a bark of a laugh. "Hardly! He weren't no gutter rat, but he sure the hell weren't no hero."

"And how would you know?" I demanded. "You've been here a fortnight, at best!"

"I know," he drawled, "Because I seen it a million times before.

Kelly's a man who tries damn hard to hide his follies, and sticks out like a sore thumb because of it. He's too clean and tidy, dontcha think? Too quick to rush to anyone's aid. Naw," and he poked at the fire, speaking easily, "Yer constable is the kinda fella who tries too hard to be a saint, because he knows deep down inside that he lacks the qualities that make an honest-to-god gentleman." Jack took up a twig and added it to the hungry fire. "He has his secrets – gambling and opium, most likely – and he considers them to be grave and grievous sins." Jack folded his hands over his bent knees. "Had himself a religious father, I wager, or maybe he comes from a military family."

I was impressed by his perception, then chilled by it. Jack might appear rough and uneducated, but he wasn't stupid.

"Naw," he continued, tossing another stick into the flames, "He ain't the kind of man he hoped to be, that's for sure. A constant disappointment to himself. Too afraid of authority to piss on a wall, never mind kill a woman."

"So you don't think this was a crime of passion then."

He scowled in thought. "I think it mighta been done quick. I'd bet she was dead before she even knew she was in danger. But passion? Naw, I don't know about that." He thought about this for a moment, considered it, mused over what I had told him. Then, Jack asked, "How was she killed?"

"Drowned."

"You positive?"

I paused, and then said, "Yes."

Jack's smile caught the meager light of the small, quavering fire. "Now, that don't sound like the answer of a girl who knows for sure. C'mon, sweetheart, tell me: how did she die?"

It was an ugly question, asked in a salacious voice. "Why do you care?" I asked harshly. "What does it matter, how Mr. Kelly murdered my sister? What next? Are you going to ask if she was ravaged? If she was whole or in pieces?"

His smile vanished. "Now, I don't mean no disrespect—"

"Everything about you stinks of disrespect, Mr. Hunter," I

accused. “You’re a leech and a gawker. My sister is dead, and while I was trying to find you at a whorehouse, instead I found my letter to my grandfather,” I said, “That’s what I came here to ask, and I intend to get a straight answer from you. Where’d you get it?”

“Well, a short little question like that? I thought that would be simple to figure, Liz.” Jack reclined back against the sandstone wall and stretched his legs out, and folding his hands behind his head. “I got it from yer grandfather.”

I scoffed. “You don’t know my grandfather.“

“Oh, I do,” he replied, taking obvious delight in my confusion. “Captain Worthington; there’s a good man! He is a fine gentleman. I was much honored to make his acquaintance.”

“How would a man like you ever meet my grandfather?” I asked.

Jack laughed. “I’ve met my share of upstanding gentlemen, Amaryllis, of all sorts and persuasions. I’ve spent the last few years in Wiltshire, in fact. It was your grandfather that told me about yer family, and said I’d know yer father by the tools in his medical bag. Pearl-handled, he said, and finely-made. There may be lots of doctors in British Columbia, and maybe even a few called ‘Saunders’, but Captain Worthington assured me: his son-in-law would never let go of them knives and walrus-hide bag.”

“I still don’t get how an American ends up in Westbury, and in my grandfather’s confidence,” I spat.

He leaned in closer, and said, “Would ya even believe me if I told ya, I was born in the upstairs room of a boarding house on Commercial Road, only a step or two from Aldgate Station, down in the darkest gutters of London?”

I would not have been more surprised if I’d just discovered Queen Victoria to be a New Guinea tribesman.

“You? English? I don’t believe it.”

“Oh, it’s true, alright,” he confided, grinning with satisfaction to see my astonishment. “My mother was from Wolverhampton, and my father was a cotton broker, drummin’ up business for the Confederates during the last years of the Civil war. I’m the proud result of a thrupenny knee-trembler in the alley behind the Boar & Cockerel.

But my pa was long gone back to Huntsville by the time I came out a-squalling into the world." Jack plucked a piece of gravel from the ground and bounced it absently off the wall of the hollow. "I spent my boyhood digging pure out of the gutters of Houndsditch, and poisoning rats for 50p in the factories along Brick Lane. Yeah, I know London; better'n you, I wager. I called Flower and Dean Street my home 'til I was six, when my ma shipped me off to the States to live with my respectable father, to have a better life hauling cotton bales. Even after the war was lost, he was a man of modest means, and well-respected, although he weren't no doctor." He caught my glance to his tattered coat. "Yeah, well, fortunes turn, don't they. I don't mind. I may not have fancy clothes and a nice horse," he threw a rakish grin to Shao, "But I've found my calling in life, my purpose for being, and that's more than most poor bastards in this company town can say."

I tried to judge if his story was true. He spoke easily, candidly, fluidly, as if the memories were there, easily accessed. But if it was a lie, perhaps it was well-constructed, a devised fiction which he clung to, and which became more true with every telling.

Still, I thought, if you were going to devise a fiction of your childhood, why would you imagine yourself collecting dog turds in a London slum, to sell for a few pennies to the tanneries? Why would your father be aligned with the losing side of a war? I considered this as Jack bounced another stone off the wall. No, I decided, if Mr. Hunter was going to lie to impress me or beguile me, he would've made a spectacle of it – he would have made it worthwhile. He wouldn't have bothered with rats and shit; he would've made himself into royalty.

"Let us entertain the thought that your story is true," I began, "When did you return to London?"

"Oh, let's see," he mused, "My father died in '82, and my stepmother, well," He chuckled, "She weren't so happy to keep me around, seein' as how I was flesh-and-blood evidence of her husband's dallying overseas. She weren't the kindest stepmother a boy could have," he said, and his right hand drifted to his left, and grazed the stump of a finger there. "So she booted me out. I made my own way 'round the Union for a while, then found my way back to England when I was in my early-twenties, looking to find my blood relations. Why would you wanna know something personal like that?"

"Because, Mr. Hunter, I imagine you are the contemptible cur who begged for his sister's job to be reinstated, and when my father refused, you ruined my mother's reputation."

The cocksure grin on Jack's face instantly vanished. "What?"

"My father told me what happened in London, and why we had to flee, first to Wiltshire and then Canada."

Jack's face became stern, guarded. "He told you? All of it?"

"Enough."

A pensive silence filled up the hollow.

"Well, there are two sides to every story, ain't there," Jack said softly, thinking.

"And I've come to hear yours." I said.

Jack sized me up, seemed to consider it briefly. Then he shook his head. "It's my own private business, girl. I'd rather leave you outta it."

"I want this ugly mess to be resolved," I said, "I want your private business, as you put it, to be finished and done to that I can go back to my life." I rocked forward and crossed my wrists over my knees. "You, George Pibbs, and your malicious accomplices drove my family to ruin, but I understand the allure for vengeance. I assure you that, in my own childish way, I loved Hannah, too."

He squinted at me, as if he didn't understand a word I'd said, as if I'd suddenly swapped the King's English for Finnish or Portuguese.

"Sorry, kid, but," Jack glanced between me and Shao, suspecting we were sharing a joke at his expense, "Who the hell is Hannah?"

The silence of the forest, the crackle of the fire, the peal of water against pebbles as it splashed down nearby waterfalls; all of these I heard as a minute of silence stretched between us. Jack waited for clarification. I fumbled for something, anything to say, to snap the whirl of thoughts that paralyzed me.

At last, I said,

"You ARE George Pibbs, aren't you? And Hannah was your sister?"

"When I got back to London," he said, "I found I didn't have no family left." He spoke slowly, as if I were an idiot, and must be treated kindly and gently. "I don't have a sister, Miss Saunders, and my name ain't George Pibbs, and your family had fled outta London by the time I ever docked there." He paused. "But this Hannah... did she wear a purple dress?"

I leaned forward. "Yes. It had been my mother's."

He savored this piece of information. "And Hannah, she was the maid?"

"She was a friend of my mother's."

Jack laughed wickedly. "Oh, she was more'n just a friend!" He plucked up another stone, weighed it in the palm of his hand as he weighed his own thoughts. "Liz, my girl, your past ain't a pretty one, and it don't seem right that I'm the one to tell you the story. But for the life of me, I can't see who else would do it." A sly smile spread over his face.

"If it's any consolation, Mr. Hunter," I said, "I doubt I'll believe you anyway."

He nodded in acquiescence. "How much you know about... Jesus, you're just a kid." Jack took a fortifying breath, shifted his seat uncomfortably in the gravel. "How much you know about the birds and the bees?"

I did not look at Shao, though it was difficult to resist. "I know a little."

"Well," Jack replied, leaning forward. "Your mother was a bit of a tuppence-licker, if you get my meaning."

I thought about this, my brow furrowed. "No, I don't."

Jack groaned. "Molly Worthington had... unnatural lusts. She was of the wrong persuasion. She preferred the company of her own fair sex." He plucked up another stone. "Captain Worthington knew his daughter wasn't right, and he married her off to the first man who'd take her, but it weren't enough to change her perversions. She had a bit of a fling with the maid, and them sort of indiscretions just aren't tolerated."

I wasn't quite sure of what he meant. I heard his words, but they didn't fit together right. How could such a liaison work? Weren't men and women made to compliment each other? The mere idea of any deviation to this pairing had never crossed my mind.

Then again, I thought, Violet had been fond of reminding me that women ought not to wear pants, and that such a deviation was an affront to good society, but I found them quite comfortable. Just because my mother's preference was different did not mean it wasn't possible.

"You get my meaning now, kid?"

"I think so," I replied. "But, how could my mother love a woman, when she was happily married to my father?" I leaned forward, shaking off the stunned expression which seemed to give Jack such obvious amusement. "My mother had no friends. She hadn't even kept female acquaintances. She shunned all efforts to connect with her own gender, and rejected any woman who offered her a hand in friendship."

Jack shrugged one shoulder. "We all gotta figure out our own ways to dodge temptation," he replied. "Molly Worthington was a fingersmith, my girl, through and through; a female inversion, to use the medical term, and once that sort of sickness takes hold, there ain't no cure."

"So my father found out?" I said carefully, "And dismissed Hannah?"

Jack tossed the stone against the wall. "I didn't want to tell you 'bout yer mother. Didn't seem proper."

"But you told Alexander Kelly," I said, "You told him, and Father was furious. He thought Molly's indiscretions went with her to the grave, but you had to come and tell—"

Jack spoke over my shoulder to Shao. "I told you before, Jim boy, that Violet died 'cause she knew too much. If you wanna keep yer Amaryllis here safe, I suggest you talk sense into her, and tell her to keep her head down, and leave a man's business to the men."

"There's very little I can say to keep Lizzie safe, when she doesn't seem to care herself," Shao growled.

I stood up, my fists at my sides. "If you hadn't said a word to Kelly, Violet would still be—"

"I didn't think Kelly would run to your father with all that I told him," Jack replied. "I thought the man had a spine and knew the value of discretion. It weren't my intention for your sister to die."

"But she did die, and it's your fault." My voice remained calm, sedate, like the deep and treacherous waters of a rip tide. My hands clenched, my back stiffened. The anger rose in me, but it was matched with that gentle tranquility, too. The light of the fire quavered, grew sharp-edged and crisp. "Why are you here, Mr. Hunter? My mother is dead and her reputation ought to die with her. What could you possibly want?"

Jack's eyes fell onto me again, I felt myself being appraised. "Yer grandfather warned me about you," he said, almost as a threat, "Told me you weren't like other girls, and never would be." This time, he didn't find my indigence to be entertaining. His eyes ranged over my expression and balked at it. "He told me you were like a mirror: you appear to the casual observer like every other child, but there's nothing in yer heart, and all you can do is reflect the world around you."

A trickle of dread percolated down my spine. He was looking at me like one might examine a wasp, curious and cautious. His hand moved until his fingers brushed on the hilt of his knife.

"No, Mr. Hunter. I am not like other girls," I admitted.

His hand gripped the hilt.

My eyes narrowed.

"And I suspect," I said with dawning realization, "That you are more afraid of me, than I am of you."

His face paled in the firelight. For a fraction of a heartbeat, I saw that it was true: my words struck him, pierced him, laid him bare. Then the bravado swept over him and he snarled. The knife hissed as it slid from the sheath, and the flames danced in the reflection along the blade as he held it before him. He jumped to his feet, intent on me.

"I didn't believe Worthington," Jack said, "I didn't believe any child could have the devil in her heart."

"My grandfather said that about me?"

"That, and worse."

I rose to my feet, unarmed and small before him. I lowered my chin, studied every tiny detail revealed by the fire light. Beads of sweat gathered on his neck, the pulse of blood danced in his carotid.

He feared me. I saw it, clear as the flash of flames against the blade. I didn't know why, but Jack Hunter feared me.

But I felt no fear – only a warmth sweeping over my skin and a clarity of my own power. I welcomed, embraced, savored it. My hands clenched at my side and my body braced itself for the impact of his attack, and in an instant, I already knew how I would strike back at him. Let him come, I thought, though it was so quick and instantaneous that it was less a thought and more an instinct, blade-sharp and programmed into every fiber of my bones. I would tear out his eyes and eat the tongue directly from his maw.

Jack's huge figure blocked out all light from the stars above and the fire below. The knife drew back. He charged at me, as formidable and unstoppable as an engine.

Then, like a bolt from heaven, like a lightning strike dashed down by a vengeful goddess-wife, a missile struck the middle of his head. Jack gave a yelp, both hands flying to his brow. The knife fell to the ground and stuck up at an odd angle from the gravel. From between his fingers, a trickle of blood sprouted from his hairline.

"God damn!" he screamed. His voice cracked with the shock of it.

Shao grabbed my hand. He yanked me up and out of the pit, then whipped another stone at Jack's head, striking the man in the bridge of the nose. We flew down the path, blundering blindly through the trees. The fading howls of Jack's curses followed us all the way down the river.

. . .

SHAO, too, cursed and fumed, but his words were in Cantonese, and I could only translate the gist of his muttering by the flush that had risen to his cheeks, the thunderous scowl across his face, and the tightness with which he clenched my hand in his. I stumbled to keep pace. He moved at a fast clip, and refused to slow down for me. We reached the farm on the edge of the swamp, where he tossed me against the roots of a pear tree. I fell heavily into the bower's embrace.

"What the hell!" he finally burst in English, turning on me, cornering me against the tree. "What was that all about!"

"My father dismissed our maid, and her brother begged for her to be reinstated," I explained, pointing back the way we'd came. "When Jack said he'd been to London, I thought he must've been the one to ruin us!"

He paced for a while longer, back and forth through the gloom, until at last he collapsed in the grass. I pressed against him, and discovered that he was shivering.

"Are you cold?"

Shao recoiled from me. "Ai ya! I'm angry! I'm terrified! He pulled a knife on you, Lizzie!"

"Yeah, well," I replied, hunching back against the tree, "It isn't the first time."

"And you stood there!" he burst, " You just... just stared at him! And your eyes looked... looked... " He searched her expression. "Even now, you look like you've done nothing more exciting than a bit of knitting! Zao gao!" He clutched his knees to his chest and pressed a palm to his brow.

I gave an audible sigh.

"I did not know that about my mother," I said quietly, more to myself than to Shao. "I didn't think such a thing was possible."

"That women can love other women? Or men, other men?" He crossed his arms over his chest. "There are no boundaries for the human heart, Liz."

He waited, to gauge if I was upset, but my face remained still and calm. My breathing was quiet and even.

"Are you angry?"

"No."

"What do you feel?" he probed, for my expression gave nothing away.

I leaned back against the tree. "I don't know. Puzzled, I guess."

"Puzzled?" Shao said, "That's it? Puzzled?" He gave a harsh laugh. "Jack holds a knife to you, threatens your life, insults your mother by calling her preferences a perversion, and this... this is all you can muster? You're slightly puzzled?"

"I guess I'm upset—"

"You don't GUESS you're upset, Liz. When you're upset, you know it!" He gripped my shoulders. "Is this what Jack meant? When he said you were a mirror?"

I nodded.

"So..." Shao couldn't find a delicate way to phrase his question, so he asked plainly, "What's wrong with you?"

I lowered my face until my gaze rested on the scorched grass. "There's nothing wrong with me," I decided, "My father assures me, I am the way I'm supposed to be."

"But your eyes," he continued. Shao pulled back and stared into my face, but he did not look at my spirit or soul or whatever alchemical process occurs that animates a human being. He studied the physical structure of which I was comprised, the moist ocular orbs of fluid and lenses and hazel green irises, but did not look at *me*. "When he drew the knife on you, and you stared back at him, I've never seen..." Shao's sentence faded into silence.

"Never seen what?" I urged.

Now his focus snapped back to the girl within the body, to the mind behind the eyes. "When I was a boy in San Francisco, my uncle took me down to the wharves to collect offal and fish heads for stew. And one time, there was a great vat full of thrashing water, and men were gathered around it, poking at the contents with their cane poles, causing the water to splash and bubble. I wanted to see what was in the vat, so jiu fu held me up to see over the edge, and inside, swimming in a soup of seawater and its own blood, was a great silver-grey shark, the biggest fish I'd ever seen, dredged up from the deep, half-dead from its capture and its torture. Suspended above it, I looked down into its face, and it looked up at me with one eye, appraising me with one black disc, completely fearless." He swallowed. "That shark had lived a life without ever feeling fear -- it was incapable of being afraid. Even trapped in a vat, without hope of escape, it felt nothing, and when they hauled it by its tail and let it hang until dead, you really couldn't tell when the life had left it, or whether it was just keeping very, very still, waiting for an unwary boy to creep close enough for it to bite. Even alive, those eyes were dead. I'd never seen anything like it before, or since." He rocked back, retreated from me. "Until now."

"I'm sorry," I said, although as the word formed, I knew it was not the right thing to say. He needed an explanation, or an assurance that it was a trick of the light, or a promise that he would never see that ugly void again.

None of these could I give him.

He watched me for a long time, charting the changes in my expression as I diminished into the humble form of a stick-limbed, bedraggled girl, my hair snagged with twigs, a smudge of dirt on one cheek. At last, Shaozhu stood, and brushed the bits of grass and twigs from his pants. "How can you possibly feel sorry, Bai SuZhen?" he asked, and turned to leave. "How can something without a soul feel remorse?"

58

When I arrived home, just after midnight, I found Father sitting in the horsehide chair with book in hand, reading, keeping vigil over the body with reverential silence.

He looked relieved as I entered.

"Thank goodness you're home!" Then his welcoming grin faded, seeing the smudge of mud on my face and the bits of twigs in my hair. "You are well?"

"I suppose."

"Where have you been?"

"Up in the woods."

"Why would you be in the forest at this hour?"

"I went for a walk. I needed time to think."

"Well, as long as you're safe, it doesn't matter to me where you ramble," he said, "I know well-enough by now that you can take care of yourself."

I glanced at the coffin on the table. I took a fortifying breath and asked boldly, "What happened to the man who ruined you?"

A heavy silence filled the parlor. Father grew stern. He closed his book to hold it on his lap.

"I beg your pardon?" he began, though he'd heard well enough. "Of what consequence is that to you, Lizzie?"

"I'm curious."

"There's no need for us to ever mention the name of George Pibbs," he spat, "May he rot in his grave and burn in the fires of hell."

"He's dead?"

"A decade ago. He died of cholera, so I heard on good authority, just a month or so before we left for Canada. I still have friends in my gentleman's club, and they were kind enough to relay the news."

I pondered this, wondered at the truth of it. "You're sure he's dead?"

Father leaned forward and rested his elbows on his knees, the book dangling from his hand. "As sure as I trust my own eyes, for your grandfather and I went to view the body, to close that sorry chapter of our lives. Why, Lizzie? Why would you need to know?"

"I thought –" I considered my assumptions. "What if the man had followed you here?"

Father shook his head. "Impossible."

"Is it?"

"Completely." He tossed the book so that it landed expertly on the side table. "Unless the Devil gave him leave, which I highly doubt. No, Lizzie, George Pibbs is dead and buried and, by now, reduced to bones and worm food."

I didn't believe him. But I didn't believe Jack, either. Something rang false between the claims of both men.

There had been a pantry maid named Hannah – of that, I could trust my own memory. I fervently wished Mother was here, to sort it all out. I'd rather rely on an adult's recollection, instead of my own childish glimpses of the distant, foggy past.

"If someone followed you, or if Grandfather sent someone, or—"

He clucked in the back of his throat. "Lizzie, you're too tired. You need to sleep."

"No, I'm fine! But if --"

"Sit down, girl," he invited, then tented his hands and cast me a kindly smile. "There is no one following us. You sound like your mother."

I realized, with a start, that he was right.

"No, Liz, whatever your grandfather said to Mr. Kelly, well… it is gone with him, wherever he has fled. The best we can do is move on with our lives."

"You are not concerned? Even in the slightest?"

"Your mother has taken her scandalous ways to the grave, and Violet is safe from the sting of her shame. Neither you nor I are the sort to let improprieties hamper us." He set his book on the lamp table. "We'll accept the offer of Mr. Fish and Dr. Briggs, and start afresh. Your mother and I did it before, and that was with two small girls in tow. You and I, we'll move on, re-build, live and thrive again. You'll see."

I considered it. I had no schooling to tie me here, and no friends, and now that Violet and Mother were dead, no family either. And maybe Shao would be relieved to be rid of me, an odd gangly urchin with the black, soulless eyes of a dead shark.

But the thought of leaving Shao made my stomach hurt.

"After George Pibbs died, what happened to Hannah?"

Father shrugged. "I don't know. Lost amongst the tide of unfortunates, I imagine. Sit down, my girl, have yourself a bite to eat and take ease," he suggested, interpreting my fatigue for sorrow. "Agnes made biscuits, and I've made tea, and it should keep us through the night. Here, you may have my chair." He stood and yawned, and stretched his arms above his head. "It has been a long, distressing day for both of us, but time marches on. I'm told it heals all wounds. Can I get you anything, before I retire?"

I unbound my hair from its braid and kicked off my boots. "No. I'm alright."

"I can stay longer, if you wish."

"I'll be fine. Go to bed."

Purple shadows ringed his eyes, his cheeks were wan. He caressed the top of the casket with one hand. "I had thought to finish my work tonight in the surgery, but I'm just too weary." Then, wiping the sleep from the corner of his eyes, he said softly, "Will you miss Violet?"

"Yes," I replied, taking the chair. "Terribly."

"I'm sorry, then, for your loss," he replied. "She was a good sister to you, and a dutiful daughter. She loved you greatly." He stared at the coffin. "Your mother and your sister, all within the space of a year. Most girls would crumble at the prospect of such loneliness. Your strength under duress is admirable, my girl."

Maybe he meant it as a compliment, but his observation stung. It only underlined to me, once more, how different I was.

"Did you love Mother?"

His eyebrows arched. "Of course."

"Did she love you back?"

John considered this, and said, "As best she could, given her illness."

I took a scone and nestled down into the warmth left by his body and captured by the chair. The question lingered on my lips: what was the true nature of Molly's illness? But then, I decided against asking; it didn't matter to me, and wouldn't change anything. I let the question die and said, "I do miss Mother, very much."

He pressed a kiss to my cheek. "If you need anything, or if you're afraid, you call me. But of course," he said with a measure of pride, "You won't be afraid."

"I'll be fine," I replied, "I sat vigil for Mother, too, not so long ago."

There were three of us to sit vigil then, I thought, but did not say it.

"I'll see you in the morning, Liz."

And with that, he retired upstairs.

I fetched a cup of tea from the kitchen and a book from the library, and installed myself in Father's place in the chair, to read absently as I ate the humble food. The sound of footfalls on the second floor gradually ceased. The house fell into a comforting, ecclesiastical peace. Nothing shifted or moved, and all that could be heard was the ticking of the clock on the mantle and the gentle flip of pages under my fingers.

But the stillness grew in weight until the silence pressed heavily on my shoulders, and I could no longer concentrate on the words before me. Eventually, I set the book aside and let my eyes drift to the casket on the table.

I did feel sad, terribly sad, and I nurtured the clenched sorrow that seemed to be growing in the pit of my stomach. I thought a bit about what Hunter had claimed, and decided he was a liar and a thief, and I shouldn't put any stock in his words. He wanted to upset me, he wanted to leave me with doubts – he delighted in it. Shao had warned me from the very beginning that Jack was not a man to be trusted; he had read my intentions as easily as he'd read Mr. Kelly's personality, and had told me things designed to upset me.

But the letter in my pocket spoke of a concrete connection. Even if Jack had stolen it from my grandfather, it meant he had come a great distance to find my family. And if what he said about Mother's inclinations was true, then he was privy to secrets that had long been buried. This thought did, indeed, rattle my composure.

And why would Mr. Kelly flee? The tale of Mother's indiscretions was hardly enough to cause a man to abandon his post and his community.

"I wish you could tell me, Vi: why leave with Kelly?" I said to the box. In the stillness, my whisper was as loud as the rapport of a gun. "Why him, Violet?"

With no answer forthcoming, my mind dredged up an answer in a voice that was not my own, and I heard Jack say, "...Too afraid of authority to piss on a wall, never mind kill a woman."

And then I wondered, again, about the dirt and blood caught under Violet's nails, and questioned how the deed had been done. How had Kelly lashed out against a defenseless woman? I tried to imagine the struggle between them, but the vision refused to manifest – the more I considered the possibility, the more I found it impossible to believe. Maybe Kelly lacked moral fiber, as Jack claimed, but not in any manner that would result in violence, and certainly not against someone he cherished so openly. I rose and crossed the room, and stood next to the casket for what felt like a very long time. At last, emboldened to break tradition and the sacred seal of a closed casket, I took up the poker from the hearth.

The lid levered open with a pop. I gripped the edge to raise it. The hinges squeaked, the wood creaked and groaned. I pushed with my shoulder, shut my eyes with the effort, until the casket lay open.

Violet's face, grotesque and bloated, stared upwards, but her misty eyes had rolled partially back in a mimicry of religious ecstasy. All the color had drained out of her skin, and it matched the white of the linen folded underneath her slack body. Her hands displayed the same dull luminosity of an old tallow candle, half-melted in the sun.

I held aloft the coal oil lamp from the tabletop. The light pushed away the shadows as I moved it slowly over the midline of the body, cataloguing what I saw. A wreath of purple and black marks encircled Violet's throat. I saw the clear fingerprints where strong hands had wrung the life from her. No scratches or cuts betrayed a weapon. The swollen neck was deeply bruised with the force of the murderer's grip.

Then I took one waxy hand and studied it, but the traces of dirt, blood and hair were gone, meticulously washed away by Father. I began to look more closely at the minutiae of Violet's clothes, from the buttons and hooks on her split corset to the laces of her boots. Her hair seemed ragged, uneven.

I peered closer. The blonde curls that cradled Violet's blue cheeks were not the same length. On the left side, her hair was two inches shorter.

Rufus said she'd left a note and a lock of her hair. Alexander Kelly rushed to meet her at their undisclosed location, assured of his sweetheart's intentions by the presence of her golden locks.

I lifted the hem from around the white ankles and began to study it, finding nothing there. It was clean and fresh. If Kelly had killed her by the lake, wouldn't there be briars snagged in the folds of her skirt, bits of grass and burrs, collected as they walked together to the place of her murder? Or at least a few strands of horsehair, or manure from crossing the roads? But there was nothing. The fabric was as clean as if Violet had pulled the dress fresh from her closet.

A trickle of water, stained pink against the linen wadding of the coffin's floor, dribbled from between the slack thighs.

A foreboding tremor skittered up my body.

I pressed my hands against Violet's hips and shifted the corpse again. The meager line of rosy liquid flowed down to the base of the box, where it curled like a serpent in the folds of the fabric.

My breath stuck in my throat. I lifted the skirts, which had been so carefully tucked around her ankles. The knees showed pale and puffy, the thighs were translucent. I folded back the black skirts over Violet's waist and held the lamp aloft for a better view.

Almost instantly I reeled back, eyes wide, before turning and vomiting a thin gruel of biscuit and tea across the carpet.

In the warm light cast by the coal-oil lamp, the skin of Violet's belly lay open like the gut of a cleaned pig. The sharp excised lines of flesh showed nothing but an empty cavity, washed clean of gore and blood, and hidden under the generous padding of skirts, petticoats and slips. Violet Saunders had been sliced open with a sharp tool and gutted with precision. The grey-pink scoop of her pelvis, shaped to cradle her visceral organs, now framed a shallow puddle of lake water in a hollow bowl of bone.

59

I FELL HEAVILY BACK against the chair and the wall. The vision of my sister's empty husk burned in my eyes, and I scrubbed the back of my hand to my face. My shoulders trembled, and the light of the coal oil lamp wavered; I put it down quickly on the table, before I dropped it and caused a fire.

Then I turned, raced down the hall and vaulted up the steps to the second floor, and pounded upon Father's bedroom door with both fists.

He opened it, dressed in his night shift and cap.

"Dear God, Liz!" he exclaimed, "You've gone as white as a sheet!"

I pointed down the stairs, to the parlor. "Kelly gutted her," I choked.

John took my shoulders in his hands and held me still, studying my face for signs of shock. "Sit, Lizzie, and take deep, easy breaths."

He guided me to his bedside and sat next to me. A sheen of cold sweat still tingled on my skin, and the image of that horrific emptiness remained in my mind.

"There was no need to look further at the body," he said with reproach, but his voice was kind, too, and he drew me under his protective arm.

"He gutted her, left her empty, tore open her belly and—" I took a great rattling breath to fill my lungs. "I thought she'd drowned, he'd held her under, but he—"

"Liz, calm down!"

"How could he do that to her?!?"

John startled at my cry. "Calm yourself! This is unbefitting, Lizzie!"

"It isn't enough that he'd kill her to keep her quiet – he savaged her! Kelly left her in pieces! What kind of sick, disgusting beast could do that to someone who loved him?" My voice cracked. "She trusted him!"

"I've never seen you so angry—"

"Why shouldn't I be angry?!" I screamed, "God damn it, look at what he's done to her!"

John lowered his chin. "I saw what he did to Violet. I tucked her skirts around her ankles, to give her dignity in death."

"This was no dignified death!"

"Lizzie, please," he persisted, speaking over me, drowning my protests with his own even-tempered words. "This isn't like you, Lizzie. Center yourself." His words were soft and soothing, hypnotic and reassuring. "Now, Lizzie, I insist that you look no more upon Violet, for her mortal coil has shuffled off all that we loved about her. I beg you, let her body rest in solitude."

I trembled with rage and bit my lip to keep from arguing.

"It is not quite what you think," John continued, "Yes, Mr. Kelly has taken your beloved sister from you, but Violet's death came from strangulation. These woods are filled with wolves and cougars and bears, and what easier meal for a scavenger than the soft belly of a woman?" He looked at me with disappointment. "Think rationally, Lizzie. It is my opinion that Kelly killed her at the shore, and she was mauled by carnivores before the torrential rains swept her body into the lake. I didn't want to spell it out for you so clearly."

"Nessie says that Tsonakwa eats the soft bits of the body, where the soul resides."

He gave a small groan. "Lizzie," he began, disgusted. "Frequenting séances? Talking about ghosts and devils? This isn't like you either!" Father shook his head. "Don't tell me your embracing all that religious, superstitious nonsense!"

"No, but—"

"This will just fuel McGill's self-righteous crusade to lever me into a church pew," he continued. "Please, Lizzie, your mother endeavored to make a God-fearing man out of me, and it didn't work. Father McGill knows I'm a hopeless case, but if he catches wind of your interest in the ethereal, he might try to plant his theolologies in you. I humored the whims of the Presbyterian church because I loved your mother, but if it sinks its talons in my house, I won't be pleased!"

I hunched over and rested my head in my hands. The shock of discovering Violet's state was beginning to fade.

"It surprised me—"

"It turned you into a quavering mess!" John replied. "Lizzie, this is not how I've raised you!" He ran one palm over my hair. "What happened to the rational child of science, of whom I am so proud? Do you think a career as a doctor will permit you such useless flights of rage and horror? You'll do no one any favors, if you persist in such rampant displays of emotion!"

"I'm sorry," I muttered.

"Do you see me, falling apart? Of course not! We must retain our strength in the face of such challenges!"

Together we descended into the parlor. Father closed the lid of the casket again, and banged it into place with the flat of his hand.

"Now, do you wish me to take the vigil again? I will, if you need sleep."

"No," I said, though now, the thought of sitting alone with an eviscerated shell in the dark gave me chills, when before it had simply been a loving sister's duty. "I'll continue."

"Violet's soul is gone," he said, "Give her body its privacy, and let her go." He gave me a cautious look, searching for any hint of a fracture in my strength. Finding none, he kissed my cheek and retired to bed.

60

August 16, 1898

At daybreak, I relinquished my vigil to Father, who urged me to retire to my room and rest. It had been a long and dreadful night, and I'd never been happier to hear the sparrows twitter their greeting to the dawn. Father said he would begin the arrangements for the funeral, and spare me the financial business of death.

For an hour or more, I lay in the lonely bed and stared at the ceiling. The image of Violet's savage wounds returned, unbidden, to the forefront of my thoughts, like a photograph rising out of the swirling chemical. The injuries had been so brutal and vicious that they almost made Violet's torso into something inhuman, like an opening flower or a foxhole dug into red earth. My mind latched onto that recurring, repeating image: peeling back the black dress to find nothing underneath.

Maybe I slept, maybe I only lay in that frustrating purgatory between sleep and waking; even I wasn't sure. Hours passed. When I rose, I heard Agnes humming in the garden, and the sun was low in the west. It cast a gooey honey-amber light; the day would soon be gone.

I had been unarmed last night, when I needed a weapon, and I would not make the same mistake again. From its box on my dresser, I withdrew the curved apothecary knife and tucked it into the back waistband of my pants. It nestled against the small of my back and pressed into the base of my spine with a comforting weight.

Father was not in the parlor.

I joined Agnes in the yard.

"Your father bid me not tae wake ye," said woman as she cracked her fingers, "He said ye had a rough night of sitting with the body."

I tried the surgery door and found it locked. "He's at the hospital?"

"Aye," she replied, and her hands returned to their task of plucking beans while her face continued the conversation. "But, God willing, they'll be bringing up no injured men at the end of the day shift, and he'll be home for supper before darkness falls."

"I'll be home for dinner, too," I said, and slipped out the gate before Agnes had any chance to admonish me, dump chores upon me, or form a question as to my destination.

Rufus, though, was no where to be found. The constabulary door was locked. In the colliery office, a young accountant told me that Rufus had continued the search, and caught wind of Kelly on the road between Courtenay and Comox. He had rented a boat and a man to row him across the bay to the town of Comox, where he would follow the lead until either he, or it, was exhausted. He was due to return that night.

When the whistle blew for the final shift at No. 5 mine, I waited by the rail station for the coal trip to arrive. Men clung to the side of the carriages, tired from the long day. It was hard to tell their coal-stained faces apart, but I stood to the side of the platform and let them notice me. One face stared at me for a fraction longer than the others, then strode close enough to touch, although he kept his hands close at his sides.

Shao said nothing. He barely tipped his head to me as he passed.

But the faint trace of a smile turned up the corner of his mouth. I was heartened.

We met at the edge of town, where a grove of plum trees abutted the railway grade. The spindly branches hung with resplendent purple fruit, and we sat in the shade with a respectable distance between us. He pulled down a handful of plums to share, and I rolled the fruit in the grass to clean off the bloom and the dust from his palms. As men trudged by on their many paths homeward, he said nothing, but listened quietly as I told him of Violet's body.

"I want to tell Rufus, but he's gone to Comox," I finished.

The coal dust, trapped in the crevasses and corners of Shao's face, defined his features in the failing evening light. "Maybe he's found Kelly, and he's bringing him in," he offered.

"Then I want to be there, when they arrive."

But Shao shook his head.

"Go home. You're safe there." He gave a great yawn. "Please don't make me run after you again: I'm too tired to go very far."

I laughed, which caused him to laugh.

"It's good to see you smile, Lizzie." He reclined against the tree. "I felt badly, about yesterday. Your sister is dead, and I'm worried about you, and people show grief in different ways. But," He took a bite from a plum. "You scared me."

"I didn't meant to. And I don't understand how I can possibly be so terrifying," I quipped, taking half of a plum in one juicy bite. "I'm just one little girl."

A couple of men on the road called out to Shao, and he raised his hand in greeting to them as they continued on. "Because you looked immoveable, Liz. No creature looks so confident unless it has the means to fully defend itself. You looked at Jack like you might look at a bug – there was no question in your mind that you could knock him down, however you chose. To you, Jack was no obstacle. And that gives a man doubts." He plucked a plum from the pile of cleaned fruit in the grass. "What, exactly, would you have done to him?"

"I honestly don't know," I replied.

A shout from further down the tracks caught our ears. I looked down the grassy slope, through the plum trees, to see three men hurrying back to town, half-running. Between two of them, they carried a strip of old canvas sacking.

We bounded down the hill slope to the side of the railway and met them as they passed. Shao recognized one of them, and hailed him in Cantonese.

The man returned his reply; one of his companions was Japanese, and the other, Italian. As the three came closer, I caught the scent of copper on the stagnant air, baked with the sun.

"What is it?" I asked, drawing close. The fabric had folded over on itself, but I saw splotches of black on the canvas. When the men laid it flat on the track and stretched it out smooth, the entire square was patterned with crusted blood.

"Ayumi spotted it, out in the swamp, hung up on some brush," said the Italian man, "And we went to go get it – good piece of canvas like this, hey? Make a good curtain."

Ayumi was young and sprightly. Mud covered his pants up to his thighs. His face was less dusty than the others -- he must work on the picking table or pull a rake in the coal yard. "I go," he said in broken English, gesturing with one hand. "I grab, I bring back. But, look!"

Look, indeed. Dried blood encrusted the fabric. Ayumi had taken care to hold it over his head and keep it from the swamp water, preserving the pattern of blood on the canvas. I crouched down to study it.

"I say, could be a hunter wrapped up a deer to carry home; it has got dust and hair on other side, from horse's back," the Italian miner continued, "It is good fabric, hey, but I know Alfio, he pull out girl from water, and we think...?" He shrugged. "Who leave good fabric like this in swamp?"

And it was, truly, a large square of good strong fabric, 5 feet on either side. I rubbed the corner between my fingers. The thread count was high; the canvas thick. This was not the kind of cloth used for clothing or sacks, but for a purpose that required durability.

Shao's thoughts had followed the same path. "A tarp?"

"No," I said slowly. Tarps were smeared with wax to make them water resistant. I looked up to him. "This hasn't been treated."

When I took the edge between my fingers and looked closely, I found evidence of stitching. A double-line of small neat holes followed the edge.

"It's upholstery fabric," I replied.

I'd seen fabric like this, not long ago. The seats of a carriage? No, not that, either. I wracked my brain for an answer, but it remained elusive.

"It looks like a hand, there," said Shao. He pointed out a smudged print on the edge of the fabric, where it had been gripped.

The rest of the blood pattern was long, smeared, oblong and surrounded by splattered droplets. A lot of blood meant a big chunk of meat.

"So you think, ya?" said the Italian man, "A hunter wrapped up a deer?"

I examined the pattern of blood, and the last bit of sunshine caught a glimmering filament of gold. I peered close, until the heady scent of blood surrounded me, and made me dizzy with its sweet rot perfume.

The glue of dried blood trapped a fringe of blonde hairs.

"The murderer wrapped Violet in this," I said to the men. "Slung her over the back of a horse or mule, and took her to the lake." I rocked back on my heels to muse over the fabric. Ayumi and the Chinese man both stepped away from the canvas, looking ill, and the Italian man crossed himself and mumbled in Latin. Shao crouched across the canvas from me, looking close.

"He would've been seen, if he rode to the lake on the railway grade," he said.

"But not if he took her up through the woods, on the other side of the swamp. You and I walked that way to see Jack; it's not impassable. He might have tossed it in the swamp from the other shore," I looked at Ayumi. "Was it closer to this shore, or the other side?"

Ayumi considered her question. "Other side. Closer to other

side." He grinned toothlessly. "I got good eyes, see little white triangle flap flap in breeze."

I looked at the fabric again, and absently flapped the corner. I remembered Agnes, beating the carpets in the back yard.

"This is the backing of a rug," I said to Shao. "The double-stitching, the weight... yes, I'm sure of it."

"Did Mr. Kelly have any rugs in his apartment?"

I shook my head. "No. When Jack and Rufus searched the apartment, their boots thumped on bare floors."

"This must be from his apartment, then." Shao replied. "He tore it off his rug, and wrapped Violet in it."

"And he dropped it where he thought no one would find it," I considered, "Maybe he hoped someone would take it, wash it, use it, and never think twice about the kind of animal it had carried."

"Or maybe," said Shao, staring at me across the mottled surface of the canvas, "Maybe he just didn't care."

61

THE MEN FOLDED the canvas into careful quarters, and gave it to me with respect. They held no doubt that it had borne my sister's corpse, and it seemed right that I should take possession of it – no matter how good the fabric, they were happy to be rid of it. But Rufus McGregor was not in town, and I didn't want to take it home.

"Come with me, then," said Shao. "I know what we need to do."

He led me down into Chinatown and along Ha Gai to the very end of the street, until we reached a little square shed with double doors, backing onto the hilly woods. He took the folded canvas and set it outside on the narrow covered porch, and put his satchel on top to mark it as his own, then opened the doors and led me inside.

A large square room spread out before us, dark and intimate, with a half-barrel full of dry sand sitting against the farthest wall. Narrow tables flanked it, carrying bouquets of wild flowers and bowls of fruit, intricately carved sandlewood boxes, and reams of curled paper decorated with Chinese characters. One candle had been left to burn in a shallow stone bowl. Behind the barrel, on a tall table, a rough wooden carving of a seated man looked down upon the room, surrounded by smaller statues, all hewn from stone or wood. Some had been carved with skill, and others were rudimentary, but most were somewhere in between: votives, idols, figures whittled with dull knives by men with arthritic hands. The air smelt heavy of perfume. Square pillows had been thrown on the ground, and Shao grabbed two and took them to the far wall, tossing them to the floor in front of the barrel.

"What is this place?" I asked in awe.

His voice was quiet and reverent. "Miu, the joss house." He smiled. "The Ancestor Hall."

Then he took the lone candle in hand and, with it, lit other candles on the narrow tables, so that the single source of illumination grew and grew, until the room was warm and cozy. When all the candles were lit, he opened one of the boxes and withdrew a handful of sticks, coated with a sticky resin.

"Here," he said, offering me five sticks.

I recalled the burnt ends of sticks in sand, on the box at the end of Shao's bed.

"What is it?"

"Incense."

"What do I do with it?"

Shao smiled at the child-like simplicity of my question, when he was so familiar with the answer. "You light them, blow them out, and stick them in the sand in the barrel to smolder."

"And then?"

I watched him carefully light the end of the incense from the nearest candle, then blow out the little flames that crowned the sticks. Torpid ribbons of fragrant smoke curled through the still air. He set them in the sand. The glowing ends became eyes of light in the gloom. Shao knelt on the pillow. "And then, you pray."

"To God?"

Shao shook his head. "To Violet."

I mimicked his actions, thrusting the ends of the sticks into the sand next to his. "What do I say?" I asked as I knelt beside him.

He rested his hands on his thighs. "Wish her well, and ask for her guidance for whatever life holds next for you."

"I don't believe in ghosts."

"Do you believe that Violet had a consciousness, and a spirit, and a soul?" He smiled at me. "Pray to whatever it was that made Violet, Violet. And if it is there, it will hear you and give you comfort. And if it isn't there?" He shrugged, "Then at least you've had a moment of peace and reflection before you continue on your way."

I couldn't suppress a smile. I had no other place to go until Rufus returned to town, so I let the smoke of the incense envelope my senses. I lowered my head and relaxed into the serenity of the Ancestor Hall, with Shao kneeling in quiet meditation at my side.

THE CLEAR SKY wicked away the heat of the day and replaced it with a chill that whispered of autumn. In the wetlands behind the Ancestor Hall, a soft chorus of frogs sang: the hour was late and the moon cast narrow slivers of light through the gaps in the shed walls. Nevermind that all women of my bearing and age ought to be tucked firmly into bed. I had grown used to my liberties and refused to suffer any infringement on my freedom, no matter what society dictated. Violet had been my voice of reason, whom I often ignored but still heard, yet Violet was dead. My conscience was silent, but its absence also gave me wings.

I knelt in front of the carved statues, listening to the gentle rhythm of Shao's breath, and thought of Violet. This was much better than sitting next to a dull casket. That box only held mauled, mortal remains. If that which made Violet, Violet was anywhere terrestrial, it would be here, in a place of sweet tranquility.

A soft step in the open doorway directly behind us caught my ear. I turned on my knees to see three men blocking the doorway. Two were Chinese, one was white. All three were young and roughly-garbed, and they looked sickly and spare, craven, with shifty manners.

Shao stood quickly and greeted them. "Ni hao?"

They looked from Shao to me. One spoke authoritatively in Cantonese.

I stood, too, unwilling to be on my knees.

"He says," Shao translated, "That we're to go with them."

"I don't think so," I replied.

But Shao shook his head. "Jiu fu sent them to find us."

"Then jiu fu can come and get us," I said. To the men, I added, "Tell Mr. Tao to come speak with us, if he that is what he wishes."

Shao cringed, but the tallest one laughed, and after making a ribald comment to his associates, he said in practiced English, "You are a guest here, and I will ignore your disrespect. I insist that you follow us." And, with a quick bow of his head, he tacked on a sarcastic "Please."

"I have no interest—"

A rough chortle rippled through them. "I do not care what interests you," he replied. With two steps to cross the floor, he reached for my collar and seized it in a tight grip. His rough calloused palms felt like sandpaper.

Shao took a step forward, but the other men grabbed his arms, and wrestled him forward.

"Come, come," the tallest man whispered in my ear. His breath smelt of tobacco and salted pork. One sinewy arm encircled my waist and tightened uncomfortably. "You are requested."

THEY HALF-DRAGGED Shao onto Ha Gai, but I would not be dragged. I wrenched a few inches of space and stood upright, still ensnared in the man's skinny arms, but no longer fumbling at his side like a marionette. He laughed and jostled me again, and I pushed back, which earned me a clout across the back of my head.

They shepherded us along Ha Gai to a tall three-story building washed white and garlanded with ivy and hawthorn bushes. Four men sat on the porch on chairs cobbled together out of branches. They sat half in shadows, and the thin bowls of their clay pipes glowed like tiny orange lanterns as they puffed. Three of the men were well-dressed in clean trousers and coulter shirts, but the fourth man, who was older than the rest by many years, wore a grey tweed suit of comparable quality to any in Father's wardrobe. His queue shone white and silver, and his beard was wispy but trimmed.

When the four men saw Shao, they glowered at him, and with a gesture from the eldest, Shao was escorted inside. I made a step to follow but the arm around my waist squeezed painfully close held me back. The door slammed shut.

The tall man deferred to the four seated men. Their conversation volleyed back and forth in rapid bursts of Cantonese and the fierce grip on my waist never slackened. I listened for words I might recognize, but they spoke so rapidly that anything I understood was quickly eclipsed by words I did not, so I studied the building and the lay of the land.

The house was detached and flanked by narrow vegetable gardens. A strip of woodland ran behind it towards the swamp to the southeast. If I could wrestle free, that would be the best direction to run.

I was so engrossed in assessing my surroundings that I failed to notice when the men switched to English. It wasn't until a question was repeated, loudly and strictly, that I realized it was directed to me.

"Why do you pester Shaozhu?" demanded the oldest man on the porch. He scowled as he lowered his pipe and exhaled a thin line of dense, floral-scented smoke through his wispy beard.

I bowed my head respectfully. “I don’t pester him, sir,” I said, “I count him as my friend.”

"You are Dr. Saunders’ daughter." he said.

"I am."

The man at my side released me instantly.

But, as his companions muttered amongst each other and traded worried glances, the elderly man remained unconcerned. He sucked on his pipe and rolled the smoke around in his mouth as he considered the implications of their visitor. "Your father gives you great latitudes, to be running around at night, and here, in this part of town," he said with staid scorn. I felt a greater blush rise to my cheeks than all of Agnes's nagging could ever have achieved. He leaned to the figure on his right, a bulky man of middle-age with a face that had once, long ago, been scorched in a fire. They traded opinions; the man with the scarred face stroked his chin, grinding his teeth. The elderly man took another long sip from his pipe, letting the smoke trickled through his lips, then nodded.

"Do you know who I am?"

I stabbed at an answer. "I think you must be part of Guan Yu Tong."

"I am the Grandfather, Ah Kung, and Shaozhu's benevolent protector," he explained, "And I do not approve of his associations with white women." He sipped from his pipe again as his eyes roved up and down my frame. "Certainly not girls as young as you. It is inappropriate, and invites bad fortune to all of us."

I made to speak, but he silenced me with one hand held briskly up.

"No one cares what has or has not happened between you -- I certainly don't. But let us be absolutely clear: others will care greatly." He regarded me coolly. "The white miners will beat him for being Chinese. The other benevolent societies will beat him, for bringing shame on our community. And his jiu fu will beat him, for all the trouble he causes." The man lowered his pipe and traded stern glances with the burned man. "If you follow him any further, Miss Saunders, his young bones will lie in a cold grave. And no one will mourn the loss of him, because he brought this trouble to himself."

I clenched my teeth but said nothing.

"As for you, only your father's good reputation keeps you safe. There are some here," he began, and his eyes rose to the man behind me, "Who see only a little girl to be raped, robbed, killed and thrown in the swamp. And who can blame them? Why should they care who you are? A woman, wandering into a town of desperate men at such an hour, gives herself willingly and openly." The old man turned to the man sitting to his left, who possessed a broad, bony face with deeply-set eyes, more black than brown. They spoke softly in Cantonese, and the man gave a curt nod before standing. "I am not without a softness in my heart, Miss Saunders; I am not so old that I don't remember the sweet foolishness of youth." He smiled faintly.

"Xiu Han will take you to Shaozhu. You bid your farewell to him, and when you leave, you will never see him again. Understand?"

"Yes, sir," I said bitterly.

Xiu Han led me into the house, through a hallway bounded on either side by two parlors. In each room, men clustered around tables, swapping little ivory tiles and shouting at each other in victory or defeat. Curtains of sweet smoke hung heavy in the air. Long languid bodies lay on couches, or on pillows across the floor, barely raising their heads as we passed. Xiu Han gave no attention to the opium addicts, but stepped over them where he must. We ascended a crooked stairwell to the second floor and, along the short corridor, the doors of the upper rooms lay open. Inside, men of all nationalities lay collapsed on the ground in stupourous ecstasy, drowsy smiles on their faces. The soothing plunk plunk of discordant music drifted from the end of the hall.

Finally, Xiu Han stopped outside a room. He gave a slight tap on the doorframe, barely loud enough to disturb the torpid stillness.

I glanced inside.

The woman's body was freckled, pocked and angular. Her skin sagged in folds over her hips like a half-starved hag's, but her black hair had retained a youthful ebony gloss, and swung buoyant over her knotted, weary shoulders. She said nothing, gave no indication of joy or pleasure as the man shuddered below her. His dilated eyes focused on some distant, imaginary place. He gave a groan from the depth of his belly, then slumped back to the floor, utterly spent.

She rose on stiff knees and helped herself to his money from his belt. Without a word, she snagged her dress from the floor, but she didn't bother to dress. In the next room, she would ply her trade on whatever man waited there. To dress was a waste of time.

As she brushed passed, Xiu Han held out his hand. She slapped the money into it and glanced briefly at me, then rattled a shrill question to Xiu Han. He chuckled as an answer. "My wife asks if I'm looking to hire a younger face," he said as he pushed me along the hall. We reached an open door, and he pushed me through. His laughter faded as he closed the door and returned downstairs.

The small chamber, bare of any furnishings, had only a single window without glass. Shao stood with his hands resting on the window pane, alone. He looked over his shoulder at the sound of the door closing, and I saw the purple stain of a rising bruise on his jaw.

"What did they do—"

"You have to go," he interrupted. His voice was hard and stony, but his eyes held anguish and grief.

And regret.

I drew next to him. I reached out to slip my fingers into his.

"No," I replied, "I can't leave you. I don't know what they'll do to you."

"They won't do anything to me."

I reached up to touch his chin. "But they already—"

"This?" he said, with a mocking laugh, "This is jiu fu's kindly suggestion that I take my leave of this place, and never come back."

"Wherever you go, I'll follow."

"Then I won't tell you where I'm going," he said, recoiling. "We can't see each other again, Liz." He cast his eyes to the floor. "Some stories are not meant to have happy endings."

The boards in the hall creaked underfoot. Mr. Tao stood in the threshold.

"When the gods looked down," Mr. Tao began, "And saw the travesty that had happened between the scholar and the serpent, the Eight Immortals sent a plague to earth, spreading like a blight over the landscape and killing every living creature in its path. In desperation, a monk seized the white serpent by her throat and cast her down into the deepest well, entrapping her forever, and saving humanity from extinction." Mr. Tao regarded Shao with disgust. "The serpent was punished for breaking the laws of nature, to ensure she would never forget her proper place."

"You have no right to send him away," I demanded. "He owes you nothing!"

But his face was closed, as engaging as a block of concrete. "What must I do to ensure you never forget your place, Bai SuZhen? I fear there is no well deep enough." Tao asked. He stood to one side of the door, and the three men who had collected us gathered in the hall. As the tallest man passed, he pressed a few coins into Tao's hand.

"Good bye, Miss Saunders," said Tao. He gave a clipped bow.

I reached out to Shao as strong fingers clutched a fistful of my hair and dragged me roughly backwards. I clutched at the door frame. Shao took a single step but no further: his uncle lashed one arm out, and a closed fist smashed into Shao's chin, snapping his head back. Shao buckled to one knee, dazed.

I roared as the three men wrangled me out of the room and dumped me unceremoniously on my back in the hall, and I caught one last glimpse of Shao, rising to his unsteady feet, as jiu fu slammed the door closed. A body hit the doorway – whether it was Shao, attempting to open it, or jiu fu, blocking it, I couldn't tell. Two enraged voices erupted from within. There came the smash of a chair against the door, and a sudden, ugly silence.

I cried out for Shao once more, but the hand entangled in my hair gave a brutal pull, and my shout changed into a scream of pain. The three men grabbed my limbs, pulled me in all directions, then dragged me down the corridor.

They were not evicting me from the building. The unrelenting grip on my arms trembled with an unmistakable eagerness.

62

THE MEN, the same half-starved jackals from the street, grabbed at my clothes and breasts as they dragged me along the hall and through the last door, into a narrow chamber with a plank floor. The white man kicked the door shut behind them. "We need us a little privacy, if you please," he laughed.

The room was cramped and small. It stank of mildew and rotting fabric. A single window on the far side showed a square of night sky. There was no bed or chair, but in one corner of the room was a reeking, fetid nest of pillows, blankets, and cast-off jute sacks. The only illumination came from a slumped tallow candle on a small table near the corner. Next to the candle, on the table, lay a coil of rope.

"Do you know who I am?" I demanded, but they laughed and traded lascivious glances. A boot pressed into my belly, squeezing my spine against the floor. Pinned underneath me, the apothecary knife pressed into the small of my back.

"Yeah," said the tallest. He grinned toothlessly, panting with the exertion of holding me down. "Don't matter much to me."

"God damn tragedy, to let a bit of flesh like you go to waste," said the third. His grey skin covered his bones like onion paper, and his eyes were ringed with blue; I recognized the tell-tale signs of smallpox in the open sores on his neck. "The grave don't care if you're a virgin or a whore. It'll take you just the same."

The man at the door flipped the latch and stormed over. "We didn't pay for the damned conversation!" He took a hank of my hair in hand to pull me from the ground.

When I sunk my teeth into his hand, I tasted sweat and manure, and the bright sharp flavor of blood.

A clout across my temple caused stars to burst across my vision.

Momentarily dazed, I felt six hands fumble at my clothes. I shook the stars from my sight and launched forwards, scratching at their faces. I raked my nails across one cheek with such force that fresh blood warmed my fingertips. A kick to my side pushed the air from my lungs in a huff. One man clutched at his bleeding face as the other wrenched the fabric of my shirt. Buttons flew in all directions, exposing a V of naked skin from my shoulders to my navel. Cold air rose gooseflesh to my skin.

For every thrash or struggle I made, they laughed harder at my distress, and one lurched forward to run his tongue over my cheek, leaving a slug's trail of saliva over my neck and jaw.

By luck more than skill, I managed to connect a solid knee to his kidney.

He crumpled, coughing and clawing at his side, and he become a barrier between myself and the tallest man. I took the few valuable seconds to scramble out of their grasp.

The one with grey skin and pox sores shoved his injured companion to the side and lashed out to box me on the ear, but instead, he swung wide and clipped me on the back of my head. Ropy with muscle, he positioned himself directly between me and the door. His face was peppered with sweat. Blood wept from three parallel gashes running from ear to chin. Spots and speckles covered his skin, and a couple of oozing sores garnished his chin. The exertion had taken its toll on him, more than the other two; he'd anticipated a struggle but not a fight. He'd expected a frantic, panic-stricken girl, easily subdued.

But his punches were no worse than the ones that Buster

Gillingham dished out. Buster was younger and well-nourished. This man was ill, desperate, and hadn't eaten a full meal in days.

I did not panic. He collapsed on me, pinning my shoulders to the ground, pressing his knee into my hip. I reached back to wrap my fingers around the knife handle, fumbling to free the blade from its sheath, but our combined weight kept the knife from sliding free. I wriggled under him, then shunted backwards over the floor and, with every ounce of strength, purposefully kicked one boot against the table legs.

It cracked and crumpled.

The candle toppled to the floor.

The pillows and blankets, greasy with the cumulative oils of a thousand nights and a hundred bodies, burst into blue-green ribbons of flame. Curls of black smoke rolled up the walls. The wood panels were tinder-dry in the August heat, and the first tongues of fire snaked up the wooden boards to hungrily lick at the rafters.

The man clenching his kidney cried out an alarm, his eyes wide, and his pox-ridden companion tripped backwards and landed in a heap. The white man scrambled backwards, away from the flames, and flung himself at the door.

A wall of flame roared and sucked at the air. Smoke billowed. My eyes stung and tears rolled down my cheeks. The sudden heat crackled, boards split, and I smelt roasted pork.

I rolled to my feet and threw open the tiny window at the far side of the room.

The men screamed behind me. From beyond the roiling flames I heard more voices in the hall, crying out in horror, and the whole building seemed to heave on its foundation. Doors slammed as the occupants fled from every room. I heard Xia Han's wife screeching as her home and business burned.

I dove for the open window, the ruins of my shirt fluttering after me.

A hand grabbed my right ankle. Looking back, the pox-stricken man snarled at me, his fingers biting into the flesh of my leg. Smoke wreathed him but he still had one purpose in mind, and he was determined to keep a firm grip on his prize.

This time, the knife slid free of its hilt. I slashed out, swinging the blade in a perfect descending arc, a conductor bringing to close a silent orchestra of motion.

A muffled, moist cry rang out. The grip slackened on my ankle. When I looked back through the window, I saw him grab at a bloody slash gaping like a second mouth across his cheek. Clouds of smoke and flame swallowed him.

I dashed across the roof of the porch as the brothel patrons poured out of every door and window. Xia Han raced back and forth, his hands clenched, his face a mask of pale horror. Men ran with buckets full of swamp water. I paused for a moment on the corner of the building, a tiny gargoyle hunched on the eaves, and scanned the crowd until I saw Mr. Tao stumble to the side of the street, coughing but alive, and dragging Shao by his hair.

He was not exactly safe, but he was alive, and for that I was thankful. I shimmied down a hawthorn bush at the corner of the building, and vanished into the dark strip of trees to the southeast.

63

A FAINT BREEZE, blowing down the valley from the lake, rustled the canopy of cottonwood leaves. I wandered between their narrow trunks across the soft low marshes: in winter, these hollows were flooded but in summer, they provided a meandering path between stagnant pools where mule deer could browse on summer shoots. My torn pants and shirt snagged on spindly huckleberry twigs, my boots caught on exposed roots and stones. I moved with as much stealth as a drunken dog, and at one turn in the trail, I startled a doe and two fawns from their foraging. The flash of their white tails disappeared into the darkness, up towards the mountains where the ancient forests shut out all moonlight, and the shadows were as thick as engine grease.

I felt sick, cold, paper-thin. The air reeked of smoke and an orange glow filled the sky behind me. I hadn't wanted to abandon Shao, but nor could I go back, and in despair I realized I was alone, small, and frail, armed with only a single knife against an entire community. I could not save him, if he even wanted to be saved: the benevolent society would band together to shut me out. No one from my own community would help me, either – Ah Kung had spelled it out in plain and simple terms, so forthright and direct that he could only be right. Shao would be vilified by all parties involved, Chinese and white. If I returned to plead for his safety, he would only be punished more severely.

The tattered remains of my shirt hung around my waist, so I tied the ends closed over my chest to ward away the chill of the night air. I crouched at a pool and splashed water on my face. When the waves stilled, my grimy reflection stared up at me.

I was alone, I realized – horribly alone. Violet was gone, so was Shaozhu. I rejected any thought of going to Father for help: I'd failed him by never trusting in him, right from the very beginning. With a single letter, I'd begun this terrible sequence of events, and I realized, Father's aspirations for me had been too high. The disappointment that John Saunders would suffer, if I admitted to him the fullness of what had happened, was too much for me to bear.

My grandfather had rejected me fully, and had even sent a man to destroy the last traces of my mother, to indelibly wipe away any threat of further embarrassment. I began to tremble. I wrapped my arms around my torso to ward away the chill I felt in my bones. The men had wrenched my arms painfully and landed a few punches to my face, but the dull ache of my injuries paled beside the ache in my belly. If what Jack said was true, then my grandfather had recognized that something was fundamentally wrong with me, that I was nothing but a mirror, reflecting the world around me. He knew I was broken on the inside, fractured, disconnected.

Mr. Tao had seen it, too. He knew I could never have happiness. He was right to save Shaozhu from me. The breath hitched in my dry throat as I accepted the truth: I would bring Shao nothing but misery.

The first tears dripped from my cheeks and disturbed my reflection. I watched the distorted face in the pool sniffle and wipe its nose on its sooty sleeve.

For a while, I sat at the edge of the water, sore and shivering, enveloped in despair. I wanted nothing more than to sit at Violet's side, watching the stars, talking about the endless possibilities that we had believed the future held for us – now gone, all vanished, for Violet.

A lifetime of grief stretched out before me. How could I possibly continue, without Violet to show me the way?

But hadn't I found comfort in the Ancestor Hall, talking to Violet? I knew I couldn't go back to Chinatown, but perhaps there was a place equally silent, where I could once more reach out across the gulf between the living and the dead. I wanted to seek council from Violet, but even more, I needed to talk with Mother. I needed to ask what part she had played in this circus, even if she couldn't reply.

I viciously rubbed my tears away with the back of my hand and stood. I began to walk east. I knew exactly where I needed to go.

The moon passed overhead. The great wheel of stars revolved over the tree tops. I fought through the dark woods, holding the knife in one hand, consumed by sorrow but afire with a need to reach the cemetery, to sit at the side of Mother's grave and seek her company. I looked to the sky and steered through the lowlands by the light of the stars, circumventing Chinatown on my right, crossing the train tracks, and circling around the northern edge of Cumberland. It was a long route, slow and twisting. One hour passed, and then another. The woods grew dark and secretive, painted blue with moonlight, but I had always felt more at home in their depths than on a city street or in a fancy parlor, and I felt no fear. Small creatures rustled in the ferns as I passed. Sometimes I heard the trickle of water echoing off a cliff face, and I came close enough to Number Five to hear the men at the picking tables chatting to each other.

I edged over a crest in the land as the moon sunk low in the west, and I stopped to gain my bearings. I had left the soft swamplands far behind me; the ridge was hard stone under my feet. Hemlocks grew tall around me. I heard the wind in the branches and the distant splash of gentles waves. Through the trees, the twinkle of starlight on water told me exactly where I stood.

Maple Lake was a round dollop of muddy water in a bowl of gravel hills. Hemlock and cedar surrounded it, and for most of its edge, the underbrush of huckleberry bushes and sword ferns reached to the shore and hung over the water, reminding me of Dr. Gould's generous tummy spilling over the waistband of his pants. There simply wasn't enough space on land to contain the abundant vegetation bursting forth. The excess greenery, forced to bubble over the boundaries between dry and wet, left no sandy shore to sit or picnic. The water was murky and smelly, not fit to swim or drink when Comox Lake provided a clearer source nearby, and even the trout pulled up from the shallows of Maple Lake tasted musty.

The graveyard was a short distance from the lake's eastern shore. A trail followed the lake, and if I hiked down this ridge, I was bound to cross it, and from there I could easily make my way—

A noise caught my attention.

I startled and gripped my knife.

The steady rhythm of breath, big and powerful, came from somewhere to my left. This was no small creature in the ferns.

My eyes scanned the darkness for a shape as I listened.

The sound of its presence rose like the stealthy advance of a fogbank creeping through the lowest reaches of the trees. It gave no cry or hue. I heard only the gentle rise and fall of breathing, but there was no doubt in my mind that it was there, and certainly, I was no longer alone. I braced my feet and lifted the knife. If it was following me, it had been as silent as a cat for longer than I could tell.

When I paused to listen, it paused, too. I heard it hold its breath, knowing that it had been discovered. Then it swept a few paces through the bushes – a heavy and solid body, but graceful, too. It was not far behind me.

Hope rose in me as I mistook it for Shao, and raised a hand to greet him. But no, the sound of footsteps stopped. It waited without showing itself.

I thought, then, that it might be Jack, but when I called out to him, there was no answer.

I looked down into the hollow to my left, away from the lake. Through the hemlocks, amid brakes of salal bushes, I saw a faint white glow.

The sight of it moving startled me more than the sound. The faint illumination hovered amongst the leaves, a huge square patch of pale ghostly light, the same pallid grey as the moon. I stood still, but it knew I was here -- after all, it had seen me first. The wraith paused. I felt it watching me.

I remembered Nessie's tale of Tsonokwa, the cannibal woman who eats the soft parts of children: the liver and heart and gut. My right hand drifted over my bare stomach and my left clenched the knife tightly.

"Violet?" I called softly. I heard the strange quiver of fear in my voice. "Is it you?"

It did not move. It shifted a little but stayed down in the hollow, surrounded by salal and ferns. The moon shadows of the trees painted cobalt stripes across its wide white back, and I crept a few paces closer, down the hill. The phantom grew in size as I edged towards it. It became a massive illumination, bigger than any will-o-the-wisp. I pushed between the ferns and bushes, reaching out one hand and extending my fingers.

And touched warm flesh. I raked my fingers over its soft hide. Only when it gave a breathy snort did I recognize it by name.

Kelly's pale mare snuffled its soft nostrils over my palm, asking for affection after long days trapped in the woods. I released my held breath and laid my cheek against the horse's warm neck, scratched my fingers over its withers in a gesture of equine affection. Its tack was dull and scuffed from the sun. The reins were wrapped around a piece of bracken, which had tangled and trapping the animal as it had run through the woods. Now that I was close, I saw clearly its track through the underbrush, where it had plunged headlong through the bushes before coming to an abrupt stop.

"Sandy calls you Calliope, yes?" I breathed into the mare's nose, and she responded to my breath with an answering grunt.

I struggled to untangle the reins and finally, when I'd managed to free a decent length, I cut them off to release the horse. Calliope skittered to one side, tossed her head, then calmed as I patted my palm against her shoulder and spoke quietly. Briars tangled her mane and the creamy coat was unkempt and ragged. The tail was a matted mess of branches and pitch. The soft, long ears wheeled in all directions even as the mare lowered her head to push lovingly into my chest, still alert for danger after her lonely imprisonment in the woods. I sheathed the knife and ran my hands under the edge of the saddle; nothing had snagged there and the horse's hide was whole and unblemished, even if her ribs were pronounced and her stomach empty.

But across the mare's pale neck, a resplendent splatter of black liquid had dried. I turned the horse so that the moonlight fell squarely upon the plumes of ink that marred the white fur. The splash was thickest at the base and tapered towards the ears. I leaned close to it, and both the color and the smell proved it to be a crust of dried blood.

I ran my palms down the arched neck, the muscular croup, the solid legs. I found no injuries on the animal, save for a few shallow scratches across the polls. The blood on Calliope's neck came from elsewhere. I stood in front of the arc and studied it. From the trajectory of the spray, I judged that it had come from someone standing alongside the animal's shoulder. They were injured, and bled profusely forward.

I gathered the remains of the reins in my left hand and clicked my tongue as I urged the horse to back up, through the bushes, until we were free of the salal and standing on more open ground. She grabbed hungrily at weeds as I gazed across the landscape towards the lake.

Looking directly east, I found myself staring down the gullet of a salmon-pink sky, ribbed with diaphanous ivory clouds as thin and brittle as fish bones. A lusty, melodramatic choir of starlings began to sing in tandem, one to the other, from their roosts high in the forest canopy, welcoming the pure dawn light.

As the color seeped up through the grey gloom around me, I easily saw where the spooked horse had pushed through the bushes, ripping up the loam with her galloping hooves.

"I promise you, Calliope," I said, urging her forward with a gentle pull of the reins, "You'll get a warm stall and a bucket of oats as soon as possible. But we need to follow your trail, and see if it leads us to Kelly."

Calliope's tracks took us towards the lake. When we reached the main trail from Cumberland, I clearly saw the deep ruts where the horse had changed direction and veered off into the bushes. We went slowly, for she was very hungry and would not let a luscious clump of grass go by uneaten, but she seemed happy to have my company and didn't want to be left behind.

Finally we reached a small beach, a meager crescent of sticky grey sand that clung to the southern shore. I saw a man's footprints in the soil alongside deep hoof prints where Calliope had started, wheeled around, and propelled herself into a full gallop back along the trail. I looped her reins over a low branch and studied the view of tiny hills which stretched for miles unbroken, rising into the mountain parapets brushed blue and gold with sunlight. There was nothing to give me a clue to why Calliope had been here: no cabin or house, no shed, not even a bench. But Kelly had dismounted on this beach, of that I was sure.

Everywhere I looked, foot prints and hoof prints scuffed the ground. I walked up from the shore, my eyes cast down. Patches of dried soil were stained red, like ochre, where the rain and sun had cemented the blood into the earth. I brushed aside pine needles with the toe of my boot and saw red in all directions: a great amount of blood.

Was this where Violet was murdered?

Why would Kelly kill Violet here by a stagnant lake, and then ride three miles, through town and along a busy rail corridor, passed mine sites and hamlets, to dump the corpse in a different lake? It made no sense.

Then the breeze capered down from the land, carrying the sweet sickly scent of rotten meat. The mare pawed at the soil and lowered her head to whinny, and the sound skittered across the oily surface of the water.

Ravens cawed – many, many ravens. I glanced up from the footprints, up into the trees, and saw hundreds of black birds, hunched against the last cold snap of night, waiting for the sun to warm their wings.

The smell grew as I followed the blood. Away from the edge of the lake, the land sloped gently upwards and the maple trees stretched high -- their lofty canopy allowed me to see in all directions. Nothing larger than a few tangled branches broke the view. The thunderstorm had brought down the weakest deadwood. I paused and crossed my arms, considering the actions of the killer, and I heard the creak of wood as the wind moved the canopy.

But to my left, the creak was a little louder. I listened, and looked up.

"Oh, Mr. Kelly," I said softly, "I would not have thought you capable of this."

64

August 17, 1898

High above the forest floor, ten or twelve feet in the air, hung the ragged, wretched remains of a man, dangling by his neck and flanked by ravens. His legs swung loose. The birds had feasted on the carrion, and all that remained of his left leg was an exposed femur and a knee bone. Rats had gnawed upon his calves, and his foot had been twisted free and dragged away. The paw prints of persistent carnivores dotted the ground underneath him and encircled the tree. He had swung in this precarious position for a few days, baking in the summer sun over an oven of stone and sand. The perfume of death was chokingly thick.

Reaching up to grab the nearest branches of the tree, I shimmied up the trunk, taking pains to breath through my mouth.

A deliberating jury of ravens congregated nearby, augmented by a bevy of crows. Two swooped at me but I swatted them away with curses, and they returned blithely to their perch to watch this lithe creature climb up and meddle with their breakfast. I shimmied on my belly along the branch from which Mr. Kelly swung, pausing until

I was certain that it would hold me. Then, looking down, I devoted my attention to the body.

His head lolled. One eye had been plucked from the swollen socket by a resourceful bird. His skin was purple-black, and the noose bit into the meat of his neck so deeply that it had almost been swallowed by his flesh. His arms hung free at his sides.

The rope ran over the branch and down to the base of another tree, where it was secured with a hefty knot.

Alexander Kelly had found an accessible yet desolate wilderness to hang himself; close to town, but in a place where few bothered to come.

I lay along the branch above him, looking down at the spatter of blood on the ground. From this aerial view, I saw scuffs in the dirt, long lines of red mud, and Calliope's hoof prints. I considered the patterns and colors. If he'd killed Violet here, then dumped her elsewhere, he might have come back to die in the same spot where she'd last taken breath – it made a strange sort of sense. Perhaps the tragic conclusion to an unrequited romance? The smell was beginning to bother me, and I shifted my weight to gain a better perspective.

Still, murder-suicide seems inelegant. Would a man like Mr. Kelly bother to think such things? And why take her to Comox Lake, where she'd be found?

"Because she'd be *found*," I said aloud. Mr. Kelly, in his shame, had wanted to be forgotten, but he couldn't bear for his love to be forgotten, too.

I grunted and sat upright, swinging my legs back and forth. "Well, maybe it seemed a romantic location for you, Mr. Kelly," I said to the corpse below me, "But it presents certain problems for me."

If I cut him down, I would have a hard time loading him up onto the back of the horse to return him to town, but if I left him on the ground, he was likely to be gone by the time I returned. He'd provide an easy meal for any carnivore that happened to be lurking nearby.

But nor did I want to leave him dangling in the wind, either – it seemed so horribly undignified.

"What do I do?" I said to him.

The only reply was a snort of impatience from Calliope.

The dead can be stubborn, I reflected when he didn't answer. A gust of air caught him and he swung a while, like a pendulum on a chain, and I perched on the branch in a patch of sun and pondered what to do. Finally, I decided that I couldn't leave him quite like this. It wasn't proper. I'd have to try to get him on the horse and bring him back to town myself.

I studied the rope, looking for the best place to slice it free. It had worn a deep rut in the branch, peeled back the thin bark, creating a groove in the wood like a pulley.

With Shao's knife, I sawed through the taut fibers until the rope snapped. Mr. Kelly's rag doll limbs fluttered and flapped to the forest floor. His awkward tumble to earth liberated a pattering, splattering rain of fluids.

I held on as the branch bucked, then scrambled like a monkey down the tree to the knot of human limbs on the ground below. His dead hand had clenched tightly in its last moments, but the jar of striking the earth knocked something from his palm. I grabbed the object which had fallen from between his fingers: a scrap of paper wrapped around a lock of Violet's blonde hair.

The note unfurled in my hands, written on black-edged stationary.

A.,

Must I cast myself into this abyss? I shall wait at the little beach on Maple Lake's southern shore, where we lingered after Mother's funeral, for whatever fate brings me. God willing, it is you.

Love,

V.

I PUZZLED over the letter as I turned it over in my hands. The printing was legible, but erratic. The lines were crooked. Blobs of ink marred the edges.

Violet had been upset, but I knew my sister was proud and dignified, too. For Violet, handwriting was an art form, never to be rushed or dismissed, and the smallest notice was an occasion for pomp and flourishes. This letter would have been more important to Violet than most. Yes, time was a factor, but she would have taken more care to write to Mr. Kelly, the man whom she loved.

Time was a factor.

My mind worked furiously. I had assumed that Kelly had brought Violet here, to this place of silence and solitude, to kill her – but why follow Violet here? Why would Violet choose this place, of all places? An alley, a church yard, the stables behind the constabulary – there were a million places between here and home where Violet could arrange to meet Kelly. Why here, in a desolate location? Maple Lake was a place that I, in good health and full of energy, had no difficulties reaching, but Violet was not so fond of Shank's pony, and rarely walked any farther than the Willard Block to mail her letters.

I looked at the hem of my trousers. They were snagged with burrs. Violet's hem had been clean, pressed, and free of grass or nettles.

Violet had never set foot here. This was not Violet's letter, wrapped around a lock of Violet's hair.

In my left hand, the note was feather-light and fragile. In my right, the apothecary knife weighed heavy and solid.

The chronology was wrong.

Violet had left the house after me, but somewhere on her way to the constabulary, she'd been intercepted. In her place, someone had left a forged letter and a lock of her hair in the constable's doorway.

The rising sunlight trickled through the forest and along the lake shore, turning the low forests from dark green to a luminous jade, the fresh leaves tinged with gold. Kelly stared up at me with his one remaining iris. The man had become a broken doll with half a face staring up at the birds wheeling through the blue sky. It was an ugly, brutal conclusion for anyone, but I reflected that it was doubly so for Kelly, who had always been so gentlemanly, so clean and proper, and terribly at odds with the natural world surrounding him. He had been a man of civilized decorum, yet here he lay, exposed to the wild elements, for wolves and rats to gnaw his bones. His pride could not have stood it, knowing he'd end so.

I crouched down and looked closer.

The rope around the neck had sunk deep into his flesh.

I wriggled my fingers under the noose and pried it open, so that it gained enough slack to be peeled from its bed.

Underneath, I saw the white-edged lip of a sliced throat. The terminus of his carotid artery hung like an empty crimson worm amid a nest of pale muscles and skin.

I looked up at the mare, standing a hundred feet away. The pattern of red across the arched white throat was unmistakable.

Kelly had come here to meet Violet, a clandestine spot perfectly placed for most young women to reach by foot, and when he'd arrived, he'd dismounted. With his back turned, the murderer had fallen upon him and slit his throat. The blood spurted out and splattered the side of Calliope. The horse, spooked, had fled into the trees.

I stood and looked again at the branch, high above. With a bit of rope and strong muscles, and the assistance of time and carnivores, it would be easy enough to turn a slit throat into a desperate suicide, especially when such an end to the tragedy was not only expected, but welcome. The murderer had slipped the noose around Kelly's neck and, tossing the rope over a high branch, hauled him up until he dangled above the forest floor. The weight of the corpse cut a deep groove in the thin bark of the stout branch.

'Yes,' I decided, 'That chronology worked. Violet had died first, and Mr. Kelly was lured here, with the promise of her affection.'

A whiney from the mare attracted my attention.

Simultaneously, a movement through the bushes caught my peripheral vision. I raised my head, and my gaze locked with the steel-grey eyes of Jack Hunter.

65

JACK STOOD ALONGSIDE THE HORSE, one hand holding the mare's reins, the other patting the animal's shoulder.

"Mr. Hunter," I said quietly, "Why am I not surprised?"

"Did Kelly off himself," said Jack, leading the mare closer, "Or was he murdered?"

"The killer cut his throat." My eyes narrowed, my hand clamped around the handle of Shao's knife. "But you already know that, I'm sure."

He was silent for a long, long time. His eyes ranged from my face to the blade swinging from my right hand.

"You suspect me?" he asked with one eyebrow raised.

"Who else would it be?"

He backed up a step. "Well, I don't know, girl, but Death seems to follow you around like a god-damned puppy, and you're the one with a knife in her hand."

"Me?" I dared not break my gaze from him, to look back at Mr. Kelly's broken remains. Instead, I tipped my head in the general direction of the tree, where the frayed end of the rope swayed lazily in the breeze. "You think I could do this? That I would have the strength to pull Mr. Kelly up so high? Or worse," I swallowed, "That I would brutalize my own sister?"

"Ain't no one gonna believe it, but I would," he replied. "You got the blood of the devil in you, Lizzie Saunders."

"I'm horrified, Mr. Hunter, that you would think so low of me."

"Well," he began, "Yer grandfather did warn me, yer funny in the head. Seems to run in the family."

"Leave my mother out of this," I snarled, raising the knife to him. "If you didn't kill Mr. Kelly, then how the hell did you know where to find the body?"

He shook the reins. "I followed you. I caught sight of you skulking down the trail to the lake, and you led me straight here!"

"I was on my way to my mother's grave when I discovered the horse, and she led me straight here." I replied, "That, sir, is Mr. Kelly's devoted mare, Calliope. Look all around us! Her prints on the ground are as clear as handwriting on a white page!"

He dropped the reins and held up his hands, both of them empty. "Look here, Amaryllis, you were kind enough to give me a warning, once. So," He swept his hands to the side, "Here's your head start. You take this horse and go, and by the time I've done walked my way back to town to find Rufus McGregor, you can be long gone. Understand?"

I strode across the clearing and took the reins sharply in hand. Jack backed up as I approached. His coat swung open; I caught sight of the pistol handle against his hip.

"As soon as I turn, you'll shoot me in the back," I said.

"I won't shoot," he said, "This time."

"Why should I believe you?"

"I may be a thief and a cheat, Miss Saunders, but I ain't about to lie to a little girl," he replied. He held out his hands, palms up. "Go on, get. And pray to God I never lay eyes on ya again."

I swung lightly into the saddle, scowling at him. His steel-colored eyes betrayed nothing; no guilt, no remorse. I nudged the horse into a quick trot toward the road. When I reached the road and turned out of his sight, I let out a long breath. I hadn't even realized I'd been holding it, waiting for the bang.

66

It was almost noon when the horse cantered passed the mule farm and the boarding houses, and trotted up the length of Dunsmuir Avenue. I intended to go directly to Father, but as the mare stumbled into town, I became aware of a din rising from the buildings at the top of the street. The general clatter sounded like a celebration: the chatter of hundreds of voices, clipped shouts and the ringing of church bells filled the air.

But as I drew closer, the voices solidified into cries of anguish. I heard tones of dismay and despair, the shrieks of women caught in hysterical grief, the keening of small children. The horse shied but I urged it forward. A great crowd of people congregated in the crossroads of Camp, and hundreds of stricken faces looked in horror to the platform behind the Company Store.

Every mining town holds its share of disasters, but the miners were no where in sight, and I could see by the closed doors of the fire station that the draegermen had not been dispatched. Surely if there had been an explosion underground, the workers of all mines would have come to the surface, and be fighting to reassure their families that they were alive.

"What's going on?" I asked a young boy.

He lifted a face that was streaked with tears. His mouth pulled down and he struggled to find words.

"Is it another explosion?" I demanded, "Is it a cave-in?"

"No, miss! The train!" he gulped, jabbing his fingers towards the empty station, "One of the boys just ran back from the trestle!"

"The trestle?" I repeated, "Spanning the Trent River? That's nine miles away!"

A run of that distance, along train tracks through wilderness, would take a strong heart. I looked over the heads again to the station platform. Women fluttered around a crumpled figure on one of the station benches. His skinny face was blotched crimson with the effort. He held a glass of ale in hand, and it trembled so violently that beer stained the wooden boards and the knees of his pants.

"But what happened?" I urged, "Where's the train?"

The boy began to sob. A sturdy man with grizzled hair, wearing a heavy leather apron, grabbed the reins to hold the horse steady. I recognized him as Bobbie Donaldson, the livery blacksmith. "The whole damn thing collapsed into the river!" he said. Perspiration stained his collar and he dabbed at his brow with a blue kerchief. "The morning train to Union Bay pitched headlong into the canyon! They're assembling a rescue now. They say there's six dead, and more injured so bad, they don't know yet if they'll make back alive."

A racket of noise at the station demanded my attention. I stood in the stirrups and craned my head towards the tracks as one of the smaller switching engines clattered into the bay. Grim-faced men carrying picks and shovels boarded the tippler, hastily latched onto the engine, and boys worked like dogs to load coal into the tender, flinging shovels of rock into the air, caring nothing for where, exactly, the smaller stones fell. Behind the dusty engine, boys at the furnace stoked the fires as if the devil himself had ordered hell hotter. Beads of sweat dripped off their brows. I saw Father climb aboard the tippler with his walrus-hide case, followed by five nurses from the hospital carrying boxes of linens and medical supplies, but before I had time to call out to him, the train whistle pierced the cacophony of noise. Droves of birds startled from the trees. The train began to pull from the station. There was no time to wait -- lives hung in the balance.

The blacksmith slapped his palm against the horse's neck. "This here's Kelly's mare," he said, and his face shone with hope. "Is the constable back?"

I jerked the reins from his hands, thinking wildly. Father was gone and could be busy now for days. I'd have to go elsewhere for help.

"I need to speak with Mr. McGregor," I replied, and urged the mare to wade through the crowd. Away from the edges of the train station and on the deserted main street, I nudged the mare to a trot. By the time I reached the constabulary, the sounds of the crowd had faded to a dull and rhythmic roar, like the distant churning of an angry sea.

67

Trent River Train Disaster - An Accident On The Coal Railway At Union Results In The Death of Seven! The Central Span Collapsed & Train & People Plunged Into Trent River

By the collapse of the centre span of the Trent River railway bridge yesterday morning, while the first loaded train of the day from the Union colliery was crossing it on its way to the shipping point at Union Bay, the locomotive and 20 cars dropped full 100 feet into the stream below, the cars piling upon each other in the rocky ravine, and the majority of those on board the train meeting death or receiving injuries so serious as to make their recovery problematical.

The dead are:

Alfred Walker, engineer: Leaves a widow and five children. His death was practically instantaneous, for a terrible cut on the head made his agonies short. His intestines were also protruding when his quivering body was picked up, and life was quite extinct;

Alexander Mellado, brakeman: Leaves a widow and infant. He was a son of Bruno Mellado, head carpenter at the mines. Both his legs and one arm were cut off, and his internal injuries were also of a necessarily fatal nature;

Richard Nightingale, contractor: Leaves a widow and family resident in Nanaimo city. He had been paying a visit to the mines on business, and was returning home;

William Work: The son of James Work, another local contractor, and the only unmarried man among the white victims of the accident, was on his way to Union, and was killed by falling upon his head. It is reported that his neck was instantly broken;

Two Japanese workmen, names not given as yet, complete the death roll.

The injured are:

Hugh Grant, fireman: Has both legs broken and one arm. He is not expected to live;

Miss Frances Horne, daughter of William Horne, blacksmith, of Union wharf: Badly scalded and cut, but may recover;

Mrs. Jeanie Hughes, wife of Reginald Hughes, mine manager: scalded with one arm broken, but expected to recover;

Miss Villa Grieves, daughter of George Grieves: Is also badly cut and burned, but hopes are entertained for her recovery;

Matt Piercy, the second brakeman: Saved himself almost miraculously by jumping on the swinging wreck of the bridge as the locomotive went over, and crawling back over the trembling timbers to safety. He can give no connected description of the accident, for it was to him all over in an instant. He heard a grinding and splintering of timbers, a crash, a plunge of heavy bodies, a sound of rushing steam, and a chorus of shrieks as men were hurried into eternity. When he jumped he could see the train falling, and he looked and called for his mate. Then his vision was shut of by the clouds of steam and coal dust coming from below.

The Trent River bridge is on the Union Colliery Co.'s coal railway, a private line connecting the mines and the wharves. The bridge, approached by trestles, spanned a deep ravine, through which the river pours between steep and wooded banks at a point seven and a half miles from Union Bay. The bridge was a wooden structure, ten years old, but well maintained and regarded as thoroughly safe for the traffic put upon it. Yesterday's train consisted of the locomotive and twenty cars, each with 23 tons of coal, every one of which went through. It was the long, or river span, that failed.

When the first rescue party reached the scene, the engine lay on its side, a mass of tangled iron spread over a pile of boulders, and surrounded by the debris of the bridge. On the other side were heaps of coal and coal cars; while twisted rails, pipes from the engine, tangled timbers, and beams were strewn everywhere.

Nicholas Walker and William Bell were under the bridge when the train went through, waiting for contractor Nightingale, who was coming to inspect the structure and make repairs where they were found necessary. He was on his way down to the bridge when he met his fate. Bell ran to Union Bay to report the accident, and Walker ran to Cumberland. In a very short time hundreds of willing hands commenced to take the dead and injured out of the ruin. All the district is naturally thrown into deepest sorrow, and the families of the victims of the tragedy have the sincerest sympathy of the entire community.

During the afternoon a special train went up from Victoria bearing Mr. Dunsmuir, Mr. Bryden, Mr. Pooley, Mr. Joseph Hunter, Mr. Prior, Mr. Bell and others prominently connected with the colliery. These gentlemen will do all that is possible to facilitate the recovery of the injured.

The locomotive is damaged beyond repair, and the majority of the cars are in the same condition.

- Victoria Daily Colonist, Thursday, August 18, 1898

68

McGregor listened to my story and gave me license to tell it freely, without any questions to distract me. When I was finished, he folded his hands over his stomach and reclined in his chair, musing over all I'd said.

"It was Kelly, dead?" he asked, "You're sure?"

"Yes."

"You say he was purple and picked over by the crows, though. He might've been a man in Kelly's coat. Nothing to say it couldn't have been stolen—"

"It was Kelly," I insisted, finding his resistance frustrating. "He was missing a bit of his face, certainly, but I recognized the part that remained."

This caused a little tremor to traverse his shoulders. His lips curled in revulsion.

"You're taking this all very well, Miss Saunders."

"My father is a doctor. I've seen death before."

McGregor narrowed his eyes to study me more closely. "I don't know if I could look on half a man's face, especially one I knew, and remain so calm."

"My sister is dead, the constable is murdered, I was accosted by a group of scoundrels earlier in the evening, and then accused of killing Kelly by the actual murderer himself. Very little can happen to upset me, Mr. McGregor, that wouldn't already be dwarfed by current events." I crossed my arms and glowered. "I assure you that Mr. Kelly isn't going far, but Jack Hunter is still able and willing to move freely, and if you hope to catch him and arrest him for the murders, I suggest you chase him, first."

"I'll round up a few men, and we'll find his camp and bring him down."

"I can lead you directly to —"

"No," he refused as he stood, "You go home. There's no good reason to entangle a lady in this matter."

"I will remind you that two ladies are already entangled, Mr. McGregor," I replied, "My sister and myself. I refuse to be cast aside—"

"I insist." The steel of his voice and stance made clear that he would brooch no argument on the matter. "You've already made a point of the harrowing events of your day. I'm sure you agree, miss, that you need to go home, take ease, and let the men handle the rest." He was in the middle of gesturing to the door, urging me to leave, when it banged open. A group of young men burst through. Most of their faces were flushed with exertion, and they exploded into a babble of voices.

McGregor, taken aback, hesitated a moment before yelling above the rabble of the crowd, "One at a time! One at a time!"

"They got the murderer!" shouted one over the rest, a brash brown-haired man in his mid-twenties, afire with the excitement in the air. "They got him!"

"Who?" replied McGregor as he grabbed his hat from the back of his chair and pulled down his gun from the hook on the wall.

My thoughts fumbled over themselves. Jack had returned? And decided to give himself up to the law? I couldn't believe it: he wouldn't submit to a mob – even he wasn't so overbearingly brave and daring as to be utterly stupid.

The procession tumbled out of the building as McGregor

elbowed his way through. I followed in his wake. One young miner, tripping over his boots, dogged McGregor through the crowd. "Frank Gillingham and his boys, they were told about the murderer, they went and found him and hauled him into town—" he panted. More men jumped in to tell their version. The answers came in a rapid volley of facts from all directions.

McGregor still hadn't heard what he wanted. "Who? Who did Frank and his boys haul into town?"

"A Chinaman!" shouted one of the men, "One of them goddamn heathens!"

The crowded began to surge down the hill to the crossroads, and a wiry boy at McGregor's elbow added, "They found evidence on him and everything! If Kelly ain't here to do it, Mahoney says the town's gotta hang him!"

McGregor's eyes flashed back to me. "Go home, girl!"

"But Hunter is the—"

"Go home!" he roared again, and dropping his gaze to the boy, he said, "Gillingham isn't the company's constable. Right now, that's me, and I'll be damned if I let anyone else do my job! And I say, we won't be hanging anyone, until we can prove it's the right man, and even then, he goes to Nanaimo for trial." He rose his voice into a commanding roar. "You hear me? No one hangs until proven guilty. I don't care if he's white, Chinese, Japanese, Indian, nothing! Understand?"

A grumble rolled through the group that surrounded him, but they continued down the hill at a run, and I fell behind, jostled out of the way by larger bodies. When I reached the crossroads, the crowd had swelled to an immense size. Men and women who had gathered to collect news about the train now found themselves spectators to a second event. McGregor bullied his way through to a small clearing in the centre of the multitude.

I caught a glimpse of Frank Gillingham and his two eldest sons. All three were muscular, work-hardened men, each possessing the same stubble of black-brown hair over their narrow scalps. Buster hung back, not as brawny as his older brothers but still eager to take partial credit for the capture. The Gillingham boys had suspended between them a lithe and lean man, his head bowed, his clothing stripped away except for the ruins of his grey shirt and trousers. His shoulder-length black hair covered his face, and his tawny skin was raked and bruised. Blood covered his chest. He'd struggled to escape their clutches and paid dearly for the attempt.

Frank Gillingham, a lanky old vulture with a cleft chin and crooked patrician nose, greeted McGregor with a smile that was both cheerful and cold. He reached out one brawny hand and clutched the prisoner's mess of black hair. He yanked back the head, cruelly and quickly, to show off his prisoner.

I clamped my hands to my mouth to keep from screaming Shao's name.

McGregor circled them: Shao's silent figure, stretched between Gillingham's two sons, each one speckled with blood. Gillingham cleared his throat to speak, and spat a wad of tobacco-stained phlegm to the dirt. A hush fell across the crowd as they strained to hear.

"We found this with him --"

He threw down the swath of canvas, blood stained and dusty, that had lain abandoned on the porch of the Ancestor House. It crumpled in the street, clearly showing the dried, flaked residue of blood.

"-- And when we asked about it, old Tao gave us these." He beckoned to Buster.

The boy reached into his pocket and pulled out a pair of flimsy, filmy things, the color of coral and stained with sweat. He tossed them to McGregor. The air caught them, separated them into two silken hands. I swallowed.

A cold spear of dread pierced my heart.

"These are fine ladies gloves," he said cautiously. McGregor crouched down in front of Shao. "Where'd you get these, boy?"

I craned forward, desperate to hear his reply.

Shao rose his dark, bruised eyes to the deputy constable. He took a breath as if to speak, but hesitated.

One of Gillingham's sons reeled back and clouted Shao across the face, underhanded, and an arc of spit and blood caught the sunlight.

Shao went limp between them. A stream of blood ran from his mouth into the dust of the road.

"Where were you, the night that Violet Saunders disappeared?" McGregor demanded. Shao lifted his head, spat out a wad of blood, and grimaced.

"He don't speak English," said Gillingham. "Trust me, deputy, you can hit him all you want, he ain't gonna tell you a thing."

And, as if to prove the point, the second son landed a sharp blow to Shao's side. The crack of a rib snapped in the still air. He screamed, high and bestial.

I surged forward, hands clenched, but an arm encircled me and held me back.

"Stay put, girl," whispered Jack into my ear, and released me as he pushed through the crowd, shoving men and women roughly out of his way. As Gillingham reeled back to deliver another punch, Jack gave a roar of rage.

"What the hell you done now, Jim boy?" he burst as he strode into the clearing. Mutterings shifted through the crowd. Gillingham kept his fist in check and McGregor reeled around on one boot heel. Shao, supported only by the two men holding him up, squinted through the pain and the blood on his face. He gaped, and looked unmistakably confused.

"Jesus H. Christ, boy, what the god damn hell—" Jack rounded on McGregor, "Look here, I don't know what he's done, but I'll pay for the damages, seeing as how he's been under my employ."

"You know him?" McGregor said.

"He's been my work boy, running errands and keeping my stuff safe, but he ain't been worth the penny, if this is the kinda trouble he brings with him." Jack wrenched Shao's wrist from one of the men, to give him a disciplinary shake. "What's the charge against him, lawman?"

"Murder."

Jack's eyebrows rose in astonishment. "God damn. I wouldn't have thunk it."

"You are doubtlessly aware, sir, of the disappearance of Violet Saunders, and her subsequent murder?"

"Now, if you're thinking my boy here did it, I can tell ya, he didn't do no such thing." Jack gave him another shake. "He's been followin' me around since last Sunday." Jack rounded on Shao. "From Sunday until this morning, at least, when he went running back to Chinatown, claiming I ain't the best of employers. I been looking for him all morning, god damn it, to get back the money I paid him." He peered close to Shao's face. "You understand? I want my money back, if you ain't able to work!"

"He's been with you?" said McGregor, "And someone can vouch for this?"

Jack looked defiantly at the crowd. "I dare say, they can."

But I knew they couldn't – not because they hadn't seen Shao with Jack, but because a Chinese man disappears into the scenery. Maybe Jack had hired him, maybe not. And looking at Shao's swollen, bruised face, who amongst these members of quality society could possibly identify him? He was one of an anonymous horde of workers that came and went, flowing in and out of this place like ants, worth nothing to anyone save for his ability to perform the worst of jobs and never complain.

As well as I knew this, McGregor did, too. He stroked his lop-sided chin with one finger. "Let the kid go, Frank."

The men released Shao into Jack's arms.

"But you keep an eye on him, Hunter. We've got other tragedies to deal with this morning, but when I call on him for questioning, I expect you'll give him up to me." He looked Jack up and down, scowling. "And I've come into a matter concerning you, Mr. Hunter, of which we ought to speak."

"Someone spinning tales about me again?" Hunter replied, "Well, then, I guess we oughta speak, and get some of these questions of yours squared away."

The crowd pressed close. McGregor's eyes scanned the people, and seeing me amongst them, he narrowed his gaze. Emotions already ran high. Half the men here were armed and ready to hang someone. A single spark would ignite a riot.

So he turned back to Jack, and said, "I think it would be best for us to speak in private, don't you?"

"Sure thing, squire," Jack replied. "I've been enjoying the hospitality afforded by Mercy at her boarding house. When you're done keepin' the peace, you'll find me and the boy there."

Jack hoisted Shao's bruised body up under his arm and half-dragged him through the crowd. Spectators parted to let them through, and hushed conversations held a mix of relief and disappointment. Jack's steely eyes caught mine as he passed, but he said nothing to me, and the two men continued at a slow, agonized pace down the street.

To his credit, McGregor knew he would get no truth at the hands of the mob. He was eager to move this circus of events away from the station, where it would only serve to entertain those waiting for information about the Trent River disaster. The air practically crackled with excitement, and an audience would be of no help in determining Shao's part in Violet's death. A parade of onlookers followed Jack at a distance, but when they reached the boarding house at the end of town, he slammed the door on them.

69

I KNOCKED on the back door. Mercy opened it, revealing a scene of shrill chaos inside.

"And now you," she snapped, throwing her hands up. She reeled on Jack, who was propping Shao carefully into a chair in the parlor. "Don't put him on the good furniture, damn it!" She left the door open, which I interpreted as a welcome of sorts, and followed her into the entertaining room of the house.

Girls in fine dresses, plastered with stage make-up, clustered around the stairway and balustrade. They twittered like a flock of sparrows on a line.

"Lizzie, get me a cloth, wouldja?" Jack shouted, "He ain't breathing right."

I knelt next to Shao and let Mercy fetch the cloth from the kitchen. Lifting Shao's bloodied shirt revealed a pattern of fierce bruises over his frame. I ran my fingers over his ribs and felt the awkward angle of one on his left side, like the strut of a ship knocked askew.

But it felt good to touch his skin again, and I savored the perfume of his body, which I thought I'd lost forever.

"Breath as deeply as you can," I said, pressing my ear to his side.

Shao's eyes closed against the pain as he inhaled, and I listened to the length of it, filling his lungs and straining against the bone. It was not a long or easy breath. Still, I heard no tell-tale gurgle of a punctured lung. The rib was cracked, but it would heal. Mercy appeared with a rag and a bucket of cool water, freshly pumped from the well out back.

"Can you bring me a ream of cloth – a bed sheet, maybe," I said, "Something long."

A worn white sheet was brought with mutters of contempt. I withdrew my knife and sliced the fibers at the end, then jerked the fabric until it ripped along the grain, pulling it into a strip one foot wide and six feet long. With the rag and bucket of water, I washed the grime and boot prints from Shao's torso, then wound the bandage around him tightly, cinching it closed with as much mercy as Violet had once cinched a corset. The fabric supported his chest, and his breathing eased.

"Better?" I asked.

He nodded and tried to smile, but winced at the pain of his bruised and battered face.

"Care to tell me why you brought this shitload of trouble to my doorstep?" Mercy aimed at Jack.

He rocked back on his heels and regarded me for a moment. Then he turned to the madam, who's eyes blazed like Medusa's. "Because I paid you for two week's lodging, and I figured I still had a room here to call my own."

"You didn't pay me near enough to shelter a Chinaman, and one who's just had the shit beat outta him, and liable to get my house burned down by an angry mob," Mercy barked. She spat at Shao's feet. "They got the leprosy, y'know."

From the coat of his pocket, Jack pulled out a leather pouch. He peeled it open, reached inside, and pulled out a wad of Dominion bills. The corner of each one read '100'. He slipped two off the top, stuffed the rest back in the pouch and then into his pocket, and crammed the bills into her hand. She regarded it dumbly with wide eyes.

"That enough?" he snapped. "If this one burns down, you can buy yourself a new god-damned House of Mercy." He turned back to Shao. "You better, boy?"

Shao nodded.

"Care to tell me how you went and got caught up in this?" he asked, then added, "You've been an ace at keeping your head down so far, you musta done something real stupid to get a big ol' target slapped on your back."

I looked out the window. Gillingham and his sons loitered across the street, blocking the main escape should their hard-won quarry attempt flight.

"This hasn't got anything to do with them," Shao said, "They're just in it for the glory of bringing in the murderer. But I have made enemies," Shao took a small, strained breath, and continued to form each word with extreme care between swollen, blood-encrusted lips, "I threatened the harmony of our community. There are some who wish to see me cast out, and others who prefer to see me hung by my neck until dead." Emboldened, he added with bitter ire, "They're willing to use your system of justice, if possible, to get rid of me. There's less to explain to the company, that way, when one Chinaman goes missing from the work roster."

"Xiu Han did this?" I asked, but Shao only looked askance at me.

"And how did you threaten the harmony, as you put it?" said Jack.

Shao lowered his face and said nothing.

"He associates with me," I replied, "This is my fault."

"Lizzie, it isn't—"

"Of course it is," I insisted. "Ah Yung was polite enough to ask me to leave, but your uncle wanted to teach me a lesson I wouldn't easily forget."

Shao bowed his head. "You slashed open a man's face and burned down Xiu Han's house," he said, "And I was the one responsible for bringing you into our community. So when I said I was going after you, Ah Yung decided I wasn't worth the trouble of sheltering any longer. His men cut off my hair, dragged me out of the house--" He swallowed.

"And pinned the murder on ya, that it?" said Jack. "Ain't that kind of him."

Shao nodded. He wasn't eager to say another word. Each syllable was agony.

"Well, you can't stay here," said Mercy, "You'll scare away business."

"You just made more money off of me, in two minutes, than you will in a week," Jack said to her as he helped Shao to his unsteady feet. "So consider me your only customer today, Mercy, and give the boy a goddamned bed."

70

"WHAT WOULD YER FATHER SAY?" said Jack to me.

We sat across from each other in the parlor of Mercy's boarding house, drinking beer from brown bottles. Shao slept on a cot upstairs, ushered into a dreamless sleep with a dash of laudanum from Mercy's medicine cabinet. Even though he was far down a hall and behind a closed door, I still heard his painful, gurgling snores.

"My father has gone with the train accident. I doubt he'll be back soon," I said, "And I think he would applaud me for being charitable and helping Shao get to safety after Gillingham and his boys were so unaccommodating."

"You ain't worried about ruining your father's good name?"

"Violet was more concerned with good conduct than me."

He grinned and took a long, leisurely swig.

"When'd you sleep last?" he asked.

"I don't know. Yesterday? It's been a while."

"You look like hell, kid. And those bruises on yer face sure ain't helping."

"Thanks, Jack."

"I may not be the finest diamond in the bloody tiara," he said, tipping his bottle to me, "But I'll always tell ya the truth."

I grinned at him over the rim of my bottle, half-full. I was not fond of beer and it made my head fuzzy, but I'd neither eaten nor drank anything for a long, long time, and it satiated both my hunger and my thirst.

"Alright, tell me the truth," I dared, "Why did you come so far to find my family?"

He swirled his drink and drained it, and set the empty bottle on the floor. "I'll make a deal with you, Lizzie. For every truth I tell you, you gotta tell me one in return. Agreed?"

I still had a number of unanswered questions, and I suspected that Jack might be the only avenue to their conclusions. I nodded.

"Right, then," he said, clapping his hands together with glee, like we'd agreed to a game of cards, "You asked why I'd come so far to find your family, but the truth of it is this: I never met your father or mother before. But your father, he's a very famous man, y'know."

"He is?"

"Ah, ah, ah!" He held up one finger. "I answered yer question, now you gotta answer mine." Jack leaned forward and set his glass on the table between us, then reclined in his chair, folded his hands behind his head, and rested his feet on the table. "Why did you and yer family leave London?"

I furrowed my brow, considering the pieces of the puzzle, "Because my mother ruined our reputation with her unnatural obsessions, and my father's practice was destroyed."

"Really, now?"

"Yes," I replied, but uncertain and confused. "My father claims my mother was insane, and that Violet and I would inherit her sickness, if we hadn't been cured by a malarial infection in Panama."

"Well, now, that's an interesting cure, if a little drastic." Jack said, his brows arching.

"Do you really know my grandfather?"

"I do," Jack replied. "And a fine fellow he is."

"How did you meet him?"

"Ah, now, it's my turn. Your mother's friend, Hannah. How did she leave?"

"Leave our employ? My father dismissed her. One day she was there, and the next she was not." I sipped my beer. "I was only five. It's not like I had much to do with the staffing of the house."

"But when?"

"I don't know... some time in August. I remember, it was very hot outside." I waggled my finger at him. "Now that's two questions in a row. My turn. Why are you so interested in Hannah?"

He chewed his lip in thought. Then, he reached into his shirt pocket and pulled out a scrap of fabric. He handed it to me.

It was a faded square of aubergine taffeta.

"This is a piece of Hannah's dress!" I whispered.

"That it was."

"Where did you—"

"Yer grandfather," Jack said.

"I don't understand—"

"You ever seen a big box in yer father's possession?"

"A box? Like, the wooden chest for his ophthalmoscope?" I held out my hands to show him the rough dimensions of the box, as large as a hardbound book.

"Bigger," Jack replied, holding out his hands. "Maybe the size of a loaf of bread. He woulda brought it with him from England."

I shook my head.

"I looked all through his surgery, and I didn't find it. Maybe it's in a bigger box," he mused, then nodded. "Yeah, it must be, idaknow, like a crate. Big, like."

"The trunk," I said, nodding, "Yes, he does. Why?"

Jack took this information and considered it. At last, he said, "There's something in it that belongs to me."

I resisted the urge to ask him what object in Father's possession could possibly belong to a man like Jack; I had other, more pressing, queries.

"Do you honestly believe me capable of killing Mr. Kelly?"

Jack shook his head. "Naw." Then he paused. "Maybe. But I wanted you gone, girl. I wanted you to leave this place and never look back. I hoped you'd take the hint and run like hell."

"Mr. Hunter, please," I said, leaning forward, "Will you do me the courtesy of telling me what is going on? My sister is dead, and now Kelly, too. What terrible past links you to my family, and why do you think I'm the next to die?"

Jack's face drew down into a pensive, thoughtful mask. "Do you know," He stopped, stuttered, almost retracted his question, but with clenched fist, continued. "Do you even know what you are?"

"What I am?" Our voices were low and intimate. It seemed like such a foolish question, requiring nothing more than the simplest explanation. "I'm Amaryllis Saunders, the youngest daughter of a scholar and gentleman."

Jack shook his head, almost imperceptibly. "No, girl. If that's what you think, you're sore mistaken."

"Then enlighten me, Jack," I said, "Tell me what I am."

He leaned even closer.

"You are evil made flesh," he said. "You are spawned from the fires of Hell's mouth, and set upon this earth to unleash chaos upon the world. You, Lizzie m'dear, are the child of the Devil."

A tense moment pulled between us like a silvery thread. When it snapped, I leaned back on the couch and laughed, laughed like I'd never laughed before, laughed the gut-wrenching laughter that can only be forged from a combination of fatigue, strain, a breakfast of beer, and the ridiculous punch line of an absurd joke I hadn't fully heard.

It took a long time for my laughter to dissolve into a mellow chuckling. When I rolled onto my side on the couch and wiped the tears from my eyes, I saw that Jack was studying my reaction, his hands tented, his face solemn and grave.

"You finished?" he asked.

"Are you're insane?!?" I sat upright, but it was difficult; the couch was so comfortable, and I was so very tired. "Do you honestly believe that I'm some sort of denizen of hell? That I'm a demon? That I'm—"

"I know what you are, Lizzie -- I'm quite certain what you are."

"When you told me I had the blood of the devil in me, you were being literal?" When he didn't immediately answer, I laughed again, and said, "You honestly believe such nonsense? A bunch of dusty old myths? And that I – that I might be—that's preposterous!" I pressed the heel of my palm to my head and muttered, "Why does every man in my life think I'm a demon?"

He didn't answer. But his hand drifted to his holster.

"Are you scared of me, Jack?"

"Hell, yeah," he replied without pause.

"Why?"

"Because you ain't got no soul, and that means you're capable of anything," he said, "Anything, except love."

My mirth dripped away.

"I love," I said, but it sounded petulant, like a command rather than an admission. "I love Shao."

Jack considered this. "Do you?"

"But it's not like what Violet said, " I stammered. How does one quantify and catalogue a feeling? "It's not romance and flowers, it's not a warm and beautiful emotion, like spring sunshine. It burns in my heart, it compels me to go against my better judgment. I do love Shao, but maybe it's not like the love that other people feel."

"Naw, that's a good description," he replied. "If all yer sister knew of love was flowers and sunshine, then she was foolin' herself. Love makes you do stupid, stupid things. Love hurts." He mused on this, and said, "Love is an obsession, and it blocks out every good sense. It destroys a person."

"When my grandfather gave you the letter, and told you I was not like other girls," I began slowly, forming the question carefully, "Did he know you think I'm the devil?"

"Did he know—" Jack broke off the sentence and laughed. "He told me, sweetheart!" Jack folded his hands over his knees. "The old captain knew he'd unleashed a foul darkness on the world, and he wants to make all right before he goes to confront his Maker. We came to an agreement, he and I: he'd pay my way, help me find yer family and get back what belongs to me, and I'd make sure to rid the world of the evil he brought into it."

"And what is it that belongs to you, Jack?" I asked. "What would compel you to risk life and limb, and travel halfway around the world to the farthest edge of the British Empire, to seek and find my father's traveling trunk?"

"Why don't you take me to it, and I'll show you," he replied.

71

The hospital lay empty, with only the barest skeleton crew to attend to the few patients. All waited with breath held for the train to return, bearing its burden of injured and dying, and no one yet knew how many to expect.

I led Jack to Father's office and found the door locked. I turned to him, to apologize for the inconvenience, but he had already raised his boot. The lock shattered under the force of his kick.

"Dear God!" I exclaimed, "Are you mad!"

But Jack was a man possessed and paid no attention to me as he entered. He prowled around the gurney in the centre of the room, looking wildly at the cupboards and desk.

"Where is it?!?"

"The chest?" I replied, "It's right –"

But the corner next to the desk was empty. Only a scuff mark on the ground showed where the battered traveling trunk had once sat.

"It's gone!"

"Where would he have taken it?"

"I don't know – I don't know why he'd bother—"

He seized my shoulders. "Where is it?"

"I honestly don't know!" I replied, angry, "It's sat there since we first arrived in Cumberland, years ago! There's no reason at all for him to move it now!"

"There's every reason," Jack barked, "He knows I've come for it. Think, girl – where's the safest place he could move it?"

"Our home, I guess," I began, and as soon as the words left my lips, he snapped up my hand in his and dragged me after him, out of the hospital, half-running over the hospital grounds towards the doctors' houses.

Agnes flew into the hall when she heard the front door bang open, and when she confronted Jack, towing me behind him, she released such a blood-curdling scream that the dust shook from the curtains and the roses ruffled in the vase. I wrenched my hand free and cast Jack an ugly look before running to the frantic woman's aid.

"I'm alright, I'm fine," I cooed.

"Guld Lord hae mercy on us!" Agnes screamed again, "You, gone all the night, and your father in fits that you've been lost as well, and now I find you dragged home by some strange craitur, and—" Agnes's voice fluttered, her face ashen. "Who wuld yeh be, man?" she demanded, "What wuld yeh want?"

I took her by one arm. "Here, sit down, breath deeply. I'm fine, Agnes. I'm perfectly fine."

The woman sank into the wooden chair, her knees trembling. "Now, aye, you're fine as a feather, home and safe in our keeping! Your father wuld have a fit if he ken you'd been out gallivanting all through the nicht!"

"Shut-up, woman!" Jack ordered as he ranged through the library, ripping drawers from desks, overturning furniture.

"Guld Lord, help us!" Agnes screeched.

But I cast a fiery glare at Jack. I softened my voice when I spoke with the housekeeper. "Where has father put the traveling trunk?"

Agnes looked between us, flustered and confused. "Get you abuin tae yer room, miss!" the woman demanded, pointing one stubby finger towards the back stairwell. "I'll nae be an accomplice tae your fool adventures again, ye hear? We've already lost one chick in this house," and before she could finish her statement, Agnes' voice broke into uncontrolled sobbing. She covered her face with her tea towel and swabbed the tears from her eyes, leaning heavily against the wall to support herself under the burden of her overwhelming grief. "Oh, Lord, how I prayed that you wuld be returned tae us before your father came home! All the nicht he was fretting – back and forth, back and forth! All the nicht! So that, in the morning when the bells tolled, he was as worn out as if he'd worked all evening, and here he had tae go tae the disaster, and Lord knows how many dead from the fall, and—"

Jack appeared from the side of the room with a glass of brandy in hand, poured from John's crystal decanter. He pushed it into Agnes' grip and she, without a word of protest, downed the entire glass.

"Oh, thank you, sir! That is kind of ye."

"Mrs. Gunn," I said, kneeling at her side, "Would you know where Father moved the traveling trunk?"

She shook her head. "I've nae seen it."

"It's not on the main floor," Jack growled.

"He can't have moved it far," I said.

"The great beast of luggage?" Agnes scoffed. "There's nae guld room in the house for such a thing, and besides, it's too heavy and cumbersome for a man tae move himself! It wuld take two or three at least!"

I ran to the kitchen window and looked out into the yard. In the soft garden soil, the wooden wheel of the barrow had cut deep, leaving a clear scar which ran to the surgery door from the front yard and, I surmised, the hospital beyond.

"But not impossible," I said, "With a wheelbarrow."

I flew down the steps to the surgery. The curtain was drawn over its lone window, and the door was locked.

I rattled at the latch. A furious buzzing rose from the eaves, but I saw no wasps.

"Outta the way," Jack said, giving me a rough shove.

It was more secure than the office door, and took Jack three solid kicks to break; each kick brought a yelp of horror from Agnes.

The door burst down with a rending, splintering crack. A stench roiled out, thick and heavy like iron. A buzzing hum seemed to come from all directions.

Inside the surgery, all was dark. The covered window let in a gently diffused light, and I reached around the threshold to pull open the thin curtain, admitting a shaft of golden sunshine.

Every surface was crimson-black. At first, I wondered if it had been painted: the neat, clean wooden table was dark, lumpy, foul. Blood covered every surface, mostly dried but still sticky where pools had collected, thick as tar in the summer air. The stench was more than blood; yes, the iron-filing scent of blood was everywhere, but the earthy perfume of digested food and the vinegar sting of stomach acid lent a pungency to the fragrance. It was the worst of bodily fluids, fermenting together in a closed room under days of August heat. The gagging smell reminded me of a stewpot left unwashed for far too long.

I heard retching. When I turned, I saw that Jack had buried his head in the marigolds.

So I left him behind, and stepped into the dark chamber. The incessant buzzing continued, grew and flowed, ebbed and eddied from one side of the surgery to the other. Under my boots, the floor crunched and crackled. I grabbed a paper box of lucifers from the shelf and lit the lamp on the table. It guttered, coughed, then cast out a circle of quavering illumination.

The floor was an undulating carpet of insects, moving and shifting. They feasted like wildebeest on the wild savannah, sipping at watering holes of crimson tar. The walls, too, heaved with life. The air was thick with wings. In the close, cramped, claustrophobic space, blowflies bred by the thousands. When I held up the lamp, they pinged into the glass.

A furious storm of red crossed the wooden table. There were no knives: he'd taken his kit with him on the train. But tracts and pools and a delta of blood had dried there, next to a pink-grey rope of intestine, impossibly long and thin, crusty at the edges from days of exposure to air. On the floor, bowls and buckets had caught the drips from the table, and the congealed blood had turned black as pudding. Bits of blonde hair, cemented into the blood, shivered in the draught from the door.

Beside the door sat the travel trunk, fresh and clean, newly stashed here this very morning. In the far corner of the room, collapsed in a heap, were the remains of the blue Persian rug, stripped of its canvas backing and tossed aside.

"He killed her here," I said to no one, for Agnes had retreated to the porch in a fit of banshee wailing, and Jack was still trying to muster his strength in the garden.

I caressed the rug's blood-stiff edges as the events fell into place. After I had left, Violet had confronted Father here, in the surgery, and backed him into a corner, both physically and psychologically. She would not let the rumors go. She insisted on running to Kelly, to coerce him into silence, but instead, John Saunders killed her and took a lock of her hair. He wrote the letter in haste to bait his trap. Kelly fell for the ruse, followed the letter to Maple Lake, and lost his life. Then, in the days following, John had spent his leisure hours gutting his own daughter in the privacy of his surgery before wrapping the empty husk of a body in the rug's backing. On horseback, he carried her along the edge of town and through the trails to Comox Lake. It was now clear to me why he didn't chose the same spot to hide both bodies: by this time, the search parties would have been scouring the roads between Cumberland, Courtenay and Union Bay. The route to Comox Lake lay in the opposite direction, and the trails behind Chinatown offered a way to skirt any busy road or train tracks.

John had dumped her in the lake and headed home. Maybe he'd considered keeping the canvas - it had been a good piece. Maybe he'd reconsidered half-way home, knowing he'd never be able to explain to Agnes where those stains had come from.

The blowflies, accustomed to my presence, had settled on the table, but the furious buzzing rose again as Jack entered.

"Violet must've lain in here for days, until my father could rent a horse under the auspices of looking for me," I said, "He suggested I go to Union Bay and back, searching for her, but she was here, the whole time."

"God have mercy," he whispered low.

"How can he have done this?" I asked, stunned. "He's a good man."

But Jack didn't answer. He seized the edge of the trunk and pulled it with brute strength out the door, into the fresh air, where he could breath without retching.

"Jack, tell me," I demanded, "Why would my father kill Violet, rather than let her speak with Mr. Kelly?"

But Jack only grunted with the effort of dragging the heavy trunk.

"Tell me!" I cried, "This is more than just my mother's indiscretions! God damn it Jack -- *what did Mr. Kelly know?*"

In the garden, where the birds sang and the breeze played in the apple branches, all the goodness in the world turned a blind eye to the pit of evil bound within those four brick walls. Sadness seeped through me, dripping like cold rainwater. I didn't feel any urge to cry, though I desperately wanted to.

The porch was empty. Agnes had fled. I knew with certainty that she'd return with Rufus McGregor in tow, just as soon as she could find him.

Jack's full attention fell to the traveling chest. He shimmied the tip of his bowie knife behind the lock, levering upwards until the rusted contraption snapped in two. I drew close to his elbow. Even after the assaultive stench in the surgery, I smelt Jack's sweat and his warmth, but as he lifted the lid, another smell now drifted up from the trunk: the clean and crisp fragrance of ethanol.

With care and patience, Jack pulled a series of glass containers from the trunk, studied each and put it on the ground beside him, searching.

"These are... teaching specimens?" I asked, but the words sounded hollow, childishly naïve, as I said them. Each container was meticulously labeled, but none carried the Latin inscription of the organ inside, as any doctor with a collection would provide for ease of instruction. The contents were slashed, savage, discolored. Kidneys were crammed into small jars like preserved plums. An ear lay wizened on a glittering bed of salt in an artfully-crafted glass-topped box. Another container held a heart, the size and shape and color of a pomegranate. Jack withdrew each item with care and laid it with its fellows on the grass until a collection of jars congregated there, a whole body or more of bits, and each one marked with a date.

He pulled out a wide-mouth bottle, adorned with a yellowed label, and ran his thumb over it. Over his shoulder, I read, "September 30, 1888" written in a flourish of sepia ink. Inside the bottle, floating in a clear sea of spirits, was a fleshy, grey-red pear. Yellow streamers of fat trailed from its edges, and drifted with the movement of the liquid like the tentacles of a tropical jellyfish. Jack held the bottle in both hands. His eyes studied every fissure and swell, his mouth turned down.

I drew close and watched it sway with the trembling of his grasp.

"This? You came for this?" I asked.

He nodded. It took Jack a long time to form an answer. The words were there, but he had no breath to speak them.

"You know what this is, kid?"

"Yes," I replied, "It's a uterus."

Then, in a harsh rasp that was little more than a whisper through a clenched throat, Jack said, "Here is where I started in the world."

He took the jar and stood, and coughed to clear his throat as he made to leave.

"You can't go!"

He stopped at the gate, and the light caught a glimmer of moisture on his cheek, which he quickly wiped away with the back of his hand.

"How many?" I cried. I was shaking now, and I wrapped my arms around my chest to support myself, to stop the trembling. "How many did he kill?"

"I don't know," Jack replied. "I've identified twelve as his work, but I'll be damned if that's the final tally." He clutched the jar to his chest. "Your grandfather told me 'bout the maid – an arm and a torso in a purple bodice , that's all they ever found of her. The rest of the women, he had no connection to 'em. He could leave 'em in the street if he wanted, and no one would put it to him. There were enough suspicious characters, down in the dark belly of Whitechapel, to keep the detectives busy." Jack rotated the jar in his hands. "But if the cops identified Hannah, it woulda led them straight to his door. So she's the only one he bothered to hide."

I cast about, confused, my head whirling. "You must be wrong—"

"He killed Hannah early in August, and yer mother fled to Wiltshire, taking you with her. But he kept coming back to London, didn't he. He couldn't stay away."

"His clients, at the hospital... he had clients—"

But I knew I was wrong. How could I argue? I was surrounded by the fragments of fallen women, and the blood of my sister clung to the soles of my boots. Father had killed them all, ripped them to pieces, and vanished into the New World, as far has he could go from the Old.

"But... but why?"

"I figure he discovered your mother and Hannah, and that would make any man sore angry." Jack said, "But he just couldn't seem to stop, and that I can't figure. You'll have to ask him that question yerself, if you can find him." He gave a bitter, tired, resentful chuckle. "And trust me, Liz, he's been a difficult man to find. If it weren't for your grandfather's guilty conscience, I wouldn't have been so lucky."

I knelt in the grass and threw my hands to my head. For long minutes I watched the shadows of the apple branches drift across the yard, and the ethanol in the jars sparkled like diamonds around their flowery cargo. I thought Jack had gone, and startled when a warm hand lay itself upon my shoulder.

He sat beside me.

"You're like him, aren't you," Jack said, like a priest coaxing a confession, "You got that same coldness in your eye. You don't flinch or feel fear. You're wrong in the head."

"No," I denied, but I knew he was right.

"You don't feel things like you ought," he continued, "You're not cryin'; you're cold and unfeeling."

"I'm not unfeeling," I said, and looked up at him, "I do have feelings, but they're buried deep. I know they're there, but I can push them away for a while, so that they're easy to ignore. And when I feel too much, when I split in two --"

Suddenly, I grasped his fingers in my hands and held them tightly.

"Get rid of me," I implored, "I know you're thinking of it. Violet's gone, my mother's gone, and they were the only conscience I had in the world. Without them, I'll turn out like him. It's better to kill me and be rid the world of me completely."

"I've spent the last eight years, trying to find him." He bowed his head. "I was gonna kill him and collect the reward, and I told Kelly so's I'd have the law on my side, but—" He stared at me, regret and dismay etched into the lines of his face. "But God damn it, it'll ruin your life, if people knew what you was."

"So kill me, too," I urged. "Please."

He winced. "Yer just a kid." He ran his palm over my tangled hair, and his touch was warm, concrete. "I ain't gonna kill you, Lizzie, because I came for him, not for you."

And without another word, he strode out of the yard and down the alley, and left me sitting in the sunlit garden, surrounded by pieces of broken women.

72

When Rufus arrived on horseback, almost an hour later, he first smelt smoke. He threw the reins of the raw-boned chestnut over the front fence and ran into the back yard, calling for me but finding no one. The door to the surgery hung on shattered hinges, and black greasy smoke billowed from inside the small space. Tongues of flame licked at the books on the shelves, the papers, the wooden furniture within. The compact brick building was an incinerator.

He shouted to the houses across the alley and threw his weight on the pump handle. Cold water filled the first bucket, and men arrived, carrying more. They threw bucketful after bucketful on the savage flames. A trickle of diluted blood snaked across the lawn, but not much, not as much as the sobbing and hysterical Agnes had led him to believe, and if there had been buckets of blood inside, the fire had consumed them. By the time they'd doused the inferno, the roof was gone and almost everything inside reduced to charred rubble. The men congratulated each other on stopping the fire so quickly. They'd managed to spare the house and the yard, even if they hadn't saved the surgery.

"Thank God the building was brick," yelled one of the men, " Kept the fire from spreading!"

Rufus pushed his cap to the back of his head and mopped a cold sweat from his brow.

"Damn it," he whispered to himself.

Dr. Saunders surgery was utterly destroyed. Nothing remained to validate Agnes' claim. If the room had been soaked with blood, it was turned to ash now.

Agnes had left before Jack had dragged the trunk out of the surgery; she had no reason to mention the trunk or the wheelbarrow, so Rufus had no reason to look for it. He gave little attention to the fresh ruts in the soft earth which lead from the scuffed grass and charred remains of the surgery, through the bean patch to the outhouse.

And only after Rufus thanked the neighbors for their quick assistance, and finished a cursory examine of the burned remains, did he notice his chestnut horse had been stolen.

I PUT heels to the horse's flanks and spurred it to a gallop, down the street to the train station, then pulled hard on the reins to the left and flew on four thundering hooves along the trail following the tracks. McGregor's horse knew only to run, ears flattened, eyes wide. I clung to the saddle with my knees and held the reins in white-knuckled fists, and aimed the terrified creature in the general direction eastward.

East, where the night had already begun to seep up through the celestial arch, and the first bright pin-pricks of stars pierced the velvety indigo depths. McGregor's horse plunged headlong into the purple twilight of the woods, following the train tracks.

I didn't know how long I'd sat, surrounded by the tranquil glass jars, watching the failing sunlight flicker in the ethanol. I stared at the beautiful remains and reflected that, while I'd asked Jack why my father had killed, I didn't need an answer.

I already understood. The obsession, the need to collect, the impulse to horde. I understood Father's desire to feel the life ebb away under his own fingertips. I'd felt that desire, too.

I knew why he'd gathered these trinkets together, why he kept them safe. Gathering the flotsam and jetsam of my life, sealing it up together in the humble tin biscuit box, and jealously guarding it for my own pleasure – other people might keep their memories inside their minds, but each one of these jars carried a moment to be savored. Each curios resurrected that elusive pinnacle of transient happiness which flared in the moment it was gathered, to be savored like sips of summer wine on the darkest night of winter. These were pieces of art, painted in reds and golds. I could close my eyes and feel the butterfly fragments of life trapped in them still. They shimmered and pulsed with a vitality of their own.

I struggled to not understand – a good person would not understand. A good person would be horrified.

I replaced the jars in the trunk, taking care to keep the glass from tinkling together, and gently packed straw and dried leaves from the garden around them.

Moving the trunk took great effort, but I couldn't bear the thought of the collection falling into the hands of a good man like McGregor. He wouldn't treat them with care. I didn't know exactly what he would do with them, but they had been entrusted to me until Father could be consulted. The trunk needed to be hidden.

But it was heavy, a monstrosity of iron-bound wood and leather. Jack had been big enough to pull it from the surgery, but I was half as tall and a fraction of his weight – to wrestle it onto the wheelbarrow took all my strength. I could only push it a few feet across the yard, beads of sweat stinging my eyes, so I heaved it into the outhouse, propped up on its end. They might look in the house and the surgery, but I doubted they'd look here.

The surgery was a mess, it could not be cleaned, and I saw only one clear option: to burn it to the ground. Time was of the essence now: Agnes had fled when the door was first smashed open. If McGregor had not yet gone to fetch Kelly's body, Agnes would quickly find the deputy constable, and even if she couldn't find McGregor, she'd surely bring someone to show them. I took the scuttle from the kitchen, filled it with embers from the stove, and placed the coals in a nest of pages from Father's books. The paper caught quickly. I fed the fire with the furniture, the rug, the books. In the dry August air, the flames blossomed and thrived.

Jack was gone, but he was resourceful - he'd find a horse easily. I'd never catch him on foot, so I hid amongst the rose bowers in the front yard. When McGregor arrived, I had no option but to take the chestnut gelding.

I was halfway to the trestle when a light on the tracks ahead shook me out of my stupor. The train crawled along the rails, bearing injured men whose crushed bones were unable to bear a rattling pace. I guided the horse into the woods to wait at the verge, and flagged the attention of one of the nurses.

"Dr. Saunders?" I called out. "Is Dr. Saunders there?"

The nurse, a young spry woman, her neatly pinned hair framing a face that was black and smeared with oil and grit, shook her head.

"Still pulling bodies!" she cried back, "He stayed behind! Only Dr. Gould and Dr. Briggs on board!"

And then the train shuddered passed, leaving a wake of thick smoke and cinders.

I reeled the horse back onto the trail and slapped the reins against its haunch. It took off at a gallop.

I heard the sounds of the disaster site long before I approached. The horse's chest heaved for breath. It had run too far. It stumbled on the sloping trail, so I slipped from its saddle and ran the rest of the way, following the tracks until they discharged me at the northern rim of the canyon.

Below, the ravine was full of orange stars. Fires burned, here and there, where lumps of coal had been thrown from the furnace and ignited isolated brush fires. Two boys extinguished them with buckets of water hauled out of the river, but there were torches, too, illuminating the scene of the disaster. Shattered timbers poked up from the debris. A mountain of rocks and twisted iron crawled with men, and the great engine of No. 14 lay on its side in the late-summer trickle of water. An acrid mist of steam and smoke filled the air.

I crawled down the embankment to the edge of the Trent River, where men appeared and vanished like apparitions through waves of steam and smoke.

"Where's Dr. Saunders?" I asked one.

He turned to me, dazed and exhausted. "He ain't here," came the reply, "He went back with the train."

But no, he hadn't: the nurses were clear, he'd stayed behind.

The man took this opportunity to press the heels of his palms to the small of his back. "Look, be a good girl and get fetch me a bucket of water upstream, wouldja?" Digging out the dead was thirsty work.

I balked.

"He wasn't on the train," I replied, "I passed the train, going to Cumberland, and he wasn't on it."

"Well, I don't know!" he replied, exasperated, "Just get me some god damned water!"

I left him and prowled around the perimeter. The few men who remained were intent on clearing debris, but the light was almost gone. They worked by torchlight on unstable stones and the fatigue had stolen their strength; every minute they worked was an open taunt to Fate. A misstep and a broken bone and the resulting septicemia could kill a man, so they crawled down off the trestle reluctantly, but knew that those left under the stones were beyond earthly assistance. There was little to do but retreat to the farm houses nearby and take their rest, and begin to dig again at dawn.

I loitered in the shadows of the ruins. They took the torches with them and disappeared up the north side of the canyon.

But one man with a torch in hand hung back, then diverged away from the others. Jack moved along the edge of the stream towards the ocean, driven and head down. His boots splashed in the water.

I waited until he had reached the river delta before I stepped into the stream. The water reached up to my ankles. Far enough to evade his hearing, I began to follow.

73

THE STREAM BED widened into a shallow, grassy delta. The forest opened up to reveal a sky that glittered with stars, and I stepped out of the woods to the pebbled ocean shore like an actor onto the open stage. A slight breeze carried the scent of kelp and salt to my nose. The rustling of branches came from the stately Douglas fir trees that lined the shore, sounding not unlike a velvet curtain closing. I turned my back to the trees and looked left, northward to Comox Bay, but saw nothing.

I walked farther into the open, to a rocky point of land that gave a better view. The tide was out, and the silvery fringe of the waves had recoiled a long distance from the trees to expose a wide swath of rocky beach. I looked southward, to my right. A plateau of sea grasses, stones, logs, bracken and kelp stretched in a crescent, and a tiny speck of flame hovered, far out on the tidal flats.

I followed at a brisk, but cautious, trot.

Jack moved methodically, bending down now and again, holding the torch to the ground before rising and advancing to follow the shore. We passed a rocky promontory and entered a small, sheltered bay, bounded by the line of black firs and a few billowing pastures of camas blossoms. Only the stars illuminated the sand and stones, but it was enough for me to distinguish a second, solitary figure ahead, moving swiftly and carrying a portmanteau.

Jack stopped and stabbed the torch into the sand. He rose his right hand straight ahead of him.

A flash of light and an explosion. The pistol rapport snapped through the silence.

I almost cried out, but the distant figure didn't crumple. The shot had flown wide.

Instead, the figure stopped and turned.

I heard Father's familiar, blithe laugh from across the broad expanse of sand and pebbles. "Were you trying to warn me, sir, or do you possess a terrible aim?"

I saw Jack fumble. He checked his bullets and I heard the barrel snap as it closed. The hammer of the gun clicked as he cocked it. The light of the torch danced off the polished steel of the barrel, and I saw for the first time that he trembled.

But Jack's voice was strong. "It might surprise ya, squire, but I'm not the sort to shoot a man in the back."

I crept closer as Father began to stroll leisurely towards Jack, each step casual and unconcerned.

"Mr. Kelly said he had come into information but refused to divulge how." Father sauntered along the sand, closing the distance between he and Jack without any sense of wariness. "He led me to think that Captain Worthington had contacted him directly: a letter from the senile father of my half-wit wife, whom he could not quite believe, but could not quite dismiss, either. I admit, he was clever to let me think so!"

"It seems I owe Mr. Kelly my life, then," Jack replied.

"Well, what little is left of it," John replied. "So who was it? A wife? A sister?" He gave a derisive chuckle. "Maybe a whore you met in Panama, and felt some misguided need to avenge?"

Jack stiffened and stood a little straighter. "It was my mother." His voice wavered a little. "Her name was Kate, sir, though I doubt you'd care."

"You ought to let go of the past," John suggested, "You're wasting your life on a damn fool quest to dog me to the end of the earth."

"Well, now, we find ourselves at the end of the earth," Jack replied, holding out his hands to encompass the Pacific beach, "So I guess that means I'm almost done."

Father approached. At the gravel shoreline, he set his bag gently down on the butt of a log.

"Come, come," he began, no longer speaking as loudly, "You could've had a family and a good career by now, if you hadn't bothered to follow me. Don't you think that would've made your old mum happier?"

Jack did not falter, but nor did he answer.

"A foolish obsession, this is," Father replied. "Let it go."

"So you can kill again? No, sir." Jack raised the gun again. "I made a promise to Captain Worthington, and I aim to see it through."

"When he heard Molly was dead, he had himself a change of heart, did he?" Father snorted derisively. "The old man was never fond of me, it's true. But he took what he could get, and he never complained when I kept his girl in good style, or gave him two fine grand-daughters."

"The captain told me things about you that would make most men run t'other way."

"But you aren't running."

"You said it yerself, sir," Jack replied, "This is the end of the earth, and there just ain't no where I can go." He moved away from the torch, out of the circle of light, so that his aim wouldn't be blinded by its illumination.

I crept closer with my back to the logs, but both men were intent upon each other. In the darkness, I was nothing more than a rustling of sand and gravel, no louder than the wind in the towering trees or the distant splashing of the surf. They had drawn close together, less than ten paces, and I didn't know what to do: rush to Father's help? Call out to distract them?

"He told you, then, that he brought me here himself?"

Jack moved forward. "He claims he prayed to God for a decent man to marry his sick daughter, and that he thought, at first, you came direct from heaven, an answer to his prayers. But he said you don't got a soul at all, and as time wore on, he came to think you'd crawled up to earth from the bellies of Hell." Jack shivered. "And lookin' on your handiwork, I damn well think he's right."

"My handiwork..." Father considered the term. "Molly understood that some forces can not be stopped, sir. She was deficient in many ways, but she possessed a great insight into my character, and in her devotion to our daughters, I never found her wanting. She excelled at ensuring the safety of our family, when even I could see no farther than my own... as you put it... handiwork."

Jack's pistol lowered a fraction. "She was your accomplice?"

"She was my wife, sir," John continued, strolling closer, "Not an accomplice, but a partner, in all respects of the word." At the mention of Molly, he grew agitated. His words took a savage edge. "It's called 'devotion', Mr. Hunter. I should think the son of a cheap whore might struggle with the concept."

Jack grimaced. He lowered his chin and bared his teeth.

"Yer wife possessed an odd sense of devotion, doncha think?" he needled, "Or have you forgotten about Hannah?"

The name rose a black shadow over Father's face.

"Molly learned, very quickly, the price of her failure," he seethed, "And she remained cautious and careful, to the very end, to keep her lust in check."

Jack suddenly realized how close John had come. He raised the gun and took no time to aim. The blast rang out, and I saw Father dodge to the right. The epaulet of his coat dissolved into tatters, but the bullet had missed his flesh. Jack cocked the hammer for a second shot, but before he could draw a bead, John rushed forward. A flash of steel in his right hand caught the torch light, but he punched with his left. The blow fell on Jack's arm with surprising strength. The gun skittered over the rocks, clattering metal on stone, and splashed into a tidal pool.

Jack retreated two steps. He unsheathed the bowie knife from his side and lifted the blade to block the downward slash of Father's knife. They parried. Jack had weight and youth to his advantage, but he was tempestuous, too, and easily enraged. Father was calculating and cold. The sharp ring of metal against metal howled into the still air, and a reflection of light follow in Father's hand in a wide arc: the slender, agile and double-edged blade of a lancet, as long as the palm of his hand.

Jack threw himself to one side. As Father regained his footing, he twisted around and held out both arms to steady himself. He grinned madly. His eyes danced.

A long slash opened the left side of Jack's coat. I heard his breath catch and knew he'd been struck. When he stumbled back, droplets of dark liquid splattered over the grey sand.

"You are a fool, sir, if you believe everything the captain says." Father stood erect as a gentleman ought and wiped the blood from the lancet on inner lining of his coat. "My wife's father is a drunk and a syphilitic, most likely from his mad excursions to East Indian brothels in his youth. He has a penchant for rambling."

"Worthington assures me," Jack said, trying to hold the shallow slash across his side together, "That you are the devil."

"My father-in-law struggles to understand things that are beyond his meager comprehension," John replied, "He squeezes reality into the narrow tubes of his religion in a vain attempt to catalogue all that this diverse world can offer. The captain prayed for a solution to his daughter's condition, and he got it, in full." Father tipped his head to the wound. "You're hurt, sir. I suggest you sit on a log there and let me be on my way. I don't like killing men: it gives me no pleasure. But I'm willing to stomach it," He lifted the knife again, "If you insist that I chop you to pieces."

Jack lowered his shoulder and rushed towards him like a charging bull.

But he was injured, clumsy, in pain and angry. Father dipped easily to the left and dodged the falling knife. In one sweeping motion, he reached out, seized the torch from the sand, and swung it around. The stock connected with a resounding clunk to the back of Jack's head. He collapsed to the wet sand, his hair singed. The bowie knife thudded into the wet sand, a few feet from his outstretched fingers.

Dazed, Jack dragged himself to his knees. His face was ashen.

Father jabbed the torch into the sand again. He circled the man on the ground, the doubled-edged knife in his grasp, and when he rolled up his sleeve in preparation of work to be done, I saw the parallel scratches running from wrist to elbow. John straddled him, seized a hank of blonde-brown hair, and wrenched the head upward to expose the full length of Jack's neck.

The light of the torch flashed on the descending blade.

"Stop it!" I screamed.

Father held his hand. He glanced towards the dark land for the source of the voice. Jack, his eyes still rolling in their sockets, tried to focus on the form running down the pebbled slope of the beach. When the light revealed me, Father regarded me with a warm and welcoming grin.

I half-stumbled down the rocky scree and onto the pad of sand, and my feet sank in the soft surface. "Don't," I said to Father, "Don't kill him. Please." I grabbed his wrist and shook him. "You've already ruined enough!"

"I haven't ruined anything," he replied, appalled at my pleas, "Place blame where blame is due, Lizzie. This man, this scrap of filth -- he ruined it!" A look of pity crossed Father's face. He let go of Jack and, stepping off of him, planted a solid kick into his side. "We were doing so well, we were settled – how can you possibly argue? It wasn't until this," And he kicked Jack again, "Came into our lives that our world fell apart."

"But don't kill him!"

"Why not?" Father narrowed his eyes, as if he didn't understand my request. "He was bound and determined to kill me!"

I threw my palms to my head. My heart beat, my mind reeled in confusion. I heard the rushing roar in my ears. "I don't, I can't—"

"Quit your simpering, Liz, it isn't like you at all," Father ordered. "Violet was prone to hysteria, but that's not how I designed you."

"You killed her!"

"I didn't have much choice, did I," he replied, looking bitter, "But if it makes you feel better, know that I didn't enjoy it. It was only an act of self-preservation, it didn't satisfy any need."

I fumbled for a reply, but the corner of his mouth kinked upwards.

"You know what I mean, Lizzie, don't deny it. I saw the look on your face when you slit that animal's throat – it struck you. It inspired you. It connected you to something greater than yourself." His smile spread, his brows drew down. "It made you feel infinite and sublime."

"No," I lied, "It didn't! I killed it because I had to!"

He leaned forward, and spoke so softly that the wind in the trees almost eclipsed his words.

"So do I."

Jack had crawled up to his knees. Passed my father, I saw him groping across the sand for his knife.

John lifted his eyes to the stars. "I tried to cure your mother, and she tried to cure me, but neither of us were entirely successful. The best we could do was keep each other in check, manage our urges, watch each other's movements and hide anything that might trigger our desires. But when she was gone, I began to see my way to freedom again, and when I watched you kill without remorse or regret, I knew! I knew you were truly my progeny!" He dropped his gaze from the heavens to meet mine. "And I dared to hope that, in time, there would be no need to hide my nature from you, because you are exactly like me."

"But," I began, "You'd abandon me, without another word?"

His face hardened. "That little outburst of your's at the sight of Violet's body... I realized there's more of your mother in you than I cared to admit. Despite all I've done, you're still sick, Liz. You're weak and ineffective, and Molly's perversion still burns in you. I'm finally free of your mother's disgusting ways; why would I want to chain myself again, to something like you?"

The darkness surged behind him, blocking out the stars, blocking out the light of the torch.

Father noticed the shadow and wheeled around as the bowie

knife lashed forward. He dodged to the right and felt to one knee, dropping the lancet, as Jack's knife bit deeply into his exposed forearm. Father screamed and wrenched his right arm back. The knife came with it.

He whipped his left arm up and dashed a handful of sand into Jack's face.

Jack cried out, stumbled and fell back, clawing at his eyes.

Gritting his teeth, Father levered the bowie knife out of his arm and flung it aside. It skidded to a stop, far out of the circle of illumination, somewhere in the blackness.

"God damn it!" he raged. His gentlemanly stoicism fractured. The fury boiled out of him and burst through the dam of his scholarly façade. "I'm talking to my daughter, you miserable piece of shit! Have some manners!"

Father grabbed the lancet in his left hand. Blood pulsed from the wound on his right arm but he didn't react to the pain. I saw it in his eyes, in the way he held his shoulders, in the exposed tendons in his neck – he was no longer in control of himself. The rational part of himself was gone: he had broken in two.

"You CAN! NOT! KILL me!" he screeched. His voice rose to a wild, wicked, inhuman pitch, "I would never allow myself to be killed by someone as pathetic as you! If you persist in your ridiculous attempts, you vile son of a bitch, you force me to remove you!"

Jack scrubbed the sand from his face, leaving behind smears of his own blood, and tried to peer blindly at the figure advancing towards him. Father's coat swirled behind him like stygian wings. The long, slender blade of the lancet rose. Jack scrambled backwards for anything to grab, but his pistol and knife were gone. His hands clenched handfuls of damp sand. There was nothing to save him, no rock or stick, nothing to serve as a weapon.

Did I scream? I don't know. I only heard the roaring in my ears, the thunderous pulse of my blood. All I saw was the flash of a descending knife ripping through the darkness.

74

For a split second, I counted two blades, mirrored reflections of each other as they arced down from the apex of the sky. But they did not fall in synchronicity. The farthest fell faster. As it buried itself between Father's shoulders, it pushed up the scrawny body that powered it. I watched in horror, only realizing a moment later that the body I saw was my own.

A face as white as pearl, holding eyes that were too large, too black, too empty to belong to any living thing. I could not tear myself from its unblinking stare. Jack, too, stared at the creature as if those black pupils would swallow him up, seize him and hold him with the force of their grip. We were staring into the abyss. Nothing lay there. Nothing but cold, impassionate emptiness. They held no fury, no rage, no anger, no feeling at all. They were pure action. They wrapped us in freezing winter and bound us with chains forged from the cold fires of Hell.

And Jack screamed.

Alongside Jack's prone body, Father fell face first into the damp sand and did not move. The hilt of the bowie knife protruded from the base of his neck.

75

THE AVENGING ANGEL EVAPORATED. I gasped, felt pain, returned to myself like a sleeper jerked cruelly awake. I was standing before Jack and watching him scream, and as the stars wheeled overhead, the blackness in my eyes began to fade. After a moment or two, he couldn't scream anymore. He knelt in the sand and panted and clutched at his wounded side, unable to flee.

"Are you okay, Jack?" I said.

In a cracking voice, he replied, "Jesus Christ, are you?!?!"

I held out my hand to him. He flinched and did not want to touch me but, when I grabbed his hand, I proved I was nothing more than flesh and bone. He felt warmth and the pulse of blood under my skin.

"You're hurt."

"I'm... not..." He tried to stand but stumbled back to one knee.

"You've lost too much blood," I replied, and helped him drag his sorry body up to the rocky shore to prop him heavily against a log. "Here, wait." I ran down the beach and grabbed Father's bag, then wrenched the bowie knife from his neck and collected the guttering torch. I brought these to Jack's side. By the fire's light, I opened the bag and rummaged within, pausing once as my fingers struck something smooth and cold.

"What?"

"Nothing," I said and resumed my search. At length, I found a needle and a thread, and with brine from the nearest tidal pool, I bathed the gash across Jack's side. It was long but not deep. It bled profusely, but it would not kill him.

I stitched him quickly and efficiently, even in such poor lighting. Every time I touched him, he shied away.

And when I was done, I sat at his side. He might have slept a little, then, for his breathing slowed and his shoulders relaxed. I leaned into the warmth of his body and my head lolled against his shoulder. I was tired, too – beyond tired, I had moved into that state of transcendence, where the world is a watery dream and every motion is torpid and disconnected. The tide rose and covered Father's body. I watched it float for a while below the surface, a dark fish buoyed up by the force of the current, and eventually it drifted out and away, cleansed of blood and life, to wash ashore in some isolated cove or desolate island, or to be dragged to the depth of the black strait and devoured by crabs and eels. As Jack slept, I withdrew a glass jar from Father's bag, hidden underneath his tools and a spare set of underwear. He had left to assist with the train disaster, but he had known he would never come back.

The glass jar in my hand reflected the flickering torch. Inside, the womb swam back and forth, rotating on its axis as I turned the jar slowly, examining every fissure and swell.

He'd killed Violet, but he'd still deemed her the only treasure worth saving.

76

August 18, 1898

"How are you?"

"Quit asking me that, Jack."

At dawn, we found a trail along the edge of the beach and, in the clear cool light, stumbled with heavy steps back to the trestle, where the sound of men at work could be distantly heard.

I propped myself under his left arm to support him, and carried Father's portmanteau under my own left arm. The perspiration rolled down my forehead in glistening beads. My sweat-damp clothes clung to my skin.

"I just need to know, that's all," he panted.

"I'm fine. You're not. Quit wasting your breath."

We crossed the river and I loaded him onto the waiting train, and when the engine began to pull back to Cumberland, I finally curled in the crook of Jack's arm and slept deeply.

I woke in the whorehouse, on a bed next to Shao.

Dust motes danced in shafts of sunlight, sliding through the open windows. The room was small and cramped, with only a bed and a humble wooden dresser in the corner, but a lavender feathered fan had been pinned to one wall and the bed frame was wrapped with gauzy mauve scarves, lending a theatrical ambiance to the space. The house was very quiet, very still. When I startled to my elbows, looking wildly at my surroundings, he reached out to stroke my naked shoulder.

"How long have I slept?" I asked.

"It's three in the afternoon," he replied. He leaned to me, gave me a kiss. "I can't possibly tell you how happy I am to see you."

I ran my hand along his chin and kissed him in reply. "I thought you were dead."

"I thought I was, too!" he grinned. "If it wasn't for Jack, I – hey, wait!"

Without a word, I'd leapt to my feet and began to dress.

Shao rolled to his side, his breath catching with pain. "Where are you going?"

"I need to talk to Jack."

Shao's eyebrows leapt upwards. "Now? Right now?"

"Yes, right now," I replied, pulling on my pants. I grabbed Shao's shirt from the floor, as my own was in tatters, then dipped down again to place a quick kiss on the tip of his nose. "Where is he?"

"I don't know," Shao said, stammering slightly with the suddenness of my departure. "He isn't looking so good, but he wouldn't tell me what happened. He said he needed to go out--"

"I'll be back," I promised, and I rushed from Mercy's house without a word of explanation.

A fresh hole in the back of my yard showed where the grave had been dug, hastily and poorly by a man with little strength. It was shallow and crooked, dredged out of the garden where the soil was already broken, but aesthetics had been farthest from Jack's mind: his only goal was to give a decent burial to the contents of the trunk.

I stood at the edge of the freshly-turned earth, surveying the charred husk of the brick surgery. The scent of yesterday's soot and smoke still hung in the apple branches.

I entered the kitchen carefully, and as I advanced through the hall, I averted my eyes from the casket on the dining room table. The air smelt stale, sweetly rotten, and empty. The house felt abandoned.

'Of course it does,' I thought, 'No one lives here anymore.'

A train's shrill whistle carried up from the station.

My breath caught in my throat. I didn't pause to close the door, but vaulted across the back porch and ran down the road. As I passed the constabulary, I dashed through a gathering of people, men and women in finery, reading a proclamation pinned to the door. Most looked relieved and assured, and a few of the women held their gloved fingers to their mouths in horrified surprise. A hand snagged my arm and pulled me to an abrupt stop. Standing with his hand on my elbow, Mason Briggs wore a celebratory grin.

"They say Rufus found Kelly, out by Maple Lake!"

The dangling body, cut from the branches; I had to blink twice. It seemed like so long ago, in a distant country, in another life.

"Yes," I began, and was suddenly swept into Dr. Brigg's arms.

"Jolly good!" he replied, "Though I never thought I'd say such a thing! But a suicide!" He sighed at the macabre thought. "Let our good Lord met out the justice that Kelly deserves, I say!"

"Rufus has ruled it a suicide?'

He cast me a pitying glance. "Oh, Lizzie, I am sorry for you. This whole trial, you've borne with enviable fortitude."

You have no idea, I thought, and nodded.

"But it's over now!" He held me at arms length. "I want to give your father a word of congratulations – is he back from the train accident?"

I looked down the hill to the station, where boys in aprons loaded the day's mail and deliveries onto the cars, but until the trestle was repaired, there would be no shipments of coal. At the accident site, both passengers and cargo would be discharged onto ox wagons, to be hauled the distance from the trestle to the Union Bay docks by bumpy roads. "He has gone on ahead to prepare the way for us," I said quickly, "I'm afraid he left late last night, suddenly, and without much notice."

Mason's face fell in surprise, then he nodded in understanding.

"I'm glad to hear it. Tell him, when you see him again, that I look forward to renewing our acquaintance when I return to Victoria."

"If you don't mind, Dr. Briggs," I said, easing away from his embrace, "I really must catch this train."

"Oh, of course!" He released me as a man might release his dance partner when the music has ended: smiling, merry, with a brief clap of his hands. "Good luck! Good luck!"

By the time I reached the train station, the engine was pulling away. I ran the length of the platform, dodging the stock boys and boxes, frantically searching the windows for a familiar face. My boots thudded on the wooden boards. At last, I saw him in the passenger car, and cried out, loud enough to carry over the rising chuff of steam and clatter of iron.

"Jack! Jack Hunter!" I cupped my hands around my mouth and screamed again, "JACK HUNTER!"

But he did not turn his head. He sat, looking straight ahead, his unshaven face empty and tired.

The whistle cried out as the train left me wreathed in coal smoke. I stood on the end of the platform, watching him leave, vanishing as surely from this place as the silvery wisps of steam now evaporating around my ankles. I wondered if I could find him again, trace him through the boat registry, follow him to Victoria and demand all the answers I'd need from him.

And then I realized, with a jolt, that I was a fool. I would never be able to find him again.

All this time, 'Jack Hunter' had never been his name.

It had been his calling.

EPILOGUE

Dear Grandfather,

I hope this letter finds you and my grandmother in good keeping, and that it comes as a welcome correspondence, rather than an uncomfortable surprise.

I admit, I hesitated to write you, but eventually I felt it prudent to inform you of recent events. You will be saddened to hear that my beloved sister Violet has met an unfortunate end, and now rests with the angels. Her passing was quick and unforeseen, and my life is poorer for the lack of her good judgment and friendship. I know that I shall miss her dreadfully to the end of my days.

For your own peace of mind, I also wish to assure you that Dr. John Saunders is no longer of any threat to the health and safety of anyone, and has (reluctantly but fully) conceded to my wishes that he cease his practice. He has been withdrawn from polite society. I'm afraid I can not be more clear, but rest assured: he is without physical means or ability to practice his particular expression of medicine in any country, landscape, dell or haven upon this earth. To this, I have seen personally.

Concerning my own position, I have left Cumberland and retired, for a time, to the harbor city of Victoria, where I find myself under the generous guardianship and hospitality of Mr. Harris Fish, originally of Birmingham by way of Australia. He has provided both me and my companion with a roof over our heads, and to him I am most grateful. You need not worry about his intentions, for he is a decent gentleman of good breeding, and I have enclosed his references herewith. I invite you to inquire as to his character if you are concerned for my safety. Given your previous letter, I trust you are not, but I include them regardless. If you wish to contact me in future, please direct any correspondence to the address on the envelope, which is Mr. Fish's fine residence in the borough of James Bay.

If you are concerned for my ability to provide for myself, I will assure you that my personal finances have been advanced by none other than yourself. Your agent, whom you sent earlier this year, has left all the monies you paid him in my care. With his task finished, he left Cumberland in great haste. It was only upon returning to my home, and opening the tin box under my bed, that I found your wallet, containing a goodly sum of bills inside.

I am terribly afraid that I did not catch his name. If you find yourself in future correspondence with him, please convey my thanks to him, whomever he may be. I have no doubt that he saved the life of me and my companion. I believe to the marrow of my bones that his valiant pursuit has saved the lives of many others, too, whose future paths would otherwise have crossed with my father's.

WITH FOND REGARDS and no regrets,
Your loving grand-daughter,
Amaryllis

MARK OF THE MAGPIE - CHAPTER ONE

October 15, 1898

Another murder of the foulest kind was committed in the neighborhood of Whitechapel in the early hours of yesterday morning, but by whom and with what motive is at present a complete mystery.

At a quarter to 4 o'clock Police constable Neill, 97J, when in Buck's Row, Whitechapel, came upon the body of a woman lying on a part of the footway, and on stooping to raise her up in the belief that she was drunk he discovered that her throat was cut almost from ear to ear. She was dead but still warm. He procured assistance and at once sent to the station and for a doctor.

- London Times, September 1, 1888

The tattered copy of the London Times had arrived by post from San Francisco only a few days ago. I'd scarcely put it down since its arrival. I'd read it so many times that the paper had gone soft, like old cotton, and the words had emblazoned themselves upon my mind. Most arresting of all was the single phrase ending the first paragraph, "... by whom and with what motive is at present a complete mystery."

For everyone else, that might be true, but not for me.

My hands trembled a little as I laid the clipping gently in the enameled tin jewelry box, where I had carefully organized a sheaf of articles by date. They were of varying lengths, and the paper quality ranged wildly, from thick expensive rag to paper so thin the light leaked through it. Some articles had cramped text, and others had wide set type spattered with spelling errors and lurid illustrations. They'd come from the street corners of London, New York, Montreal and Toronto, but all had arrived in my possession by way of Miss Rose Fish, a woman obsessed with collecting newsprint, who (according to her brother) was drowning in a sea of broadsheets. The generous and accommodating Rose had sent me twenty-three newspapers in total, and I had carefully snipped the articles that had caught my fancy to assemble my own, more precise collection. All manner of stories filled her tabloids and broadsheets, but I only cared for the ones detailing the rise and disappearance of Jack the Ripper. I especially cherished the ones describing the heinous crimes he'd inflicted upon the wayward women of Whitechapel, ten years ago. Anyone who opened this jewelry box would doubtlessly think me to be a girl obsessed, seized with a gloomy fascination for gore and terror, titillated by murders unsolved.

But they would be wrong. I took no pleasure in reading these words. They were shards of glass. As I read about the women who had been left to die in bloodied pieces in dark London alleys, each detail wormed its way deep into my brain. The lurid stories reduced them to featureless shapes with blunt words like 'whore' and 'prostitute' and 'unfortunate victim', and I could not bear that they been stripped of their humanity, so I committed their names to memory: Martha Tabram, Mary Ann Nichols, Annie Chapman, Elizabeth Stride, Catherine Eddowes, Mary Jane Kelly, Rose Mylett, Elizabeth Jackson.

More and more, on and on, woman after woman. I filled my mind with them, tried to rebuild them from newspaper rumors and gossip. Maybe only five, maybe thirteen, maybe any number in between.

Or, I suspected with dread, maybe even more, and their names lost forever.

I kept a careful tally of each incident, each missing organ, each slice, gash, and stab, because Jack the Ripper was not a mystery to me. He was a monster, an obsession curdled by self-importance. He was a warning of the path where my own impulses might lead me.

He was my father.

A knock at the door broke my focus. I closed the lid and set the box on the bedside table, and through the wood slats came the puzzled voice of Mr. Fish.

“Lizzie?” he said, "I don't wish to intrude. Are you awake?"

“Yes, sir," I replied, "Please, do come in."

The door opened. He smiled to see me.

Mr. Harris Fish was not the sort of fellow to show happiness openly. The expression sat ghoulishly on his narrow features. He was a hawkish, peevish sort of man, possessing few friends and having no hobbies beyond his beloved island railway line. For the last week, he'd been discussing its future construction with agents of the provincial government, which meant that most afternoons, he disappeared in meetings, debates, and arguments; to the best of my knowledge, his ideas had met with fierce opposition from both sides of the legislative house, and the war had given him a spring in his step and a blazing fire in his bright brown eyes. He came from a long line of railway industrialists, and his brother had amassed a fortune in Australia constructing transportation networks, so I suppose the love of trains resided in his blood, spurred to a froth by fraternal competition. No one would dare call Mr. Fish 'friendly' or 'warm', but neither would they call him 'weak' nor 'easily discouraged'. He was churlish, contrite, and unforgiving of those he deemed as fools, and most of his neighbors knew to avoid him. As thin and unyielding as an iron rail spike, Mr. Fish used his sour demeanor and vast investments to fight battles with the tenacity of a pit dog.

But I was neither an adversary nor an ally in his railway battle, so he didn't know what to do with me. He lingered in the doorway, unused to having a guest in his house. He'd never married and most people thought that was a blessing -- he'd make a most cantankerous husband. But, while he had only a few close friends, he possessed a very loyal staff, and during the last four weeks that I'd been living under his roof, it became clear that he preferred the company of his housekeeper to any wife or paramour. An unmarried elderly bachelor was often the topic of much speculation, but Mr. Fish didn't seem to give a fig what others thought, and I rather like that quality in a person.

I'd taken residence in one of the attic rooms of his grand James Bay mansion. The series of sparsely-decorated chambers had once been furnished for staff, and now served me quite comfortably. I had a private space with a wrought-iron bed, a full-length mirror, and a chest of four drawers that provided me with far more storage than I needed. A small window looked east over the garden and alley, and another offered a southward glimpse of the sea. At night the room could be quite cold and silent, but with a thick wool blanket and a clay pig warmed by the kitchen stove, I was very comfortable.

He spied the clipped newspapers on the bed and floor. "I've interrupted. You're pouring over the package from Rose. You carry the expression of a pensive scholar, Amaryllis, and your hands are black with printing ink."

I glanced to the remains of the paper, strips and squares scattered like streamers and confetti. "Your sister was very kind to send me these back issues, especially of the London Times. I must write a letter to thank her."

"Don't bother. It will only be lost in the piles of papers towering around her apartment," he huffed, "Really, I ought to thank you, Liz! Rose's hoarding has grown worse with age, but you've been kind enough to put her stacks of rubbish to good use. If my sister's trash aids your research on The London Match Girls' Strike, then so much the better!"

Ah, the match girls. I smiled and mustered my story before I spoke.

"I've learned a great deal, sir," I said. "The prohibition of white phosphorous has not yet come to pass, and those poor girls still work in atrocious conditions. Our work is not yet done!" I brandished my small fist. "I shall not be content until they've won their fight."

Lifting the plight of the lower classes was a noble cause, taken up by many girls my age. It provided a perfect excuse.

"I dare say, the suffragettes are lucky to have you on their side, Lizzie," he said as his face squished into an ungainly smirk. Then he waved one long hand in dismissal and said, "But, I didn't come to debate the atrocious living conditions of the poor. I came to tell you, you have a visitor."

"I do?"

"Indeed. And you will be very pleased to see who it is." Without waiting for my reply, he turned and descended the stairs, trusting that I would follow.

Because the attic was designed for the accommodation of servants, the rear stairway was steep and dark, and led directly to the kitchen on the first floor. With his long legs, Mr. Fish was able to descend them two at a time, and he reached the bottom long before I did.

I was still only half way down the case when I heard him say, "Here is your guest, Liz, right where I left him."

I thumped into the kitchen as Chen Shaozhu rose from the table.

To see him, my heart lifted from the shadows like a sparrow taking wing. His smile was a ray of sunlight slicing through my gloomy thoughts.

I hadn't seen Shao in five days. I tried not to count the passage of time; I knew he was busy working, building a place for himself in this city, establishing a business network that would provide him with much-needed security, but some things are difficult to ignore. His absence was like a sliver of wood in my thumb: persistent, uncomfortable, and relentless. Now that he stood before me in the sunny kitchen, my eyes ranged over every feature, every nuance, every movement, ravenous for the sight of him.

His plain grey suit had no adornment except for carved bone buttons, but the simplicity of his clothes only accentuated the handsome features of his face. His blue-black hair had been cut short, except for one wayward lock that persisted in falling over his brow. Mischief sparkled in his eyes. When he smiled, I felt my pulse race.

"*Ni hao, Lei Zi*," he said.

"*Ni hao ma*," I replied, stumbling over the inflection. Up, or down? God's teeth, it was hard to remember!

To Mr. Fish, he said, "Good afternoon, sir. You're well?"

The man scoffed. "Why waste time asking after my health, boy? We all know, you're here for her." He lowered his voice theatrically. "And who can blame you? Liz is a far more attractive host than me."

"I certainly agree," said Shao.

Mr. Fish raised his head and yelled through the kitchen doors, into the parlor. "Jess, my girl? Be a dear and make enough tea for all. But I'll take mine in the study." To me, he cast a wink. "The sun is shining full and bright upon the back porch, Liz. Best to enjoy it before the winter arrives." He strode out of the kitchen, leaving us together, rasping a chuckle under his breath.

Shao and I moved out to the porch. The rich October sunlight cast a honey-thick glow over the dry leaves of the oak trees, and a fresh sea breeze ruffled the last roses in the bowers. There wasn't much of summer left. The season wished to expel one last burst of sunshine before the cold rain arrived. I sat next to him on the top step, not so close to be improper, but I set my hand down next to his, close enough to feel the warmth from his skin. Oh, how I missed him! The mere presence of him made me giddy, and the rational part of my brain scolded my heart for being so ridiculous, romantic, simpering. I tried to stamp down the gallop of my pulse, but then I felt the touch of Shao's smallest finger against my own, and my blood was set racing again.

"How have you been?" he asked. He kept his voice low, but I heard a tension there, as if he was having trouble keeping his own happiness restrained.

"Well enough," I replied.

"You've been practicing your vocabulary?"

"A little," I replied. "But Xi laughs at my accent. I spend most of my time talking to myself in the mirror. Mr. Fish seems very amused by my efforts."

"He's a strange old fellow, isn't he."

“He’s been very accommodating,” I replied. "And Eddy's a wonderful cook. I think I'm gaining weight."

I saw clearly in his face that he didn't believe me. Mr. Fish's housekeeper, Edwina, was very skilled in the kitchen, that part was true, but I never had much of an appetite these days. Before Shao could press the issue, I said, "What about you? How’ve you been?”

“The rib still hurts.”

“Let’s see,” I urged.

He faltered. "But the neighbors..."

We might not be able to show affection, but there were loopholes. I mustered up any sense of authority a 15-year-girl can hold, and scowled fiercely.

"I'm your physician, Mr. Chen," I reminded him, then added, "Sod the neighbors."

He chuckled as he removed his grey coat, turned his back to me, and lifted his white cotton shirt.

I ran my palms down the left side of his lean bare torso, where the fierce bruise in the shape of a boot had almost completely vanished. Shao flinched but said nothing. I felt the strong, well-defined muscles covering a brace of bones, each one straight and well-healed.

“Breath in,” I instructed.

His rib cage rose evenly. He released his breath, wincing a little.

I let my touch linger, then helped him replace his shirt, but I was reluctant to hide away his handsome form. I ached to wrap my arms around him. I felt so few strong emotions that it was an agony to stifle these delicious desires. However, I leeched any passion from my voice and said, in a most scientific and scholarly way, “I think your pain may simply be the last of the healing process.”

He settled back on the step before shaking his head in wonder and frustration. "Three months!" he snapped. "It's been almost three months since..." The furious words snagged in his throat.

Since he'd been beaten at the hands of vengeful, hateful, spiteful men. I brought my head close to his.

"You're getting better," I reminded him. I ran my fingers over his hand, caressed the small bones of his wrist, let myself take delight in the touch of his skin. "Rib injuries take a long time to heal properly."

"*Pok gai*," he muttered through clenched teeth.

For the last two weeks, I'd barely seen him; his work at Mr. Lim's apothecary shop kept him too busy for social calls, if such a thing would even be allowed between him and me. Shao's infrequent visits to James Bay came in the form of deliveries to wealthy patrons, and when he could spare a moment, he'd drop by the house to see me. He seemed content, very happy with the job he'd secured. I suppose Mr. Lim recognized a valued employee when he saw one, and considered Shao to be an investment worth nurturing, rather than a slave to drive hard. The two of them ran a neat little shop on Herald street, and Shao spent almost every day in the bustling alleys and dens of Chinatown, where he could practice the arts of pharmacy in the company of men who respected him. He'd left English society behind, and after the beating he'd received at the hands of white miners, I couldn't blame him.

But he'd left me behind, too. The thought stung. I missed him terribly.

He straightened his white shirt, turning his gaze to me. "Liz, how are you, really?" he asked, and before I could craft a lie, he said, "You look terrible. You've got shadows under your eyes."

"Newspaper ink, I bet."

"You look like you haven't slept in days. You're as pale as custard."

I shrugged.

How could I tell him he was right – I hadn't slept, I didn't eat – without explaining to him why? Maybe it was better that our lives were drawing apart. With Shao engrossed in his own life, it meant I never had to tell him about mine.

"Have you heard from your father?"

I winced. "No."

"He left for Europe last August!" he exclaimed, his eyebrows arching in surprise. "And not a single word to you?"

"I don't wish to talk about it."

"He's abandoned you, Liz. *Zao gao*! Does he even know where you are?"

"Stop it," I hissed.

Shao recoiled, only a fraction, but it was enough: I saw from the look on his face that my own expression had changed. The mask had fractured, the dark beast peeked out. I closed my eyes, willed the warmth of human emotion back into my features.

Since the events of last summer, I'd begun to suffer lapses in my composure, and I hated the flash of rage and sense of detachment that now rose quickly in moments of anger. I feared that those last minutes in my father's company had dredged something sinister from the depths of my soul. I was hardly eager to recognize it. I dared not name it. I felt as if confronting it was tantamount to giving it power, and I didn't want to lose control. With my eyes firmly shut, I struggled to suppress the rising dark -- I struggled to forget how good it had felt to plunge that knife into firm, living flesh.

I am not like him, I thought, banishing the memories to the basement of my soul. *I will never be like him.*

When I opened my eyes, Shao was watching me, concerned and perhaps a little afraid.

I took his hand in mine. "Please," I said quietly, "I don't want to talk about it."

We sat for a moment in awkward silence.

Then, Shao stood. He fidgeted, he faltered. "I should leave," he said, "Mr. Lim is expecting me back. I... I only wanted to know how you were doing."

He didn't look back as he walked down the stairs and across the lawn, towards the back gate leading to the alley. He'd crossed the garden path and was reaching out for the latch when I called out, "Shao, I'm sorry."

He paused, turned.

"I'm sorry," I repeated.

"For what?"

For not being honest with you. For not telling you everything. For not admitting I killed my own father and dumped his body in the ocean. For lying again and again to you, never admitting you into my confidence, for not trusting you. For ripping your life apart and putting you in harm's way. For loving you.

For everything, really.

My throat hitched.

"I… I don't know."

He frowned, puzzled by my answer, then disappeared out the gate. I heard his footfalls on the hard clay of the alleyway, disappearing towards the harbor.

A light step in the kitchen door caught my ear. I looked up to see Jess, standing in the doorway, holding a silver tray.

She looked much younger than her twenty years, with soft, rounded features and wide-set eyes. There were very few negro people in Victoria, and the complexion of her skin set her apart from other women her age, but I think Jess' childlike face was more arresting than any other difference that divided us. Her body showed every clue that she was older than me, taller and shapely and womanly, but her face seemed so much younger and girlish than mine.

"Um, miss?" said Jess in her soft, timid voice, "Would you still like your tea?"

"No thanks."

She hesitated. Jess only spoke after great thought, and she rarely did anything impulsive. Rarer still was speaking her mind, or telling someone what to do.

"I think you ought to have something to eat, miss," she insisted. "I've made you an egg salad sandwich."

"I'm really not hungry—"

"You're heartsick, miss, nothing more. He's a lovely boy, but he ain't your type, and this heartsickness, it'll pass." She laid the blue-and-white china plate next to me on the step. "Trust me, I been through it myself." She smiled warmly, and her voice adopted a motherly tone. "Now, I shall not interrupt you as you eat, but I'll be watching you from the kitchen window, miss, and I'll know if you throw it to the birds."

I scrubbed one hand over my face, feeling hollow inside. "Thank you, Jess."

"There's a sing-along at the theatre tonight. You're coming with me."

"I'm not really the musical type —"

"Of course you ain't, miss," she agreed, "You're the type to lock yourself in an attic and turn your back on the people who wish to drag you into the light." She set a cup of tea alongside the sandwich. "I've told Mrs. Thornton to expect us. We'll leave by 6:30, the show begins at seven. We'll be taking the trolley, and Mr. Fish said he'll pay our fare." She gave me a pert smile to show that she would accept no refusal, and before I could protest further, she left.

Her soft, steely resolve brought a small smile to my own lips, and I begrudgingly took a bite of the sandwich. A quick glance at the window showed that yes, she was watching, so I nodded in thanks and continued to eat. I did like Jess, very much; I wonder if she would've allowed me to not like her? She was headstrong in a quiet way, so that she could steer a person's opinion without them even noticing, and she kindly guided Mr. Fish to compromises when her fusty employer and her mother would have otherwise argued. Jess was a soothing spring breeze, and I had liked her since the first moment I met her, on a sunny afternoon in mid-September, only four weeks ago...

ACKNOWLEDGMENTS

Goodness, has it really been 10 years since Bucket of Blood was first published? How time flies when you're having fun!

Time has passed, but my acknowledgments remain the same: I'd like to thank the staff and board of the Cumberland Museum, who have dedicated themselves to telling a fascinating, gritty, and complex people's history: Flo Bell, Frank Carter, Meg Cursons, Brian Charlton, Lindsay Chung, Colleen Dane, Toni Gore, Jackie McCauley and Michelle Peters. Thank you to my dad, Ron Bannerman; my mom, Cindy Bannerman; and my grandparents, John and Alice Bannerman, who taught me from a very early age to love the stories of the past, to share those stories, and to pass them along.

I wish to thank Kate Blood, Jennye Holm, Tracy Jenneson, and Laurie Farkas for providing feedback and editorial comments, and to Frank Zafiro, Adele Wearing, Jodi Cleghorn and Pauline Trent for their professional encouragement. Many thanks, too, to the staff of North Island College for their support—Susan Auchterlonie, Alex Khan, Jolean Finnerty, Christiana Wiens, Michael Johnson, Matt Rader and Beth Turner have been generous beyond measure. Thank you to the

Canada Council for the Arts for their support, and thank you to Claire Fisher at Red Bird Graphics for her amazing original cover design.

I'd also like to thank all of the book clubs, community organizations, writing groups, and bibliophiles who have supported me and inspired me over the last decade. Thank you, too, to the Canada Council of the Arts for supporting this project.

Lastly, I wish to thank Shawn Pigott for his ardent support and encouragement. He never complains when we tromp through the swamps of Chinatown or prowl the dark, cobwebbed corners of old bookstores and archives. He is patient, generous, and always supportive. To him, I give a lifetime of appreciation and love.

xoxo, Kim

Manufactured by Amazon.ca
Bolton, ON

45883578R00302